PENGUIN CLASSICS

JULES VERNE was born in France in 1828 and died in 1905. His collaboration with the publisher Pierre-Jules Hetzel was wildly successful, producing many brilliant novels in the burgeoning genre of science fiction: *Twenty Thousand Leagues Under the Sea*, *Journey to the Centre of the Earth* and *Around the World in Eighty Days*, among others. Verne is the second most translated author in the world, after Agatha Christie and before Shakespeare.

DAVID COWARD is Emeritus Professor of French at the University of Leeds and has translated many books from French for Penguin Classics.

JULES VERNE

Twenty Thousand Leagues Under the Sea

Translated with an Introduction and Notes by
DAVID COWARD

PENGUIN BOOKS

PENGUIN CLASSICS

UK | USA | Canada | Ireland | Australia
India | New Zealand | South Africa

Penguin Books is part of the Penguin Random House group of companies
whose addresses can be found at global.penguinrandomhouse.com.

First published in French as *Vingt mille lieues sous les mers: Tour du monde sous-marin* in 1870
This translation first published in hardback in Penguin Classics 2017
This edition published 2018

002

Translation and editorial material copyright © David Coward, 2017

The moral rights of the translator have been asserted

Set in 10.25/12.25 pt Adobe Sabon
Typeset by Jouve (UK), Milton Keynes
Printed in Great Britain by Clays Ltd, St Ives plc

A CIP catalogue record for this book is available from the British Library

ISBN: 978-0-141-39493-0

www.greenpenguin.co.uk

MIX
Paper from
responsible sources
FSC® C018179

Penguin Random House is committed to a
sustainable future for our business, our readers
and our planet. This book is made from Forest
Stewardship Council® certified paper.

Contents

TWENTY THOUSAND LEAGUES
UNDER THE SEA

PART ONE

PART TWO

Chronology

1827 27 February: marriage at Nantes of Pierre Verne, a Nantes lawyer, and Sophie Allotte de la Fuÿe.

1828 8 February: birth, at Nantes, of Jules-Gabriel Verne, who was followed by brother Paul and sisters Anna, Mathilde and Marie.

1834–46 Attends schools in Nantes, sitting his *baccalauréat* examination on 29 July 1846.

1840 The family moves nearer to the River Loire, where Verne learns to love boats and water.

1847 29 June: completes *Alexandre VI*, a verse tragedy, the first of a score of plays in various genres written before his first play is performed in 1850.

Falls in love with his cousin Caroline Tronson and then her friend Angèle Desgraviers. Neither reciprocates his feelings.

Autumn: after some months of apprenticeship in his father's office, Verne completes the first year of his legal studies in Paris. It is assumed that he will eventually take over his father's legal practice.

1847–8 Writes love poems to Herminie Arnault-Grossetière, who marries another in 1848.

1848 February: fall of the monarchy. Verne's sympathies favour conservative, constitutional monarchy rather than republican, parliamentary government.

November: with a Nantes friend, Verne settles in the Latin Quarter, though he never becomes part of student Bohemia.

1849 An uncle introduces him to the salon of Madame de Barrère, where he meets leading literary figures, including Victor Hugo and Alexandre Dumas *père* and *fils*. He subsequently provides secretarial help with the affairs of Dumas' Théâtre Historique and consults Dumas about his plays.

1850 12 June: *Les Pailles rompues* (*The Broken Straws*) performed at the Théâtre Historique. Between 1850 and 1856, he writes a further fourteen plays, only three of which are performed.

1851 First tales published in the *Musée des Familles* (*The Family Enquirer*) but make little impression.

1852 Begins work as an unpaid secretary at the Théâtre Lyrique to further his career as a dramatist.

1853 April: production at the Théâtre Lyrique of *Le Colin Maillard* (*Blind Man's Bluff*), the first of four performed comic operas with music by Aristide Hignard (1822–98) and libretto by Verne.

1854 19 April: the family's law office is sold after Verne tells his father that he has decided against a legal career.

April: Verne shaves off his beard to treat the facial paralysis which would recur intermittently for the rest of his life.

1855 November: finally ceases work at the Théâtre Lyrique.

1856 20 May: at Amiens meets Honorine de Viane, a widow aged twenty-six, with two daughters. With money from his father, buys a share in the de Vianes' stockbroking firm.

1857 10 January: marries Honorine in Paris and becomes a stockbroker.

Summer: publishes eight long articles devoted to the Academy's annual art exhibition in the *Revue des beaux-arts*.

1859 26 August–6 September: accompanies Hignard on a short tour of Scotland. An account of their journey is published posthumously in 1989.

1860 Autumn: joins the Cercle de la Presse scientifique, a forum for the discussion of new scientific advances.

1861 15 June: begins a five-week tour of Germany and Scandinavia with Hignard.

3 August: birth of Michel, the Vernes' only child.

1862 Accepts that his ambition to succeed as a playwright will come to nothing. Completes his 'balloon story', shows it to Dumas and offers it to the publisher Pierre-Jules Hetzel.

23 October: signs the first of the six contracts he will have with Hetzel.

1863 31 January: publication of *Cinq Semaines en ballon* (*Five Weeks in a Balloon*).

December: *Paris au vingtième siècle* (*Paris in the Twentieth Century*), written in 1860, is rejected by Hetzel and remains unpublished until 1994.

1864 20 March: the first issue of the *Magasin d'éducation et de récréation* prints the first instalment of *Les Voyages et aventures du capitaine Hatteras* (*The Adventures of Captain Hatteras*). The *Magasin* will run until December 1906 and serialize many of Verne's books.

April: publishes a study of 'Edgar Poe et ses œuvres' ('Edgar Poe and His Works') in the *Musée des familles*.

Summer: publication of *Voyage au centre de la terre* (*Journey to the Centre of the Earth*). Verne gives up being a broker to devote all his time to writing.

1865 14 September–14 October, *De la terre à la Lune* (*From the Earth to the Moon*) serialized in the *Journal des débats*.

Start of serialization *Les Enfants du capitaine Grant* (published in English as *In Search of the Castaways*) in the *Magasin d'éducation et de récréation*.

A letter from George Sand mentions the idea for a voyage of undersea exploration.

1866 January: starts work on an illustrated geography of France.

March: moves to Le Crotoy on the Somme estuary, 10 miles north-west of Abbeville.

September: sails his converted fishing boat, the *Saint Michel*, to Bordeaux and back.

1867 16 March: travels to New York on the *Great Eastern*. Visits Niagara Falls. The brief trip provides material for *Une Ville flottante* (*A Floating City*, 1870) and inspiration for some thirty works set in the US.

1868 *Géographie illustrée de la France et de ses colonies* (*Illustrated Geography of France and Its Colonies*), published in three volumes by Hetzel.

1869 20 March: start of serialization of *Vingt mille lieues sous les mers* (*Twenty Thousand Leagues Under the Sea*) in Hetzel's *Magasin d'éducation et de récréation*.

1870 May: sails up the Seine to Paris just weeks before the start of the Franco-Prussian war.

15 August: Honorine first suspects that Verne has a mistress.

19 August: awarded Légion d'honneur.

November: too old for mobilization, joins the National Guard.

1871 March–May: Paris Commune, which dismays Verne.

3 November: death of Pierre Verne.

1872 Settles definitively in Amiens.

28 June: elected to the Académie des sciences, des lettres et des arts of Amiens.

6 November–22 December: serialization of *Le Tour du monde en quatre-vingts jours* (*Around the World in Eighty Days*) in *Le Temps*.

1873 First balloon ascent.

1874 Édouard Cadol, who collaborated with Verne on the novella and stage adaptation *Le Tour du monde en quatre-vingt jours*, sues Verne for plagiarism and wins compensation.

7 November: *Le Tour du monde* staged with great success. *L'Ile mystérieuse* (*The Mysterious Island*), in which Captain Nemo reappears, is serialized 1874–5.

1875 Elected president of the Académie d'Amiens.

Verne sends his son for treatment for his behavioural problems at a clinic at Tours.

1876 April: illness of Honorine. Michel is aggressive and violent.

1877 2 April: to please his wife, Verne gives a reception and ball at Amiens, but Honorine falls ill with pleurisy, does not attend and makes a slow recovery.

First of several attempts to canvas support for his election to the French Academy, which come to nothing.

1878 4 February: Michel is sent as a cabin boy on a ship bound for India, in the hope that he acquires self-discipline.

Writing a *Histoire générale des Grands Voyages et des Grands Voyageurs* (*General History of Great Journeys and Great Travellers*), published 1878–80 in three volumes.

1880 1–24 July: sails his boat, the *Saint Michel III*, to Ireland, Scotland and Norway.

1884 May–July: last cruise of the *Saint Michel III* to Vigo, Gibraltar, Algiers, Tunis, Malta, then to Italy. He visits Rome and meets the Pope (7 July).

1885 8 March: holds another ball at Amiens, for which Verne dresses as a head waiter.

1886 15 February: sells the *Saint Michel III* and never buys another boat.

9 March: his nephew Gaston shoots him in the foot.

17 March: death of Hetzel, who is succeeded by his son.

1887 15 February, death of Verne's mother.

Autumn: gives a series of readings in Belgium and Holland.

1888 15 May: elected as a centre-right conservative in the municipal elections at Amiens and is re-elected in 1892, 1896 and 1900.

1895 Publication of *L'Ile à hélice* (*Propeller Island*), unusually written in the present tense.

1896 Eugène Turpin (1848–1927), a French chemical engineer, sues Verne for basing Thomas Roch, the mad scientist of *Face au drapeau* (*Facing the Flag*), on him. Verne wins but privately admits the libel.

1897 Complains of dizziness, writer's cramp, bronchitis and rheumatism.

27 August: death of Paul Verne, his brother.

1898 Death of Aristide Hignard.

1905 24 March: death of Jules Verne, aged seventy-seven, from diabetes.

2 May: Michel publishes in *Le Figaro* a list of all his father's unpublished writing and undertakes to revise, complete and publish most of them.

1909 9 May: bust of Verne unveiled in Amiens.

1910 29 January: death of Honorine, aged eighty.

1918 Michel Verne founds Les Films Jules Verne, a production company, and subsequently adapts several novels for the screen.

1925 Death of Michel Verne.

2005 A statue of Verne is erected in Vigo (Spain) to commemorate the famous episode in *Twenty Thousand Leagues Under the Sea* (Part II, chapter 8).

Introduction

If the seventeenth century in France was the golden age of theatre, the second half of the nineteenth belongs to the novel.
Literary history has adjudicated upon the question of which
writers produced the finest and most enduring examples of the
art of fiction. But in the history of reading, the great names are
not Balzac, Stendhal, Flaubert or Zola but a succession of lesser
authors who acquired huge popular followings. Until about
1830 the light touch of Pigault-Lebrun's *roman gai* and the ris-
qué novels of Paul de Kock (devoured, it was said, by 'concierges
and ladies' maids') enjoyed greater commercial success than
most Romantic poets and playwrights. Then in 1836 newspapers began taking advertisements as a way of halving their
cover prices. Their circulation rose dramatically. But it soon
became apparent that serialized fiction of the right sort could
attract even more readers and both earn and retain their loyalty.
Fortunes were paid to writers who had the knack of turning
out sensational tales of mystery and adventure in gripping,
cliff-hanging instalments. In the 1840s the masters of the new
serialized fiction (the *roman-feuilleton*) were Eugène Sue, author
of *Les Mystères de Paris* (*Mysteries of Paris*), and Alexandre
Dumas *père*, creator of the Musketeers and Monte Cristo. These
first *feuilletonistes* were the 'kings of romance', and their
names were known not only throughout France but from San
Francisco to darkest Russia. When their hour passed, the public
hailed new tellers of tales. After 1850 it was Paul Féval and
Ponson du Terrail who supplied the new low-priced newspapers
with what the critic Sainte-Beuve had in 1839 called 'industrial

literature'. Sensation, sentiment, violence and escape found a ready market. High art did not.

Among these new Second Empire wholesalers of high-octane fiction was Jules Verne, who, after fifteen years of trying and failing to make his name as a playwright, scored an overnight success in 1863 with *Cinq semaines en ballon* (*Five Weeks in a Balloon*). He avoided the *feuilletoniste*'s stock subjects – history, contemporary manners, crime and murder – and inaugurated a new kind of fiction: the 'scientific romance'. His 'balloon story' made his name. Having found his niche in the market, he went on, over the next forty years, to produce sixty-three novels and a score of long tales. He also found time to add a further ten titles to his previous tally of about twenty-five plays and librettos, of which barely half a dozen had been performed. When he died in 1905 he had long been one of the small number of Frenchmen (others include Voltaire, Alexandre Dumas and Victor Hugo) whose names were, and still are, known all over the world to people of all ages and circumstances.

Jules Verne was born in Nantes in 1828, the oldest of the five children of a conservative, devoutly Catholic lawyer. He had a happy childhood and learned to love the sea, boats and tales of adventure. After attending local schools, he moved to Paris in 1847 to study law on the understanding that one day he would take over his father's legal practice. But the law bored him, and he set his sights instead on a literary career. Through family connections he acquired a toehold in artistic circles in Paris, where he met his idols, Victor Hugo and especially Alexandre Dumas *père*, who helped him get his first play performed in Paris in 1850. Between 1852 and 1855, he worked as an unpaid secretary-cum-administrator at the Théâtre Lyrique, which staged three comic operas for which he wrote the librettos to music composed by Aristide Hignard, an old friend from Nantes. He also published a few tales in the manner of E. T. A. Hoffman, Edgar Allan Poe and James Fenimore Cooper. Unhappy in love, he finally married in 1857. Honorine de Viane was twenty-six, a widow with two daughters. Despite his absorption in his work and her cool temperament, the marriage lasted nearly fifty years.

A son, Michel, was born in 1861. To support his ready-made family, Verne found work as a stockbroker, though without abandoning his literary ambitions. He rose at five, worked on his current tale or play until ten, then walked to the stock exchange for the day's business.

By 1862 he finally accepted that he would never become a successful playwright. Instead, he put all his mind to writing a novel, which, when it was published in 1863, would catch the mood of the times. He had joined the Cercle de la Presse scientifique, where he met travellers, scientists and inventors, and particularly the photographer Nadar, who had used balloons to take the first aerial pictures. He informed himself about the latest developments in technology, advances in the pure and applied sciences and the discoveries of explorers newly returned from polar, oriental and exotic regions of the globe. He shared the widespread enthusiasm for the latest journey of the explorer John Hanning Speke, who was then in Africa attempting to confirm his claim that he had found the source of the Nile. In the summer of 1862 Verne offered his manuscript to a publisher, P.-J. Hetzel, who liked what he read and in January 1863 published *Five Weeks in a Balloon*, the dramatic story of a journey by balloon across Africa from Zanzibar to Senegal, filled with thrills but also with descriptions of strange animals and exotic landscapes. It was a great success. Hetzel offered Verne a contract for three volumes of fiction a year against a fixed but not over-generous monthly stipend. Over the years, Verne would renew his contract half a dozen times, always on better terms. Even so, Hetzel was the main beneficiary of their partnership, with Verne accepting the arrangement because he valued Hetzel's friendship and because, after so many years of rejection, he welcomed the security offered by a regular income.

His 'balloon story' was based entirely on secondary sources. But borrowed fact was so skilfully built into his fast-paced tale of adventures that many readers believed what they were reading was a true narrative of a real expedition. In reality, the vivid descriptions were taken from books, the proceedings of learned societies, lectures and newspaper articles. Verne loved the sea, lived for many years at Le Crotoy on the Somme estuary and bought three boats, which he sailed enthusiastically, relishing stormy weather. But he was always an armchair traveller who sent his heroes on journeys to the four corners of the globe, while he himself never ventured further north than Scotland and Scandinavia, further east than Germany and further south than the Mediterranean. He did once cross the Atlantic on the *Great Eastern* but managed a stay of only one week in the United States.

Verne's appetite for knowledge was shared by a generation coming to grips with a world that was being transformed by technology. Readers were regularly required to accept implausible novelties in the form of cable telegraphy, iron ships (why did they not sink?), railways and rotary printing presses, which put cheap newspapers within the reach of all. The public was curious about events at home and abroad, from wars and the fate of John Franklin's lost expedition to find the icy North-West Passage to the natural history and customs of the lands which France was busily colonizing. Verne, as much a man for facts as Dickens's Gradgrind in *Hard Times*, was completely at home in an age of scientific vulgarization and encyclopedias such as Pierre Larousse's *Grand dictionnaire universel* (*Great Universal Dictionary*), which began appearing in 1866. He himself published several such compilations, including a three-volume *Géographie illustrée de la France et de ses colonies* (*Illustrated Geography of France and Its Colonies*, 1868).

Verne's particular fascination with science and technology has led to his being thought of as a 'father of science fiction'. It is a title which he rejected. He certainly used the applications and implications of science in his fiction. But he denied any expertise in chemistry, physics, botany, zoology, mechanics, engineering or mathematics, although he worked hard to inform himself and made technical accuracy a key element of his stories (he asked qualified friends to check his calculations). He also kept too tight a rein on his imagination to be thought a writer of science fantasy. The 'what if' question (which often makes the first chapter the most interesting of many sci-fi novels) was answered by most contemporary exponents of the 'anticipation novel' in super-normal terms which defied the laws of the universe. H. G. Wells, for example, invented an invisible man, a time-machine, invaders from outer space and 'cavorite' (a material that cancelled the force of gravity), which, though ingenious and intriguing, were entirely fanciful. On the other hand, Verne's rockets, dirigible airships, Captain Nemo's *Nautilus*, even the amphibious flying motor-car of *Le Maître du monde* (*The Master of the World*, 1904) were solidly based on contemporary science and were all technically feasible. They were no more or less fantastic than electric light or the amazing new express trains which travelled at a staggering 26 miles an hour. At times, he was remarkably prescient. The calculations for the angle and escape velocity of the missile which, in *De la Terre à la Lune* (*From the Earth to the Moon*, 1865) and its sequel *Autour de la Lune* (*Around the Moon*, 1869), flies Verne's doughty heroes into space and brings them back again, were so accurate that he chose to situate the launch of the space vessel in Florida at a site not a stone's throw from Cape Canaveral, which a century later the Americans also chose as the optimal location for a moon shot.

All Verne's stories are firmly planted in the facts of the world, of which he had only second-hand knowledge. His detailed descriptions of flora and fauna he had never seen were taken from authoritative published sources, just as his use of latitude and longitude were based on the latest maps and charts. His personal library was as comprehensive as that assembled by Captain Nemo on board the *Nautilus* in *Twenty Thousand Leagues Under the Sea* (Part I, chapter 11). He used different sources according to the requirements of each book: earth sciences and earth history for the *Voyage au centre de la terre* (*Journey to the Centre of the* Earth, 1864); polar expeditions and Arctic lore for *Les Voyages et aventures du Capitaine Hatteras* (*The Adventures of Captain Hatteras*, 1864–5); and for the most intensively documented of all his novels, *Twenty Thousand Leagues Under the Sea* (1869–70), he combed volumes of physical geography, oceanography, malacology, marine zoology and so on by authorities both old and new. He regularly borrowed descriptions of fish from La Cépède's *Histoire naturelle des poissons* (*Natural History of Fish*, 1798–1803) and used M. F. Maury's *Physical Geography of the Sea* (1855) to enable the *Nautilus* to navigate accurately in exotic waters. Occasionally, he quotes his sources directly. He mentions, for example, H. C. Sirr's *Ceylon and the Cingalese* (1850) when providing details of the pearl fisheries of Manaar. But he also borrowed without acknowledgement from many more. He occasionally begs the reader to excuse his 'dry' catalogues of fish, molluscs, corals and marine vegetation, which modern readers can skip but sorely try the translator's patience. The writer Apollinaire argued that his style consisted entirely of nouns, though Georges Perec, that connoisseur of words, considered it to be 'poetry'. But in the days before film-makers revealed distant lands and the secret life of nature in moving pictures, Verne's public were less inclined to quibble: they found his guided tours of worlds at, above and below sea-level both fascinating and educational.

If Verne was at all a writer of science fiction, it was in a few forays into fantasy and a handful of dystopian ventures into a future where computer-style calculators, photographs, electric power, urban transport, dirigible airships and ocean-going vessels which no longer depended on sail had long ceased to be wonders and were presented as routine features of advanced societies. But science remained subservient to his endless curiosity about the physical world and the wonders of nature, which led him to send his heroes travelling on, over and under the earth by balloon, sail, submarine, canoe, horse, coach and elephant, to the poles, the centre of the earth, Africa, the United States, Russia and the bottom of the sea. Wherever they went, he ensured that their thrilling adventures were set in the physical world whose realities he translated in dramatic, visual terms. Geology, climatology and zoology were not just subjects of study but became erupting volcanoes, deadly hurricanes, sharp teeth and wildly waving tentacles.

Verne's publisher did not object to his lists of facts and didactic digressions. On the contrary, he approved wholeheartedly. Pierre-Jules Hetzel (1814–86) was a fervent republican who had been *chef de cabinet* to the minister of foreign affairs, the writer Alphonse de Lamartine (1790–1869), after the 1848 revolution and had spent much of the 1850s in exile in Belgium until he returned under the amnesty issued by the materialistic Second Empire, which he despised. Since the age of twenty-three he had been a commercial publisher of, among others, Balzac, Baudelaire, Hugo and George Sand. But convinced that dispelling ignorance was the best way of fighting social injustice, he turned to magazines dedicated to making modern scientific ideas exciting. He had published *Five Weeks in a Balloon* in book form, but in March 1864 he began serializing Verne's next work, the entirely fictional but apparently real adventures of Captain Hatteras, in the first issue of his new periodical aimed at younger readers: the *Magasin d'éducation et de récréation*. Thereafter, it serialized most of Verne's books, though a small number first appeared in other papers.

The *Magasin* was Hetzel's greatest success. In 1867, it was awarded the Montyon Prize by the French Academy for its role in encouraging an interest in modern ideas among the young. The following year the Bishop of Paris, who believed that education should be in the hands of the Church, not of secular government, attacked the *Magasin* for being anti-Christian. Hetzel replied energetically, restating his liberal case, and there was no lasting harm. But he continued to be aware of the power of such adverse publicity to damage his crusade for secular values and his business. From the start, he commented extensively on Verne's manuscript and called for changes, some very substantial. He wanted more, not less, pedagogic material and ran a red pencil through political and social comment on the affairs of France and on anything which might offend powerful interests and affect circulation. He also changed anything he judged unsuitable for young people. In the final version of *Twenty Thousand Leagues Under the Sea,* for instance, he even replaced the 'half-clothed female figure' which Verne had included in the art collection on board the *Nautilus* with 'a nymph' (Part I, chapter 11). Yet Hetzel had good reason to tread warily. In 1875 he felt concerned enough that Verne's *Michel Strogoff* might be judged hostile to the Tsar that he submitted the manuscript to both the Russian ambassador and the Paris-based Russian novelist Ivan Turgenev for their comments. Despite

xxii   INTRODUCTION

these precautions, the Russian translation of the novel was banned in Russia. There was a similar scare in June 1877, when Zadoc Khan, Chief Rabbi of Paris, objected to the anti-Semitism he detected in the portrait of a Jewish character in Verne's *Hector Servadac*. Hetzel penned a firm reply, and matters were left there.

But Hetzel carried his hands-on approach to extremes of interference. He toned down Verne's sense of humour, ruled out romantic interest and pared female characters to the palest of pale stereotypes, justifying his disapproval of departures from decorum and good taste on the grounds that he stood *in loco parentis* to his youthful readers. He also called for changes in characterization and tampered with plots, insisting on revisions which altered the mood, shape and often the point of Verne's narratives. The manuscript of *Hector Servadac*, for example, ended with a cataclysm in which all the survivors of an accident of nature are killed in accordance with the laws of physics, a logical if somewhat gloomy climax. Hetzel felt that this conclusion would upset his readers, and Verne was obliged to write a new, quite unconvincing ending in which the characters escape miraculously in a balloon. However, the most serious damage of all was that inflicted on *Twenty Thousand Leagues Under the Sea*.

Verne originally conceived of Nemo as an aristocratic Polish nationalist whose family had been brutally murdered or exiled to Siberia and their estates confiscated during the Russian repression of the anti-Tsarist uprising of 1863. His personal history provides the motive for his hatred of humanity in general and explains why his attacks on vessels which threaten him are so merciless. Hetzel would have none of it. He thought Nemo should be American, an opponent of slavery who has lost both family and property in the recently concluded Civil War, so that his misanthropy would have its root in a right-thinking, morally sound cause. Hetzel's reaction was partly prompted by his fear – not without foundation, as we have seen – of offending Russia. But the change he had proposed was also in line with his own liberal principles, for he raised no objection to Nemo's role in financing the 1866 Cretan insurrection, in which the freedom-loving islanders rose against the oppressive regime of the Turks.

In a letter of 17 May 1869 Verne explains why Hetzel's desired change was at odds with his own view of Nemo as a man of 'generous nature' crushed by injustice who defends himself when attacked. For Verne, Nemo was not a democrat, but an individualist, a patriotic nobleman bent on avenging his honour, not the enemy of nationalism or a champion of the sacred rights of peoples. Nemo might hold certain views that make him sound like an opponent of capitalism and colonialism: he abominates man's destruction of nature for profit and hates the navies kept by developed nations to protect their territorial and economic interests. But when Nemo declares himself master of the world beneath the waves and raises his personal flag over Antarctica, he does so not on behalf of any country or cause or ideology, but by the right of conquest earned by his own determination, industry and courage. Verne refused to give way to Hetzel's demands on this point and opted instead to leave Nemo as a man with no name and no nation, a powerful symbol of self-reliance and detachment from politics and vested interests. Even so, Hetzel did not surrender entirely. Verne's manuscript ends by saluting in Nemo an 'homme libre'. In the printed version, his freedom has been curbed, and we are left ponder these anguished words: 'Almighty God! Enough! No more!', which Aronnax, clearly prompted by Hetzel, tentatively describes as an expression of remorse and a tormented conscience. When Nemo reappears in *L'Ile mystérieuse* (*The Mysterious Island*, 1874–5), his last word is 'Independence!', which, in the printed text, becomes 'God and my country!' (Part III, chapter 17). In other words, Nemo the free spirit, the rebel and avenger who uses his genius to escape the world and retreat into a state of splendid isolation, is turned into the representative of orthodox, liberal moral values, which are Hetzel's, not Verne's.

At times, Verne complained of what amounted to censorship by Hetzel and, in old age, regretted that he had been confined to the requirements of a juvenile readership. His life would have been much easier, he said, without Hetzel's puritanism, which denied him adulteries, crimes and innocent maidens cheated out of their inheritances – the stuff of popular fiction. He also regretted the strict injunction to avoid political or social comment which Hetzel believed was unsuitable for the young and bad for business. This was partly why Verne rarely raised the great issues of his times, from the policies of Second Empire France, the Franco-Prussian War of 1870 and the 1871 Paris Commune to the Dreyfus affair in the 1890s. It also explains why his novels were rarely set in France. But despite everything – Hetzel's miserly contracts and over-liberal use of his red pencil – Verne remained on friendly terms with his publisher, valuing his advice, his careful reading of his work and his suggestions, which Verne usually found helpful and stimulating.

He was also wise enough to leave the business side of their partnership to Hetzel, although he is known to have stepped in to plug financial holes in the company's accounts and even occasionally ran the business for short periods when Hetzel was ill. He was well aware that his success was due in no small measure to the shrewd way Hetzel promoted and packaged his books. He kept Verne's name before the public by reissuing them in various forms. First came serialization in the *Magasin d'éducation et de récréation*, then publication in low-priced volume form and finally a large-format edition, lavishly illustrated with engravings executed by a small team of talented artists recruited and paid for by Hetzel. The illustrated volumes were attractively bound in embossed boards in bright colours, and decorated with gold lettering. It was also Hetzel who came up with the running title for Verne's works of *Voyages extraordinaires*, which first appeared on the cover and title page of the illustrated *Les Enfants du capitaine Grant* (usually translated as *In Search of the Castaways*, 1868). Hetzel's strategy of bringing out these handsome books in the late autumn ensured good Christmas sales for what very quickly turned into an immediately recognizable product.

The novels published in the 1860s made Verne famous and financially independent. His working routine dominated his life and became a refuge from family problems and the coolness of Honorine, who suspected, probably rightly, that he had taken a mistress. His main form of relaxation was in the form of summers spent sailing with friends, usually on his own boats. He kept abreast of public events and in July 1870, on the outbreak of the Franco-Prussian war, was strongly opposed to the stance of the government of Napoleon III, which nevertheless awarded him the Légion d'honneur. He was as shocked, as were most people, by the rapid defeat of France and welcomed the new Republic declared in September. He was too old for mobilization but served briefly in the National Guard. He was also alarmed by the Paris Commune in May 1871, which resulted in the breakdown of social order and brutal repression by the authorities.

By this time, he had settled into a regular routine for writing. He would begin a new novel by sketching the outline of a story which had perhaps been suggested by an idea he found in a conversation, a book or a newspaper. The kernel of *Twenty Thousand Leagues Under the Sea* may well have been an admiring letter he received in 1865 from the novelist George Sand, who observed that the world beneath the waves awaited his inventive pen. Verne would then decide in which part of the globe to set his story, the kind of characters he needed and the purpose of their journey. Next came the research to establish authentic backgrounds against which his story would be set. Only when he had completed thorough research would he produce a draft, which he then revised and rewrote half a dozen or more times before submitting it to Hetzel. After Hetzel's comments were incorporated, a proof was sent to him. As William Butcher has shown, Verne would then make extensive revisions at this proof stage before the text was finalized and sent to the printer. Verne may have written for a popular audience, but as a writer he spared no pains.

In time, without abandoning the basic format of the documented travel adventure, he branched out into other styles of fiction. *Le Tour du monde en quatre-vingts jours* (*Around the World in Eighty Days*, 1872) provided scope for his light, comic touch; *Le Rayon vert* (*The Green Ray*, 1882) was a romantic comedy with a happy ending; *Le Château des Carpathes* (*The Carpathian Castle*, 1892), set in Transylvania, was a gothic melodrama; *Les Cinq cents millions de la Bégum* (*The Begum's Fortune*, 1879), was a *revanchiste* novel featuring a mad scientist, the evil Schultze who, like Roch of *Face au drapeau* (*Facing the Flag*, 1896), was a threat to the future of the entire human race.

For though he admired progress, ever-expanding knowledge and the benefits of technology, Verne had always been aware of the dangers of science. *Paris au vingtième siècle* (*Paris in the Twentieth Century*), written in 1860 but rejected by Hetzel as too pessimistic and published only in 1994, pictured a future dominated by the materialistic worship of unrestricted progress. In the imagined Paris of 1960 there is no art or kindness, and private life, like social living, is governed by scientific, commercial and industrial values. Verne did not object to science and the spirit of inquiry, but to the way they can be used for negative, destructive ends and result in unintended consequences.

Religion played no part in these reservations. He was not a man of sincere faith, though at first he generally opposed enemies to the strict Catholicism in which his father had raised him. After the death of Pierre Verne in 1871 he became more critical of the Church, although on a visit to Rome in 1884 he was commended by the Pope for upholding Catholic values. Opinions vary about his religious views, some claiming that he retained an essentially Catholic mentality, although most argue that he was a deist and able to reconcile a respect for his positivist age with a belief in a deity. Politically, he was right of centre, believing in the virtues of individualism and personal merit and generally assuming the superiority of his heroes over the backwardness of the natives they encounter. But equally, he disliked the materialism of the Second Empire and defended republican values as the best recipe for democracy and social cohesion. In the same spirit, his respect for the British Empire declined when it ceased bringing progress to remote parts of the globe and became expansionist and exploitative, and he admired American energy and technology but loathed its Barnum-style big business. Yet he also mistrusted socialists, revolutionaries and anarchists because they too were a threat to civilized values, and he opposed the liberal republicans by affirming the guilt of the Jewish officer Dreyfus in the scandal that shook France in the 1890s.

Hetzel's censoring of Verne's religious and political views makes it difficult to decide exactly where he stood. As a result, he has been called subversive, a radical, a closet revolutionary and an enemy of capitalism and colonialism. However that may be, it is a fact that between 1888 and 1902 he served four terms as a conservative councillor in his adopted town of Amiens, which repaid his active role in the social and cultural life of the community by raising a statue to him in 1909. Perhaps he is best described as a sceptical idealist, fully aware of the fragility of any system that is based on trust and goodwill. For Verne, progress came from work, patience and collective ambition, not from violent revolution or the hope of reward. Both sides of the argument are put in *Twenty Thousand Leagues Under the Sea*.

Verne completed his synopsis of the novel in January 1866 but, distracted by other projects, did not start the first draft until the spring of 1867. By then he had decided that there would be three protagonists, as in his first success, *Five Weeks in a Balloon*. Professor Aronnax is the man of science; his valet, Conseil, is a mechanical classifier whose limited understanding of the wonders of nature will grow with time; and Ned Land is the practical man of action. Verne was not interested in their past or their inner lives, only in their function as motors of his plot. Captain Nemo, however, is full of tensions and contradictions. When Verne returned to him in *The Mysterious Isle* (Part III, chapters 16–18), he was at last revealed not as a Polish noble but as an Indian Prince whose family were murdered by the oppressive British. But in *Twenty Thousand Leagues Under the Sea*, he is a man with no past, no allegiances, an enigma, a force of nature with whom Aronnax and his friends must struggle if they are to escape from the prison of the *Nautilus*.

Their underwater circumnavigation is made to seem not just plausible but real. First, there are the facts. Aronnax's dates provide a detailed record of passing time, just as the log of their progress marks their exact latitude and longitude. Nemo explains the workings of the ship (though he does not say how exactly he produces electricity from sea-water), and Aronnax, abetted by Conseil, never tires of explaining and cataloguing the wonders of the sea. These facts are not encyclopedic asides but regularly become part of the drama. What seems incredible becomes perfectly convincing when we discover exotic places through the eyes of believable characters and see creatures with Latin names come startlingly to life. At regular intervals, Aronnax confesses he does not know what is happening: what kind of sea monster is attacking the world's shipping? What does Nemo plan to do with them? Where will he go next? What is the purpose of their expeditions on the sea-bed? What are the ruins deep under the Atlantic? The reader has no privileged information. We learn the answers when Aronnax does and are made to feel that we too are discoverers and equally involved in mortal dangers from tempest, giant squid and angry tribesmen. We are drawn into Verne's fictional world and cease to question its implausibility.

Unlike peddlers of fantasy, the supernatural or the bizarre (like Edgar Allan Poe), Verne's characters live in a world that is made authentic by science and mastered by men – almost always men – who are practically minded and resourceful. They are down-to-earth men, scientists and engineers with the survival instincts of Robinson Crusoe, but they also have the trapper spirit and life-saving skills of the heroes of James Fenimore Cooper, author of ripping frontiersmen yarns.

They are, however, no match for Nemo, who, like so many of Verne's heroes, is silent, impassive and always in control. Having rejected humankind, he has found refuge under the sea, for which he has endless admiration. Yet he has strange blind spots. He sees no contradiction in depriving his 'guests' of their liberty in order to protect his own privacy. He rails against sealers and whalers who exploit the sea for gain, but savagely massacres whales and sharks whenever their instincts conflict with his purposes. He hates the human race and kills sailors by sinking their ships; yet at various times shows great humanity, rescuing the pearl fisher and solemnly burying his dead comrade in the coral cemetery. Some of these contradictions are the result of Hetzel's meddling with the text, yet they also reinforce the image of Nemo as an unpredictable, frightening, mysterious force.

Twenty Thousand Leagues Under the Sea, part vulgarizing travelogue and part adventure yarn enlivened by comic moments, thrills, surprises, mortal dangers, narrow escapes and brisk, lively dialogue (the secrets of which Verne had learned as a playwright), is Verne's most enduringly popular novel. It has never been out of print and has been translated 147 times into many languages. It has been adapted (not always with advantage) for radio and television and made into nine films: the first, *Amid the Workings of the Deep*, was released in 1907.

In 1886 Hetzel died, and the family business was carried on by his son, who maintained the same, if less censorious, relationship with its most valuable asset. Such was Verne's industry that he completed novels long before they were due, so that after his death in 1905 new titles kept appearing at the usual rhythm until 1910. Meanwhile, his domestic life was soured by Honorine's lack of interest in his work and the strange affair of a favourite nephew who, in a fit of madness in 1886, shot him in the foot, leaving him with a permanent limp. His greatest worries were supplied by his son, Michel, who was unruly and could be violent. He married against his father's wishes, floated various business ventures that in all cost Verne 200,000 francs and opposed him during the Dreyfus affair. Yet after his father's death Michel supervised the publication of his remaining manuscripts, editing and sometimes rewriting them to an extent now difficult to assess. In 1918 he set up Les Films Jules Verne, a production company that adapted several titles for the silent screen until it was wound up in 1925, when Michel died.

In old age Verne became a familiar, friendly figure in Amiens, where he had lived permanently since 1872. He played a prominent role in the social and cultural life of the town, joining learned societies and associations and, in particular, supporting the town's theatre. He died of diabetes in 1905 and was buried at Amiens. His funeral was attended by 5,000 people, but no representatives were sent by the government or the French Academy, which had rejected him. But though he was denied official recognition during his lifetime, the list of his admirers is long, and runs from Théophile Gautier, George Sand and Baudelaire to H. G. Wells, Arthur C. Clarke and the best exponents of sci-fi. And he has never lost his loyal popular following at home and abroad among readers young and old. A hundred years on, his name has become a global symbol for intelligent, white-knuckle yarns of adventure. Jules Verne is the world's second most translated author. In UNESCO's *Index translationum*, he ranks one place below Agatha Christie and one place higher than William Shakespeare.

David Coward, 2016

Further Reading

Much has been written about the life and work of Jules Verne. The following selection includes some of the more recent and most helpful.

BOOKS

Correspondance inédite de Jules Verne et P.-J. Hetzel 1863–86, ed. Olivier Dumas, Gondolo della Riva and Volker Dehis, 3 vols. (Geneva: Slatkine, 1999–2002).

Butcher, William, *Verne's Journey to the Centre of the Self: Space and Time in the 'Voyages extraordinaires'* (New York: St Martin's Press, 1990).

—, *Jules Verne. The Definitive Biography* (New York: Thunder's Mouth Press, 2006). (A tour de force of scholarly investigation and the indispensable starting-point for anglophone readers of Verne.)

Chesneaux, Jean, *Une Lecture politique de Jules Verne* (Paris: Maspero, 1971); translated as *The Political and Social Ideas of Jules Verne* (London: Thames and Hudson, 1972).

Compère, Daniel, *Jules Verne écrivain* (Geneva: Droz, 1991).

Dumas, Olivier, *Jules Verne* (Lyon: La Manufacture, 1988); revised edition, *Voyage à travers Jules Verne* (Montreal: Stanké, 2000).

Evans, Arthur B., *Jules Verne Rediscovered: Didacticism and the Scientific Novel* (Westport, CT: Greenwood Press, 1988).

Huet, Marie-Hélène, *L'Histoire des voyages extraordinaires. Essai sur l'œuvre de Jules Verne* (Paris: Minard, 1973).

Jules-Verne, Jean, *Jules Verne* (Paris: Hachette, 1973); translated and adapted by Roger Greaves, *Jules Verne: A Biography* (London: Macdonald and Jane's, 1976).

Lottman, Herbert, *Jules Verne: An Exploratory Biography* (New York: St Martin's Press, 1996).

Martin, Andrew, *The Mask of the Prophet: The Extraordinary Fictions of Jules Verne* (Oxford: Clarendon Press, 1990).

Martin, Charles-Noël, *La Vie et l'œuvre de Jules Verne* (Paris: Michel de l'Ormeraie, 1978).

Unwin, Timothy, *Jules Verne: Journeys in Writing* (Liverpool: Liverpool University Press, 2005).

ARTICLES

Belloc, Marie C., 'M. Jules Verne at Home', *The Strand Magazine* (February 1895).

Evans, Arthur B., 'The Illustrators of Jules Verne's *Voyages extraordinaires*', *Science Fiction Studies*, vol. 25, no. 2 (July 1998), pp. 241–70.

—, 'Collaboration and Conflict', in *Science Fiction Studies*, vol. 28 (March 2001), pp. 240–55.

Le Men, Ségolène, 'Hetzel ou la science récréative', in *Romantisme*, vol. 19, no. 65 (1989), pp. 69–80.

Sherard, R. H., 'Jules Verne revisited', in *T. P.'s Weekly* (9 October 1903).

Verne, Jules, 'The Story of My Bayhood', in *The Youth's Companion* (Boston), vol. 64 (9 April 1891), p. 211; reprinted in *The Eternal Adam and Other Stories*, ed. Peter Costello (London: Phoenix Books, 1999).

WEBSITES

Verniana, Jules Verne Studies, at http://verniana.org.

For the *Bulletin de la Société Jules Verne* (1935–8 and since 1967): http://sociétéjulesverne.org.

The covers of Verne's *Voyages extraordinaires* can be viewed at http://vernehetzel.free.fr.

A Note on the Text and Illustrations

Two manuscripts of *Vingt mille lieues sous les mers* have survived and are now deposited in France's National Library. One of these, in handwriting which ranges from neat italic to near-illegible scrawl, has been posted online at http://gallica.bnf.fr/ (follow *Jules Verne Vingt mille lieues sous les mers*). The novel first appeared in instalments in the *Magasin d'éducation et de récréation* between 20 March 1869 and 20 June 1870 before being published in book form in two separate parts, Part I in October 1869 and Part II in June 1870. The illustrated edition, with 111 plates by Riou and Neuville went on sale in November 1871. The text used for this translation is that of the 1871 edition as reproduced by Christian Chelebourg for the Livre de Poche edition of *Vingt mille lieues sous les mers* in 1990. The forty-two illustrations are based on those in the 'popular' edition in two volumes, many times reprinted, published for the first time in the 'Collection Hetzel' in 1901.

Most of the *Voyages extraordinaires* appeared first as a serialization in a periodical, followed by publication in volume form, and finally in a large-format, hardcover, fully illustrated edition. The pattern was established early on in Verne's career. His publisher, the shrewd Hetzel, used illustrations as part of his marketing strategy. He and, after his death, his son financed an average of sixty-five per volume, a total of around 4,200 (some with added colour from 1887 onwards) by about thirty illustrators, who were served by an unknown number of engravers. All were men, and most were painters, though not of the first rank. But the bulk of the illustrations were produced by just six artists. Édouard Riou (1833–1900) and Henri de

Montaut (1830–90), working mainly in tandem, illustrated the first six titles (1866–8), supplying over 700 plates between them. Alphonse de Neuville (1835–85), an ex-pupil of Delacroix, and better known as a painter of military and patriotic subjects than as a book-illustrator, briefly replaced them between 1870 and 1873, supplying 158 illustrations, just over half this number being drawn for *Twenty Thousand Leagues Under the Sea*. He was followed by Jules Férat (1829–89?), who between 1871 and 1877 provided 445 plates for six novels. Thereafter, nearly all the illustrations for Verne's novels were the work of just two men. The most prolific was Léon Benett (1839–1917), who also illustrated novels by Victor Hugo, Tolstoy, Fenimore Cooper and others. He specialized in exotic scenes for which he drew on his wide experience as a government administrator in far-flung French colonies. Between 1878 and 1910, with a gap of seven years (1896–1903), he illustrated twenty-five Verne titles, a total of about 1,530 full-page plates. Benett overlapped with the almost equally productive Georges Roux (*c.*1850–1929), who, between 1885 and 1919, illustrated twenty Verne titles, containing over 950 plates in all.

Working in pairs or alone, they created an image for a Verne novel which was carefully managed by Hetzel. It is not clear how free a hand they had in choosing their subjects but they were certainly given firm directions. There is evidence to show that, with input from Verne and his canny publisher, they created an overall house style of detailed line-drawings which is as evocative and as distinctive as the association which links Tenniel to Lewis Carroll, or Cruikshank and Leech to the early Dickens. There was always an intriguing frontispiece, designed to lure the buyer, and the text was invariably illustrated in accordance with the goals of instruction and entertainment, the twin aims of Hetzel's *Magasin d'éducation et de récréation*. Different categories of illustrations are repeated: formal portraits of the main characters, painterly views of the places where their adventures are set and dramatic scenes showing crucial moments of the action. The educational intention was served by maps and accurate technical illustrations of flora and fauna, which are faithful to the old tradition of the plates that had appeared in books of natural history since the seventeenth century. Traditional too are the views showing the geography and geology of remote regions. Graphic representations of travelling machines followed Verne's written descriptions but were also 'instructive', being in the style of the line drawings of machinery then beginning to appear in the popular press and works of science. The inclusion of so many 'educational' plates was also intended to reassure the wealthy elite that a Hetzel novel was not illustrated merely as a sop to an audience with poor reading skills but was 'improving', respectable and suitable for all classes of book-buyer. In particular, Férat's ninety-one illustrations for *Michel Strogoff* (1876), which showed views of Russia, contributed significantly to its success.

Verne was no less committed to the illustrated book than Hetzel. His correspondence reveals how closely he monitored the work of the artists employed by Hetzel. In 1869 he was prepared to travel at short notice to Paris from Amiens to discuss Férat's illustrations for *Une Ville flottante* (*A Floating City*, 1871) and later that year, when preparations for the illustrated *Twenty Thousand Leagues Under the Sea* were in hand, he wrote to his publisher:

> I have received Riou's sketches. I have a number of suggestions to make which I shall put to him by return of post. I think he should make the figures larger and the rooms smaller. He also needs to add much more detail . . . But what an excellent, marvellous idea of yours to use Colonel Charras as a model for Captain Nemo. How stupid of me not to have thought of it myself![1]

He approved of the use of models and posed for Riou's portrait of Professor Aronnax in Part I, chapter 3 (page 19). The images of Michel Ardan of *De la Terre à la Lune* (*From the Earth to the Moon*, 1865) were based on his friend, the photographer and balloonist Nadar ('Ardan' is an anagram of Nadar), and twenty years later he reacted strongly against the way the hero of *Mathias Sandorf* (1885) had been made to look: 'Benett has given the doctor a face like a convict's,' he wrote to Hetzel. 'It's not right at all. The young Sandorf is modelled on you aged

thirty-five.' In 1879 he instructed Benett to make an eastern
caravan look 'more ornate and more oriental'. He intervened
mainly when an illustrator used his imagination too freely and
departed from his text. He corrected errors and, for example,
drew attention to Neuville's representation of the giant squid
as having ten arms instead of the eight specified in the text. In
fact the illustrator was right: it is the octopus which has eight
tentacles. The change of illustrator from Riou to Neuville after
Part I, chapter 11 was seamless, though later there are occasional inconsistencies. Thus, the 'iron ladder clamped to the
wall' of page 100 becomes a 'central stairwell', and a wide
staircase which is shown with a handrail (page 203) that later
disappears (page 435). On the whole, Verne found making
such corrections tedious, and Hetzel, who adjudicated between
him and his artists, always had the casting vote, especially in
matters of taste and decorum.

The illustrated editions masterminded by Hetzel ensured that
the volumes became instantly recognizable and formed a series
to which he gave the running title of *Voyages extraordinaires* in
1868. But the illustrations were not merely a smart marketing
ploy which packaged Verne as a uniform, branded product, nor
were they simply an addition to the novels, providing some relief
from all those words: they were essential ingredients of their
literary success. By visualizing what was strange, unknown and
beyond ordinary imagining, they shone a light on the unfamiliar and made the unlikely seem credible. By showing Verne's
heroes discovering and conquering undiscovered worlds, they
reinforced the positivist message that reality is stranger than fiction and that nature is tamed once it is understood.

NOTE

1. See Charles-Noël Martin, *La Vie et l'œuvre de Jules Verne*
    (Paris: Michel de l'Ormeraie, 1978), p. 76. Charras (1810–65)
    was a soldier and ardent republican who had been jailed (as had
    Hetzel) for his opposition to Louis-Napoleon's coup d'état in
    December 1851.

Twenty Thousand Leagues
Under the Sea

PART ONE

I

A Runaway Reef

The year 1866 was marked by a strange occurrence, an unexplained and indeed inexplicable phenomenon which surely no one can have forgotten. Though rumours abounded which alarmed the populations of ports and inflamed public sentiment in the interior of every continent, it was seafaring folk who felt the most afraid. Merchants, shipping companies, the captains of vessels, the skippers of boats and the marine commanders of Europe and America, officers of the navies of every nation and, in their wake, the governments of various countries of both continents, all gave their whole attention to the question and allocated it the highest priority.

The fact of the matter was that, for some time past, various ships at sea had encountered a long cigar-shaped object which could at times be phosphorescent and was infinitely larger and faster than a whale.

The facts concerning this mysterious apparition, set down in various ships' logs, all more or less tallied as to the structure of the object or creature in question, its unprecedented speed, its amazing locomotive power, and the particular vitality with which it appeared to be endowed. If it was a cetacean, it was infinitely larger in size than anything science had recorded up to that time. Not Cuvier nor Lacépède, nor Monsieur Duméril nor Monsieur Quatrefages[1] would have admitted the existence of such a monster – unless they had seen it for themselves, in other words had observed it through their own scientific optic.

Taking the average of the observations recorded at different times – and discounting both the conservative estimates which attributed to the object a length of 200 feet and the exaggerated reports which made it a mile wide and 3 miles long – it could be stated that this phenomenal creature surpassed by far the dimensions considered possible hitherto by ichthyologists – if, that is, it existed at all.

But exist it did, it was an undeniable fact and, given the ready tendency of the human brain to detect marvels everywhere, it will not be difficult to understand the excitement produced all over the globe by the supernatural apparition. Any thought that it could be relegated to the ranks of fable could not be entertained.

And then, on 20 July 1866, the steamship *Governor Higginson*, of the Calcutta and Burnach Steam Navigation Company, encountered this travelling mass 5 miles off the coast of Australia. At first, Captain Baker believed that he was dealing with an uncharted reef and was preparing to note its exact position when two gouts of water, released by the inexplicable object, rose 150 feet into the air with a great roar. Thus, unless the reef was subject to the intermittent eruption of a geyser, the *Governor Higginson* had happened upon a species of a hitherto unknown aquatic mammal, which was in the habit of blowing columns of water, mixed with air and steam, through its spiracles.

A similar encounter was recorded on 23 July of the same year, in Pacific waters, by the *Cristobal Colon*, of the West India and Pacific Steam Navigation Company. It followed that this cetacean was able, within a space of just three days, to move under its own power from one location to another with astonishing speed, for the *Governor Higginson* and the *Cristobal Colon* had observed it on two points on the map which were more than 700 nautical leagues apart.

Two weeks later and 2,000 leagues from the last sighting, the *Helvetia*, of the Compagnie Nationale, and the *Shannon*, of the Royal Mail, on opposite tacks in that part of the Atlantic which separates the United States from Europe, both reported sighting the monster at latitude 42° 15' north and longitude 60° 35' west of the Greenwich meridian. These simultaneous sightings allowed the minimum length of the mammal to be set at more than 350 English feet,* for neither the *Shannon* nor the *Helvetia* was as big, though both measured 100 metres from stem to stern. The largest whales, those to be found in the seas around the Aleutian Islands, the Kulammak and the Umgillick, never exceed a length of 56 metres and rarely achieve that.

These reports, arriving fast on the heels of each other, plus a new sighting made by the transatlantic steamship the *Pereire*; a collision between the *Etna* of the Iseman Line, and the monster; a detailed report from officers of the French frigate *La Normandie*; an unimpeachably accurate signal sent from senior officers under the command of Commodore Fitz-James, of the *Lord Clyde* – all brought the interest of the public to fever pitch. In countries inclined to the frivolous, jokes were made about the phenomenon. But in sober, practically minded countries, such as England, America and Germany, the matter was taken extremely seriously.

In every large centre of population, the monster was all the rage. Songs were sung about it in cafés, journalists mocked the very idea that such a thing existed, and plays featuring it were staged in theatres. Hoaxers of every shape and form had a field day. When newspapers were short of copy, they resurrected all the old tales of legendary, gigantic creatures, from the 'White Whale', the so-called fearsome 'Moby Dick' of hyperborean latitudes, to the colossal Kraken, whose tentacles could encircle a ship weighing 500 tons and drag it down into the depths of the ocean. Reports dating from ancient times were reprinted, the pronouncements of Aristotle and Pliny, who believed in the existence of monsters, the Norwegian accounts of the Bishop Pontoppidan, the travels of Paul Heggede and, not least, the reports of Mr Harrington, whose good faith is above suspicion when he claims to have seen, while a passenger on board the *Castillan*, in 1857, the enormous serpent which until that moment had only ever swum in the seas of the old *Constitutionnel*.[2]

And of course interminable arguments broke out in learned societies and scientific periodicals between believers and

* About 106 metres. An English foot measures just 30.4 centimetres. (Verne's notes included here as footnotes.)

unbelievers. The 'Monster Question' inflamed opinion. Journalists of a scientific bent locked horns with colleagues of a more spiritual disposition and used up gallons of ink in the course of this memorable campaign. Some even spilled a few drops of blood, for from spinning old yarns of sea-serpents they soon graduated to exchanging the most virulent insults.

For a whole six months the war of words continued, spurred on by chance happenings. To the weighty articles issued by the Brazilian Geographic Institute, the Royal Academy of Science in Berlin, the British Association, the Smithsonian Institute in Washington, to the discussions published by *The Indian Archipelago*, the abbé Moigno's *Cosmos*, Petermann's *Mittheilungen*, and to the scientific studies which appeared in the leading French journals – to all these the popular papers replied with inexhaustible energy. Their witty writers, parodying Linnaeus' remark, much quoted by the monster's detractors, took the view that 'Nature never created a fool'[3] and called on readers not to contradict nature by admitting the existence of Krakens, sea-serpents, Moby Dicks and other fantasies spawned by the fevered imaginations of sailors. Finally, the favourite contributor of a much-feared satirical magazine reviewed the whole matter in an article. He set about the monster like Hippolyte,[4] and administered the final *coup de grâce* to much general hilarity. Wit had vanquished science.

All through the first months of 1867, it seemed that the topic was as dead as a doornail, and that there was no likelihood of its being resurrected. And then new facts were brought to the attention of the public. It ceased to be a scientific problem which needed solving but became a very serious and real danger which had to be countered. The affair took on a new complexion. The monster reverted to being an island, a rock, a reef, but a moving reef of indeterminate and elusive dimensions.

On 5 March 1867 the *Moravian*, of the Montreal Ocean Company, sailing at night at latitude 27° 30' and longitude 72° 15', ran its starboard side against a rock which did not appear on any chart of the area. Propelled by the combined power of a following wind and its 400 horse-power engines, it was making 13 knots. No doubt it was due to the exceptional strength of its hull that the *Moravian* was not holed by the collision and sunk with the loss of the 237 passengers it was bringing back from Canada.

The accident had happened around five o'clock in the morning, just as dawn was beginning to break. The officers of the watch rushed to the stern of the vessel. They examined the ocean with the closest scrutiny. They saw nothing, save a strong agitation of the water three cables' length away, as though deep layers of the sea had been violently disrupted. The exact bearing was noted, and the *Moravian* continued on her way without any apparent damage. Had it struck a submerged rock or some large remnant of a wrecked ship? No one could tell. But when her hull was inspected in a dry dock, it was observed that a section of the keel had been splintered.

This occurrence, though very serious in itself, might have been forgotten along with all the others if, three weeks later, the same thing had not happened again and in identical circumstances. But this time, owing to both the nationality of the ship involved in this new collision and the name of the company which owned her, the incident attracted widespread attention.

There is no one who has not heard the name of the English shipping magnate Cunard. In 1840, this intelligent entrepreneur established a postal service between Liverpool and Halifax, with three wooden ships each of 1,162 tons and equipped with paddles driven by 400-horse-power engines. Eight years later the company's fleet was increased by four 650-horse-power vessels weighing 1,820 tons apiece and, two years later, by two additional ships of even greater power and tonnage. In 1853 the Cunard Company, whose licence to carry mail had just been renewed, expanded its fleet with the addition of the *Arabia*, the *Persia*, the *China*, the *Scotia*, the *Java* and the *Russia*, all vessels of the very highest specifications and, after the *Great Eastern*, the largest ships that had ever sailed the seas. Thus in 1867, the company owned twelve vessels, eight with paddles and four with propellers.

If I give these very brief details, it is so that readers understand the full importance of the Cunard shipping company, known the world over for the superior way in which it is run.

No other transoceanic navigation company has ever been managed with such skill, and no other enterprise has met with such success. During the last twenty-six years, Cunard ships have crossed the Atlantic 2,000 times. No scheduled voyage has been cancelled, all boats have arrived on time, none has been held up, no letter or passenger ship has been lost. The result is that travellers, despite the strong competition put up by France, continue to choose the Cunard Line in preference to all the rest, as becomes clear from an examination of publicly available accounts of the last few years' trading. This said, no one will be surprised by the enormous outcry that followed the accident which happened to one of its finest steamships.

On 13 April 1867, with a calm sea and a moderate wind, the *Scotia* was proceeding at longitude 15° 12' and latitude 45° 17' and, driven by her 1,000-horse-power engines, was making 13½ knots. Her paddles were turning with perfect regularity. Her draught was 6 metres and 70 centimetres and her displacement, 6,624 cubic metres.

At 4.17 in the afternoon, when passengers had gathered for lunch in the main saloon, there was a barely noticeable thump on the *Scotia*'s hull, on the quarter, a little aft of the portside paddle-wheel.

The *Scotia* had not struck anything: it had been struck, and by something that was sharp or piercing rather than blunt. The contact had been so slight that no one on board would have been alarmed had it not been for the stevedores in the hold who emerged on deck shouting:

'We're sinking! We're sinking!'

At first the passengers were very frightened. But Captain Anderson wasted no time in reassuring them. And indeed there could be no immediate danger. The *Scotia*, divided into seven separate watertight compartments, would not be seriously threatened by an isolated inrush of water.

Captain Anderson immediately hurried down to the hold. He ascertained that the fifth compartment had been flooded by the sea and the speed at which it had filled was evidence that the quantity of water taken on board was considerable.

Fortunately, this section was not where the boilers were located. If it had been, the fires would have been suddenly been put out.

Captain Anderson gave the order to stop the engines, and one of the sailors dived into the hold to report on the extent of the damage. Moments later, it was confirmed that there was a hole 2 metres across in the ship's bottom. There was no way a leak of that size could be fothered, and the *Scotia*, its paddles now partly under water, had no choice but to continue on her way. She was then 300 miles from Cape Clear and after a delay of three days, which caused considerable anxiety in Liverpool, she finally tied up at the company's wharves.

The engineers proceeded to inspect the *Scotia*, which was laid up in a dry dock. They could not believe their eyes. Two and a half metres below the water line was a neat puncture in the form of an isosceles triangle. The hole in the sheet-iron plating was cleanly cut and could not have been made more precisely by a metal punch. It followed that the piercing object which had done the damage was no common implement – and having been thrust forward with a force prodigious enough to penetrate metal plate four centimetres thick, it must have been withdrawn by a backward motion of a truly inexplicable nature.

This last occurrence had the effect of galvanizing public opinion afresh. From that moment on, any disaster at sea with no definite cause was attributed to the monster. This fantastic creature was made responsible for all such shipwrecks, which unfortunately are very numerous. For of the 3,000 ships whose loss is recorded each year by the Veritas Bureau,[5] the figure for sailing and steam vessels which, in the absence of information, are assumed to be lost with all hands and a full cargo runs to no less than 200!

So, rightly or wrongly, the 'monster' was held responsible for their disappearance, and with crossings between the various continents becoming increasingly dangerous, the public made its views felt and demanded categorically that every effort be made, whatever the cost, to rid the high seas of this formidable cetacean.

2

Pros and Cons

At the time when these events occurred, I had just returned from a scientific expedition to the badlands of Nebraska in the United States. In my capacity of assistant professor at the Museum of Natural History in Paris, I had been added to its complement by the French government. After six months in Nebraska, I reached New York towards the end of March with a number of valuable collections. My passage to France was booked for the start of May, and I was occupying the time until then cataloguing my wealth of mineralogical, botanical and zoological specimens when the *Scotia* incident occurred.

I was thoroughly acquainted with the leading topic of the day. How could I not be? But while I had read and reread all the reports in the American and European press, I was no further forward. The mystery puzzled me. Being in no position to form an opinion, I swung from one extreme to another. That there was something there was not in doubt, and unbelievers were invited to place their hand on the hole in the side of the *Scotia*.

When I reached New York, the story was on everyone's lips. The hypothesis of a floating island, of an elusive reef, which was advanced by a handful of unqualified commentators, had been completely discredited. For unless this reef had a motor in its entrails, how could it travel at such prodigious speeds?

Also rejected was the idea of a floating hull, some huge wreck, and for the same reason: the speed at which it travelled.

That left two possible solutions to the problem, which led to the rise of two distinct sets of advocates. In one camp were those who held out for a monster of colossal strength; in the other were those who supported the idea of a 'submarine' vessel with extreme locomotive power.

The latter hypothesis, which was after all theoretically plausible, did not stand up to investigations undertaken on both sides of the Atlantic. That any such motor engine could be available to a private citizen was highly unlikely. Where and when would he have built it and how could he have kept its construction secret?

Only a government could possess such a destructive machine, and in these disastrous times, when human ingenuity has been devoted to increasing the power of its arsenal of war, it was quite possible that some state was testing out a terrifying new weapon without the knowledge of the others. After the chassepot rifle came the torpedo, after the torpedo came the underwater battering-ram and after that will come revulsion. At least I hope so.

But the war machine hypothesis also collapsed after governments issued public denials. Since what was involved was a matter affecting the public at large, since all transoceanic traffic would be affected, the truth of these official statements could not be doubted. Moreover, how could it be imagined that the construction of this submarine vessel had escaped public notice? Keeping a secret in such circumstances is fearsomely difficult for a private citizen; but it is quite impossible for a state whose every action is tenaciously scrutinized by powerful rivals.

And so, after investigations undertaken in England, France, Russia, Prussia, Spain, Italy, America and even Turkey, the theory of an underwater *Monitor*[6] was definitively shelved.

The monster idea was therefore refloated despite the endless jokes made about it in the popular press, and once again imaginations ran wild with absurd stories based on ichthyological fantasy.

When I reached New York, several people had done me the honour of consulting me on this same phenomenon. In France, I had published a work in two quarto volumes entitled *Mysteries of the Great Ocean Depths*. My book, particularly well received by the scientific community, made me an expert in this rather abstruse area of natural history. My opinion was canvassed. As long as I felt able to deny the reality of the story, I stuck to repeating my negative statements. But soon I was backed into a corner and had to explain my position in unambiguous terms: 'the distinguished Professor Pierre Aronnax of the Museum of Paris' was invited by the *New York Herald* to get off the fence and express a view.

I did so. Unable to maintain my silence, I spoke. I discussed the problem from every angle, politically and scientifically. Here I shall print part of a very full article which I published in the issue of 30 April:

And so, having analysed the various theories one by one, all other assumptions having been discarded, I believe there is no other possibility than to favour the existence of a marine creature of enormous strength.

The great ocean depths are totally unknown to us. Soundings have not plumbed them. What goes on in those extreme gulfs? What kinds of creatures live and are able to live 12 or 15 miles beneath the surface of the water? What is the organic nature of such forms of life? We can barely guess.

However, a solution to the problem I have been asked to consider may well affect the nature of our inquiry.

Either we know all the species of creatures which inhabit our planet or we do not.

If we are not acquainted with all of them, if nature still has ichthyological revelations to make, then there is nothing unreasonable in admitting the existence of fish or cetaceans of new species or even new genera, all designed for 'bottom-dwelling', which inhabit strata beyond the reach of our soundings and which some kind of accidental occurrence, some whim or caprice of nature if you will, may at long intervals bring nearer to the surface of the ocean.

If, on the other hand, we are familiar with all living species, we must look for the animal in question among the marine creatures which are known and classified, in which case I would be inclined to admit the existence of a *Giant Narwhal*.

The common narwhal, or marine unicorn, often attains a length of 60 feet. Multiply this figure by five or ten, attribute to this cetacean strength commensurate with its size, increase its weapons of attack and you have the animal in question. It will have the proportions estimated by the officers of the *Shannon*, the piercing tool needed for the holing of the *Scotia* and the power required to penetrate the hull of a steamship.

For the narwhal is actually equipped with a sort of ivory 'sword' or 'halberd', to adopt the terms used by a number of naturalists. It is a principal tooth and is as hard as steel. A few such teeth have been found embedded in the bodies of whales, which the narwhal attacks, invariably with success. Others have been removed, not without difficulty, from the keels of ships which they had gone clean through, the way a gimlet pierces a barrel. The museum of the Faculty of Medicine in Paris possesses one of these tusks 2 metres and 25 centimetres long and 48 centimetres wide at its base!

Now, imagine this weapon to be ten times stronger and the animal ten times more powerful, launch it at a speed of 20 miles an hour, multiply its mass by its speed and you will have the potential for an impact capable of producing the required damage.

Therefore, until we have more information, I would favour a marine unicorn of enormous size, armed not with a halberd but with a spur, like armoured frigates or 'war rams', which it would equal in size and striking power.

In this way we would have the explanation of this inexplicable phenomenon – unless there is something over and above what has been imagined, seen, sensed and conjectured, which is still a possibility!

These last words were an equivocation on my part. For I wished up to a point to preserve my professorial dignity and not give the Americans too much of an opportunity to scoff, for when they laugh they laugh loudly. I allowed myself a loophole. But basically I was backing the 'monster' theory.

My article was hotly debated and attracted considerable attention. It drew a large number of supporters. Actually, the solution it proposed offered wide scope for the imagination. The human mind is naturally drawn to grandiose notions of supernatural beings, and the sea is the ideal medium for them, the only environment where such giant creatures – compared with which terrestrial animals such as elephants or rhinoceroses are mere midgets – can exist and prosper. Great masses of water can support the weight of the largest known species of mammals and may yet reveal the existence of molluscs of incomparable size, crustaceans fearsome to behold, lobsters, for example, 100 metres long or crabs that weigh 200 tons! Why not? Long ago, terrestrial animals living in ages corresponding to the geological epochs, quadrupeds, quadrumanes, reptiles and birds, were on a gigantic scale. The Creator had designed them in conformity with the principle of the gigantic, whose dimensions time has gradually reduced. Why, in its unknown depths, should the sea not have preserved these huge forms of life from another era, for the sea never changes, whereas the the earth's core is in an almost constant state of flux? Why should it not still conceal the last varieties of these titanic species for which each year is one of our centuries, and their centuries our millennia?

But I am allowing myself to be drawn into speculations which are no longer mine to encourage! Let us have no more talk of these fantasies that time has converted for me into fearsome realities. I repeat: opinions were formed at that juncture about the nature of the phenomenon, and the public accepted without question the existence of a prodigiously large creature which had nothing in common with the sea-serpents of myth and legend.

But if there were those who regarded the matter as no more than just another scientific problem in need of a solution, others, reacting in a more positive way, especially in America and England, set out to rid the ocean of this dangerous monster in order to safeguard intercontinental traffic. The industrial and economic press approached the issue mainly from this point of view. The *Shipping and Mercantile Gazette*, the *Lloyd*, the *Paquebot* and the *Revue maritime et coloniale*, all periodicals reflecting the interests of insurance companies that were threatening to raise their premiums, were unanimous on this question.

Public opinion having delivered its verdict, the States of the Union were the first to take action. In New York, preparations were put in hand for an expedition to hunt the narwhal. A fast frigate, the *Abraham Lincoln*, was made ready and scheduled to sail at the earliest opportunity. The arsenals were made available to Captain Farragut, who did all he could to ensure that the vessel was fully armed.

And then, as invariably happens, once the decision had been taken to hunt the monster, the monster failed to reappear. For two months, there was no mention of it. No boat encountered it. It was as if the unicorn had got wind of the campaign which was being mounted against it. There had been so much talk of it, some of it via the transatlantic cable. Consequently the wits claimed that the cunning creature had somehow intercepted a telegram, which it was now using to its advantage.

So the frigate was armed for a long campaign and equipped with formidable fishing tackle, but no one knew in which direction it should be dispatched. Impatience mounted. And then, on 3 July, it was learned that a steamship of the line sailing from San Francisco to Shanghai had sighted it several weeks earlier in the seas of the northern Pacific.

The excitement caused by the news was extreme. The authorities granted Captain Farragut less than a day to take final stores on board. The ship's bunkers overflowed with coal. No member of the crew defaulted on his duties. It only remained to light the boilers, let them come up to pressure and get under way! Not even half a day's delay would have been tolerated! But in any case, Captain Farragut could not wait to be gone.

Three hours before the *Abraham Lincoln* sailed from its Brooklyn pier, I received a letter which read as follows:

To Professor Aronnax, of the Museum of Paris, Fifth Avenue Hotel, New York

Dear Sir,

If you will consent to join the expedition of the *Abraham Lincoln*, the government of the Union will be most happy to see

France represented by you in this great enterprise. Captain
Farragut has ordered a cabin to be put at your disposal.

With every good wish,
J. B. Hobson
Navy Secretary

3
As Monsieur Wishes

Three seconds before J. B. Hobson's letter arrived, I was no more thinking about going after the unicorn than of trying to find the North West Passage. Three seconds after reading the missive from the honourable navy secretary, I finally knew my true vocation: the sole object of my whole existence was to hunt this troublesome monster down and rid the world of its presence.

However, I had only just returned from an exhausting journey and was weary and in need of rest. All I wanted was to set my eyes once more on my homeland, my friends, my small apartment in the Jardin des Plantes and my beloved, precious collections! But nothing could stop me. I forgot everything, fatigue, friends, collections, and accepted the invitation of the American government without a moment's hesitation.

'Besides,' I thought, 'all roads lead to Europe, and the unicorn will surely be kind enough to take me back to the shores of France! For my personal benefit, the worthy beast will allow itself to be caught in European waters, and I fully intend to take not less than half a metre of its ivory halberd back to the Museum of Natural History!'

But in the meantime I would have to look for the narwhal in the northern Pacific, which, if I was to return to France, meant taking the route via the antipodes.

'Conseil!' I shouted impatiently.

Conseil was my man. He was a devoted fellow who always went with me on all my travels, a good Fleming whom I liked a lot and who returned the sentiment. He was phlegmatic by nature, methodical by principle, keen by habit, calm in face of life's surprises, good with his hands, able to apply himself to any task, and, despite his name, he never gave advice even when asked for it.

From his frequent contact with scientists in our small circle at the Jardin des Plantes, Conseil had managed to pick up more than a smattering of learning. In him I had an extremely capable specialist in natural history classification who could scale with the agility of a circus performer the ladder of branches, groups, classes, sub-classes, orders, families, genera, subgenera, species and varieties. But that was where his knowledge ended. Classification was his whole life and his competence, and he knew nothing else. Well versed in the theory of classification and not at all in the practice, I suspect he would not have been able to tell a cachalot from a whale! Yet he was willing and so very dependable.

For the previous ten years, Conseil had followed me wherever science had directed my steps. Never a complaint from him about how long or tiring a journey might be. Never an objection when asked to pack a case for some foreign country, be it China or the Congo, no matter how far away it was. He would go wherever he was bidden without question. In addition, he enjoyed rude good health which resisted all forms of illness. He had strong muscles but no nerves, or any appearance of nerves – temperamentally speaking, that is.

He was thirty years old, and his age was to his employer's as fifteen is to twenty. The reader will forgive me for saying in this way that I was forty.

Conseil had one fault: he was a stickler for formalities. He always addressed me in the third person, which at times I found most irritating.

'Conseil!' I shouted again, as I feverishly set my hand to my preparations for departure.

I always knew, of course, that I could count on his loyal service. Ordinarily, I never asked if it was convenient for him to go with me on my travels. But this time, the proposed expedition was an enterprise which might be indefinitely prolonged and was also dangerous, for it meant hunting an animal more than capable of sinking a frigate as easily as a nutshell. It was something that even the most equably tempered man in the world needed to think about. What would Conseil say?

'Conseil!' I called for a third time.

Conseil appeared.

'Did monsieur call?'

'Yes. Pack for me and pack for yourself! We leave in two hours!'

'As monsieur wishes,' said Conseil, as calm as you like.

'There isn't a moment to lose. Pack a trunk with all my usual travel articles: suits of clothes, shirts, socks. Don't worry about how much to take, just pack as much as you can, and quick about it.'

'And monsieur's collections?'

'We'll worry about them later.'

'What! Including the archiotherium, hyracotherium, oreodons, cheropotamus and other specimens?'

'The hotel will look after them.'

'And the live babirusa?'

'They'll feed it while we're away. Anyway, I shall make arrangements for our collection of live specimens to be sent to France.'

'So we will not be returning to Paris?' asked Conseil.

'Yes ... of course,' I said evasively, 'but we'll be making a detour.'

'A detour which will be to monsieur's liking?'

'Oh, just a small one. A slightly less direct route, that's all. We'll be travelling on the *Abraham Lincoln*.'

'As monsieur thinks best,' was Conseil's unruffled answer.

'Actually, old friend, it's all to do with the monster, the famous narwhal. We're going to rid the seas of its presence! The

'*As monsieur wishes*'

author of a quarto work in two volumes on the *Mysteries of the Great Ocean Depths* cannot afford to turn down the chance of sailing with Captain Farragut. A glorious mission but also a hazardous one. We do not know where it will take us. Those creatures can behave very unpredictably. But go we shall! We have a skipper who has all his wits about him.'

'What monsieur does, I shall do also,' said Conseil.

'Have you thought about this? I have no wish to keep anything from you. It will be one of those voyages from which a man does not always return.'

'As monsieur wishes.'

A quarter of an hour later our trunks were ready. Conseil had packed them in the twinkling of an eye. I knew that nothing had been left behind because he classified shirts and clothes as carefully as he did birds and mammals.

The hotel lift carried us down to the spacious lobby on the mezzanine. I descended the few steps that led to the ground floor. I paid my bill at the long counter, which was always besieged by a large number of people. I made arrangements for my crates of stuffed animals and dried plants to be forwarded to Paris. I opened an account sufficient to cover the expense of keeping the babirusa and, with Conseil close on my heels, jumped into a cab.

The twenty-franc fare took us down Broadway to Union Square, followed Fourth Avenue as far as the junction with Bowery Street, turned into Katrin Street and drew up at Pier 34.* From there, the Katrin ferry took us – men, horses and cab – to Brooklyn, the grand annex of New York situated on the left bank of the East River, and within minutes we had reached the pier, where the twin funnels of the *Abraham Lincoln* were making vast amounts of black smoke.

Our luggage was immediately carried on to the deck of the frigate. I rushed on board and asked for Captain Farragut. A sailor led the way to the poop, where I came face to face with a hearty-looking naval officer, who offered me his hand.

'Professor Pierre Aronnax?' he said.

* A special kind of jetty provided for each individual vessel.

'The very same,' I replied. 'Captain Farragut?'

'In person. Welcome aboard, professor. Your cabin is ready for you.'

I bowed and, leaving the captain to attend to the business of getting the ship under way, I was shown to the quarters which had been assigned to me.

The *Abraham Lincoln* had been well chosen for her new role. She was one of the very fastest frigates, fitted with super-heating steam engines which created a steam pressure of 7 atmospheres. With such high pressure, the *Abraham Lincoln* could reach an average speed of 18 3/10 knots, an impressive speed, but one which was nevertheless no match for the giant cetacean.

The on-board design of the frigate was of the same high standard as its nautical features. I was very happy with my quarters, which were situated aft and opened directly into the officers' ward room.

'We shall do very well here,' I said to Conseil.

'As well, begging monsieur's leave,' said Conseil, 'as a hermit crab in the shell of a whelk.'

I left Conseil to stow away the contents of our trunks and went back out on deck to watch the preparations for departure.

Just then Captain Farragut was giving the order to cast off the last moorings holding the *Abraham Lincoln* fast to its Brooklyn pier. Which meant that if I had been a quarter of an hour late, or even less, the frigate would have sailed without me and I would have missed that extraordinary, supernatural and highly implausible expedition, of which an exact account may well meet with some scepticism.

But Captain Farragut was determined not to waste a day, an hour, in his eagerness to take up a station in the seas where the creature had been sighted. He called to the chief engineer.

'Are we up to pressure?' he asked.

'Yes sir!' the man replied.

'Then make full steam!' said Captain Farragut.

At this order, which was transmitted by means of the compressed-air communication system, the chief engineer turned the wheel that started the engines. The steam hissed as it rushed into the half-open slide-valves. The long horizontal

'The armada continued to follow the frigate'

pistons protested as they moved the crank-arms. The blades of the propeller beat the water at an increasing rate, and the *Abraham Lincoln* slid majestically through a hundred or so ferry-boats and steam tenders* loaded with spectators that were escorting her on her way.

The wharves of Brooklyn and the whole of that part of New York bordering the East River were lined with sightseers. We were given successive rounds of three cheers as we sailed past the 500,000 spectators. Thousands of handkerchiefs were brandished above the heads of the tightly packed crowds, saluting the *Abraham Lincoln* until she reached the waters of the Hudson at the southern end of the elongated peninsula which forms the city of New York.

Then the frigate followed the coast of New Jersey along the river's magnificent right bank, tightly packed with villas, and passed between the forts, which honoured her by firing their largest guns. The *Abraham Lincoln* returned the salute by showing and thrice raising the American flag, whose thirty-nine stars[7] fluttered gaily from the peak of the mizzen top-mast. Then, changing course to negotiate the curving channel marked by buoys in the inner bay formed by Sandy Hook Point, she skirted the sandy tongue of land, where several thousand spectators added more cheers.

The armada of boats and tenders continued to follow the frigate and did not turn back until they came abreast with the lightship whose twin beacons mark the entrance of the New York channels.

By then, three o'clock was striking. The pilot disembarked into his small boat and rowed back to the small schooner waiting for him on our lee side. The boilers were stoked higher; the screw churned the water more quickly; the frigate moved along the low, yellow shore of Long Island and, at eight in the evening, when to the northwest the lights of Fire Island had at last dropped from sight, she was steaming at full speed over the dark waters of the Atlantic.

---

* Small steam launches which service large steamships.

4

Ned Land

Captain Farragut was a fine seaman and worthy of the frigate he commanded. He and his boat were as one. He was its soul. As to the cetacean, there was no doubt in his mind, and he banned all arguments about the existence of the creature on his ship. He believed in it as certain devout women believe in the Leviathan[8] – by faith, 1st reason. The monster existed, and he had sworn to rid the sea of it. He was a kind of Chevalier de Rhodes, a Dieudonné de Gozon,[9] sallying forth to fight the serpent which was ravaging his island. Either Captain Farragut would kill the narwhal or the narwhal would kill Captain Farragut. There could be no other outcome.

His officers shared their captain's opinion. You had only to hear the way they talked, discussed, argued, calculated the various chances of meeting the creature and see them scanning the vast expanse of the ocean. More than one volunteered to keep a look-out in the crow's nest who would have cursed being sent aloft in any other circumstances. For as long as the sun followed its daily course the crosstrees were crowded with sailors so eager to join the hunt that they simply could not stay on deck, even though the *Abraham Lincoln* had yet to set its prow anywhere near the suspect waters of the Pacific.

The whole ship's company wanted nothing more than to come upon the unicorn, harpoon it, hoist it on board and slaughter it. Every eye scoured the sea with the closest attention. Moreover, Captain Farragut had made it known that a reward of $2,000 would be given to whoever first sighted the animal, whether it was a ship's boy, sailor, able seaman or officer. I leave it to the reader to decide if eyes on board the *Abraham Lincoln* were kept permanently peeled.

I myself was no different from the others and never ceded my part of each day's observation to anyone else. The frigate would have been justified many times over in calling herself the *Argus*.[10] Of the ship's complement only Conseil, being utterly indifferent to the question which fascinated everyone, demurred and thus was the exception to the general enthusiasm shown by all concerned.

As I said, Captain Farragut had carefully fitted out his ship with tackle adapted for catching the cetacean. A whaler would not have been better armed. We had all the latest equipment, from the hand-thrown harpoon to the barbed variety which is shot from a blunderbuss and explosive heads fired by a swivel-gun. On the fo'c'sle was positioned the latest type of breech-loading cannon, thick-barrelled and small-bored, a specimen of which is to feature in the Universal Exhibition of 1867.[11] This invaluable weapon, made in America, could easily fire a cone-shaped projectile weighing 4 kilos an average distance of 16 kilometres.

The *Abraham Lincoln* thus lacked no form of destructive weaponry. But it also had something even better. It had Ned Land, prince of harpooners.

Ned Land was a Canadian, uncommonly skilful with his hands and unrivalled in his dangerous occupation. Skill and a cool head, courage and astuteness: he possessed all these qualities at the highest level. It would take a cunning whale indeed or an unusually wily cachalot to escape his harpoon.

Ned Land was about forty years old. He was very tall – he was over six English feet – strongly built, sombre in manner, naturally taciturn, sometimes violent and capable of great rages when contradicted. His appearance commanded attention, and in particular the directness of his look gave his face a most striking expression.

I believe it was very shrewd of Captain Farragut to engage his services. He was worth more than the rest of the crew put together in the keenness of his eye and the strength of his arm. I could not do better than to compare him to a powerful telescope which was simultaneously a loaded gun ready to go off.

To call someone Canadian is the same as saying they are French. Although Ned Land was not very communicative, I must admit that he took a liking to me. My nationality was doubtless part of the attraction. It provided him with an opportunity to talk and me with a chance to hear the old language of Rabelais,[12] which is still used in certain Canadian provinces. The harpooner's family came originally from Quebec, a tribe of bold fishermen in the days when the province still belonged to France.

Gradually Ned became more talkative, and I loved to hear him speak of his adventures in the polar seas. He told me about his fishing trips and his colossal struggles with great natural poetic flair. His tale was cast in an epic mould, and I had a sense that I was hearing a Canadian Homer singing the *Iliad* of those hyperborean regions.

I describe this bold companion as I know him now. The fact is, we have become firm friends, bound together by the unshakeable comradeship born of, and consolidated in, the most fearful ordeals. Ah! Brave Ned! I would only ask to live for another hundred years to hold the memory of you longer!

And now, what was Ned Land's opinion of the sea-monster question? I will admit here that he was not much taken with the idea of a sea unicorn and that he was the only man on board who did not share the general view. In fact, he deliberately evaded the subject when one day I tried to tackle him on it.

On the splendid evening of 30 July, that is, three weeks after our departure, the frigate was sailing off Cape Blanc, 30 miles in the lee of the coast of Patagonia. We had crossed the Tropic of Capricorn, and the Straits of Magellan lay 700 miles to the south of us. Within a week, the *Abraham Lincoln* would be ploughing through the waves of the Pacific.

Ned Land and I were sitting on the poop, chatting of this and that, looking out over the mysterious sea, whose depths have so far remained inaccessible to the eye of man. I brought the conversation gently round to the giant unicorn. I ran through the various chances of success or failure that our expedition might meet with. Then, realizing that Ned was allowing me to ramble on without saying very much himself, I decided to press him more directly:

'How is it, Ned, that you won't be convinced of the existence of the cetacean we are hunting? Do you have any particular reason for being so dubious?'

The harpooner looked at me for a few moments, struck his broad brow with one hand in a habitual gesture of his, closed his eyes as if to gather his thoughts and finally said:

'Maybe I have, Professor Aronnax.'

'But Ned, you, a whaler by profession, are familiar with the larger marine mammals and able to stretch your imagination far enough to include the hypothesis of gigantic cetaceans; surely you should be the last person to have doubts in the circumstances!'

'That's where you're wrong, professor,' replied Ned. 'If ordinary folk believe that there are strange comets travelling through space or antediluvian monsters living in the centre of the earth and other such fantasies, astronomers and geologists do not. The same goes for whalers. I've hunted many cetaceans, harpooned a large number of them and killed a good few, but however powerful and well armed they were, neither their tails nor their tusks would ever have broken through the iron plates of a steamship's hull.'

'Still, Ned, you do hear of ships which have been holed by a narwhal's tusk.'

'Wooden ships, maybe,' replied the Canadian, 'but there again, I never saw such a thing myself. So until there is evidence to the contrary, I shall deny that whales, cachalots or sea unicorns can produce such an effect.'

'Listen, Ned . . .'

'No, professor, I won't. On any other subject, yes, but not that one. Perhaps a gigantic octopus? . . .'

'Even more unlikely, Ned. The octopus is a mollusc, and the very word suggests the lack of firmness of its flesh. Even at 500 feet long it would still not belong to the class of vertebrates and would be harmless to ships like the *Scotia* or the *Abraham Lincoln*. So the ravages of the Kraken and other monsters of that kind must be relegated to the realms of legend.'

'So as a naturalist,' Ned went on in a sarcastic tone of voice, 'you persist in believing in the existence of an enormous cetacean.'

'I do, Ned, and I'll say it again with a conviction based on the logic of fact. I believe in the existence of a mammal which is powerfully built, a member of the class of vertebrates, like the whale, the cachalot and the dolphin, which is armed with a horn or tusk with colossal penetrative power.'

'Hm,' said the harpooner, shaking his head with the air of a man who has made up his mind not to be convinced.

'And note further, my good Canadian friend,' I continued, 'that if such an animal does indeed exist, if it lives at the bottom of the ocean, if its habitat is the watery deep miles beneath the surface of the seas, it must of necessity have a physical form so strong as to defy all comparison.'

'And why should this form need to be so strong?' asked Ned.

'Because it requires incalculable strength to survive in those lowest depths and withstand the huge pressures.'

'Is that a fact?' asked Ned looking at me with a doubtful wink.

'It is a fact, and a few figures will easily prove it.'

'Oh, figures!' said Ned. 'You can prove anything with figures!'

'In business, Ned, but not in mathematics. Now listen here. Let us agree that the pressure of one atmosphere is represented by a column of water 32 feet high, though actually, the column of water would not be quite as tall as that, since we're talking about sea-water, which has a higher density than fresh water. Now, when you dive, Ned, the number of times 32 feet of water you have over your head is the same as the number of times your body is withstanding the equivalent of atmospheric pressure, that is, the same number of kilograms per square centimetre on the surface. It follows that at 320 feet down this pressure is 10 atmospheres, 100 atmospheres 3,200 feet down and 1,000 atmospheres 32,000 feet below the surface, which is about 2½ leagues. This is the same as saying that if you could go down to such a depth, each square centimetre of the surface of your body would be subject to a pressure of 1,000 kilos. Now, Ned, do you have any idea of how many square centimetres there are on the surface of your body?'

'Probably not, professor.'

'About 17,000.'

'Who'd have thought it?'

'And since in reality atmospheric pressure is slightly higher than the weight of one kilogram per square centimetre, those 17,000 square centimetres are subjected to a pressure of 17,568 kilos.'

'Without me noticing?'

'Without your noticing. But if you are not crushed by such pressure, it is because air is entering your body at the same pressure. This achieves a perfect balance between internal and external pressures, which then cancel each other out, and this allows you to bear them without difficulty. But it's quite another matter under water.'

'I see that,' said Ned, now paying more attention. 'It's because the water is all round me and does not get inside me.'

'Exactly, Ned. So when you're 32 feet beneath the surface of the water, you will be experiencing pressure of 17,568 kilos; at 320 feet down, ten times that figure, that is 175,680 kilos; at 3,200 feet, the pressure is 100 times greater, 1,756,800 kilos; at 32,000 feet, it is 1,000 times greater again, making 17,568,000 kilos – which means that you would be squashed as flat as if you'd been put through the rollers of a hydraulic mill!'

'I'll be damned!' said Ned.

'So, my harpooning friend, if vertebrates several hundred metres long and of a corresponding size and whose surface is to be measured in millions of square centimetres, can survive at such depths, then it is in billions of kilos that we must estimate the pressure they have to withstand. Now calculate how great must be the strength of their skeletal structure and the strength of a carcass required to withstand such pressure!'

'They'd have to be made,' said Ned, 'of steel plate 8 inches thick, like armoured frigates.'

'As you say, Ned, and just think of the damage that would be done by a mass that size when propelled with the speed of an express train against the hull of a ship.'

'Yes . . . well . . . perhaps,' replied the Canadian, shaken by these figures but not quite willing to surrender.

'Well, have I convinced you?'

'You've convinced me of one thing, professor, which is that if indeed such animals do exist at the bottom of the sea, then they must of necessity be as strong as you say.'

'But if they don't exist, you stubborn man, how do you explain what happened to the *Scotia*?'

'It could be . . .' said Ned uncertainly.

'Out with it, man!'

'Because . . . it isn't true!' answered the Canadian, unwittingly echoing the famous reply given by Arago.[13]

But this answer merely confirmed the harpooner's obstinacy, nothing more. That day, I did not push him any further. What happened to the *Scotia* was undeniable. The hole was real and had to be repaired – and I don't think that the existence of a hole can be more clearly demonstrated. Now the hole had not appeared all by itself, and since it had not been made by submerged rocks or underwater weapons, it had to have been caused by the penetrative power of an animal's weapon.

Now, in my view, and for all the reasons previously adduced, the animal belonged to the branch of vertebrates, to the class of mammals, to the pisciform group and ultimately to the order of cetaceans. As to where it ranked exactly in the family among whale, cachalot or dolphin, as to what genus it belonged and the species to which it should be assigned, these were questions to be settled later. But for us to find the answers, the unknown monster would have to be dissected; to dissect it, it would have to be caught; and to catch it, it had to be harpooned – which was Ned Land's department; to be harpooned it would have to be sighted – which was the business of the boat's crew; and to sight it we would need to find it – which was a matter of chance.

5
Adventure Ho!

The voyage of the *Abraham Lincoln* continued for some time without incident. However, an event occurred which demonstrated Ned Land's remarkable skills and showed just how much confidence could be placed in him.

We were off the Falklands on 30 June when the frigate exchanged signals with some American whalers. We discovered that they had no knowledge of the narwhal. But one of them, the captain of the *Monroe*, learning that Ned Land had shipped on the *Abraham Lincoln*, asked for his help in hunting down a whale they had in sight. Captain Farragut, curious to see Ned Land in action, gave him permission to go on board the *Monroe*. Luck was so much on the Canadian's side that instead of one whale he harpooned two in quick succession, hitting one clean in the heart and hooking the other after a pursuit lasting only a few minutes!

One thing is clear: if the monster ever comes up against Ned Land's harpoon, I would not bet on its chances.

The frigate sailed down the south-eastern coast of South America at a prodigious speed. On 3 July, we were at the entrance to the Magellan Straits, abreast of Cabo Virgenes. But Captain Farragut was not minded to venture through that winding route and set a course that took us round Cape Horn.

The crew gave him their unanimous backing. For was it at all likely that we would have encountered the narwhal in that narrow channel? A good number of the sailors were sure the monster would not be able to get through it as 'it was far too big for that'!

On 6 July, around three in the afternoon, the *Abraham*

Lincoln, then 15 miles to the south, passed the uninhabited island – little more than an isolated rock – which was the far-thermost tip of the American continent to which Dutch sailors had given the name of their home town: Cape Horn. A north-westerly course was set, and the next day the frigate's propeller was at last churning a passage through the waters of the Pacific

'Keep your eyes open! Keep 'em peeled!' was the repetitive refrain of the crew of the *Abraham Lincoln*.

And keep them open they certainly did! Eyes and telescopes, somewhat dazzled it must be said by the prospect of the 2,000 dollars, were barely still for a single moment. Night and day, they scanned the surface of the ocean, so that even true nyc-talopes, whose ability to see in the dark would have increased their chances by fifty per cent, would have been hard put to win the prize.

Though I myself was not tempted by the lure of money, I was not the least enthusiastic observer on board. Sparing only a few minutes for meals and a few hours for sleep, indifferent to sun and rain, I never left the deck of the ship. Stationed at the bow or leaning aft over the taffrail, I hungrily scoured the fleecy wake which whitened the tops of the waves as far as the eye could see. And how many times did I share the excitement of the ship's officers and crew when the dark-hued back of a playful whale broke the surface? Then the frigate's deck would suddenly become crowded. The companion hatches would dis-gorge a torrent of sailors and officers. Their chests pounding, each of them followed the movements of the cetacean through blurry eyes. I looked, I looked hard enough to wear out my retina and blind myself, while Conseil, as phlegmatic as ever, kept repeating calmly:

'If monsieur would be good enough not to open his eyes so wide, he would be able to see much better.'

But our excitement was soon confounded! The *Abraham Lincoln* would change course, overtake the animal we had sighted, and it would turn out to be a common whale or just another cachalot, which would then disappear quickly amid a chorus of oaths.

Meanwhile the weather continued fair. The voyage was

enjoying the most favourable conditions. It was then winter in the southern hemisphere, for July in those regions corresponds to our January in Europe, but the sea remained calm, allowing its entire vast circumference to be easily scanned.

Ned Land still maintained the same stubborn incredulity. He even pretended not to scour the surface of the sea outside his official watches – at least when no whale had been sighted. Still, his almost miraculous eyesight would have been a great help. But that obstinate Canadian spent eight hours out of every twelve reading or sleeping in his cabin. I kept reproving him for his indifference.

'Bah!' he would say, 'there's nothing there, Professor Aronnax. And even if there was, what chance have we got of spotting it? Aren't we just sailing around more or less at random? They reckon that this elusive creature has been seen in the high latitudes of the Pacific. I'm quite prepared to believe it. But it's already been two months since it was sighted there, and if we can go by the nature of your narwhal, it doesn't like hanging around in the same place for long! It's prodigiously endowed with the ability to move from one place to another. Now you know far better than me, professor, that nature never contradicts itself. It would never give an animal that is essentially slow-moving the ability to travel at high speed unless it needed to use it. So if this beast does exist, then it's already a long way away.'

I was hard put to reply to this. Obviously, we were searching blind. But what other way was there? This meant our chances were very slim. Still, no one doubted that we would succeed and no sailor on board would have bet against the existence of the narwhal and its next appearance.

On 20 July, we reached the Tropic of Capricorn at 105° longitude, and on the 27th of the same month we crossed the equator on the 110th meridian. After taking a bearing, the frigate set a more specific course due west and began entering the waters of the central Pacific. Captain Farragut thought, and rightly so, that it would be better to patrol the deep water and keep away from continents or islands, which the animal had always seemed reluctant to approach, 'doubtless on account of there not being enough water for it', as the bosun said. Accordingly, the frigate kept well away from the Pomotou Isles, the Marquesas and the Sandwich Islands, crossed the Tropic of Cancer at 132° longitude and headed into the China Seas.

We had now at last reached the scene where the monster had last disported itself and, to be frank, those on board hardly dared breathe. Our hearts beat wildly, doubtless setting ourselves up for a future of incurable aneurisms. The whole crew was in a state of nervous over-excitement that I can scarcely convey. The men stopped eating, they did not sleep. A dozen times a day some misreading of the signs or a false sighting on the part of a sailor high in the crosstrees caused unbearable alarm, and these shocks to the system, repeated over and over, kept us in a state of heightened tension far too violent not to produce a reaction sooner or later.

And indeed a reaction was not long in coming. For three months – three months when each day lasted a century! – the *Abraham Lincoln* had been patrolling the northern Pacific, pursuing whales which had been sighted, making abrupt changes of course, changing tack suddenly, stopping without warning, making full steam ahead then going into reverse, time after time threatening to throw the engines out of kilter. We had left no compass point unexplored from the shores of Japan to the coast of America and had found nothing, nothing except the vastness of the empty waves, nothing that looked like a gigantic narwhal or an underwater island or a derelict wreck or a runaway reef or anything that was remotely supernatural!

At last the reaction came. Discouragement began to creep in and opened the way to doubt. A new feeling spread through the ship which was three parts mortification and seven parts fury. The men felt stupid for having let themselves be taken in by a fantasy, but more than that they were furious! The mountain of arguments which had been built up over the past year now suddenly collapsed, and everyone thought only of how they could make up for the time that had been so idiotically sacrificed by doing as much eating and sleeping as they could.

With the fickleness that comes naturally to the human mind, they jumped from one extreme to another. The most enthusiastic supporters of the undertaking now became its fiercest critics. The reaction rose from the bowels of the ship, from the stokers in their bunkers to the officers on the bridge. It is certain that had it not been for Captain Farragut, who remained stubbornly steadfast, the frigate would have turned and set a course south.

But clearly this useless search could not go on for much longer. The *Abraham Lincoln* had nothing to reproach itself with, having tried everything in pursuit of success. No crew of any ship in the American Navy had ever showed more patience and zeal. Failure could not be laid at its door. There was no alternative but to return to port.

A proposal to this effect was put to the captain. Captain Farragut held firm. The sailors made no attempt to hide their discontent, and their work suffered. I am not saying that there was a mutiny on board but, after digging his heels in for a reasonable period, Captain Farragut, as Christopher Columbus once did, asked for the men to be patient for three days. If in that time the monster had not appeared, the helmsman would give the wheel three full turns, and the *Abraham Lincoln* would steer a course for the waters of Europe.

This promise was made on 2 November. It had the immediate effect of reviving the crew's flagging spirits. Again, the ocean was scrutinized with renewed zeal. Each man was eager to have that one last look that sticks in the memory. Telescopes were worked feverishly hard. It was a final challenge to the giant narwhal, which in all reasonableness could not fail to respond to this 'summons to appear'.

Two days passed. The engines of the *Abraham Lincoln* moved slowly. Everything possible was tried to attract the animal's attention or rouse it from its torpor if it should happen to be somewhere close. Huge sides of fat bacon were towed in the ship's wake – much to the delight, I must add, of the sharks. The ship's boats fanned out in all directions around the *Abraham Lincoln* as she lay to, leaving no quarter of the sea unexplored. But the evening of 4 November came round, and still the answer to the underwater mystery had not been found.

The following day, 5 November, at noon, the agreed time

would be up. After that point, if Captain Farragut was to keep his promise he would have to order a southeasterly course to be set and leave the waters of the northern Pacific once and for all.

At that time, the frigate's position was latitude 31° 15' north and longitude 136° 42' east. The coast of Japan lay less than 200 miles to leeward. Darkness was falling. Eight bells had just been struck. Large clouds veiled the face of the moon, then in its first quarter. The sea heaved gently under the frigate's stern.

I was leaning over the fo'c'sle rail on the starboard side. Conseil, standing next to me, was looking straight ahead. Members of the crew, perched aloft, were scanning the horizon, which was slowly growing fainter and darker. The officers were peering through their night glasses into the gathering gloom. At intervals the murky ocean glinted as a beam of moonlight slanted down between the edges of two clouds. Then all trace of light was swallowed up by the blackness.

As I watched Conseil, I was aware that even my valiant servant was falling under the same spell as everyone else. At least I thought so. Were his nerves pulsing with feelings of curiosity, perhaps for the first time?

'Look lively, Conseil!' I said. 'This is your last chance to pocket 2,000 dollars.'

'If I may be permitted to say so, monsieur,' Conseil replied, 'I have not been counting on winning the prize. The government of the Union could have offered a reward of 100,000 dollars and been none the poorer.'

'You're quite right, Conseil. This is a very foolish business, and one which we entered into far too lightly. It's been such a waste of time, an unnecessary expenditure of energy. We could have been back in France six months ago.'

'In monsieur's modest apartment,' replied Conseil, 'in monsieur's own museum. And I would have already classified monsieur's fossils. And the babirusa would have been settled in his cage in the zoo and attracting all the inquisitive citizens of Paris.'

'Exactly, Conseil, not to mention the fact that I suppose they'll all have a laugh at our expense.'

'Very true,' Conseil said coolly. 'I think that monsieur will be a butt of their jokes. And need I say . . . ?'

'Say it, Conseil.'

'Well, monsieur will have got no more than he deserves.'

'Really!'

'When a man has the honour, as monsieur has, of being a person of learning, he does not go out of his way to . . .'

Conseil was unable to finish his compliment, for a voice had just burst into the general silence. The voice belonged to Ned Land, and Ned Land was shouting:

'The object we're hunting! There, on the beam, amidships!'

6

Full Steam Ahead!

When they heard him shout, the full ship's company rushed to where the harpooner was standing, captain, officers, petty officers, sailors and ship's boys, everyone down to the mechanics who abandoned their engines and the stokers who deserted their furnaces. The order to heave to had been given, and the frigate was being carried forward by nothing more than its own momentum.

It was now pitch dark, and however keen the Canadian's eyesight, I wondered how he had been able to see at all and what it was that he had seen. My heart was thumping as if it was about to burst.

But Ned Land had not been mistaken, and we all saw the object he was pointing at.

Not two cables' length from the *Abraham Lincoln*, off the starboard beam, the sea looked as if it were being lit from below. It was not just a straightforward occurrence of the phenomenon of phosphorescence, there was no possibility of error over that. The monster now lying a few fathoms beneath the surface of the water was emitting the same intense but inexplicable illumination which had been mentioned in the reports of a number of ships' masters. Its fierce radiance could only have been produced by some hugely powerful means. The part which was lit formed a great, elongated oval in the centre of which was the source of the blinding incandescence. Its unbearable brilliance was then progressively reduced in a series of decreasing stages.

'Why, it's just a mass of phosphorescent molecules!' exclaimed one of the officers.

'The monster now lying a few fathoms beneath the surface of the water'

'Not so,' I replied with conviction. 'Neither piddocks nor salpae ever give off such intense light. This brilliance is essentially electric in nature. Anyway, look there, it's changing position! . . . It's moving forward . . . now back . . . it's making straight for us!'

A general shout went up from the frigate.

'Silence!' cried Captain Farragut. 'Lay the helm hard over! Make full astern!'

The crew rushed to the helm, and the engine men to their posts. The steam power was immediately reversed, and the *Abraham Lincoln*, beating to port, described a semi-circle.

'Right the helm! Make full ahead!' cried Captain Farragut.

His orders were executed with alacrity, and the frigate, making speed, sailed away from the source of the light.

But I am mistaken: we attempted to move away but the supernatural creature caught us up, travelling at twice our speed.

Our breathing was shallow and rapid. But it was astonishment, not fear, that froze our tongues and rooted us to the spot. The animal gained on us and started playing with us. It raced round the frigate, which was then making 14 knots, and covered us with electric charges like so much luminous dust. Then it shot off to a distance of 2 or 3 miles, leaving a wake of phosphorescence similar to the clouds of steam that trail the locomotive of an express train. And now, from the dark edges of the horizon where it had retreated to start its run, it suddenly bore down on the *Abraham Lincoln* with terrifying speed, pulled up just 20 feet short of our gunwales and extinguished its light – not by sinking beneath the waters, because its brilliance did not fade gradually – but instantly, as if the source of the blinding light it gave off had suddenly failed! Then it reappeared on the other side of the ship, either having sailed round us or under the hull. At any moment, there could be a collision which might have proved fatal to us.

But I was amazed by the frigate's response. Instead of attacking, we beat a retreat. The ship which was supposed to pursue was itself being pursued! I turned and put this to Captain Farragut. His face, normally so impassive, was suffused with an expression of indescribable amazement.

'Professor Aronnax,' he said, 'I have no idea what kind of formidable opponent I am up against and I do not intend to do anything in this darkness that would put my ship at risk. Besides, how am I to attack an unknown enemy? How can I defend my ship? Let us wait for daylight, and the roles will change.'

'Do you have any remaining doubts, captain, about the nature of the animal?'

'No, professor, it's obviously a colossal narwhal which also happens to be electric!'

'Perhaps,' I added, 'we should no more try to approach it than we would an electric eel or an electric ray.'

'Quite right,' said the captain, 'and if it does indeed possess colossal electric power within it, then it is quite certainly the most terrifying animal ever put on this earth by the hand of the Creator. That is why, professor, I intend to stay on my guard.'

The entire crew remained on the alert all night. No one thought of sleep. The *Abraham Lincoln*, unable to outrun the creature, had slowed and was maintaining half-speed. The narwhal, tracking the frigate, let itself be carried along by the action of the waves but appeared quite determined not to quit the field of battle.

But around midnight it disappeared or, to put it more accurately, it 'extinguished itself' like some huge glow worm. Had it run away? This was something more to be feared than hoped for. But at 12.53 in the morning, a deafening whooshing noise was heard. It was like the sound made by a column of water being shot up into the air with extreme violence.

Captain Farragut, Ned Land and I were then on the poop, peering avidly into the pitch blackness.

'Ned Land,' asked the captain, 'you have often heard whales exhaling through their blow-holes?'

'Frequently, sir, but never the kind of whale whose sighting has netted me 2,000 dollars.'

'Ah, yes! You're entitled to the reward. But tell me, is this the same noise that cetaceans make when they blow water out through their spiracles?'

'It is, sir, but incomparably louder. There's no way I can be mistaken. There is definitely a cetacean there, in our waters.

With your permission, captain,' added the harpooner, 'we'll have a little word with him tomorrow when the sun is up.'

'If, that is, he's in a mood to listen to what you have to tell him, Mr Land,' the captain replied, sounding less than convinced.

'Let me get to within four harpoon lengths of him,' the Canadian retorted, 'and he'll have to listen.'

'But if we want to get near it,' the captain went on, 'will I need to break out a whale-boat for you?'

'Certainly, sir.'

'Would I thereby be putting the lives of my men at risk?'

'And mine too,' the harpooner said simply.

Around two in the morning, the source of the light reappeared, just as bright, 5 miles windward of the *Abraham Lincoln*. Despite the distance and the noise of wind and sea, we could distinctly hear the fearsome beating of the creature's tail, even its rapid breathing. We had a sense that when the huge narwhal finally came to the surface of the ocean to blow, air would rush into its lungs the way steam is sucked into the huge piston cylinders of an engine capable of generating 2,000 horse-power.

'Hm!' I thought, 'a whale with the strength of a cavalry regiment must be a pretty large whale!'

We remained on full alert until daybreak and got ready to do battle. The special fishing tackle was set up along the side of the ship's rails. The second officer gave the order to load the guns that can fire a harpoon a distance of a mile and likewise the swivel-guns that shoot explosive shells, causing injuries fatal even to the largest animals. Ned Land kept himself busy sharpening his harpoon, a terrible weapon in his hands.

By six, dawn was just breaking, and with the first rays of the sun the electric light given off by the narwhal disappeared. At seven, the day was well advanced, but a very dense morning mist reduced our horizons so that even the most powerful telescopes could not see through it. The result was disappointment and frustration.

I climbed up the mizzen mast. A number of officers were already there, perched around the masthead.

At eight, the fog still sat heavily on the waves, but gradually its swirling eddies lifted. The horizon receded and as it did grew clearer.

Then, exactly like the night before, the voice of Ned Land rang out:

'The object we're hunting! There, astern, on the port quarter!'

All eyes turned in the direction of his pointing finger.

A mile and a half from the frigate, a long blackish object was showing about a metre out of the water. Its tail was beating furiously, making the water boil. No mortal tail had ever lashed the sea with greater power. A huge wake, blindingly white, marked the passage of the animal in the form of an elongated curve.

The frigate approached the cetacean. I was able to examine it, keeping an open mind. The reports made by the *Shannon* and the *Helvetia* had rather exaggerated its size: I judged its length to be not more than 250 feet. As to its overall bulk, I found it hard to come up with an estimate, but overall, the animal seemed to me admirably proportioned in all three dimensions.

While I was observing this phenomenal creature, two jets of vapour and water were released from its spiracles to a height of 40 metres. This drew my attention to the way it breathed. I came to the definitive conclusion that it belonged to the branch of vertebrates, the class of mammals, the subclass of monodelphia, to the pisciform group, the order of cetaceans, the family of . . . At this point I found I could not proceed with certainty. The order of cetaceans is made up of three families – whale, cachalot and dolphin – and it is among the last that the narwhals is classified. Each of these families is divided into several genera, each genus into species and each species into varieties. The precise variety, species, genus and family still eluded me but I had no doubt that I would complete my classification with the help of Heaven and Captain Farragut.

The whole crew were waiting expectantly for the captain's orders. After observing the animal closely, Captain Farragut summoned the chief engineer, who arrived at the double.

'Well, chief?' said the captain. 'Do we have full pressure?'

'Yes sir!' said the chief engineer.

'In that case, stoke your fires high and make full steam ahead!'

The order was received with three cheers. The hour for battle had struck. Only moments later, torrents of black smoke poured from both the frigate's funnels, and the deck shook with the judder of the boilers.

The *Abraham Lincoln*, urged forward by the thrust of her powerful propeller, made straight for the animal. The creature let it come within half a cable length. Then, showing no interest in diving, it turned and moved a little way off and seemed content to keep at the same distance.

This pursuit went on for about three-quarters of an hour, during which time the frigate did not gain more than a couple of fathoms on the cetacean. It was obvious that if we continued at the same speed we would never catch up with it.

Captain Farragut was furious and kept tugging at the tuft of whiskers that adorned his chin.

'Mr Land!' he called.

The Canadian answered the summons.

'Well, Mr Land?' said the captain. 'Would you still advise me to lower my boats on to the water?'

'No, sir,' replied Ned Land, 'because that animal will not allow itself to be taken unless it is good and ready.'

'So what do we do?'

'Maintain full speed if you can, sir. Meanwhile I, with your permission, of course, will take up a position under the butt-end of the bowsprit. If we get within range, I shall harpoon the animal.'

'Go to it, Ned,' replied Captain Farragut. He then shouted to the engineer:

'Chief! Increase pressure!'

Ned Land took up his position. The boilers were stoked even higher. The screw built up to forty-three turns a minute. Steam pulsed through the valves. When the log was trailed, it was noted that the *Abraham Lincoln* was making 18½ knots.

But the cursed animal was also moving at 18½ knots.

For another hour, the frigate kept up the same speed, without gaining so much as a single fathom's length! It was complete humiliation for one of the American Navy's fastest ships. An angry murmur swept through the crew. The sailors swore at the monster, which did not deign to respond. Captain Farragut was no longer satisfied with pulling on his goatee: he started biting it.

The chief engineer was summoned once more.

'Are you up to maximum pressure?' the captain asked.

'Aye, sir.'

'And your valves are coping?'

'At 6½ atmospheres.'

'Take them up to 10!'

Now there was an American order if there ever was one! No Mississippi steamboat trying to outdistance a 'competitor' would have gone one better!

I turned to my man Conseil and said: 'You do realize, don't you, that we are probably about to explode?'

'As monsieur pleases,' he replied.

I don't mind admitting that it was a risk I was very happy to take.

The pressure dials rose. Coal was piled into the furnaces. The fans blew torrents of air though the fires. The speed of the *Abraham Lincoln* increased. The masts shook in their stepping holes, and there was hardly room for the billowing smoke to escape through the narrow funnels.

The log was trailed again.

'Speed, helmsman?' asked Captain Farragut.

'Nineteen and three-tenths knots, captain.'

'Put on more steam!'

The chief obeyed. The pressure-gauge now showed 10 atmospheres. But the cetacean must also have put on a spurt because, without extending itself, it too was now moving at a speed of $19^3/_{10}$ knots.

The chase was on! I cannot begin to describe the feelings which made my very being pulsate. Ned Land remained at his post, harpoon at the ready. Several times, the animal allowed us to come nearer.

'We're gaining on it! We're gaining on it!' cried the Canadian.

Then, just as he was poised to strike, the cetacean would make off at a speed I cannot estimate at less than 30 miles an hour. And when we were going at maximum speed, it toyed with the frigate by sailing in a ring around us! A cry of fury rose from every man on board.

At noon, we were no further forward than we had been at eight that morning.

At this point, Captain Farragut decided to use more direct methods.

'So,' he said, 'this animal can travel faster than the *Abraham Lincoln*. Very well! We'll soon see if it can outrun explosive shells. Master-gunner! Order your men for'ard!'

Without more ado, the gun in the fo'c'sle was loaded and aimed. The shot was fired but the shell passed several feet above the cetacean, which was half a mile distant.

'Give the gun to someone who can shoot straight!' cried the captain. 'And there's 500 dollars for the man who pierces the hide of this infernal animal!'

An old gunner with a grey beard – I can still see him – calm eyes and a cool expression on his face, stepped up to the plate, adjusted the settings of the gun and took a long time aiming. Then there was a loud detonation, which was accompanied by a loud cheer from the crew.

The shell hit its target. It struck the animal but not in the usual way, for it bounced off its curved surface and ended up in the sea 2 miles away.

'I don't believe it!' the old gunner exclaimed furiously. 'The brute must be armour-plated with 6-inch steel!'

'Hell and damnation!' cried Captain Farragut.

So the pursuit began again, and, turning to me, the captain said: 'I'm going to chase the brute until my frigate explodes!

'Yes,' I replied, 'and you'd have every justification!'

We could only hope that the animal would wear itself out and be affected by fatigue the way steamships are not. But it was not so. The hours slipped by, and there was no indication that it was tiring.

But it says much for the *Abraham Lincoln* that it battled on with indefatigable tenacity. I reckon that the distance it travelled during that ill-fated 6 November could not have been less than 500 kilometres. Night came on and wrapped the surging waves in shadow.

I believed at that moment that our expedition was at an end and we would never again set eyes on that extraordinary animal. I was mistaken.

At 10.50 that night, the electric luminosity reappeared, 3 miles windward of the frigate, as clear and bright as the night before.

The narwhal appeared to be stationary. Perhaps, after its exhausting day, it was sleeping, surrendering to the rise and fall of the waves? Here was an opportunity that Captain Farragut was determined not to miss.

He gave his orders. The *Abraham Lincoln* was kept down to low steam and edged forward cautiously so as not to wake its opponent. Now, it is by no means rare to find whales deeply asleep in the middle of the ocean. They are then successfully attacked. Ned Land had harpooned a number while they were sleeping. The Canadian resumed his position on the butt of the bowsprit.

The frigate crept noiselessly forwards, stopped engines two cable lengths away from the animal and continued by its own momentum alone. On board, no one dared breathe. A deep silence came over the deck. We were less than 100 feet from the source of the light, which grew bigger and more dazzling as we approached.

At that moment, I was leaning over the fo'c'sle rail. I saw Ned Land just below me clinging to the jib-boom with one hand and with the other brandishing his fearsome harpoon. There were barely 20 feet between him and the motionless animal.

Suddenly, his arm straightened, and the harpoon was on its way. I heard a clang as though the point had struck a solid object.

The electric brightness was instantly doused, and two huge columns of water fell on the deck of the frigate, rushing like a torrent from stem to stern, knocking men over and snapping the lashing that held our spare masts and yards.

There was a tremendous jolt. I had no time to hold on to anything and was thrown over the rail into the sea.

7
A Whale of an Entirely
Unknown Species

Although I had been utterly taken aback by my unforeseen tumble, I nevertheless have a clear recollection of my feelings at the time.

At first I was driven down to a depth of about 20 feet. Now, I am a pretty good swimmer, though I would not claim to be the equal of Byron or Edgar Allan Poe, those masters of the art, so my ducking did not make me lose my head. Two strong kicks with my heels brought me back to the surface of the sea.

My first thought was to get a sight of the frigate. Had the crew noticed I had disappeared? Had the *Abraham Lincoln* changed tack? Did Captain Farragut intend to lower a boat? Could I hope to be rescued?

The darkness grew deeper. I spotted a dark mass disappearing in the east, its fore and aft lights gradually becoming extinguished. It was the frigate. I felt lost.

'Help! Help!' I shouted, swimming desperately towards the *Abraham Lincoln*.

I was impeded by my clothes. The water made them cling to my body and hampered my movements. I was sinking! I couldn't breathe!

'Help!'

It was the last shout I uttered. My mouth filled with water. I struggled as I was pulled down into the depths.

Suddenly, I felt a hand grab my clothes, and I was dragged violently to the surface of the water and heard, yes, heard these words spoken into my ear:

'If monsieur would be so very good as to hold on to my shoulder, he would find it much easier to swim.'

I clutched the arm of my ever-dependable Conseil with one hand.

'You!' I cried. 'It's you!'

'Indeed it is, sir,' replied Conseil, 'and awaiting monsieur's orders.'

'Did the deluge also wash you overboard at the same time as me?'

'Not at all, sir. But being in monsieur's employ, I followed him.'

And the admirable fellow considered this to be perfectly natural!

'What about the frigate?' I asked.

'The frigate!' said Conseil, turning on his back. 'I think monsieur would do well not to place too many hopes on it.'

'What did you say?'

'I said that just as I was about to jump into the sea, I heard the helmsmen shout: "The propeller and rudder are both shattered!"'

'Shattered?'

'Yes. Shattered by the monster's tusk. But I think that is all the damage the *Abraham Lincoln* has sustained. Unfortunately for us, the boat no longer answers to the helm.'

'So, there is no hope for us?'

'Perhaps,' Conseil said calmly. 'But we still have a few hours, and a lot can be done in a few hours.'

The imperturbable coolness of the man revived my drooping spirits. I swam more strongly. But, impeded by my clothes which clung to me like a cloak made of lead, I found it very difficult to stay above water, a fact noted by Conseil.

'If monsieur would allow me to make a slit about his person . . . ?' he said.

He slid an open knife under my clothes and cut them from top to bottom with a single stroke. Then he neatly pulled them off me, while I swam for both of us.

Then I did the same for Conseil, and we continued 'navigating' side by side.

But our predicament had not been made any the less desperate. Perhaps our disappearance had not been noticed, but even if it had, the frigate could not tack because it had lost its rudder. Our only hope therefore was to be picked up by a longboat.

Conseil made a reasoned case for this supposition and outlined a plan accordingly. What an amazing character! So unflappable that he was perfectly at his ease.

Thus it was decided that our only chance of being rescued was to be spotted by the boats from the *Abraham Lincoln*. We consequently had to think of what we could do to hold out for as long as possible while we waited for them to come. I resolved that we should divide our strength so that we both of us would not become exhausted at the same time, and this is what was agreed: while one of us, floating on his back, would remain still, arms crossed and legs straight out, the other would swim and push him forwards. The role of tower was not to last more than ten minutes and, by taking turns in this way, we should be able to stay afloat for several hours, and perhaps even until dawn.

It was a slim chance. But hope is so strongly rooted in the human heart! Besides, there were two of us. And I can now safely state – however implausible it sounds – that even if I had tried to destroy all my illusions, if I had wanted to give in to despair, I couldn't have done it!

The clash of the frigate and the cetacean had occurred around eleven at night. I reckoned therefore that we had to keep swimming for eight hours until the sun rose again. If we continued to take turns, this was a perfectly feasible proposition. The sea was reasonably calm and was not taking too much out of us. From time to time I peered into the impenetrable gloom, which was broken only by the phosphorescence caused by our movements. I watched the luminescent waves break over my hands, their glistening veneer freckled with bright flashes. It was as if we were swimming through a bath of mercury.

At about one in the morning I felt overcome by extreme fatigue. My arms and legs seized up, constricted by violent cramps. Conseil had to hold me up, and the task of saving us both fell on him alone. I heard the poor fellow gasping. His breathing grew short and hurried. I knew he would not be able to carry on like that for long.

'Let go of me!' I said. 'Let me go!'

'Abandon my master? Never!' he replied. 'I'd rather drown first!'

At that moment, the moon showed through the fringes of a

huge cloud which the wind was driving eastwards. The surface of the water glittered in its light. Its reassuring illumination put new heart in us. My head came up, and my eyes scoured all points of the horizon. I made out the frigate. It was 5 miles from us and now was just a dark shape, barely visible. But there were no longboats in sight!

I wanted to cry out. But from this distance what was the use? No sound passed my swollen lips. Conseil managed to pronounce a few words, and several times I heard him say:

'Help! Help!'

We ceased our efforts for a moment and listened. Was it the singing which the pressure of blood causes in the ear? Yet it seemed to me that someone had answered Conseil's shout.

'Did you hear that?' I murmured.

'Yes, I did!'

And Conseil gave another despairing cry.

This time, there was no mistake. A human voice was answering ours! Was it some unfortunate abandoned in the middle of the ocean, another victim of the buffeting that the ship had taken? Or rather one of the frigate's boats, hailing us through the darkness?

Making a supreme effort, Conseil, leaning on my shoulder while I kicked out madly with my legs in one final convulsion, rose half out of the water then fell back, exhausted.

'What did you see?'

'I saw,' he murmured, 'I saw . . . but let's not talk . . . let's save our strength!'

What had he seen? For some reason, the thought of the monster came into my head for the first time. Yet there was that voice . . . and the days are long gone when the likes of Jonah found shelter in the bellies of whales!

Meanwhile, Conseil was towing me again. From time to time he raised his head, looking straight in front of him, and gave a cry, like a signal, to which another voice, drawing closer and closer, replied. I could hardly hear. I was at the end of my tether. My fingers stiffened; my hand ceased to give me any support; my mouth opened uncontrollably and filled with salt water. I was gripped by cold. I raised my head one last time and then let myself slip.

At that instant, I was hit by something solid. I clung on to it. Then I felt that I was being hauled up, pulled up to the surface, and that my lungs were collapsing – and I knew no more.

I must have recovered consciousness quickly thanks to the vigorous friction applied to all parts of my body. I opened my eyes

'Conseil!' I murmured.

'Did monsieur call?' asked Conseil.

Then in the fading light of the moon, which was now sinking towards the horizon, I saw a face that was not Conseil's. But I recognized it at once.

'Ned Land!' I gasped.

'Here present, sir, and still on the trail of his reward!' answered the Canadian.

'Were you thrown into the sea when the frigate was hit?'

'I was, professor, but I was more fortunate than you, I managed to find my footing on a floating island almost straight away.'

'An island?'

'Or more precisely, on our gigantic narwhal.'

'What do you mean, Ned?'

'The fact is I soon saw why my harpoon had not pierced its skin and blunted itself on it.'

'Why was that, Ned?'

'Because, professor, that creature is made of steel plate!'

I must pause here to collect my wits, refresh my memories and check the statements I have made.

The last words pronounced by the Canadian had brought about a sudden turnaround in my brain. I quickly scrambled up to the highest point of the half-submerged creature or object on which we had taken refuge. I tested it with my foot. It was obviously solid and impenetrable and nothing like the yielding substance which forms the bulk of large marine mammals.

Yet the hard body could still be a bony carapace similar to those of antediluvian animals, and I would have settled for classifying our monster as some form of amphibious reptile like turtles and alligators.

But no! The sable back on which I was standing was smooth, polished and in no way scaly. When struck, it gave out a metallic clang and, incredible though it seemed, it appeared – could it be possible? – to be made of riveted metal plates!

There was absolutely no doubt about it! The animal or monster or natural phenomenon which had puzzled the world's scientific community and overwhelmed and beguiled the imagination of mariners in both hemispheres – there was no avoiding it – was a far more astounding phenomenon: a phenomenon created by the hand of man!

Discovering the existence of the most fabulous, the most mythological creature would not have been a greater shock to my reason. For the proposition that all that is prodigious comes from the Creator could not be more straightforward. But suddenly to find the impossible mysteriously and humanly wrought and staring you in the face was enough to turn a man's wits.

But there was no time to waste. We were lying on the back of some sort of underwater vessel in the form, insofar as I could tell, of a huge steel fish. Ned Land's mind was quite made up on this point. Conseil and I had no choice but to agree.

'In that case,' I said, 'inside this machine there must be some mechanical means of locomotion and a crew to operate it.'

'That goes without saying,' replied the harpooner. 'Yet I have been on this floating island for three hours, and in that time it hasn't given any sign of life.'

'The boat hasn't moved at all?'

'No, Professor Aronnax. It floats on the waves but doesn't go anywhere.'

'But we know for sure that it is capable of moving at high speeds. And since an engine is needed to produce such speeds and an engineer to drive the engine, I conclude that we are now saved.'

'Hm!' said Ned Land doubtfully.

At that very moment, as if to support my argument, the water at the stern of this strange vessel began to boil, churned up no doubt by a propeller. Then we started moving. We had time only to cling on to its highest point, which sat about 80 centimetres above the waves. Fortunately its speed was not excessive.

'As long as she stays horizontal,' muttered Ned Land, 'I have no complaints. But if she takes a fancy to dive, I wouldn't give two dollars for my chances.'

Less than two, the Canadian might have said. It was now becoming urgent for us to communicate with the people, whoever they might be, inside the vessel. I scanned the surface of the craft for an opening, a hatch, a 'manhole', to use a technical term. But the lines of rivets, tightly bonding the joints between the plates, were clean and unbroken.

Add to this that the moon disappeared just then, leaving us in complete darkness. We would have to wait for daylight if we were to come up with some way of entering this submarine boat.

And so our salvation depended solely on the whims of the invisible helmsmen who were steering the craft. If they decided to dive, we were lost! That eventuality apart, I was in no doubt about the possibility of contacting them. Because if they did not manufacture their own air, they would be obliged to return to the surface of the ocean from time to time in order to replenish their supply of breathable molecules. So there had to be an opening which connected the inside of the boat with the atmosphere outside.

As to being rescued by Captain Farragut, we had to abandon all hope in that quarter. We were being carried away westwards at a speed, which was relatively steady, of 12 knots by my reckoning. The propeller churned through the waves with mathematical regularity. At times, it rose clear and then sprayed luminous water to a considerable height.

Around four in the morning, the speed of the vessel increased. When waves smashed over us, we found it difficult to cope with being carried along at such a dizzying rate. Fortunately, Ned's hand happened on a mooring ring fixed to the upper part of the iron hull, and we all managed to hang on for dear life.

At last the long night ended. My incomplete memories do not allow me to recall everything that happened. Only one detail is clear in my mind. During certain lulls of sea and wind, I thought several times that I could hear vague sounds, a sort of elusive harmony formed of distant chords. What was the mysterious secret of this submarine vessel which the entire world had been vainly trying to fathom? What kind of people lived

inside this strange boat? What sort of mechanical contrivance allowed it to travel at such phenomenal speeds?

The new day dawned. Morning fog enveloped us but did not take long to lift. I was about to resume my close examination of the hull, which, at its highest point, took the form of a sort of horizontal platform, when I felt it begin slowly to submerge.

'Hell's teeth!' cried Ned Land, stamping his foot on the ringing metal plate, 'open up, you inhospitable lubbers!'

But it was difficult to make himself heard against the deafening thrashing of the propeller. Fortunately, however, we stopped submerging.

Suddenly, the noise of metal bolts being hurriedly drawn back came from inside the boat. An iron plate was raised, a man appeared, gave a strange shout and then disappeared immediately.

A few moments later, eight burly sailors, their faces masked, came up. Without saying a word, they dragged us inside their amazing machine.

8
Mobilis in Mobili

Our abduction was effected brutally, at lightning speed. My companions and I had not had time to take stock of what was happening. I have no idea what they were feeling as they were ushered into this floating prison. For my part, a sudden shiver chilled me to the bone. With whom were we dealing? Probably a new breed of pirates who were plundering the sea in some way.

The narrow hatch had scarcely closed behind me when I found myself plunged into pitch blackness. My eyes, accustomed to the light outside, could make out nothing. I felt my bare feet grip the rungs of an iron ladder. Ned Land and Conseil were roughly manhandled and followed. At the foot of the ladder, a door opened and was shut on us immediately with a loud clang.

Then we were alone. Where? I could not say nor hardly imagine. It was dark, a dark so impenetrable that after a few minutes my eyes still could not make out any of those faint glimmers which linger in the deepest blackness.

But Ned Land, furious at the way we were being treated, did not conceal his anger:

'Hell's teeth!' he exclaimed, 'these people must be related to the Caledonians if this is what they mean by a welcome! They're just one step away from cannibals! Indeed, I wouldn't be at all surprised if that's what they are! But I tell you, no one's going to eat me without having a fight on their hands!'

'Calm down, Ned, calm down,' said Conseil coolly. 'No need to get all steamed up before you have to. We're not in the cooking-pot yet!'

'Not in the pot, no,' retorted the Canadian, 'but definitely in an oven! It's as black as the ace of spades in here. Luckily, I've still got my Bowie-knife*[14] and I can see well enough to use it. The first of these villains who lays a finger on me . . .'

'Don't get angry, Ned,' I told the harpooner. 'You mustn't make things worse by uttering idle threats. Who knows if they're not listening to what we say? Let's try instead to find out where we are.'

I put one foot forward, then another, feeling my way. After five steps, I encountered a metal wall, built of riveted iron plates. Then I turned and walked into a table, around which there were a number of stools. The floor of our prison was hidden under thick fibrous matting that deadened the sound of our feet. There was no sign of a door or windows in the bare walls. Conseil, who had set off in the opposite direction, met up with me, and together we returned to the middle of this cabin, which seemed to be 20 feet long and 10 wide. Ned Land, tall as he was, was unable to estimate its height.

Half an hour had already gone by with no change in our situation when, all at once, from total blackness, our eyes were exposed to brilliant light. Our prison had suddenly been illuminated, that is, filled with luminous matter so bright that at first I could not bear it. By its whiteness and intensity, I recognized the illumination as the same electric light that had wrapped the underwater vessel in a magnificent display of phosphorescence. Having closed my eyes instinctively, I now opened them again and saw that the luminous agent was emanating from a hemisphere of polished glass located in the upper part of the cabin.

*A wide-bladed knife always carried by an American.

'At last! Now we can see what we're doing,' cried Ned Land, who, knife in hand, had assumed a defensive posture.

'True,' I said and, putting the opposite view, added: 'but our predicament is no clearer than it was before.'

'Perhaps monsieur might care to be patient,' said the imperturbable Conseil.

The sudden illumination of the cabin gave me an opportunity to examine it in detail. It contained only the table and the five stools. The door was invisible and was probably hermetically closed. No sound reached us. Everything seemed dead inside the boat. Was it moving, was it still on the surface of the ocean, was it diving into the depths? I could not guess.

But the luminous globe had not been lit without some reason. I therefore hoped that it would not be long before members of the crew would show themselves. You don't light dungeons when you intend to forget the occupants.

I was not mistaken. There was a sound of bolts being drawn, the door opened, and two men appeared.

One was short, solidly muscled, with wide shoulders, sturdy limbs, a head like a bull covered with thick black hair, a walrus moustache, keen, piercing eyes and overall, that aura of southern vitality which in France marks out the peoples of Provence. Diderot[15] rightly argued that all human gestures are metaphorical, and this stocky man was the living proof of this claim. You had a feeling that his normal speech would be full of prosopopoeia, metonymy and hypallage.[16] Though I was never in a position to confirm this, since in my presence he invariably spoke in a strange tongue that I found absolutely incomprehensible.

The other man deserves to be described in more detail. For a disciple of anatomists like Gratiolet or Engel,[17] his face would have been an open book, and they would have read it accordingly. I recognized his dominant characteristics without a moment's hesitation: self-confidence, for his head was admirably set on the arc formed by the line of his shoulders and the look in his black eyes was cool and measured; composure, for his skin, which was pale rather than dark, indicated that his blood was not easily stirred; energy, as was demonstrated by the rapid contractions of his broad forehead; and lastly courage, for the depth of his breathing was a clear sign of his vital powers.

I will add that the man was proud, that his calm, assured gaze seemed to suggest high thoughts and that the harmonious unity of the whole – both the physical gestures and facial expressions – produced, according to the principles of the physiognomists, an unquestionable degree of frankness.

I felt 'involuntarily' reassured by his presence and had a good feeling about our meeting.

Whether the man was thirty-five or fifty years of age, I was not able to say. He was tall and had a wide forehead, a straight nose, a firmly set mouth, splendid teeth and hands that were delicate, long-fingered and eminently 'psychic', to borrow a term from the art of reading chirognomy, by which is meant that they were perfectly suited to serve a heart that was noble and passionate. He was the most perfect specimen of manhood I ever came across. One special detail: his eyes, being set rather wide, made it possible for him to take in at any one time pretty near a quarter of the horizon. This ability – as I subsequently confirmed – was accompanied by an acuity of vision sharper even than that of Ned Land. When he wanted to see an object, his eyebrows came together, his wide eyelids crowded around his pupils, thus narrowing his field of vision, and he looked. And what a look! He magnified objects made small by distance! He could see into your very soul! He could see into the waters of the sea, which are so opaque to our eyes, and read what was contained in their depths!

The two men, both sporting caps of sea-otter fur and sealskin sea-boots, were wearing clothes made of a special kind of cloth that left the body free and allowed great freedom of movement.

The taller of the two – obviously the boat's captain — inspected us without saying a word. Then, turning to his companion, he spoke in a tongue that I did not recognize. It was a sonorous, harmonious, supple language, with vowels that appeared to be stressed in various ways.

The other man responded with a nod of the head and added two or three utterly incomprehensible words. Then he looked directly at me, quizzically, as if expecting an answer.

I replied in plain French that I did not understand his language, but he did not appear to understand mine either, and the situation became somewhat embarrassing.

'Monsieur might care to tell him our story notwithstanding,' said Conseil. 'These gentlemen might grasp a few words of it.'

So I began the tale of our adventure, pronouncing every syllable clearly and without omitting any detail. I gave our names and ranks. Then I introduced us formally: Professor Aronnax, his man Conseil and Ned Land, the master-harpooner.

The man with the gentle, quiet eyes heard me out calmly, indeed politely, and with marked attention. But there was nothing in his expression to suggest that he understood a word of what I was saying. When I had finished, he said nothing at all.

There remained the last resort of trying English. Perhaps we could make ourselves understood in that language, which is more or less universal. I spoke it, and German too, well enough to be able to read it fluently, but not to speak it correctly. And circumstances made it imperative that we should make ourselves understood.

'Look, why don't you try?' I said to the harpooner. 'Over to you, Ned. Rack your brains and try to come up with English as good as any spoken by an Anglo-Saxon and see if you can do better than me.'

Ned did not need to be asked twice and took up my story again. I understood most of it. The content was virtually the same, but the form was different. The Canadian, carried away by his temperament, put a great deal of expression into it. He complained bitterly about being imprisoned in flagrant violation of international jurisprudence and demanded to know by what law he was being held there, spoke of *habeas corpus*, threatened to prosecute anyone who kept him locked up without reason, raised his voice, waved his arms and finally, with an expressive gesture, gave them to understand that we were dying of hunger.

This was perfectly true, though we had more or less forgotten the fact.

To his amazement, the harpooner did not seem to have been

any more intelligible than I had. Our visitors did not bat an eyelid. It was obvious that they did not understand the language of Faraday any more than that of Arago.[18]

Having exhausted our philological arsenal and, as we were at our wits' end, I did not know which way to turn next. And then Conseil said:

'If monsieur will allow, I will attempt to explain our predicament in German.'

'What? Do you speak German?' I exclaimed.

'As well as any Fleming, with all due respect to monsieur.'

'It is to you that respect is due. Go to it, man.'

Then in a steady voice Conseil related the various episodes of our adventure for the third time. But despite all his elegant turns of phrase and perfect enunciation, the German language proved unsuccessful.

Finally, scraping the barrel, I gathered together everything I remembered of my schooldays and attempted to give an account of what had happened to us in Latin. Cicero would have covered his ears and packed me off to the kitchen. Still, I somehow managed to get through it. But with the same negative result.

When this last effort proved to be definitively abortive, the two individuals exchanged a few words in their incomprehensible language and left without even offering us one of those gestures of reassurance which are standard in all countries the world over. The door closed behind them.

'It's a disgrace!' exclaimed Ned Land, adding to the score of outbursts he had made. 'We talk to the rogues in French, English, German and Latin, and neither of them has the decency to answer!'

'Calm down, Ned,' I told the irascible harpooner. 'Getting angry won't get us anywhere.'

'But don't you realize, professor,' said our combustible companion, 'that we could all easily die of hunger, yes die, in this iron box?'

'Nonsense,' said Conseil philosophically, 'we can hold out for a long time yet.'

'Listen, both of you,' I said, 'we mustn't give up hope. We've all been in worse predicaments than this. So do me a favour and wait before making up your minds about the captain and crew of this boat.'

'My mind's already made up,' Ned retorted. 'They're all rogues!'

'All right. And what country do they belong to?'

'Rogueland!'

'My dear Ned, that's a country which is not yet marked on any map of the world, though I agree it's not easy to tell what country those two individuals are from. They're not English nor French nor German, and that's all we can say for sure. However, I'd be tempted to place the captain and his companion as being born in the lower latitudes. There's something southern about them. But whether they are Spaniards, Turks, Arabs or Indians is not something that can be inferred from their physical type. And their language is absolutely incomprehensible.'

'That's the disadvantage of not being able to speak all languages,' said Conseil, 'or of not having one single language.'

'That wouldn't help,' said Ned. 'Don't you see that these men have a language that's all their own? It was invented to drive good people who ask for something to eat to despair. But surely in every country on earth, opening your mouth, moving your jaws, miming with teeth and lips is something which is easily understood? Doesn't it mean in Quebec as in Pomotou, in Paris as in the antipodes: "I'm starving! Give me something to eat!"?'

'Oh!' said Conseil, 'there are creatures of little intelligence . . .'

Just as he was saying these words, the door opened, and a steward came in. He brought us clothes, sea-jackets and trousers made of a fabric which I could not identify. I donned them quickly, and my companions followed my example.

Meanwhile, the steward – who was possibly deaf and dumb – had laid the table for three.

'This is more like it,' said Conseil. 'It's a good start.'

'Get on with you,' grumbled the cantankerous harpooner. 'And what do you think they eat here? Liver of turtle, fillet of shark, dogfish steaks, that's what!'

'Well see,' said Conseil.

The platters, each under a silver cloche, were arranged symmetrically on the cloth, and we sat down round the table.

Decidedly, we were dealing with civilized people, and had it not been for the electric light that filled the place so brightly, I would have sworn I was in the dining room of the Adelphi Hotel in Liverpool or the Grand Hotel in Paris. Still, I must report that there was no bread or wine. Water was served, and it was cold and clear, but it was water. This was not to the taste of Ned Land. On some of the platters placed before us I recognized various kinds of fish all delicately prepared; I could not say what the contents of others were, though it all made excellent eating, and I could not even have said to what realm, animal or vegetable, they belonged. As to the service, it was elegant and in perfect taste. Each utensil, spoon, fork, knife and plate was engraved with a letter, and round it was inscribed a motto of which this is an exact facsimile:

MOBILIS

N

IN MOBILI

'Moving within the moving element'! The motto suited this underwater vessel perfectly, provided the preposition *in* was translated as 'within' and not 'on'. Doubtless the letter N was the initial of the name of the enigmatic individual who sailed a ship at the bottom of the sea!

Ned and Conseil did not bother with thoughts of this kind. They ate voraciously, and soon I was following their lead. However, I did feel more sanguine about our fate, for it was obvious to me that our hosts had no intention of allowing us to starve to death.

But everything has an end here below, everything moves on, even the hunger of men who have not eaten for fifteen hours. Once our appetites were satisfied, the need for sleep became overwhelming and irresistible. It was a natural reaction after that interminable night spent struggling with death.

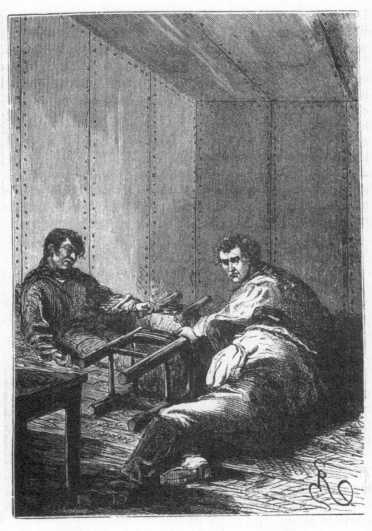

'*Both my companions stretched out on the carpet*'

'By God, I shall sleep well!' said Conseil.

'And so will I!' replied Ned Land.

Both my companions stretched out on the carpet on the cabin floor and were soon sound asleep.

For my part, I surrendered less easily to the overmastering need for sleep. Too many thoughts crowded into my mind, too many questions without answers pressed in on me, too many images kept my eyelids half open! Where were we? What strange power was leading us on? I felt, or rather I thought I could sense, the vessel sinking down to deepest levels of the sea. I was possessed by violent, nightmarish visions. In those mysterious haunts I glimpsed an entire world inhabited by unknown animals to which our submarine boat seemed a related species, alive, moving, just as formidable a presence as they were! But then my brain slowed, my imagination slipped into a fog of drowsiness, and soon I fell into a cheerless sleep.

9
Ned Land Loses His Temper

How long we slept I could not say, but it must have been for some considerable time, because we woke completely rested after our recent fatigues. I was the first to open my eyes. My companions had not moved and were still asleep in their corner: two inert shapes.

I had scarcely got up off my rather hard bed when I felt that my brain was working properly and that my mind was as clear as a bell. I at once resumed my close inspection of our cell.

Nothing about its interior appearance had altered. Our prison was still a prison, and its prisoners were still prisoners. However, while we had been asleep, the steward had cleared the table. There was therefore nothing to suggest that our situation would change any time soon. I wondered quite seriously if we were destined to live indefinitely in this cage.

To me, this prospect seemed all the more dire because, while my brain was now free of its obsessions of the evening before, I felt my chest oddly constricted. I found it difficult to breathe. The oppressive air was no longer adequate for the functioning of my lungs. Although our cell was large it was patently obvious that we had consumed most of the oxygen it contained. It is a fact that in one hour a man uses up all the oxygen in a hundred litres of air, which then, being saturated with a more or less equal quantity of carbon dioxide, becomes unbreathable.

It was therefore a matter of some urgency that the atmosphere in our prison should be replaced and, most likely, the atmosphere in the rest of this submarine vessel.

This raised a question in my mind: how did the captain of this floating residence deal with this problem? Did he obtain fresh air by chemical means, using heat to release the oxygen contained in potassium chlorate and absorbing the carbon dioxide by means of caustic potash? If so, he must have maintained a number of contacts on all five continents in order to have access to the materials required for such an operation. Did he settle for stocking air in pressurized tanks and then releasing it as and when his crew required? Perhaps. Or did he use a process which was more convenient and economical (and therefore more probable) and simply return to the ocean surface to breathe, like a cetacean, and replenish his air with a sufficient supply for twenty-four hours? However that might be and whatever method he used, I felt it would be prudent to implement it without delay.

I was already being forced to breathe faster to extract the small amount of oxygen our cell contained, when I suddenly felt the coolness of a current of pure air which carried the tang of salt. It was in fact a sea breeze, health-giving and laden with iodine! I opened my mouth wide, and my lungs filled with fresh molecules. At the same time I felt a slight swell, a rolling motion which, though not very strong, was clearly the real thing. Obviously the boat, the iron monster, had surfaced to breathe the way whales do. In this way the ship's ventilation system became perfectly transparent.

When I had drunk my fill of this pure air, I looked round for the duct, the 'aeriferous' conduit, if you will, which enabled the salutary wafture to reach us. I soon found it. Above the door was a vent that allowed a flow of fresh air to pass and thus renew the exhausted atmosphere of our cell.

I had got this far in my observations when Ned and Conseil both woke more or less simultaneously under the influence of this reviving ventilation. They rubbed their eyes, stretched their arms and were on their feet in an instant.

'Did monsieur sleep well?' asked Conseil, as polite as he was every day.

'Very well, Conseil,' I replied. 'And what about you, Mr Ned Land?'

'Like a log, professor. I may be mistaken, but is that some kind of sea breeze that I seem to be breathing?'

A sailor would make no mistake in such a matter, and I told the Canadian what had happened while he had been asleep.

'Ah!' he said. 'That explains those whooshing sounds we heard when the so-called narwhal was within sight of the *Abraham Lincoln*.'

'Exactly, Ned. That was it breathing!'

'One thing, Professor Aronnax: I have absolutely no idea what time it is, except that it's high time for dinner.'

'Dinner-time. Ned? Say rather time for breakfast, for it is patently obvious that today is the day after yesterday.'

'Which proves,' said Conseil, 'that we have slept for twenty-four hours.'

'That's what I think too,' I said.

'I won't disagree,' said Ned Land. 'But whether it's time for dinner or breakfast, that steward would be welcome whether he brought the one or the other.'

'The one *and* the other,' said Conseil.

'Quite right,' replied the Canadian, 'we're entitled to two meals and, speaking for myself, I'd do justice to both.'

'Patience, Ned, we'll just have to wait,' I said. 'It's obvious that these people have no intention of allowing us to starve, otherwise last night's dinner makes no sense.'

'Unless they want to fatten us up!' said Ned.

'Come now,' I said. 'We haven't fallen into the hands of cannibals!'

'Maybe they'll make an exception for us,' the Canadian replied in all seriousness. 'How do we know that these men haven't been deprived of fresh meat for ages, and if that is so, three healthy and well-upholstered specimens such as the professor, his valet and myself . . .'

'Don't think such thoughts, Ned,' I said to the harpooner, 'and above all don't use them as a pretext for letting fly at our hosts. It would only make matters worse.'

'Perhaps,' said the harpooner, 'but I'm as hungry as a sack-ful of demons, and whether it's dinner or breakfast don't signify, since there's no sign of actual food!'

'Mister Land,' I said, 'we must abide by ship's rules. I'm assuming our stomach clocks are fast compared with theirs.'

'Then we'll have to reset them to local time,' Conseil said calmly.

'Isn't that you all over, Mister Conseil!' said the Canadian impatiently. 'You never get angry and you don't get worked up! Always so calm! You'd give thanks before you'd got what you were about to receive. You'd rather die of hunger than complain!'

'What would be the point?' asked Conseil.

'Complaining would be the point! It would be doing something! And if these pirates – I say pirates out of politeness, so as not to contradict the professor, who won't let me call them cannibals – if these pirates think they can keep me locked up in this suffocating cage without getting an earful of choice epithets that would express my outrage perfectly, then they are badly mistaken! Come, Professor Aronnax, tell me straight: do you think they'll keep us locked up for long in this iron tank?'

'To be honest, my guess is as good as yours, Ned.'

'But you must have some idea?'

'I assume that chance has made us privy to some important secret. Now, if the crew of this submarine have some reason to want their secret to stay a secret, and if their secret weighs more heavily in the balance than the lives of three men, then I think that I wouldn't give much for our chances. But if the reverse is true, the behemoth which has swallowed us will certainly return us to our world and our friends at the first opportunity.'

'Unless they decide to add us to the crew roster,' said Conseil, 'and keep us here that way . . .'

'Until such time,' broke in Ned Land, 'when some frigate, faster and sharper than the *Abraham Lincoln*, boards this nest of buccaneers and hangs the whole crew and us included from its yard-arm once and for all . . .'

'A cheerful thought, Ned,' I replied. 'But as far as I am aware no one has mentioned any such thing. So there's no point discussing what line we should take if it happened. I repeat: let's wait, let's keep our counsel until circumstances change and do nothing, since there's nothing to be done.'

'On the contrary, professor,' said the harpooner, who was in no mood to back down, 'we must do something!'

'Like what?'

'Escape!'

'Escaping from a jail on terra firma can be difficult enough. But breaking out of an undersea prison strikes me as being quite impossible.'

'Well, Ned?' asked Conseil. 'What have you got to say against the professor's objection? I shouldn't have thought that an American is ever at a loss for an answer!'

The harpooner, visibly nonplussed, remained silent. To attempt a breakout in the situation chance had placed us in was quite out of the question. But a Canadian is half French, as Ned Land showed by his reply. After a few moments' thought, he went on:

'So, Professor Aronnax, you can't guess what men who can't get out of their prison must do?'

'No, Ned.'

'It's very simple. They must settle for staying where they are.'

'True,' said Conseil, 'we're better off inside than above or below!'

'But only after we've rid the ship of the warders, turnkeys and guards,' added Ned Land.

'Hold on, Ned. Are you serious in thinking about taking over the ship?'

'Very serious,' replied the Canadian.

'But it's impossible.'

'Why, sir? A favourable opportunity might present itself, and I can't see what could prevent us making the most of it. If there are no more than twenty men on board this vessel, I don't think they'd be a match for two Frenchmen and a Canadian!'

It was easier to accept the harpooner's plan than to argue about it. So I merely said:

'Let the circumstances arise, Ned, and we'll see. But until then, please keep your impatience under control. We'll have to rely on subterfuge if we are to make a move, and losing your temper is not the way to create an opening that will improve our chances. So promise me you will accept the situation without getting too angry.'

'I promise, professor,' answered Ned Land, not very convincingly. 'No headstrong language will pass my lips, no furious gesture will give me away – even if the steward doesn't wait at table with the appropriate standard of service.'

'So I have your word, Ned,' I said to the Canadian.

There the conversation paused, and each of us began thinking his own thoughts. I confess that, personally speaking, and despite the assurances given by the harpooner, I had few illusions. I did not believe in the favourable odds Ned Land had spoken of. To be so safely operated, the submarine boat needed a large crew, which meant that if we had to use our fists we would find ourselves up against overwhelming opposition. Besides, we first needed to be free, which we were not. I could not envisage any way of escaping from our hermetically sealed iron cell. And if the boat's mysterious captain did have some sort of secret to keep – and this seemed at least probable – he would not allow us to move freely around his vessel. Was he planning to get rid of us by violent means or would he abandon us one day on some deserted shore? These hypotheses seemed all too plausible to me, and only a harpooner would have had hopes of regaining his freedom.

Furthermore I could see that Ned Land's ideas were growing wilder under the influence of the thoughts gripping his mind. I could hear oaths snarling at the back of his throat and saw his gestures becoming more threatening. He stood up, prowled like a caged animal, struck at the walls with feet and fists. Meanwhile, time passed, the pangs of hunger became more cruelly insistent, and this time the steward did not appear. If our captors really had our best interests at heart, they were leaving it far too long to remember that we were shipwrecked survivors.

Ned Land, tormented by the gnawing of his clamouring stomach, grew increasingly irate, and, though he had given his word, I was beginning to fear the worst would happen when he eventually came face to face with one of the crew.

Ned Land's anger went on building a head of steam for a further two hours. The Canadian called out, he shouted, but to no avail. The metal walls did not have ears. I could not hear a sound from anywhere inside the boat, which seemed devoid of life. It was not moving, for I would obviously have felt the hull vibrate as the propeller turned. It was doubtless deep under the water and disconnected from dry land. The silence was bleak and frightening.

As to our being abandoned and left alone in our cell, I dared not try to estimate how long our predicament would last. The hopes I had conceived after our interview with the ship's master gradually faded. The gentle look in the man's eyes, the generous expression on his face, the loftiness of his bearing were all blotted out in my memory. In my mind's eye I now saw that enigmatic figure as he had surely been: cruel and without mercy. I sensed that he did not belong to the human race, being impervious to any feeling of pity, and was the implacable enemy of his own kind, whom he had vowed to hate for all time!

But was this man intending to let us die of starvation, still prisoners in our narrow prison and vulnerable to the ghastly temptations brought on by ungovernable hunger? This terrifying thought took hold of my imagination with horrible intensity, and, urged on by my imagination, I felt myself being overtaken by mindless fear. Conseil was calm, but Ned Land began to roar.

At that moment, we heard a noise outside. Footsteps rang on the metal floor. Someone rattled the locks, the door opened, and the steward walked in.

Before I could make a move to stop him, the Canadian had leaped on the unfortunate man and knocked him down and was holding him by the throat. Caught in that massive grip, the steward was choking to death.

Conseil was already attempting to pull the harpooner's hands off the half-throttled victim and I was about to add my efforts to his when I was suddenly rooted to the spot by words spoken in French:

'Easy, Mister Land, and you, professor, listen to me!'

The Man of the Deep

It was the master of the ship.

On hearing these words, Ned Land sprang to his feet. The steward, half-strangled, staggered outside on an order from the captain, whose authority on board was such that the man showed no indication of the animosity he must have been feeling towards the Canadian. Conseil, instinctively curious, and I, feeling bewildered, waited in silence for the scene to play out.

The captain, leaning on one corner of the table with his arms crossed, observed us attentively. Was he reluctant to say more? Was he already regretting the words he had just spoken in French? It was a distinct possibility.

After a few moments of a silence, which none of us were tempted to break:

'Gentlemen,' he said in a calm, probing voice, 'I too can speak French, English, German and Latin. I could have answered you at our first meeting but I wished to know you first and think later. Your quadruple tale, each time fundamentally the same, confirmed your identities. I know now that chance has brought to me Professor Pierre Aronnax, holder of the Chair of Natural History in the Museum of Paris, who has been on a scientific mission to foreign parts; Conseil, his manservant, and Ned Land, Canadian by birth and harpooner on board the *Abraham Lincoln*, a frigate of the National Navy of the United States of America.'

I bowed, indicating my agreement. The captain had not asked a question, and thus I was not required to answer. He expressed himself with complete ease, with no trace of an accent. His statements were clear, his words were perfectly apposite and his fluency quite remarkable. And yet I did not have the feeling that he was a compatriot of mine.

He resumed the conversation in these terms:

'You will have doubtless thought, sir, that I have allowed a good deal of time to pass without paying you a second visit. The fact is that, having discovered your identity, I wished to give due thought to what I was to do with you. I was a long time making up my mind. The most regrettable circumstances have brought you to a man who has cut all ties with the rest of humanity. Your arrival has upset my way of life.'

'Unwittingly,' I said.

'Unwittingly?' he said, raising his tone a little. 'Was it unwittingly that the *Abraham Lincoln* has been hunting me down all over the high seas? Was it unwittingly that you took a passage on board the frigate? Was it unwittingly that your shells bounced off the hull of my ship? Was it unwittingly that Mister Land struck my vessel with a harpoon?'

I detected controlled irritation in what he said. But I had an all too natural answer for his accusations and I gave it.

'Sir,' I began, 'you probably do not know how much talk there has been about you in America and Europe. You will be unaware that a number of accidents, caused by collisions with your submarine vessel, have stirred public opinion on both continents. I shall spare you the countless theories advanced to explain the inexplicable phenomenon of which only you knew the truth. But you must appreciate that in following you into the watery wastes of the Pacific, the *Abraham Lincoln* believed it was hunting some powerful marine creature of which it had at all costs to rid the seas.'

A faint smile relaxed the captain's lips. Then in a calmer voice he replied:

'Professor Aronnax, are you seriously telling me that your frigate would not have tracked and bombarded a submarine boat as readily as it has a sea monster?'

I was nonplussed by the question, for Captain Farragut would not have hesitated for an instant. He would have considered it as much his duty to destroy a vessel of this kind as a giant narwhal.

'Then you will understand, sir,' he went on, 'that I am perfectly entitled to regard you as enemies,'

I did not answer, and with good reason. What was the point of discussing such a proposition in a situation where force could trump the best arguments?

'I hesitated for some time,' the captain resumed. 'Nothing obliged me to offer you hospitality. If I were to sever all contact with you, then meeting you again would in no way serve my interests. I could return you to the platform of my boat on which you took refuge. I could dive beneath the waves and forget that you ever existed. Would I not be within my rights to proceed in that way?'

'It might be within the rights of a savage,' I said, 'but not of a civilized man.'

'But, professor,' the captain went on quickly, 'I am not what you call a civilized man! I have cut off all relations with the whole of society for reasons which I alone am entitled to judge. So I do not obey its rules and I insist you undertake never to refer to them in my presence!'

This was said categorically. A flash of anger and disdain had lit up his eyes, and I caught a glimpse of something terrible in the past life of the man. Not only had he placed himself outside the laws of men but he had made himself independent, free in the most comprehensive sense of the word, and beyond the reach of anyone and anything! Who would dare to follow him to the bottom of the sea when on the surface of the oceans he could counter every action taken against him? What boat could withstand a clash with his underwater iron-clad monitor? What cruiser, however stoutly built, could withstand the impact of its ram? No man alive could ask him to account for his actions. God, if he believed in Him, and his conscience, if he had one, were the only judges he could answer to.

While these thoughts raced through my mind, this strange man said nothing, seeming absorbed, even withdrawn into his inner self. I looked at him with a mixture of fear and curiosity, as Oedipus once contemplated the Sphinx.

After a prolonged silence, the captain began to speak once more:

'As I say, I hesitated,' he said, 'but I found that I could reconcile my interests with the natural feeling of pity to which every human is entitled. You will remain on board, since fate has brought you here. You will be free, and in exchange for your freedom, relative though it necessarily is, I will only impose one condition on you. Your word to respect it will suffice.'

'State your condition, sir,' I replied. 'I assume it belongs with those which any man of honour may accept?'

'Yes, sir. Here is my condition. It is possible that certain unforeseen events may force me to confine you to your cabins for a few hours or a few days according to the case. Having no wish to resort to violence in any circumstances, I shall expect total and passive obedience from you at those times even more than at all others. By this means I shall take full responsibility for what happens so that you shall not be held accountable for anything, in any degree, since I shall have put you in a situation where you could not see what should not be seen. Do you accept my condition?'

So things happened on board which were, to say the least, unusual, things which persons who had not set themselves outside the law ought not to see. Of all the surprises the future held in store for me, this would not be the least.

'We accept,' I said. 'However, I beg leave, sir, to ask you a question, just one.'

'Proceed.'

'You say we shall be free on your ship . . .'

'Entirely.'

'Then I would like to ask: what you mean by "freedom"?'

'Why, the freedom to come and go, to see, to observe everything that goes on here – save on a handful of occasions – in short you will have the same freedom as that which is enjoyed by myself and my companions.'

It was obvious that we were not talking about the same thing.

'Excuse me, captain,' I went on, 'but this freedom is no different from that of any prisoner to walk around his cell! It is not enough.'

'But you must make do with it.'

'What! Must we give up all hope of seeing our homeland, our friends and families ever again?'

'Yes, professor, you must. But giving up all thought of shouldering the insufferable burden of the constraints of life on dry land, which people mistake for freedom, may well prove less painful than you imagine.'

'Damnation!' cried Ned Land. 'I'll never swear that I won't try to escape!'

'I'm not asking you to swear to anything, Mister Land,' said the captain sharply.

'Captain,' I said, feeling my anger mount, 'you are taking advantage of the fact that you have the upper hand! It is cruelty!'

'Not at all, professor, it is lenience. You are my prisoners, men who fought me and lost. I am keeping you here, though at a word from me I could tip you back into the depths of the ocean. You attacked me. You came with the intention of purloining a secret which no man alive has any right to know: the very secret of my whole existence! And you think I am going to send you back to the solid earth which shall hear no more of me? Never! By holding you here, it is not you I am safeguarding but myself!'

The words revealed that the captain harboured an *idée fixe* against which all argument would be powerless.

'In short, then,' I went on, 'what you are offering us is, in essence, a choice between life and death.'

'In essence, yes.'

'My friends,' I said, 'to a choice framed in this way, no answer is possible. But we have taken no binding oath to obey the master of this vessel.'

'None whatsoever,' agreed the captain.

Then he added in a milder tone:

'And now, please allow me to finish what I have to say to you. I know you, Professor Aronnax. You, though perhaps not your companions, may well have less cause to complain of the chance happening which has bound you to my fate. Among the books which I use for my preferred area of research you will find the monograph you published on the great ocean depths. I have read it often. You have taken your work as far as terrestrial science currently permits. But you do not know everything, nor have you seen everything. Allow me to say, professor, that you will not regret the time you spend on board. You will travel through a world of marvels. Your mind will exist in a constant ferment of amazement, of stupefaction. You will not be left cold by the sights you will be continually offered. I shall undertake a new voyage round the world under the sea – who knows? It might be my last – and revisit everything I have investigated at the bottom of oceans through which I have sailed so often. You will share my studies. As of today, you will enter a new element, you will see what no man before you has ever seen – I and my men do not count – and thanks to me our planet will give up its last secrets to you!'

I will not deny it: the captain's words had a tremendous effect on me. I had been caught in my weak spot and for a moment I lost sight of the fact that seeing such sublime sights could never be a substitute for the loss of my liberty. Or rather, I thought I could let the future come up with the answer to this crucial question. I merely said:

'Captain, you may well have cut all ties with humanity, but I fully believe that you have not set every human feeling to one side. We are castaways whom you brought on board out of charity, and we shall not forget the fact. Speaking for myself, I am persuaded that if the cause of science can overcome even our need for freedom, then the benefits that I hope will come from our meeting will leave me admirably compensated.'

I thought the captain was about to offer me his hand to seal the treaty. But he did not, and I was sorry for it, on his account.

'A last question,' I said just as this incomprehensible man seemed on the point of leaving us.

'Which is?'

'By what name should I address you?'

The master of the vessel replied: 'To you, professor, I shall simply be Captain Nemo[19] while to me you and your companions will be simply passengers on the *Nautilus*.'[20]

Captain Nemo called. A steward appeared. The captain gave orders in the strange language I still could not identify. Then, turning to the Canadian and Conseil, he said:

'A meal awaits you in your cabin. Please go with this man.'

'I don't mind if I do!' said the harpooner.

Then he and Conseil finally left the cell where they had been locked up for more than thirty hours.

'And now, Professor Aronnax, our lunch is ready. Allow me to lead the way.'

'I am at your orders, captain.'

I followed Captain Nemo. Once through the door, we proceeded along an electrically lit walkway which resembled the gangway of a ship. After we had gone ten metres or so, a second door opened, and I entered a dining room which was done out and furnished in a severe style. A tall dresser of oak inlaid with ebony motifs stood at each end of the room, and on their scalloped shelves gleamed objects of china, porcelain and glass worth incalculable sums. The silver plate shone in the light from the luminous ceiling, on which were painted handsome pictures which suffused and softened the glare.

In the middle of the room was a richly laid table. Captain Nemo pointed to the chair in which I was to sit.

'Do sit down,' he said, 'and eat like a man who must be dying of hunger.'

Lunch consisted of a number of dishes whose components had been supplied entirely by the sea, and of a few others whose nature and origin I could not guess at. I confess it made good eating, though it had a particular taste, to which, however, I quickly became accustomed. I had the feeling that all these various delicacies must surely be rich in phosphorus, and I assumed they must all have come from the sea.

Captain Nemo watched me. I did not ask him anything, but he guessed what I was thinking and supplied answers to the questions which I was burning to put to him.

'Most of these dishes will be new to you,' he said, 'but you need not be afraid to partake of them. They are safe and very nourishing. I have not eaten food originating on dry land for a very long time and am none the worse for it. My crew, who are strong and hearty, eat the same diet as myself.'

'You mean all this food is the product of the sea?'

'I do, professor. The sea supplies all my needs. I trail my nets

'I entered a dining room'

astern, and when I haul them in they are full to bursting. Or I
go hunting in this watery environment, which seems inaccessible to humans, and run down the game which lurks in my
underwater forests. Flocks I have like those of Neptune's old
shepherd,[21] and they graze on the immense ocean floor, where
they have nothing to fear. I have a very large estate which I
farm myself and which is kept permanently planted afresh by
the hand of Him who creates all things.'

Somewhat surprised, I looked at Captain Nemo in silence,
then said:

'I fully understand, sir, that your nets supply your table with
excellent fish, though I understand less well how you can hunt
aquatic game in your underwater forests. But I do not understand at all how any piece of meat, however small, can figure
anywhere in your diet.'

'Which is why,' said Captain Nemo, 'I have nothing to do
with the flesh of land-based animals.'

'Then what is this?' I asked, pointing to a terrine in which
there remained a few slices of beef.

'What you think is meat, professor, is fillet of sea-turtle.
Here you have dolphin livers which you could easily mistake
for ragout of pork. My chef is very talented and particularly
skilful in dressing a wide variety of ocean produce. This is a
preparation of holothurians, or sea-slug, which a Malay would
say has no rival anywhere in the world. That is a custard made
with milk from a cetacean mother, and the sugar comes from
giant North Sea fucus. Finally, may I offer you some of this
sea-anemone compote, which is as good to eat as preserves
made from the most delicious fruits?'

I sampled it more out of curiosity than as a gourmet while
Captain Nemo fascinated me with his most unlikely tales.

'But the sea, Professor Aronnax,' he said, 'this prodigious,
inexhaustible fount of plenty does not only feed me, it puts
clothes on my back. The fabric you are wearing was woven
from the byssus of certain kinds of shellfish. They were then
dyed with the purple known to the Ancient World, which is
enhanced with the addition of violet tinctures which I extract
from the Mediterranean sea-hare. The fragrances you will find

on the dressing-table in your cabin were all distilled from marine plants. Your bed is made of the softest sea-grass in the ocean. Your pen is whalebone, and your ink the fluid secreted by the cuttle-fish or calamari. Everything now comes to me from the sea just as everything will return to it one day!'

'You love the sea, captain.'

'Of course I love it! The sea is everything! It covers seven-tenths of the world's surface. Its breath is pure and salubrious. It is a vast desert where man is never alone because he feels the constant beat of life all around him. The sea is merely the medium which supports the most fantastic, prodigious forms of existence. It is nothing other than motion and love, it is infinity in action, as one of your poets put it.[22] For nature, professor, is displayed in her three kingdoms, animal, vegetable and mineral. The first is generously represented by the four groups of zoophytes, three classes of articulata, five classes of molluscs, three classes of vertebrates: mammals, reptiles and innumerable regiments of fish comprising a numberless multitude of animals belonging to more than 13,000 species, of which only one-tenth live in fresh water. The sea is nature's vast storehouse. It was in the sea that the globe can be said to have begun, and who can say that it will not also end there, where it began? In it all is ultimate peace. The sea does not belong to tyrants. They may still exert their iniquitous rights on its surface, fight, exterminate each other and practise all the horrors they bring from the land. But thirty feet beneath its waves, their power ends, their influence fades and their power vanishes. I tell you, sir, live in the bosom of the seas. Only there will you find independence! Here I acknowledge no master. Here I am free!'

Captain Nemo suddenly fell silent in the middle of the effusion which his exaltation had produced. Had he forgotten his natural reserve and allowed himself to be carried away? Had he said too much? For a few moments he paced up and down, seeming very agitated. Then his nerves settled down, his features resumed their normal cold expression, and, turning to me, he said:

'But now, professor, if you wish to see around the *Nautilus* I am entirely at your disposal.'

11

The *Nautilus*

Captain Nemo got to his feet. I followed him out. A double door at the far end of the room opened, and I found myself in a room as big as the one I had just left.

It was a library. Displayed on the wide shelves of tall bookcases made of Brazilian rosewood with brass fittings were large numbers of volumes, all uniformly bound. They lined the walls of the room, and at their foot were divans covered in brown leather whose curved shape afforded maximum comfort. Light mobile stands which could be moved back or brought forwards as required offered rests for books being consulted. In the middle was a huge table covered with tracts and brochures and, among them, a few newspapers, which were already well out of date. The whole harmonious scene was lit by electric light from four half-globes of frosted glass each set into decorative whorls on the ceiling. I looked round in genuine admiration at this room, which had been so ingeniously fitted out. I could scarcely believe my eyes.

'Captain Nemo,' I said to my host, who had sat down on one of the divans, 'this is a library which would do honour to a palace on any of the five continents. I am truly astounded to think it can follow you down into the depths of the ocean.'

'Where could a man find greater solitude, and silence more profound, Professor Aronnax?' replied Captain Nemo. 'Does your study in the museum offer you such utter peace?'

'No, sir, it does not, and I must admit that it cuts a poor figure next to yours. You must have six or seven thousand volumes here.'

'Twelve, professor. They are the only links I still have with

'It was a library'

the land. But that world ended for me the day my boat, the *Nautilus*, dived beneath the waves for the first time. That day I bought my last books, my last journals, my last newspapers and since then I am perfectly ready to believe that mankind has stopped thinking and stopped writing. But these volumes, professor, are entirely at your disposal. You are free to make full use of them.'

I thanked Captain Nemo and began examining the shelves in the bookcases. They were filled with works of science, moral philosophy and literature, in many languages, but I could not see any books dealing with political economy, which seemed to be strictly excluded on board. There was one odd thing: the volumes, whatever the language they happened to be written in, were classified in no particular order. The fact that they were unsorted in this way proved that the captain of the *Nautilus* must have no difficulty reading whatever tome his hand chanced to pick up.

Among the books I saw the masterpieces of the great writers of Antiquity and the Modern world, that is, the best of what mankind has achieved in history, poetry, fiction and science from Homer to Victor Hugo, from Xenophon to Michelet, from Rabelais to George Sand. But science was the most prominently represented on those shelves: books about mechanics, ballistics, hydrography, meteorology, geography, geology and so forth occupied a place no less important than works devoted to natural history, and from this I took it that they were the captain's major topics of study. I saw the complete works of Humboldt, all Arago, monographs by Foucault, Henri Sainte-Claire Deville, Chasles, Milne-Edwards, Quatrefages, Tyndall, Faraday, Berthelot, Abbé Secchi, Petermann, Captain Maury, Agassiz and others, the proceedings of the Academy of Sciences, reports from various geographical and other societies and, by no means trailing the field, the two volumes which were what may have earned me a relatively warm welcome from Captain Nemo. Among the titles by Joseph Bertrand, his book called *The Founders of Astronomy* provided me with a specific date: I knew it had come out some time in 1865, so I was able to conclude that the fitting-out of the *Nautilus* could not have been completed before that date. Captain Nemo had therefore embarked on his undersea existence not more than three years previously. I also hoped that I might find even more recent books which would enable me to date that time more accurately. But I would have time to look into that matter and had no wish to delay our tour of the wonders of the *Nautilus* any further.

'Captain,' I said to him, 'I thank you for giving me the run of your library. It contains a wealth of scientific knowledge, and I shall make the most it.'

'But it's not just a library,' said Captain Nemo, 'it's also a smoking room.'

'A smoking room?' I exclaimed. 'So smoking is permitted on board?'

'Of course.'

'In that case, captain, I can only think that you must have maintained some contact with Havana?'

'Not at all,' replied the captain. 'Please accept this cigar, professor. Although it doesn't come from Havana, I think you will be impressed – if, that is, you are a connoisseur.'

I took the cigar which he held out to me. Its shape reminded me of a Havana, but the kind intended for the London market, yet it seemed to have been rolled using golden leaves. I lit it at a small brazier which stood on an elegant bronze stand and took my first puffs with all the sensual pleasure of the regular smoker who has been deprived of tobacco for two whole days.

'This is excellent, but it's not tobacco.'

'True,' said the captain. 'This tobacco does not come from Havana nor from the Orient. It is a variety of seaweed rich in nicotine which the sea supplies me with, though somewhat parsimoniously. Are you sorry it's not a London Havana?'

'From this day forwards, captain, I shall spurn them.'

'Please do not stint yourself and do not worry about where they come from. No official agency has checked their quality, but I dare to say they are none the worse for that.'

'On the contrary.'

At this juncture, Captain Nemo opened another door exactly facing the one by which I had entered the library, and I passed into a huge room. It was brilliantly lit.

It was an immense rectangle, with the corners cut off, 10 metres long, 6 wide and 5 high. The ceiling, decorated with a tracery of arabesques, was illuminated and cast a soft, clear light over all the wonders crowded into what was almost a museum. But it actually was a museum in which a generous, intelligent hand had assembled all the treasures of nature and art with the artistic confusion reminiscent of a painter's studio.

About thirty paintings by great masters, all in identical frames and separated by arrangements of ancient weapons and glinting armour, graced the walls, which were decorated with paper of a sober design. I saw canvases worth fortunes, most of which I had admired in private collections in Europe and at art exhibitions. The various schools of old masters were represented by a Raphael Madonna, a virgin by Leonardo da Vinci, a nymph by Correggio, a portrait of a woman by Titian, an adoration of the Magi by Veronese, an Assumption by Murillo, a Holbein portrait, a Velásquez monk, a martyr by Ribera, a country fair by Rubens, two Flemish landscapes by Teniers, three small genre pictures by Gerard Dow, Metsu and Paul Potter, two canvases by Géricault and Prud'hon, and a few seascapes by Backhuysen and Vernet. Among works of modern art were paintings signed by Delacroix, Ingres, Decamps, Troyon, Meissonnier, Daubigny, etc., and a handful of first-rate marble and bronze reduced copies of the finest statues from Antiquity stood on pedestals in niches of this magnificent museum. The stupefaction which the captain of the *Nautilus* had warned me to expect now began to take hold of my mind.

'Professor,' this strange man said to me, 'I hope you will excuse the informality of my welcome and the untidiness of this room.'

'Sir,' I said, 'I have no intention of trying to find out who you are, but may I be allowed to think you might be an artist?'

'An art lover, sir, at most. There was a time when I took pleasure in collecting these fine works created by the hand of man. I was an avid hunter, an indefatigable tracker, and I was able to assemble a few items of high value. They are the last souvenirs I have of the land which is dead to me. To me, your modern artists are already old masters: they are all two or three thousand years old, and I do not distinguish between them. Great masters have no age.'

'Is that also true of these composers?' I said, pointing to scores by Weber, Rossini, Mozart, Beethoven, Haydn, Meyerbeer, Hérold, Wagner, Auber, Gounod and numerous others scattered over a full-size piano-organ which filled the whole of one of the room's wall panels.

'These composers,' replied Captain Nemo, 'are the contemporaries of Orpheus. In the memories of the dead, chronological differences are erased, and I, professor, am dead, as dead as any of your friends who are at rest six feet underground.'

Then he said no more and seemed lost in his thoughts. I looked at him, feeling rather concerned as I silently analysed the strange expressions which flitted across his face. He was leaning with one arm on a valuable mosaic-topped table. He did not see me. He had forgotten I was there.

I did not intrude upon his reverie and continued my survey of the exhibits which graced the room.

After the works of art, rare objects from the natural world occupied a particularly important place. For the most part, they were plants, shells and other forms of marine life, doubtless personal discoveries made by Captain Nemo himself. In the middle of the room was a fountain, electrically lit. A jet of water rose and fell back into a basin made of a single tridacna. The circumference of the delicately scalloped edges of this shell, which had been provided by the largest of the acephalan molluscs, measured about 6 metres. It was therefore larger than the splendid tridacnae presented to King François I by the Republic of Venice which were used by the church of Saint-Sulpice in Paris as the basis for two enormous holy water stoops.[23]

Around this basin, under glass in elegant brass-framed display cases, were ranged, duly classified and labelled, the rarest specimens of marine life ever subjected to the gaze of any naturalist. You can imagine how delighted this professor was!

The sub-kingdom of zoophytes included several very unusual specimens from both its groups, the polyps and the echinoderms. From the first group were tubipores and fan-shaped gorgones, sweet-water sponges from Syria, several kinds of isis

from the Moluccas, pennatules, an impressive funiculine from
Norwegian waters, assorted umbelliferae, alcyonarians, a whole
series of the madrepores which my old teacher Milne-Edwards
has so meticulously classified, and among them I noticed some
very fine flabellinae, oculinae from La Réunion, various specimens of Neptune's Chariots from the West Indies, and lastly all
the species of those bizarre polyparies which form clumps and
entire islands and will turn one day into continents. Then came
the echinoderms, with their distinctive spiny outer cases, which
were represented by asterias, starfish, five-pointed crinoids,
comatulidae, asterophons, sea urchins, holothurians, etc., making a complete collection of the individuals of this group.

Even a moderately excitable conchologist would surely have
fainted at the sight of other, more numerous display cabinets
which classified examples of all the members of the sub-
kingdom of molluscs. I judged that they contained a collection
of incalculable value, but time does not allow me to record
them all. Among the specimens I will quote, just for the record:
the elegant royal hammer-shell from the Indian Ocean, with
regular white flashes which stand out vividly against a red and
brown background; a brightly coloured imperial spondylus,
bristling with spines, rarely found in European museums and
worth, I reckoned, 20,000 francs; a common hammer-oyster
from the seas around New Holland and very hard to come by;
exotic cockles from Senegal, bi-valves with shells so delicate
that a puff of air would burst them like a soap-bubble; several
varieties of Javanese watering-pot shells composed of calcareous tubes fringed with foliaceous pleats and much sought after
by collectors; a complete set of conical trochi, some greenish
yellow, from American waters, others reddish brown which
thrive in the seas around New Holland, together with examples
from the Gulf of Mexico most remarkable for their imbricated
shells; stellari which are found in the Southern Ocean; and,
lastly, and rarest of all, the magnificent New Zealand spur
shell. There were also wonderful sulphur-yellow tellins; precious species of cytherea and venus-shells; the latticed solarium
from the coastal waters of Tranquebar; the turban-shell marbled with brilliant mother-of-pearl; green parrot shells from

the China Seas; the little-known cone of the genus *coenodulli*; all varieties of the cowrie shells which are used as currency throughout India and Africa; the Glory of the Seas, the most precious shell in the East Indies; then lastly, littorina, dauphinules, turritella, janthina, tube shells, volutes, olividae, mitre shells, helmet shells, pourpres, whelks, harps, rock shells, trumpet-shells, cerites, spindle shells, strombs, pteroceres, limpets, hyales, cleodorae, all fragile, delicate shells for which science has found the most engaging names.

Kept apart from them, in special cabinets, were displayed ropes of pearls of the greatest beauty which reflected the electric lights in flashes of fire; rose pearls obtained from Red Sea *pinna marina*; green pearls from the blackfoot paua, together with yellow and blue and black pearls all derived from a variety of molluscs from all the world's oceans and from a certain kind of mussel found in northern rivers. Finally there were several examples, truly beyond price, of pearls grown by the rarest pintadine oysters. Some of these pearls were bigger than a pigeon's egg and comparable in value – and more – with the pearl Tavernier sold to the Shah of Persia for three million, and was worth even more than that other pearl belonging to the Imam of Muscat, which I had believed was without equal anywhere in the world.

Of course, it was virtually impossible to estimate the value of this collection. Captain Nemo must have spent millions acquiring all those different examples, and I was beginning to wonder where he had found the funds to satisfy his collecting whims when I was interrupted by these words:

'I see that you linger over my shells, professor. They are of course of interest to any naturalist, but to me they have an added charm: I collected them all myself. There is no sea on the globe which has escaped my collecting hand.'

'Captain, I understand what a joy it is to walk in the midst of such riches. You are the kind of man who amasses his own treasure. No museum in Europe has comparable holdings of marine exhibits. But if I use up all my admiration on them, what will be left for the rest of the boat which houses them? I have no wish to pry into your secrets, yet I confess that the

Nautilus, the driving power contained within it, the machinery by which it is steered, the colossal fuel which powers it, all this also arouses my curiosity hugely. In this very room I see instruments fixed to the walls whose purpose I cannot even guess at. May I be enlightened?'

'Professor Aronnax,' said Captain Nemo, 'I have told you that you have the run of my boat. This means that no part of the *Nautilus* is out of bounds to you. You may therefore proceed to examine everything in detail and it will be my pleasure to be your guide.'

'I do not know how to thank you, sir, but I shall not abuse your forbearance. I will ask only what function is served by these scientific instruments.'

'I have an identical set of controls in my cabin, professor, and there I shall be happy to explain what they are for. But first, I will show you the cabin which I have given you. You should know how you are to be accommodated on board the *Nautilus*.'

I followed Captain Nemo, who opened a door in one of the cut-off corners of the room and brought me back out on to the ship's walkways. He led me for'ard, where I found, not an ordinary cabin, but an elegant room furnished with a bed, dressing-table and various other items of furniture.

I could only thank my host.

'Your cabin is next to mine,' he said, opening a door, 'and mine connects with the large room we've just come from.'

I stepped into the captain's cabin. It had a severe, almost monastic look to it. An iron bunk, a work-table and a few lockers for clothes and toiletries. It was lit by a kind of skylight. Totally lacking in comfort. Just the bare essentials.

Captain Nemo motioned to a chair.

'Do sit down,' he said.

I did so, and he started to speak upon this wise.

12

All Done by Electricity

'Professor Aronnax,' said Captain Nemo, gesturing towards the instruments fixed to the walls of his cabin, 'these are the controls which are required for sailing the *Nautilus*. Here, as in the Great Saloon, I can always see them, and they show my course and exact position at sea. Some will be known to you, like that thermometer, which gives the temperature inside the *Nautilus*; the barometer, which measures air pressure and predicts changes in the weather; the hygrometer, which indicates the level of dryness of the atmosphere; the storm-glass, which is filled with a solution which, when it grows cloudy, warns of approaching storms; the compass, which gives me my course; the sextant, which uses the elevation of the sun to give me my latitude; the chronometers, which allow me to calculate my longitude; and lastly my day- and night-glasses, which permit me to scour all points of the horizon whenever the *Nautilus* surfaces.'

'They are standard navigational aids,' I said, 'and I know what they are for. But these others doubtless are to do with the specific requirements of the *Nautilus*. That dial I see there, with the moving pointer, isn't that a pressure-gauge?'

'Indeed, that is exactly what it is. It is connected directly to the water and, by registering the outside pressure, it tells me at what depth my boat happens to be.'

'And are these others a new kind of depth gauge?'

'They are thermometrical sounding devices, which measure the temperature of the water at various levels.'

'What about these other instruments, whose functions I cannot guess at?'

'At this point, professor, I should give you a word or two of explanation,' said Captain Nemo. 'So if you would hear me out . . . ?'

He remained a few moments without speaking, then went on:

'There is a potent, responsive, rapid, convenient form of power which is suitable for all kinds of purposes and reigns supreme on my boat. It does everything. It gives me light and warmth and is the force which drives all my mechanical appliances. That power is electricity.'

'Electricity!' I said in a startled voice.

'Yes, professor.'

'But, captain, you are capable of attaining great speeds, and that is difficult to reconcile with the power of electricity. Until now, its dynamic force has been limited and capable of generating only a low output of power.'

'Professor Aronnax,' said Captain Nemo, 'my electricity is not like the electricity other people use . . . but that is as much, if you don't mind, as I shall say on the subject.'

'I won't press you, sir. I shall settle for being amazed by what you have achieved. But one question, if I may. You need not answer if it is intrusive. The fuels you use to produce this amazing power must get depleted very quickly. How, for example, do you replace zinc, given that you no longer have any contact with the land?'

'I will answer your question,' answered Captain Nemo. 'In the first place, I will point out that there are deposits of zinc, iron, silver and gold under the sea-bed which would be eminently workable. But I have not used any of the metals which are extracted from the earth. I have made it a point of looking to the sea itself for the means of generating my electricity.'

'The sea?'

'That's right, professor, and there is no shortage of ways of achieving that objective. For example I could have created a circuit of connected rods sunk at various depths and obtained electricity from the differences in temperature between them. But I preferred a much more practical system.'

'What was that?'

'You know the chemical structure of sea-water. Of every 1,000 grams of it, 96.5 per cent is water, about 2.66 per cent sodium chloride and small percentages each of magnesium chloride, potassium chloride, magnesium bromide, Epsom salts, lime sulphate and carbonate of lime. You will observe that sodium chloride represents a substantial proportion of the whole. It is from that sodium compound which I extract from sea-water that I derive the components I need.'

'From sodium?'

'Absolutely. When mixed with mercury it forms an amalgam which is a substitute for zinc in the Bunsen batteries.[24] The mercury is never depleted, only the sodium, and the sea provides me with ample supplies of that. Let me add further that sodium batteries are considered to produce the most energy, and that their electro-motive power is double that of zinc batteries.'

'I grant you that in the conditions in which you operate sodium is superior, for it is found in the sea. Fine. But it still has to be made available, by that I mean extracted. And how do you do that? Obviously your batteries could be used in the extracting process, but unless I'm mistaken the amount of sodium required by your electrical equipment would exceed the quantities obtained. It follows therefore that in order to produce it you would consume more than the amount you would produce!'

'And that is why, professor, I do not use batteries to extract it. Instead I just use the heat of coal.'

'Coal dug out of the ground?'

'Very well, sea coal, if you prefer,' said Captain Nemo.

'And you are able to mine coal beneath the sea-bed?'

'Professor Aronnax, you shall watch me do it. All I ask of you is a little patience – and you have plenty of time to be patient. Just remember this: I owe the sea everything. It produces electricity, and electricity gives the *Nautilus* heat, light, motion, in a word, life.'

'But not the air you breathe.'

'Oh, I could easily make all the air I need for my purposes, but there is no point because I can surface whenever I like. But if electricity does not supply me with breathable air, at least it operates the powerful pumps which store it in special tanks which enable me, if I need to and for as long as I wish, to extend the time I spend at extreme depths.'

'Captain,' I said, 'I am happy to sit back and admire. You have evidently found what other men will doubtless discover one day, the full dynamic power of electricity.'

'I have no idea if they will find it or not,' Captain Nemo said frostily. 'But however that may be, you have already seen for yourself to what uses I for the first time have put this precious power. It is what lights our darkness with a steadiness and continuity which sunlight does not have. But now look at this clock; it is electric and works with an accuracy which challenges that found in the best chronometers. I have divided the dial to show twenty-four hours, as in Italian clocks, because for me there is no night, no day, no sun, or moon, but only my artificial light, which I take with me to the bottom of the sea! Look! It is now ten in the morning.'

'True.'

'Another use I make of electricity. That dial you see there gives the speed of the *Nautilus*. An electric cable connects it to the log's propeller, and the needle gives me a reading of the current speed of the engine. There you are, at this moment, we are moving at a modest 15 knots.'

'Wonderful!' I said. 'I can see, captain, why you are right to use this new power, which is sure to replace wind, water and steam.'

'That's not all, Professor Aronnax,' said Captain Nemo, getting to his feet. 'If you would be so good as to come with me, we shall inspect the stern section of the *Nautilus*.'

Indeed, I was now thoroughly conversant with the entire bow area of the submarine vessel and I here give its exact layout, going from the waist of the ship to the bow: first the dining room, 5 metres, separated from the library by a sealed bulkhead, meaning that it prevented water from getting in; the library, also measuring 5 metres; the Great Saloon, 10 metres, separated from the captain's cabin by a second watertight bulkhead; then the captain's cabin, 5 metres; mine at 2.5 metres; and finally an air-tank, 7.5 metres, which ran all the way to the bow. Total length: 35 metres. The watertight bulkheads had doors in them which were closed hermetically by means of rubber flaps which thus made the *Nautilus* absolutely safe in the event of the ship's springing a leak.

I followed Captain Nemo along one of the lateral walkways as far as the middle of the boat. There I found a kind of open stairwell between two watertight bulkheads. An iron ladder clamped to the wall led up to the top of the shaft. I asked the captain what purpose was served by the ladder.

'It leads to the dinghy,' he answered.

'What? You have a dinghy on board?' I said, rather surprised.

'Of course. An excellent ship's dinghy, light and unsinkable, which we use for short trips out and for fishing.'

'So does that mean that when you wish to use it you have to return to the surface?'

'Not in the least. The boat is fixed to the top of the hull of the *Nautilus*. It fits into a dedicated recess designed to accommodate it. It is fully decked, completely watertight and held securely in place by strong bolts. The ladder leads up to a manhole in the hull of the *Nautilus* which connects with a similar aperture in the side of the dinghy. It is by means of this double opening that I get into the boat. The hole in the *Nautilus* closes behind me, and I close the other one, the one in the boat, by means of pressure screws. I release the bolts, and the boat floats up to the surface at a tremendous rate. I open the hatch in the deck, which is kept carefully closed until that point, I raise the mast and hoist the sail or else take to my oars, and away I go.'

'But how do you get back on board?'

'It is not I who returns, Professor Aronnax, but the *Nautilus* which returns to me.'

'On your orders?'

'At my order. I am linked to my ship by an electric wire. I just send a telegram. That's all there is to it.'

'I see,' I said, dazzled by these wonders, 'it's as simple as that!'

Having passed the bottom of the stairs which led up to the platform, I saw a cabin 2 metres long, where Conseil and Ned Land, delighted with their meal, were still eating voraciously. Then a door opened into a galley 3 metres in length, located between the huge on-board storerooms.

There, electricity, more powerful and responsive even than gas, was used exclusively for cooking. Cables reached under the ranges and were connected to metal plates, which distributed the heat evenly and maintained a steady temperature. It also heated the distillation unit, which, by means of evaporation, produced excellent drinking water. Next to the galley was a bathroom, most comfortably appointed, with taps supplying cold or hot water as required.

After the galley came the crew's quarters, 5 metres long. But the door to it was shut, and I was unable to see how it was arranged, though that would perhaps have given me an idea of the number of men required to sail the *Nautilus*.

At the far end was a fourth sealed bulkhead which separated the crew's accommodation from the engine room. A door opened, and I walked into this area where Captain Nemo – clearly a first-rate engineer – had sited the engines which powered the boat.

This engine room was brilliantly lit and measured not less than 20 metres in length. It was, of course, divided into two sections: the first housed the equipment that generated the electricity, and the second the machines that transmitted motor power to the screw.

At first I was rather puzzled by the singular smell that filled this compartment. Captain Nemo noticed my reaction.

'During the process,' he explained, 'quantities of gases are released, a by-product of the use of sodium, but it's a minor inconvenience. In any case, we ventilate the entire ship each morning by blowing air through it.'

Meanwhile, I set about examining the engines of the *Nautilus* with an eagerness that will easily be understood.

'As you see,' Captain Nemo told me, 'I use Bunsen, not Ruhmkorff, batteries,[25] which would not have been powerful enough. Fewer Bunsen batteries are needed and they are powerful and big, which is better, as experience shows. The electricity produced is fed to the rear, where, boosted by very large electro-magnets, it drives a novel system of levers and gears which transmit the power that turns the propeller shaft. The propeller is 6 metres in diameter with a pitch of 7½ and can supply up to 120 revolutions a second.'

'And that gives you?'

'A speed of 50 knots.'

'This engine room was brilliantly lit'

There was still something mysterious about all this, but I went no further in trying to get to the bottom of it. How on earth could electricity be made to yield such power? What was the source of this virtually unlimited force? Was it in the extraordinary voltages achieved by transformers of some new type? Was it in the transmission process itself, which could be ratcheted up to infinity by some entirely new system of levers?* That was what I was unable to fathom.

'Captain Nemo,' I said, 'I can see the results for myself and I do not even begin to understand them. I have seen the *Nautilus* outmanoeuvre the *Abraham Lincoln* and I have been left in no doubt about the speeds it can achieve. But mere motion is not enough. You must be also able to see where you are going. You must be able to steer to the right, to the left, up and down. How do you manage to descend to such tremendous depths where you must encounter increasing pressures running to hundreds of atmospheres? How do you return to the surface? And lastly how are you able to remain at the various depths you choose? Is it indiscreet of me to ask?'

'Not at all, Professor Aronnax,' the captain answered after a moment's hesitation, 'since you cannot ever again leave my submarine vessel. Come into the Great Saloon. It's what we use for our study. There you will learn all you need to know about the *Nautilus*!'

---

* In fact, there are reports of an invention of this kind which claim that a new set of levers allows very considerable forces to be produced. Did by any chance the inventor ever meet Captain Nemo?

13
Facts and Figures

Moments later, we were seated on a divan in the Great Saloon, each drawing on a cigar. The captain spread out a blueprint showing the full layout, section and elevation of the *Nautilus*. Then he began his description in these terms:

'Here, Professor Aronnax, you see the various dimensions of the boat you are sailing in. It is an elongated cylinder with conical ends. It has the rather obvious form of a cigar, a shape already adopted in London for a number of experimental underwater craft. The length of the cylinder from end to end is exactly 70 metres, while its beam, at its broadest point, measures 8 metres. So it is not built quite in the one-to-ten proportions that are used for ocean-going steamers, but its lines are long enough and its curves sufficiently extended for the water it displaces to

flow smoothly all round it and not set up any resistance to its progress.

'These two measurements enable us to obtain by a simple calculation both the surface area and volume of the *Nautilus*. Its surface covers an area of 1,011.45 square metres, and its volume is 1,500.2 cubic metres, which means that when completely submerged it displaces 1,500 cubic metres of water and weighs 1,500 tons.

'When I drew the plans for a boat intended for underwater navigation, I intended that when floating on an even keel nine-tenths of it would be submerged, leaving just one-tenth above water. To achieve this, it would have to displace a quantity of water equivalent to only nine-tenths of its volume, that is 1,356.48 cubic metres, and weigh the identical number of tons. I could not therefore exceed this weight when building it according to the dimensions I have given you.

'The *Nautilus* has two hulls, an inner and outer. They are held together by T-shaped iron struts which ensure that the structure is 100 per cent rigid. The effect of this cellular design is to make it as strong as a dense block, as if it were solid not hollow. Its plated outer skin cannot be breached; its structure holds it intact, not the tightness of the rivets; the uniformity of its construction, which results from the ultra-accurate assembly of its parts, enables it to withstand the most gigantic seas.

'Both hulls are made of steel plate 7.8 times denser than water. The outer skin is nowhere less than 5 centimetres thick and weighs 394.96 tons. The inner skin plus the keel, which is 50 centimetres high, 25 centimetres wide and alone weighs 62 tons, together with the engine, ballast, assorted equipment and fittings, bulkheads and the interior locking struts, in all run to 961.62 tons. When added to the 394.96 tons, the total weight of the *Nautilus* comes to the required figure of 1,356.58 tons. Are you following me?'

'Every step of the way,' I said.

'So when, given these conditions, the *Nautilus* is sitting in the water, only one-tenth of her is above the surface. Now, if I add two tanks with a capacity equal to that one-tenth, by which I mean that they are capable of holding 150.72 tons, and if I fill them with water, the boat displaces a total weight of 1,507 tons and will be completely submerged. And that is exactly what happens, professor. These tanks are located one on each side of the lower level of the *Nautilus*. If I open the stopcocks, they fill, and the boat sinks until she is just beneath the level of the sea.'

'That's all very well, captain, but now we come to the hard part. I will concede that you can hold station just under the surface of the ocean. That I see. But at lower depths, when you dive beneath the surface, will not your submarine vessel encounter pressure and consequently experience an upward thrust which must be in the region of 1 atmosphere per 30 feet of water, or about 1 kilo per square centimetre?'

'That is quite right, professor.'

'So unless you completely fill the *Nautilus*, I do not see how you can take it down into deep water.'

'But, my dear sir,' replied Captain Nemo, 'you are confusing static and dynamic states, and this has led you to commit a serious mistake. Very little effort is required to reach the bottom of the ocean, for solid bodies have an inbuilt tendency to sink. Listen to my reasoning.'

'I'm listening.'

'When I began trying to work out by how much the weight of the *Nautilus* needed to be increased to enable it to dive, the only factor I needed to consider was the rate of the reduction in volume which sea-water undergoes as it sinks to ever deeper levels.'

'Obviously,' said I.

'Now, though water is not absolutely incompressible, it is at least not very compressible. Indeed, according to the latest calculations, the limit of reduction is a mere 436 ten-millionths per atmosphere or per every 30 feet of depth. So if we wish to go down to 1,000 metres, then I take into account the reduction of volume at a pressure equivalent to that of a column of water 1,000 metres high or, if you prefer, a pressure of 100 atmospheres. The figure for the reduction will then be 436 hundred-thousandths of an atmosphere. Thus I need to increase the weight from 1,507.2 tons to 1,513.77 tons. The increase needed would therefore be just 6.57 tons.'

'Is that all?'

'That's all, Professor Aronnax, and my calculation is easy to confirm. Actually I have fitted extra tanks with a total capacity of 100 tons. I am thus able to dive to considerable depths. When I wish to return to the surface and level off, all I do is expel water. If I want just one-tenth of the volume of the *Nautilus* to emerge above water level, I simply empty all the tanks completely.'

I could hardly object to these arguments, backed as they were by detailed figures.

'I accept your calculations, captain,' I said, 'and it would be churlish of me to contest them since experience bears them out on a daily basis. But at this juncture I see a very real difficulty.'

'Which is?'

'When you are at a depth of 1,000 metres, the hull of the *Nautilus* must be subjected to a pressure of 100 atmospheres. So if, at that point, you attempt to empty your tanks to lighten the boat and return to the surface, your pumps will need to overcome a pressure of 100 atmospheres, which amounts to 100 kilos per square centimetre. That requires a degree of power . . .'

'. . . which only electricity can give me,' Captain Nemo said quickly. 'I repeat, sir, that the dynamic output of my engines is virtually limitless. The pumps of the *Nautilus* have tremendous power, as you will probably have seen when the jets of water they sent up fell in torrents on the *Abraham Lincoln*. But as it happens, I only use my extra tanks to reach depths averaging 1,500 or 2,000 metres, to avoid overloading my motors. Also if I ever wish to inspect the ocean depths 2 or 3 leagues under its surface, I use more leisurely but no less infallible means.'

'And what are they?' I asked.

'This brings me naturally to telling you how the *Nautilus* is sailed.'

'I am most eager to know.'

'To turn the boat to port or starboard, in other words to sail on the horizontal plane, I use an ordinary rudder with a wide blade fixed at the back of the stern-post, which is worked by means of a wheel and pulleys. But I can also steer the *Nautilus* upwards and downwards, on the vertical plane, by using two angled rudder-blades located one on each side the hull at the exact centre of the flotation line. These blades can be manoeuvred into any position from inside the vessel by means of powerful levers. When the position of these blades is parallel with the boat, the vessel moves horizontally. When they are angled, and depending on the angle they are set at, the *Nautilus*, powered by her screw, either dives along a diagonal course for as long as I require, or else rises along a similar diagonal course. If I wish to return to the surface more quickly, I engage the propeller, and the thrust of the water pressure drives the *Nautilus* straight up, exactly as a balloon filled with hydrogen shoots straight up into the air.'

'Well done, sir!' I exclaimed. 'But, when you are at depth, how is the helmsman able to follow the course you give him?'

'The helmsman occupies a glazed cockpit which projects above the upper part of the *Nautilus*'s hull and is fitted with lens-shaped windows.'

'You mean a kind of glass able to withstand great pressures?'

'Quite so. Crystal-glass, though a shock will easily shatter it, is nevertheless remarkably strong. During trials of fishing by electric light carried out in the North Sea in 1864, glass plate of this material just 7 millimetres thick was observed to withstand pressures of 16 atmospheres while simultaneously allowing free passage to strong thermal rays which distributed their heat across it unevenly. The lenses I use are at least 21 centimetres thick at their centre, which makes them thirty times thicker.'

'I grant you all that, Captain Nemo. But if the eye is to see, the light must be strong enough to disperse the darkness, and I wonder how that can be done down there in deep, black waters.'

'Behind the helmsman's cockpit is a powerful electric reflector, a searchlight which can light the sea for up to a range of half a mile.'

'Brilliant, captain! Quite brilliant! Now I understand the phosphorescence of what we thought was a narwhal, which was such a mystery for our scientists. In this connection, may I ask if the collision of the *Nautilus* and the *Scotia*, which caused such an outcry, was the result of an accidental encounter?'

'Entirely accidental, professor. I was proceeding 2 metres below the surface when we collided. But I was able to see that the consequences were not serious.'

'Indeed they were not, sir. But what about your clash with the *Abraham Lincoln*?'

'I am extremely sorry, professor, for what happened to one of the finest ships of the United States' fine fleet, but I was under attack and was obliged to defend myself. But I restricted my response to ensuring that the frigate was in no state to threaten my boat – it will have no problem having the damage repaired in the nearest American port.'

'Captain Nemo,' I cried with total sincerity, 'the *Nautilus* is truly a magnificent boat!'

'Indeed, professor,' replied Captain Nemo, genuinely pleased, 'I feel for her the way I would feel for the flesh of my flesh! If danger is a constant companion on board any of the vessels which are subject to all the perils of the sea, if on the surface of that sea what dominates the mind is, as the Dutchman Jansen[26] puts it so well, 'awareness of the abyss', then the heart of the man who sails on the *Nautilus* beneath the waves has nothing to fear. No buckling of the hull, for my boat's double skin is as rigid as iron; no danger of rigging being frayed by the constant pitching and rolling; no sails to be blown away by the wind; no boilers to burst under the pressure of steam; no risk of fire, since my boat is made of steel plate, not wood; no coal to run out, since she is powered by electricity; no possibility of collision, since she is the only boat sailing in deep water; and no storms to face, because a few metres beneath the surface the water is absolutely calm! Now that, sir, is what makes her such an excellent ship! And if it is true that the chief engineer has more confidence in the boat than the naval architect who built it, and the architect who built it greater faith in it than the captain himself, you will understand how much trust I have in the *Nautilus*, for I am captain, architect and chief engineer all rolled into one!'

Captain Nemo spoke with infectious eloquence. The fire in his eye and the passion of his gestures quite transformed him. It was true: he loved his boat the way a father loves his child!

But one question, indiscreet perhaps, arose naturally, and I could not refrain from putting it to him.

'So you are an engineer, captain?'

'I am, professor,' he replied. 'I studied in London, Paris and New York in the days when I was an inhabitant of the continents of the earth.'

'But how were you able to build the magnificent *Nautilus* in secret?'

'Each section, professor, was delivered to me from a different part of the globe, using an accommodation address. The keel was forged at Le Creusot, the propeller shaft was made by Pen & Co. of London, the metal plates for the hull by Leard of Liverpool, and the propeller by Scott of Glasgow. Its tanks were manufactured by Cail et Compagnie of Paris, its engine in Prussia by Krupp's, the bow section in the workshops of Motala in Sweden, all its precision instruments by Hart Brothers of New York and so forth. Each of my suppliers was given my plans under a variety of names.'

'But all these different pre-fabricated sections had to be assembled and aligned somewhere?'

'Professor, I had previously built my own boatyards on an uninhabited island in the middle of the ocean. There, I and my workmen, or rather the loyal companions whom I had taught and trained, completed the construction of the *Nautilus*. Once that was done, all trace of our presence on the island was destroyed by fire. I would have blown it up, if I had been able to.'

'So am I to assume that the cost of building the boat was colossal?'

'Professor Aronnax, it costs 1,125 francs a ton to build an iron ship. The *Nautilus* has a displacement of 1,500 tons, which means it cost 1,687,000 francs, or 2 million if we include fixtures and fittings, and 4 or 5 million if we add the works of art and the various collections on board.'

'One final question, captain.'

'Please . . .'

'You must be very rich?'

'Limitlessly rich, sir, so rich that I could, without feeling it, pay off the whole of France's national debt of 10 billion!'

I stared at this strange man who had spoken these words. Was he taking advantage of my credulity? The future would answer my question.

14
The Black River

The area of the globe covered by water is estimated to be 3,832,558 square myriametres, that is 38 billion hectares. This mass of water amounts to 2,250 million cubic miles and would form a sphere with a diameter of 60 leagues weighing 3 quintillion tons. To understand this last figure, it should be borne in mind that a quintillion is to a billion what a billion is to 1, that is, there are as many billions in a quintillion as there are 1s in a billion. Now this liquid mass is more or less the quantity of water which would flow down all the rivers in the world over a period of 40,000 years.

During the geological epochs, the age of fire followed the age of water. In the beginning, the sea entirely covered the globe. Then gradually, during the Silurian period, the tops of mountains appeared, islands emerged, disappeared during partial deluges, reappeared, joined together, formed continents, and finally these land masses became geographically fixed in the form in which we now see them. The process of solidification forced the liquid element to disgorge 37,000,657 square miles of dry land, the equivalent of 12,916 million hectares.

The way the continents are configured divides the water into five major parts: the glacial Arctic Ocean, the glacial Antarctic Ocean, the Indian Ocean, the Atlantic and the Pacific.

The Pacific Ocean stretches north to south between the two polar circles, and east to west from Asia to the Americas, over a span of 145° of longitude. It is the calmest of all the seas. Its currents are broad and slow, its tides modest, and its rainfall abundant. It was this ocean that fate first destined me to roam in these strange circumstances.

'Professor Aronnax,' said Captain Nemo, 'we shall now, if you have no objection, take our exact position and fix our point of departure for our forthcoming journey. It is a quarter to twelve noon. I shall now begin to surface.'

The captain pressed the electric bell three times. The pumps began expelling water from the tanks; the needle of the pressure gauge registered the different pressures as the *Nautilus* rose and then stopped.

'We're there,' said Captain Nemo.

I proceeded to the central staircase which led up to the platform. I climbed the metal steps and through the open hatchway I arrived at the highest part of the *Nautilus*.

The platform stood just 80 centimetres out of the water. The forward and rear sections of the *Nautilus* were tapered, justifying the description of the boat as a long cigar. I noticed that its metal plates were slightly overlapped and looked like the scales which cover the bodies of the larger terrestrial reptiles. I now saw how natural it was that, despite the best telescopes, the vessel should always have been assumed to be a marine animal.

In the middle of the platform, the dinghy, bolted in its recess, formed a low swelling on the hull of the boat. Fore and aft were two knee-high structures with sloping sides inset with thick glass lenses. One was intended for the helmsman who was steering the *Nautilus* and the other was the site of the electric beam which lit his way.

The sea was magnificent, and the sky cloudless. The elongated vessel was scarcely affected by the swell of the ocean. A light easterly breeze purled the surface of the water. The horizon, now free of mist, provided the best conditions for taking observations.

There was nothing in sight. No reefs, no small islands, no *Abraham Lincoln*. Just empty, open sea.

Captain Nemo brought out his sextant, which he used to take the elevation of the sun. This would give him our latitude. He paused for a few minutes for the glowing disc to touch the edge of the horizon. He did not move a muscle while taking his reading, and the instrument would not have been steadier if it had been held by a marble hand.

'Midday,' he said. 'And now, professor, when you are ready . . .'

I cast one last look over the slightly yellowish waters of Japan's coastal seas and then went below to the Great Saloon.

Once there, the captain jotted down his reading and referred to his chronometer to calculate his longitude, which he checked against previous readings. Then he said:

'Professor, our position is 137 degrees and 15 minutes west.'

'Which meridian are you using?' I asked quickly, hoping that the captain's reply might give me his nationality.

'Oh, I have a number of chronometers which are set variously by the Paris, Greenwich and Washington meridians. But in your honour, I shall use the Paris meridian.'

His answer told me nothing. I bowed and the captain went on:

'Longitude 137 degrees 15 minutes west of the Paris meridian and 30 degrees 7 minutes latitude north, that puts us about 300 miles off the coast of Japan. So it is today, 8 November, at twelve noon, that we begin our voyage of exploration under the seas.'

'May God protect us!' I said.

'And now, professor,' added the captain, 'I will leave you to your studies. I have set a course east-north-east at a depth of 50 metres. You have here large-scale charts on which you can follow our progress. This room is entirely at your disposal. With your leave, I shall withdraw.'

Captain Nemo bowed and left. I remained alone, lost in my thoughts. They were all focused on the master of the *Nautilus*. Would I ever discover the nationality of this strange man, who boasted to have none? Who had caused the loathing he felt for humankind, the hatred which might perhaps be translated into terrible acts of revenge? Was he one of those misunderstood scholars, a genius who 'had been hard done by', to use one of Conseil's phrases, a modern Galileo, or one of those men of science like the American Maury, whose career was wrecked by political revolution.[27] This I could not yet say. I who had been delivered by chance on board his boat, I whose life he held in his hands – I had been given a cool welcome, though a hospitable one. Except that he had never shaken the hand I had held out to him. And he had never offered me his.

I remained wrapped in my thoughts for a whole hour,

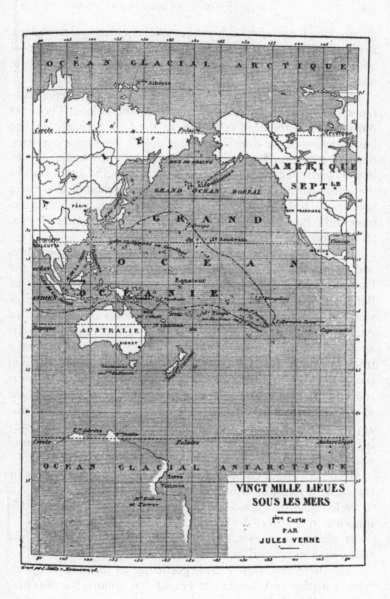

VINGT MILLE LIEUES
SOUS LES MERS

1ʳᵉ Carte

PAR

JULES VERNE

during which I tried to solve the mystery which concerned me so closely. Then my eye fell on the large planisphere that stood on a table and I placed my finger on the exact place where the observed degrees of latitude and longitude converged.

Seas have rivers just as continents do. They are special currents, recognizable by their temperature and colour. The most remarkable of them all is known as the Gulf Stream. Science has determined the direction of the globe's five major currents: one in the North Atlantic, another in the South Atlantic, a third in the North Pacific, a fourth in the South Pacific and a fifth in the southern Indian Ocean. It is more than probable that there was once a sixth, in the northern Indian Ocean, when the Caspian and Aral Seas, being then a part of the great lakes of Asia, formed a single, unbroken expanse of water.

Now, flowing under the place marked on the planisphere, was one of these currents known to the Japanese as the Kuro-Scivo, the Black River, which after leaving the Bay of Bengal, where it is heated by the perpendicular rays of the tropical sun, crosses the Strait of Malacca, flows up the coast of Asia, forms a loop in the North Pacific with the Aleutian Islands as its furthest point, carrying with it the trunks of camphor trees and other kinds of indigenous debris and making a vivid contrast between the pure indigo of its waters and the surrounding ocean. It was this current that the *Nautilus* was now about to join. I tracked its course with both eyes. I saw it disappear in the vastness of the Pacific and was feeling that I was being swept along by it, when Ned Land and Conseil appeared at the door of the Great Saloon.

Both my valiant companions looked as if turned to stone by the sight of so many wonders massed before them.

'Where is this?' cried the Canadian. 'Where are we? In the museum in Quebec?'

'If monsieur pleases,' said Conseil, 'it looks more like the Hôtel du Sommerard in Paris.'

'Ah, there you are!' I said, gesturing to them to come in, 'you're neither in Canada nor France but aboard the *Nautilus* and 50 metres below sea-level.'

'I believe what monsieur says because monsieur says it,'

replied Conseil. 'But to be frank, how could anyone expect a simple Fleming such as myself not to be surprised by a place such as this?'

'Look and be amazed. For an expert classifier like you, there is a great deal of work to be done here.'

I did not need to encourage the excellent Conseil, who was already hunched over the display cases muttering words in the language of naturalists: class of gastropods, family of *buccinidae*, genus cowrie, species *cypraea madagascariensis* and so on.

Meanwhile, Ned Land, who was not much of a conchologist, was asking me about my interview with Captain Nemo. Had I found out who he was, where he came from, where he was going, how deep he was taking us, plus a lot of other questions which I did not have time to answer.

I told him what I knew, or rather all I didn't know, and in turn asked what he had seen or heard on board.

'I haven't seen or heard anything!' replied the Canadian. 'I haven't even caught sight of any of the boat's crew. Are they by any chance electric too?'

'Electric?'

'Hell's teeth, a man might be tempted to think so! But how about you, professor?' asked Ned Land, who was always like a dog with a bone. 'Can you tell me how many men are on board? Ten, twenty, fifty, a hundred?'

'That I can't, Mister Land. But just pause for a moment, stop thinking about taking the ship over or escaping. This boat is a masterpiece of industrial-age naval architecture, and I would have been very sorry not to have seen it! Many people would be happy to be in the situation which has been forced on us, if only to be able to see all these wonderful things. So calm down and let us try to work out what is going on.'

'See?' cried the harpooner, 'but we can't see anything, nor will we see out of this metal prison! We're moving, we're sailing blind!'

Ned Land was just saying these last words, when we were suddenly plunged into complete and utter darkness! The luminous ceiling was snuffed out so quickly that it made my eyes hurt, an effect not dissimilar to that produced by moving from deep shadow into very bright light.

We stood there, not speaking, not moving, not knowing what surprise, pleasant or unpleasant, awaited us. Then there was a sliding sound. It was as if panels on the sides of the *Nautilus* were being closed or possibly opened.

'It's the end! It's all over!' said Ned Land.

'Order of hydromedusas,' murmured Conseil.

Suddenly both walls of the room were illuminated by a brightness which entered through two oblong openings. The mass of water outside became visible, brilliantly lit by electrical power. Two plates of glass separated us from the sea. At first, I went weak at the thought that these fragile barriers might break. But strong brass frames held them firmly and gave them almost unlimited strength.

The sea was clearly visible over a radius of a mile all round the *Nautilus*! What a sight! Whose pen could describe it! Who could capture the effects of the light through those expanses of transparent water and the subtlety of the imperceptible stages by which it faded as it merged with the upper and lower levels of the ocean!

The diaphanous nature of the sea is well known, as is the fact that sea-water is clearer than rock water. The mineral and organic matter which is held in suspension increases its transparency. In certain parts of the ocean, in the Caribbean, the sandy bottom is visible 145 metres down and looks amazingly clear; indeed, the sun's rays appear to penetrate as far as a depth of 300 metres. But in the marine environment through which the *Nautilus* was sailing, the brightness of its electric lights was being produced in the sea itself. It was not illuminated water, it was liquid light.

If we allow Erhemberg's hypothesis,[28] which states that the lower depths are lit by the phenomenon of phosphorescence, then nature has certainly reserved one of her most amazing sights for the denizens of the deep, as I could judge by the myriad effects of that luminosity. On each side I had an unobstructed view of those unexplored depths. The darkness of the Great Saloon emphasized the brightness outside, and we watched as if its pure crystal window was the glass pane of an immense aquarium.

The *Nautilus* did not appear to be moving. The reason for this was that there were no fixed reference points. However, now and then as we watched, lines of the water left by the prow rushed past at a tremendous rate.

Agog with wonder, we leaned on our elbows in front of our windows. Not one of us had so far broken our stunned silence. Then Conseil said:

'You wanted to see, Ned. Well, now you're seeing!'

'Curious, very curious!' said the Canadian, who, forgetting his rages and all his plans of escape, was irresistibly fascinated. 'A man would come a long way to see a sight like this!'

'Ah!' I exclaimed. 'I can understand the life our host leads! He has created a world apart which reserves its most amazing splendours just for his eyes!'

'But where are the fish?' remarked the Canadian. 'I don't see any fish!'

'Why should that bother you, Ned,' said Conseil, 'since you don't know the first thing about fish!'

'I, know nothing? I'm a fisherman!'

Whereupon an argument sprang up between the two friends because, although they knew everything about fish, each knew about them in different ways.

It is widely known that fish are the fourth and last class of the sub-kingdom of vertebrates. They have been correctly described as 'cold-blooded vertebrates which have double circulation, breathe through gills and can live only in water'. They form two distinct groups: the class of bony fish, that is, those with spines made of bony vertebrae, and cartilaginous fish, that is, those whose spine is made of cartilaginous vertebrae.

Perhaps the Canadian was aware of the distinction, but Conseil knew far more about it than he did. However, having become firm friends with Ned, he did not want him to think that he knew any less on the subject than he did. Accordingly, he said:

'Ned. You are a killer of fish, a very skilled fisherman. You have caught a very large number of these fascinating creatures. But I'll wager that you have no idea about how they are classified.'

'But I do,' the harpooner said earnestly. 'They are classed as fish you can eat and fish you can't eat!'

'Ah! The view from the kitchen!' said Conseil. 'But tell me, do you know the difference between bony fish and cartilaginous fish?'

'Now maybe I do, Conseil.'

'And the subdivision of these two large classes?'

'Not a clue.'

'Well, Ned, listen and learn. Bony fish are subdivided into six orders. First: the acanthopterygians, which have a complete, moveable upper jaw and comb-shaped gills. This order includes fifteen sub-orders, which include three-quarters of all known fish. Type: the common perch.'

'They make quite good eating,' replied Ned Land.

'Second: abdominal fish with ventral fins located under the abdomen and behind the pectorals but not attached to the bones of the shoulder. The order to which they belong is divided into five sub-orders and includes the majority of fresh-water fish. Types: carp and pike.'

'Ugh!' retorted the Canadian scornfully. 'Freshwater fish!'

'Third,' said Conseil, 'the subbrachians. Their ventral fins are attached under the pectorals and hang from the shoulder bones. This order contains four sub-orders. Types: plaice, dab, turbot, brill, sole, etc.'

'Excellent, all excellent!' exclaimed the harpooner, whose interest in fish was entirely culinary.

'Fourth,' went on Conseil, refusing to be diverted, 'the apodals, which have cylindrical bodies, no pelvic fins and are covered with a thick, often sticky skin. This order has only one sub-order. Types: eels and electric eels.'

'Medium to poor.'

'Fifth,' persisted Conseil, 'the lophobranches, which have complete, free jaws but gills made of small tufts arranged in pairs along the brachial arches. This order has just one sub-order. Types: sea-horse, pegasus sea-moth.'

'Sounds disgusting!'

'Sixth and last,' said Conseil, 'the plectognaths, whose maxillary bone is attached to the side of the intermaxilla which forms the jaw. The palatine arch is imbricated with the cranium by sutures and is thus held rigid. This order does not have ventral fins as such and consists of two sub-orders. Types: globe-fish, trigger-fish.'

'I wouldn't let them anywhere near a pan!'

'Have you got all that, Ned?' asked the learned Conseil.

'No, Conseil, none of it,' replied the harpooner, 'but carry on all the same, you make it all sound so interesting.'

'Turning now to the cartilaginous fish,' Conseil resumed imperturbably, 'they run to a mere three orders.'

'That's a mercy,' said Ned.

'First, the cyclostomes, having jaws that are fused and form a moveable ring, and whose brachiae, or gills, open through a number of orifices. An order with just one sub-order. Type: lamprey.'

'Not to everybody's taste,' said Ned Land.

'Second, the selachians. Their brachiae resemble the gills of the cyclostomes, but their lower jawbone is moveable. The order, the largest in its class, consists of two sub-orders. Types: shark and ray.'

'What!' exclaimed Ned. 'Rays and sharks in the same sub-order? Conseil, if you have the interests of rays at heart, I wouldn't recommend that you put those two together in the same tank!'

'Third,' continued Conseil, 'the sturionians, whose brachiae ordinarily function through a single slit with a gill-plate. This order has four sub-orders. Type: sturgeon.'

'Conseil, my friend, you've kept the best for last, at least in my opinion. Have you finished?'

'All done, Ned,' said Conseil. 'But remember: when you know all that, you still don't know very much, for each sub-order is subdivided into genera, sub-genera, species, varieties . . .'

'Well, Conseil,' said the harpooner, turning back to the window in the panel, 'here's a whole crowd of varieties swimming by!'

'Well, you wanted fish!' exclaimed Conseil. 'It's almost like looking into an aquarium!'

'Hardly,' I broke in. 'An aquarium is a cage, and those fish out there are as free as the birds of the air.'

'Go on, then, Conseil,' said Ned Land, 'name them!'

'Oh no,' said Conseil, 'I couldn't. That's my employer's field.'

It was true. The excellent Conseil was a furious classifier but no naturalist, and I'm not sure that he would have been able to tell a tuna from a bonito. He was, in a word, the opposite of the Canadian, who could put names to all these fish without hesitation.

'There's a trigger-fish,' I said.

'And a Chinese trigger-fish!' said Ned Land.

'Family *ballistidae*, sub-order scleroderms, order of plectognaths,' murmured Conseil.

Decidedly, put the two of them together, and Ned and Conseil would have made one first-rate naturalist.

The Canadian was quite correct. A shoal of ballistes with flattened bodies, coarse skins and armed with a dorsal sting were playing around the *Nautilus* and waving four rows of spines which bristled along each side of their tails. It would be difficult to imagine anything more admirable than their livery: grey underneath, white on top, with patches of gold that gleamed in the dark swell of the water. Rays undulated between them like sheets blowing in the wind, and among them I was delighted to see a Chinese ray, yellowish on its upper side, delicate pink underneath and equipped with three stings behind its eyes. A rare species, whose existence was still doubted in the time of Lacépède,[29] who had never seen it except in a book of Japanese engravings.

For two hours, an entire aquatic army escorted the *Nautilus*. While they played and sported and strove to outdo the others in beauty, brilliant colourings and speed, I made out a green wrasse; the barberin mullet, with its double black stripe; the elytriform goby, which has a rounded caudal fin, is white coloured and has splashes of violet on its back; the Japanese scombrus, a gorgeous mackerel and a native of these waters, which has a blue body, a silver head; azuror fish, blue and gold, with a name which makes description redundant; striped sparadas with variegated blue and yellow fins; shiner fish with bold black streaks on their caudal fins; zonifer sparadas, elegantly trim in their six belts; trumpet fish, or red oyster catchers, which are more or less mouths attached to flutes, some of which reached a length of a metre; Japanese salamanders; clouded morays, serpents 6 feet long with small quick eyes and huge mouths bristling with teeth, and many, many more.

Our admiration remained at the highest pitch. There was no end to our amazed exclamations. Ned gave the names of all the fish, Conseil provided classifications, while I was in seventh heaven just watching the speed of their acrobatics and the beauty of their forms. Until that moment, it had never been given to me to observe these creatures living freely in their natural element.

I will refrain from naming all the varieties which swam past our bedazzled eyes in a parade of all the species of the Japan and China Seas. Those fish swarmed more numerous than the birds of the air, almost certainly attracted by the bright source of the electric light.

Suddenly, the lights came on again in the Great Saloon. The metal panels slid shut. The enchanting vision disappeared. But I went on seeing it in my mind's eye for some time until I caught sight of the instruments fixed to the walls. The compass still gave our course as north-north-east,[30] the pressure gauge registered a figure of 5 atmospheres, which was the equivalent of a depth of 20 metres, and the electric patent-log recorded a speed of 15 knots.

I waited for Captain Nemo, but he did not return. By the clock it was 5 p.m.

Ned Land and Conseil went back to their cabin, and I to my room. My dinner was waiting for me. It consisted of turtle soup made of the tenderest hawksbills, the white, slightly flaky flesh of a whole surmullet, with the liver served separately, which made delicious eating, and filets of emperor holocanthus, which I thought was superior in flavour to salmon.

I spent the evening reading, writing and thinking. Then, as fatigue began to catch up on me, I lay down on my sea-grass bed and fell into a deep sleep, while the *Nautilus* glided through the fast-flowing waters of the Black River.

15
A Formal Invitation

The following morning, 9 November, I did not wake until I had slept for twelve hours. Conseil came in, as he always did, to ask 'how monsieur had passed the night' and offer his services. He had left his friend, the Canadian, snoring like a man who had never done other than sleep like a log all his life.

I let the excellent fellow babble on freely without going out of my way to respond. My mind was full of the non-appearance of Captain Nemo at our session in the saloon the previous evening, and I was hoping to see him today.

Soon I had got into my byssus clothes. Conseil commented on their fabric more than once. I told him they were made with the glossy, silky threads which anchor mussels, pen shells and various kinds of shellfish, all abundant on the shores of the Mediterranean, to rocks. Once upon a time, they were regularly used to make excellent fabrics, stockings and gloves because of their qualities of softness and warmth. So the crew of the *Nautilus* were able to clothe themselves with a very small outlay without needing to turn to the cotton plants, sheep and silk worms of dry land.

When I was dressed, I hurried off to the Great Saloon. There was no one there.

I buried myself in a study of the conchological treasures which filled its cabinets to bursting. I also wandered among vast herbariums filled with the rarest marine plants, which, though they had been dried, still retained their vivid colours. Among those precious aquatic plants were examples of verticellate cladstephus, sea pen pavonaria, vine-leaf caulerpa, *callithamnion granifero*, delicate scarlet-hued *ceramium rubrum*, fan-shaped agars and assorted acetabularia, which resemble flattened mushroom caps and were for a long time classified among the zoophytes, in other words a wide range of algae.

The whole day sped by without my being honoured by a visit from Captain Nemo. The panels in the saloon walls did not open again. Perhaps the intention was that we should not get used to so much beauty and start taking it for granted.

The course of the *Nautilus* remained east-north-east, her speed 12 knots and her depth between 50 and 60 metres.

The next day, 10 November, I was again ignored and left to myself. I saw no member of the crew. Ned and Conseil spent most of the day with me. They were amazed by the inexplicable absence of the captain. Was that singular man ill? Was he minded to change the plans he had for us?

After all, as Conseil observed, we enjoyed complete freedom and were delicately and abundantly fed. Our host kept to the terms of our agreement. We had nothing to complain of and, in any case, the strangeness of our fate had brought such wonderful compensations that we were as yet in no position to formulate charges against destiny.

That day I began a log of these adventures, which has enabled me to relate them with the most scrupulous accuracy. Curiously enough, I wrote it on paper made from marine sea-grass.

Very early on 11 November, the cool air which filled the interior of the *Nautilus* told me that we had returned to the surface of the ocean, to replenish our supplies of oxygen. I proceeded to the central stairwell and climbed up to the platform.

It was six in the morning. I found a cloudy sky and a sea that was grey but calm. There was hardly any swell at all. I was hoping to meet Captain Nemo there. Would he come? I saw only the helmsman enclosed in his glass cage. I sat on the projection formed by the hull of the ship's dinghy and took deep breaths of the delicious salt air.

Gradually, the mist cleared in the warm rays of the sun. Its radiant disc was edging above the eastern horizon. Trapped in its glare, the sea caught fire like a trail of gunpowder. Spread across the length and breadth of the vaults of heaven, the clouds scattered across the upper reaches of the sky took on bright, wonderfully varied hues, while numerous 'mares' tails'* were harbingers of winds for the rest of the day

But what could winds do to the *Nautilus*, which had nothing to fear from tempest and storm?

So there I was, admiring the joyous sunrise, so cheering, so revitalizing, when I heard someone coming up to the platform.

I was getting ready to greet Captain Nemo, but it was his first officer – I had already encountered him during that initial meeting with the captain – who appeared. He stepped out on to the platform but did not seem aware of my presence. Holding a powerful telescope to one eye, he scoured each point of the horizon with close attention. Once he had finished, he moved back to the hatchway and made a pronouncement in these exact words. I remember it clearly, for it was repeated every morning in identical circumstances. It sounded as follows:

'*Nautron respoc lorni virch.*'[31]

What it meant, I could not possibly have said.

Once he had pronounced these words, he disappeared below. Supposing that the *Nautilus* would now resume its course under water, I went back to the hatch and thence, via the walkways, to my room.

Five days passed in this way, during which the situation did not change. Every morning, I went up to the platform. The same words were pronounced by the same individual. Captain Nemo never appeared.

I had resigned myself to not seeing him again when, on 16 November, going back to my room with Ned and Conseil, I found a note for me on the table.

I opened it impatiently. It was written in a hand that was open and clear though with a touch of gothic resembling German script.

It read as follows:

* Small white clouds, fluffy, with serrated edges.

Professor Aronnax, on board the *Nautilus*
16 November 1867

Captain Nemo has great pleasure in inviting Professor Aronnax
to a hunting expedition which will be held tomorrow morning in
his forests of Crespo Island. He hopes that there is nothing that
will prevent Professor Aronnax from attending and will be grat-
ified if his companions would also accompany him.
Master of the *Nautilus*
Captain Nemo

'A hunt!' exclaimed Ned.
'In the forests of Crespo Island!' added Conseil.
'So he's going ashore, then, is he?' said Ned.
'That seems clear enough from what he says here,' I said,
reading the note through again.
'In that case, we'll have to accept,' said the Canadian. 'Once
back on terra firma, we can decide on our next move. Anyway,
I won't be sorry to get my teeth into a piece of fresh venison.'
Without trying to resolve the contradiction between Captain Nemo's stated detestation of continents and islands and
this invitation to hunt in his forests, I just said:
'First let's see where this Crespo Island is.'
I turned to the planisphere and at a position of latitude 32°
40' north and longitude 167° 50' west, I discovered a small
island which had been explored in 1801 by Captain Crespo
and was previously named on old Spanish charts as Rocca de
la Plata, or 'Silver Rock'. We were thus about 1,800 miles from
our starting point, and the slightly altered course of the *Nautilus* was taking us back towards the south-west.
I pointed out this little lump of rock lost in the middle of the
North Pacific to my companions.
'If Captain Nemo does indeed go ashore sometimes,' I told
them, 'at least he chooses desert islands!'
Ned Land shook his head without responding, and then he
and Conseil left me to myself.
After a supper served by the mute, stony-faced steward, it
was with a somewhat troubled mind that I fell asleep.

The moment I woke next morning, 17 November, I sensed that the *Nautilus* was not moving. I dressed quickly and hastened to the Great Saloon.

Captain Nemo was there, waiting for me. He stood up, wished me good morning and asked if I was disposed to accompany him.

As he himself did not refer to his absence during the past week, I refrained from mentioning the matter and answered simply that my companions and I were ready to follow him.

'However, captain,' I added, 'I would like to ask you something.'

'Please ask, Professor Aronnax, and if I can answer, then I shall.'

'Well, captain, how is it that you, who have cut all ties with the land, are the owner of forests on Crespo Island?'

'Well, sir,' the captain answered, 'the forests I own do not require the sun to provide either heat or light. They are home to no lions, tigers, panthers or any kind of quadruped. They are known only to me. They grow only for me. They are not land forests but underwater forests.'

'Underwater forests?' I exclaimed.

'Yes, professor.'

'And you are offering to take me there?'

'Indeed I am.'

'On foot?'

'And without getting your feet wet.'

'While hunting?'

'While hunting.'

'With a gun in my hand?'

'With a gun in your hand.'

I stared at the master of the *Nautilus* in a way which could not be construed as flattering.

'Decidedly, his wits have turned,' I thought. 'He has been having a bout of insanity which has lasted a week and is obviously still going on. Such a shame! I liked him better strange than mad!'

This thought could be clearly read in my face, but Captain

Nemo merely invited me to follow him, and I did so with the air of a man who is expecting the worst.

We entered the dining room, where breakfast was ready.

'Professor Aronnax,' said the captain, 'I would be glad if you would share my breakfast without ceremony. We can talk as we eat. I offered to take you on an expedition in a forest, I did not promise that you would find a restaurant there. So make a hearty breakfast as befits a man who is not likely to sit down to his dinner until very late.'

I did full justice to the meal. It consisted of different kinds of fish and slices of sea cucumber, excellent zoophytes, served with spicy and very appetizing seaweeds such as *porphyria laciniata* and *laurentia primafetida*. To drink we had water to which, following the captain's example, I added a few drops of a fermented liquor extracted, by the Kamchatka method, from an alga, *rhodymenia palmata*, known as sea lettuce.

At first, Captain Nemo ate without uttering a single word. Then he said:

'When, professor, I suggested that you might come hunting with me in the forests of Crespo, you thought you had caught me in contradiction with myself. When I told you that they were underwater forests, you thought I was mad. Well, sir, you should never judge a man lightly.'

'Captain, please believe . . .'

'Hear me out and you will judge then whether you should still bring charges of madness or self-contradiction against me.'

'I'm listening.'

'Professor Aronnax, you know as well as I do that a man can live under water provided he carries a supply of breathable air with him. Men who work under water wear a watertight suit and a metal diving helmet which encases the head. Their air comes from the surface by means of force pumps fitted with valves to control the flow.'

'It's what deep-sea divers wear.'

'Exactly, but in such conditions man is not free. He is attached to the pump, which supplies him with air through a rubber pipe, which acts like a chain and keeps him linked to the land. If we had to be so closely bound to the *Nautilus*, we would not be able to go very far.'

'And how could you be free of it?' I asked.

'By using the Rouquayrol-Denayrouze regulator,[32] which was invented by two compatriots of yours, but adapted by myself for my own use. It will enable you to venture into this new physical environment without damaging your internal organs in any way. It consists of a tank made of thick metal in which I store air at a pressure of 50 atmospheres. This tank is carried on the back by means of straps, like a soldier's knapsack. Its upper section serves as a chamber for the air, which is maintained by a system of bellows. The air cannot escape except at normal pressure. In the Rouquayrol regulator, as normally used, two rubber tubes lead out of this chamber to a kind of mask which covers the diver's nose and mouth. One pipe introduces air which is breathed in and the other removes the air which has been breathed out, with the tongue closing the first or the second according to the rhythms of respiration. But I operate under the sea at great depths and have to contend with very high pressures. So I had to enclose my head entirely, as with the deep-sea diver, in a round copper helmet to which the inflow and outflow pipes are connected.'

'I see all that, captain, but the air you carry with you must get used up very quickly and as soon as air contains less than 15 per cent of oxygen, it ceases to be breathable.'

'True, but as I've explained, professor, the pumps on board the *Nautilus* allow me to store air at very high pressures, and given these conditions the apparatus can supply breathable air for nine or ten hours.'

'I have no further comment to make,' I replied. 'I would only ask, captain, how you manage to see where you are going on the ocean bed?'

'With the Ruhmkorff apparatus,[33] professor. The tank is carried on the back, but this apparatus is attached to the belt. It consists of a Bunsen battery, which I turn on using not potassium bichromate but sodium. An induction coil collects the electricity that is generated and transmits it to a specially designed lamp. In this lamp is a fine spiral of glass which contains a trace only of carbon dioxide. When the lamp is turned on, this gas becomes luminous and gives out a steady, whitish light. And so I can both breathe and see.'

'Captain Nemo, you provide such complete answers to all my objections that I hardly dare raise another. However, though I have no alternative but to accept the Rouquayrol regulator and the Ruhmkorff lamp, you must still allow me to have reservations about the gun you propose to arm me with.'

'But it's not a weapon that requires gunpowder,' said the captain.

'So it's an air gun?'

'Of course. Surely you don't expect me to be able to make gunpowder on board my ship when I don't have saltpetre, sulphur or coal?'

'In any case,' I said, 'to shoot under water, in an environment 855 times denser than air, you would need to overcome enormous resistance.'

'That's not a problem. There are in existence certain kinds of cannon, based on designs by Fulton and developed by the Englishmen Phillip Coles and Burley, Furcy, a Frenchman, and the Italian Landi, which are fitted with a specially sealed firing mechanism that allows them to be used in precisely such conditions. But I repeat: not having gunpowder, I have replaced it with high-pressure air, which the pumps of the *Nautilus* can give me in endless quantities.'

'But doesn't that air get used up quickly?'

'Yes, but there's always my Rouquayrol tank, which can give me more, if needs be. All that's required is an improvised valve. But you shall see for yourself, Professor Aronnax, that when we go hunting under water we shall not be using large quantities of air and ammunition.'

'Yet I still feel that in conditions of semi-darkness and when surrounded by liquid which is extremely dense compared with the atmosphere above bullets won't carry very far and will have difficulty being lethal.'

'On the contrary, professor, with this kind of gun, every shot is lethal. Once an animal is wounded, however lightly, it dies as if poleaxed.'

'Why?'

'Because this gun does not fire ordinary bullets but small glass capsules invented by the Austrian chemist Leniebroek, of which I have a large stock. These glass capsules, encased in steel and weighted with a lead shot, are in effect miniature Leyden jars into which the electricity has been forced at very high voltages. At the slightest shock caused by impact, the animal, however powerful it may be, is killed outright. I should add that the calibre of these capsules is no greater than a .4 and that the breech of an ordinary gun could hold ten of them.'

'I have no more questions,' I said, getting up from the table. 'It only remains for me now to get my gun. And where you go, I shall go too.'

Captain Nemo led me towards the stern of the *Nautilus*, and as we passed by the cabin assigned to Ned and Conseil, I called to my two companions, who immediately fell in step with us.

We stopped at a chamber situated amidships, near the engine room. There we would get into the clothes for venturing outside.

16

A Tour of the Plain

Properly speaking, the chamber was the arsenal and changing room of the *Nautilus*. A dozen diving suits hanging on the wall awaited the hunters.

When he saw them, Ned Land's reluctance to get into one was obvious.

'Actually, Ned,' I said, 'the forests of Crespo Island are just forests under water!'

'Oh!' said the harpooner, visibly disappointed when he saw his dreams of fresh meat vanish. 'And are you, Professor Aronnax, intending to put on one of these suits?'

'Needs must, Ned.'

'If you say so, sir,' replied the harpooner, shrugging his shoulders. 'But, speaking for myself, I'll never put on one of those things on unless I'm forced to.'

'Nobody is forcing you, Mister Land,' said Captain Nemo.

'Is Conseil going to risk it?' asked Ned.

'I go wherever monsieur goes,' replied Conseil.

Summoned by the captain, two members of the crew appeared and helped us into the heavy, watertight suits, which were made of rubber, had no seams and were designed to withstand very high pressures. They were like suits of armour, being both flexible and strong. They consisted of trousers and jacket. The trouser legs ended as thick boots with heavy lead soles. The material of the jacket was reinforced with copper ribbing that formed a breastplate and protected the chest against the thrust of the water and allowed the lungs to function normally. The sleeves ended in the form of flexible gloves which in no way impeded the free movement of the hands.

As we could see, these suits of advanced design were a far remove from the cumbersome accoutrements, like the cork breastplates, under-tunics, mariner's body suits, floats, etc., which were invented and widely lauded in the eighteenth century.

Captain Nemo, one of his men – as big as Hercules and doubtless as prodigiously strong – Conseil and I were soon in our diving suits. All that remained now was to insert our heads in the metal spheres. But before proceeding to that stage, I asked leave of the captain to examine the guns which had been picked out for us.

One of the crew of the *Nautilus* handed me a basic-model gun, of which the butt was made of steel and hollow inside and was unusually large. It was the chamber for the compressed air which a valve, opened and closed by means of a trigger, released into the metal tube. A holder for the ammunition situated inside part of the hollowed-out butt contained around twenty electric cartridges, which, at the touch of a spring, were automatically moved into the barrel of the gun. When one shot was fired, the next was loaded and ready for firing.

'Captain Nemo,' I said, 'this weapon is perfect and easy to handle. I simply have to try it. But how are we to get out on to the sea-bed?'

'At present, professor, the *Nautilus* is resting in 10 metres of water. All we have to do now is go out.'

'But how do we go out?'

'You shall see.'

Captain Nemo put his head into the spherical helmet. Conseil and I followed his example, though not without hearing the Canadian wishing us an ironic 'good hunting!' The upper half of our suits was finished off with a copper collar with an integrated thread, on to which the metal head-piece was screwed. Three apertures, filled with thick glass, enabled us to see in all directions by simply turning our heads inside the head-piece. Once it was securely fitted, the Rouquayrol regulators, which were strapped on our backs, began to function immediately and I found I was able to breathe easily.

With my Ruhmkorff lamp hanging from my belt and my gun in my hand, I was ready to go. But to be honest, imprisoned in my heavy suit and glued to the deck by my heavy lead soles, I could not have put one foot in front of the other unaided.

But this eventuality had been anticipated. I felt myself being propelled into a small compartment situated next to the chamber. My companions, similarly hauled, followed. I heard a door fitted with seals close behind us, and we found ourselves in complete darkness.

After a few minutes I heard a loud hissing sound and experienced a mild feeling of cold spreading from my feet to my chest. Obviously a stopcock inside the boat had been opened, allowing water from outside to enter. It was now rushing in fast, and soon the chamber was completely flooded. Then a second door, this one in the hull of the *Nautilus*, opened, and we were suddenly in half-light. A moment later our feet were making contact with the bottom of the sea!

And now, how can I convey my impressions of our foray beneath the waves? Words are powerless to describe such wonders! When even the painter's brush is unable to capture the special effects produced by an underwater habitat, how can we expect the writer's pen to record them?

Captain Nemo was walking in front of us, and his companion followed a few steps behind. Conseil and I remained side by side, as if we thought we could exchange a few words through our metal helmets. I no longer felt the weight of my suit, boots and air-tank nor the burden of that thick round sphere inside which my head rattled about like an almond in its shell. Once in the water, all these items lost a percentage of their weight equal to that of the liquid they were displacing, and I was most grateful for that particular law of physics discovered by Archimedes. I was no longer an inert mass and had quite substantial freedom of movement.

The daylight which lit the sea-floor at a depth of 30 feet beneath the surface of the ocean surprised me by its strength. The rays of the sun passed easily through the aqueous mass and took the colour out of it. I could clearly make out objects 100 metres away. Beyond that, the water darkened and gradually took on the delicately graded hues of ultramarine, which turned deeper shades of blue further off before merging into an indeterminate darkness. The water which surrounded me was really the equivalent of air, denser than the atmosphere on dry land but almost as transparent. Above me, I could plainly make out the calm surface of the sea.

We were walking over fine, even sand, not rippled like beaches on which the swell leaves its mark. This dazzling carpet acted as a reflector and it returned the rays of the sun with surprising intensity. Hence the ubiquitous, vibrant luminosity which filled all the liquid molecules with brightness. Will I be believed when I swear that at a depth of 30 feet I could see as clearly as if it were day?

For a quarter of an hour, I walked over this gleaming sand, which was dusted with an intangible silt of shell remains. The hull of the *Nautilus*, resembling an elongated reef, faded gradually from view, but its beacon light, once night had filled those waters with darkness, would guide our return by projecting a beam of amazing clarity. The effect will be understood with difficulty by those who have only seen the whitish, brilliantly sharp glare of lighthouses on shore. On land, the dust which impregnates the atmosphere makes their brightness look like illuminated mist. But out at sea and under it, these electrical discharges are transmitted with unparalleled clearness.

Meantime, we walked on over the vast, seemingly endless, sandy plain. With my hand I pushed aside the liquid curtains, which closed behind me, while my footprints were immediately erased by the pressure of the water.

Soon shapes loomed up before me, their outlines scarcely softened by distance. I made out the first magnificent outcrops of rock carpeted with the finest specimens of zoophytes but was especially fascinated by an effect unique to this environment,

It was then about ten in the morning. The sun's rays were striking the surface of the water at a fairly oblique angle and, when struck by their light, which was broken down by refraction as it would if passing through a prism, the contours of flowers, rocks, plantlets, shells and polyps were all tinged with the seven colours of the sun's spectrum. The riotous admixture of different hues was a marvel, a feast for the eye, a kaleidoscope of green, orange, violet, blue, like the full palette of some

manic colourist! If only I had been able to convey to Conseil all
the strong sensations that rushed to my brain and compete with
him in expressions of admiration! If only I had, like Captain
Nemo and his companion, been able to exchange thoughts by
means of a system of signs! But, having no alternative, I was
reduced to talking to myself, shouting out loud inside the metal
sphere which enclosed my head and probably using up more air
uttering pointless words than was entirely wise.

Confronted by this wonderful spectacle, Conseil had come
to a stop, as had I. It was patently obvious that the splendid fellow, having been presented with these specimens of zoophytes
and molluscs, was busy classifying and categorizing. The
sea-bed was strewn with polyps and echinoderms. Various
kinds of isis; *cornularia* which live apart in clumps; tufts of virgin *oculina* (once known as ivory bush coral), bristling with
mushroom-shaped coral fungi; anemones anchored by muscular discs – all featured in beds studded with blue *siphonophore*
adorned in their annuli of sky-blue tentacles; constellations of
starfish in the sand; *asterophyton verrucosum*, which looked
like the finest lace embroidered by the hands of naiads and
hung in festoons which swayed in the eddies initiated by our
passing. It pained me greatly to tread on the brightly coloured
specimens of molluscs which littered the sandy floor by the
thousand: concentric combs; hammers; varieties of *donacia*
(the jumping shell); *tochidae*; red helmets; angel-wing strombs;
sea-slugs and many more creatures born of that inexhaustible
ocean. But walk we had to and on we pressed while over our
heads swam a flotilla of Portuguese men of war, their ultramarine tentacles trailing in their wake, and medusas whose
milky-white or pale-pink umbrella-shaped bells festooned with
sky-blue skirts sheltered us from the rays of the sun: if it had
been after dark, droves of *pelagia panopyra* would have lit our
way with their phosphorescent glow.

I observed all these marvels over a space of a quarter of a
mile, barely stopping and following Captain Nemo, who kept
calling me to order with a gesture of his hand. Soon the nature
of the sea-floor began to change. The sandy plain gave way to
a layer of viscous mud which Americans would call 'ooze' and

'Over our heads swam a flotilla of Portuguese men of war and medusas'

which consisted entirely of siliceous and calcareous shells. Then we crossed a meadow of seaweeds, pelagic plants which grew in wild profusion and which the surging water had not yet uprooted. These close-textured lawns, so soft to walk on, stood comparison with the most sumptuous carpets made by the hand of man. All this verdant growth extended under our feet, but it did not neglect our heads. A delicate raft of marine plants, classified in the exuberant family of algae of which over 2,000 species are known, mingled on the surface of the water. I saw long, floating ribbons of sea-wrack, some globular, others tabulate; *laurentiae*; delicately fringed *cladostephi* and *rhodymenia palmata*, which looked like cactus fans. I observed that the green plants kept closer to the surface of the water, while the red remained at a depth halfway down, leaving the black or brown hydrophytes to form gardens and beds at the deepest levels of the sea.

These algae are a prodigy of creation, one of the wonders of the world's flora. This family of plants produces the smallest but also the biggest forms of vegetation on earth. For just as 40,000 barely detectable plantlets have been counted in an area of 5 square millimetres, and examples of sea-wrack have been observed that were over 500 metres long.

We had been gone from the *Nautilus* for about an hour and a half. It was now around midday. I noted that at this time, when the sun was directly overhead, its rays were no longer being refracted. The magical colours gradually faded, and the emerald and sapphire hues disappeared from over our heads. We were maintaining a steady pace, and our footsteps on the sea-bed rang out astonishingly loud. The smallest sounds were transmitted at a speed to which the land-based human ear is unaccustomed. Actually, water is a far better conductor of sound than air, transmitting it four times as fast.

At this juncture, the ground began to fall away quite steeply. The light took on a uniform dimness. We reached a depth of 100 metres, where the pressure of the water was 10 atmospheres. But my diving suit was designed for such conditions, and I was in no way incommoded by the pressure. All I felt was a certain stiffness in the joints of my fingers, and even then the discomfort wore off pretty quickly. As to the fatigue one might have expected after walking for two hours in an unfamiliar get-up, it was non-existent. Buoyed up by the water, I was able to move with surprising ease.

When we reached this depth of 300 feet, I was still aware of the sun's rays, but only just. Their intense brightness had been followed by a reddish half-light, a halfway point between night and day. But we could still see well enough to find our way, and it was not yet necessary to turn on our Ruhmkorff lamps.

Just then, Captain Nemo stopped. He waited until I came up with him and then pointed a finger towards a number of dark shapes a short way off and just visible against the shadows.

'The forest of Crespo Island!' I thought, and I was not wrong.

17

A Forest Under the Sea

At last we had arrived at the beginning of the forest, probably one of the finest anywhere in the estates of Captain Nemo. He considered it as his personal property and claimed the same rights to it as the first men at the dawning of the world. And who would have contested his ownership of an underwater forest? What bolder pioneer would have come, axe in hand, to clear its dark thickets?

The forest was made up of large arborescent plants, and once we were moving under their vaulting arches my attention was first caught by the singular way in which their branches grew – an arrangement which I had not observed until that point.

None of the grasses carpeting the forest floor, none of the branches which sprouted on the shrubs trailed or spiralled or grew out on a horizontal plane. They all reached up towards the surface of the sea. Every filament, every ribbon, however thin, stood as straight as rods of iron. Sea-wrack and lianas grew along rigid, perpendicular lines which were dictated by the density of the element which had produced them. They did not move, yet when I brushed them to one side, they immediately returned to their original position. It was the kingdom of the vertical.

I soon got used to this strange phenomenon and also to the semi-darkness which surrounded us. The floor of the forest was littered with sharp rocks, difficult to avoid. The range of marine flora seemed to be more or less complete, and richer in fact than if it had been located in the Arctic or tropical zones. But for a good few minutes, I unwittingly confused the various kingdoms, mistaking zoophytes for hydrophytes, animals for plants. And

who would not have made the same mistake? Fauna and flora
are so closely conjoined in the realm beneath the waves!

I noticed that all these creations of the vegetable kingdom
clung to the ground by means of the flimsiest footings. Having
no roots and not caring what solid body – sand, shell, urchin or
pebble – supported them, all they required was something to
rest on, not something to draw on for life. These plants are
self-propagating, and the root of their whole existence is the
water which sustains and feeds them. Most did not have leaves
but instead put out blade-shaped lamellas in fanciful variations
and in a palette of colours restricted to pink, carmine, green,
olive, fawn and brown. Again I encountered, but not in the dried
form they had on board the *Nautilus*, specimens of peacock's
tails arranged like fans as if to catch the breeze; scarlet cera-
mies; *laminariales*, which produced long, edible, new shoots;
threads of flexuous ribbon kelp which rose to a height of 15
metres; bouquets of *acetabularia* with stems that grew downwards from the top; and numerous other pelagian plants, none
of them with flowers. 'It is an odd anomaly, a bizarre paradox,'
a witty naturalist once remarked, 'a world where the animal
kingdom flowers and the vegetable kingdom does not!'

In the watery shade of these assorted arborescent growths,
which grew as tall as trees in temperate zones, there flourished
bushes bright with flowers, hedges of zoophytes which were
home to brain corals with marbled convoluted surfaces, yellowish *caryophillia* with diaphanous tentacles, a thickly textured
sward of *zoantharia* and – to make the illusion complete –
fishflies that flitted from branch to branch like swarms of
humming birds, while yellow bristling-jawed, spiny-scaled
lepisacanthes together with *dactylopterae* and *monocantha*
flew up at our approach like a cloud of woodcock.

Around one o'clock, Captain Nemo gave the signal to halt. I
for one was not sorry. We stretched out under a canopy of large
brown alaria, whose long thin blades stood up like arrows.

That moment of rest seemed quite delicious to me. All we
lacked was the charm of conversation. But it was quite impossible to speak and out of the question to answer. All I could
manage was to bring my large copper helmet closer to Conseil's

head. I saw his eyes ashine with excitement and, to indicate his happiness, he jigged about in his suit in the drollest manner imaginable.

After our four-hour trek, I was very surprised not to feel violent pangs of hunger. Why my stomach should react like this, I could not say. On the other hand, I was aware of an insurmountable urge to sleep, as happens to all divers. And so my eyes soon closed behind their protective glass, and I fell into a state of drowsiness which until that moment had been kept at bay only by the action of walking. Captain Nemo and his strapping companion, now supine in the crystal-clear water, gave us the lead.

How long I had been sleeping so heavily I could not judge. But when I woke, I had the impression that the sun was sinking towards the horizon. Captain Nemo was already up and about, and I had begun stretching my limbs when an unexpected sight brought me sharply to my feet.

Only steps away a monstrous sea-spider, a full metre tall, was staring at me with its sinister eyes, about to pounce. Although my diving suit was thick enough to protect me against the creature's bite, I could not repress a start of horror. Conseil and the sailor from the *Nautilus* woke up just at that moment. Captain Nemo directed his companion towards the hideous crustacean, which he instantly dispatched with a blow from the butt of his gun, and I saw the repulsive legs of the monster thrash about in one last, terrible convulsion.

This encounter made me think it more than likely that there were other animals, even more fearsome, lurking in these dark places and that my suit might not protect me against their attacks. Until that moment, I had not considered this and I resolved to stay on my guard. I also imagined that this halt marked the furthest point of our expedition. But I was wrong. Instead of returning to the *Nautilus*, Captain Nemo continued on his bold foray.

The ground was still falling away, and the slope grew steeper and led us on ever further downwards. It must have been around three o'clock when we reached a narrow valley, really a cleft between two high, sheer rock walls and located at a depth

'*A monstrous sea-spider*'

of 150 metres. Thanks to the excellence of our equipment, we had now exceeded by 90 metres the limit which hitherto nature had imposed to restrict man's underwater explorations.

I say 150 metres, although we had no instrument with which I could accurately measure the distance. But I knew that even in the clearest seas, the sun's rays could not reach deeper than that. Now here, the gloom was intense. Nothing was visible further away than ten paces. I was feeling my way forwards when I was suddenly surprised by a bright, white light. Captain Nemo had just turned on his electric lamp. His companion did likewise, and Conseil and I followed their example. By turning a screw I completed the contact between the coil and the thin glass spiral, and the sea, now lit by four lamps, was illuminated for a radius of 25 metres.

Captain Nemo continued to forge ahead into the dark depths of the forest, where the smaller shrubs had become fewer and further between. I noted that plant life here was disappearing more quickly than animal life. The pelagian plants no longer sprouted from the now sterile ground, whereas animals, zoophytes, vertebrates, molluscs and fish continued to flourish in large numbers.

As I walked along, I thought that the light from our Ruhm-korff lamps was bound of necessity to attract the denizens of these dark arches. But while some did come nearer, they kept at a distance that was frustrating to our hunters. Several times I saw Captain Nemo drop on one knee and put gun to shoulder. But after taking aim for a few moments, he would then get up and continue walking.

Finally, at about four o'clock, our fantastic trek came to an end. A wall of imposing rocks of vast proportions rose before us, an enormous pile of huge stone blocks forming a gigantic granite cliff pock-marked with dark caverns. There was no climbable route up it. It was the footing on which Crespo Island rested. We had reached land.

Suddenly Captain Nemo paused. A sign from him made us halt too, and, eager though I was to scale the wall, I was forced to stop. This point marked the limit of the captain's dominion, and he did not intend cross the line. On the other side of it was that part of the globe on which he had sworn never to set foot again.

We began the return journey. Captain Nemo was again at the head of our small group, still proceeding on his way without hesitation. It seemed to me that we were not following the same route for our march back to the *Nautilus*. Our new path, very steep and consequently very demanding, quickly brought us almost to the surface of the sea. But our return to the higher levels of the sea was not so rapid that the pace of decompression was too speedy, for that would have subjected our bodies to serious harm and provoked the internal lesions which are fatal to divers. Daylight reappeared promptly and grew stronger, and since the sun was already low on the horizon, the refraction effect again encircled all things with ghostly rings.

At a depth of 10 metres we were walking through a shoal of small fish of various kinds that were more numerous than the birds of the air and nimbler too. But we saw no aquatic game worthy of pointing a gun at.

Just then I saw the captain put his weapon quickly to his shoulder and keep it trained on a moving target lurking in the shrubbery. There was a shot, I heard a faint hiss and an animal fell dead, blasted, only a few paces away.

It was a magnificent sea otter, *enhydra lutris*, the only quadruped that is exclusively marine. It was a metre and a half long and must have been worth a great deal of money. Its pelt, chestnut brown on its back and silver on its belly, would have made one of those splendid furs that are in such demand on the Russian and Chinese markets. The softness and sheen of its coat would have ensured a minimum of 2,000 francs. I looked admiringly at this unusual mammal with its rounded head, short ears, globular eyes, the white whiskers like a cat's, the webbed feet and claws and the bushy tail. This exquisite carnivore, hunted and pursued by fishermen, is becoming extremely rare and has sought refuge mainly in northern parts of the Pacific, where in all likelihood it will not be long before the species dies out altogether.

Captain Nemo's companion stepped forwards, picked up the animal and slung it over his shoulder. Then we went on our way.

For the next hour, a sandy plain stretched away before us. It often rose to within less than 2 metres of the surface of the water. At such times I could observe us all clearly reflected but upside down so that above us we could see an identical group which mimicked our movements and gestures and were in a word exactly like us in every respect except that they walked with their heads down and their feet up in the air!

One other effect worth noting: the way thick clouds formed quickly and then were gone. On reflection I realized that what I took for clouds were caused simply by the varying heights of long bottom waves, and I also saw the 'white horses', the foam which their breaking crests scattered over the surface of the water. I could even identify the passage of large birds as they flew over our heads by the shadows they cast fleetingly on the surface.

It was on that occasion that I observed one of the finest shots that ever stirred the fibre of a hunting man. A large bird, with a vast wingspan, and very visible, was gliding towards us. Captain Nemo's companion took aim and shot it when it was no more than a few metres above the waves. The creature dropped like a stone, and the force of its fall brought it within arm's length of the skilful sportsman, who immediately seized it. It was an albatross of the finest kind, an admirable specimen of those sea-going birds.

Our progress was not held up by this incident. For two hours we traversed a succession of sandy plains and meadows of seaweed, which were very difficult to cross. To be perfectly honest, I had about reached the end of my tether when I made out, about half a mile away, a faint gleam which broke through the darkness of the water. It was the *Nautilus*'s beacon light. We would be on board within twenty minutes, and then I would be able to breathe easily, for I was beginning to think that my tank was supplying me with depleted air containing low levels of oxygen. But I had not reckoned on an encounter which would delay our arrival.

I had remained about twenty paces to the rear when I saw Captain Nemo suddenly hurrying back to me. With a strong sweep of his hand he forced me to lie flat on the ground while his companion did the same to Conseil. At first I did not know what to make of his brusque action but I was reassured when I saw that the captain was lying next to me and was completely still.

So there I was, stretched out on the ground and in the lee of a large clump of seaweed, when, on raising my head, I saw large, bulky shapes which gave out a phosphorescent glow pass noisily overhead.

The blood froze in my veins! I had realized what the formidable sharks now threatening us were: they were two fearsome tintoreas, killer sharks, which have enormous tails and torpid, glassy eyes and secrete a phosphorescent substance through holes around their muzzles. Monsters as lethal as cannon which can grind a man to pieces in their iron jaws! I do not know if Conseil was whiling away the time classifying them. But I myself was able to observe their silver undersides and formidable jaws bristling with teeth, from a standpoint which was not very scientific: more prey than naturalist.

Most fortunately for us, these voracious animals have very poor eyesight. They passed on their way without seeing us, though they brushed us with their brownish fins, and we escaped, almost miraculously, from a danger which was many times greater than coming face to face with a tiger in the middle of a jungle.

Half an hour later, guided by the electric beam, we reached the *Nautilus*. The outer door had been left open, and Captain Nemo closed it after we were all back in the first chamber. Then he pushed a button. I heard the sound of pumps inside the boat and was aware that the level of water was dropping around me; in a matter of moments the chamber had been completely evacuated. Then the inner door opened, and we transferred to the changing area.

There our diving suits were removed, not without difficulty, and then, completely exhausted, fainting with hunger and lack of sleep, I returned to my room, my head full of the wonders of our amazing expedition on the floor of the ocean.

18

Four Thousand Leagues
Under the Pacific

The next morning, 18 November, being completely recovered after the exertions of the previous day, I climbed up to the platform just as the first mate of the *Nautilus* was intoning his daily message. It crossed my mind that the words were connected with the state of the sea, or rather that they meant: 'We have nothing in sight.'

And the ocean was indeed absolutely empty. Not a sail on the horizon. The highest point of Crespo Island had disappeared during the night. The sea, absorbing all the colours of the prism except the blues, which it was now reflecting in all directions, had assumed a wonderful shade of indigo. At regular intervals an area like shot silk, with widely spaced spectrum lines, would spread across the surface of the waves.

I was admiring this wonderful spectacle of the sea when Captain Nemo appeared. He did not seem to be aware of my presence and began taking a series of astronomical observations. When he had finished this business, he leaned on the rail that ran round the beacon-light housing and became absorbed in his scrutiny of the ocean.

But a score or so of the crew of the *Nautilus*, all vigorous, burly men, were now climbing out on to the platform. They had come to gather in the trailing nets, which had been set overnight. These sailors were clearly of different nationalities, although the European type was recognizable in all of them. I had no difficulty picking out Irish, French, one or two Slavs and a Greek or Cretan. The men were economical with words and among themselves used only the strange language whose origin I could not even guess at. Consequently, I had to give up any thought of asking them questions.

The nets were hauled on board. They were a type of dragnet, not dissimilar to those used on the coasts of Normandy, huge pockets with one end kept open by a floating boom and a chain laced through the bottom links. These nets, hauled on iron gantries, trawled the sea-bed and scooped up everything they encountered. That morning, they landed curious specimens from these fish-rich waters: monkfish, which have such comical movements and are sometimes known as 'fishing-frogs'; commerson fish, black and equipped with antennae; sinuous trigger-fish ringed with narrow bands of red; puffer fish, whose venom is extremely subtle; a scattering of olive-coloured lampreys; *macrorhinus*, a small shark, covered with silver scales; cutlass fish, which have an electric charge equal to that of the knifefish and the electric ray; scaly *notopteri* with brown, transversal rings; greenish gade; several varieties of goby and so on, together with a few larger species: a metre-long caranx fish with a large head; several fine scombroid bonitos fancily liveried in blue and silver; and three magnificent tuna fish, whose speed had not saved them from the trawl net.

I reckoned that the catch had landed more than 1,000 pounds weight of fish. It was a good haul but not surprising. In practice, these nets were left trailing for several hours and garnered into their mesh prison a whole range of aquatic life. So we would not be short of victuals of the highest quality, which the speed of the *Nautilus* and the power of attraction of its electric lights could replenish at will.

These various items of sea food were immediately lowered through the hatch and stowed away in store rooms, some to be consumed fresh and the rest to be salted.

When fishing operations were complete and the air-tanks replenished, I imagined the *Nautilus* would resume her underwater voyage, and I was about to go below to my room when Captain Nemo turned to me and without preamble said:

'Look at the sea, Professor Aronnax. Does it not truly possess the gift of life? Does it not get angry? Is it not capable of tenderness? Yesterday it went to sleep as we did and now it is waking after a peaceful night!'

Not a 'good morning' or a 'good night'! Would not a third-party have assumed that this strange man was merely continuing a conversation which had already been started?

'Look,' he went on. 'It is being awakened by the touch of the sun. It is about to relive its daily cycle. Studying the workings of its organism is a fascinating business. It has a pulse, it has arteries and it has crises, and I agree with the scientist Maury, who discovered that it has a circulation as real as that of the blood in animals.'

Captain Nemo was clearly not expecting any answers from me, and I saw no point in giving responses of the 'Obviously', 'Of course' and 'You're right' variety. He was in fact talking to himself, leaving long gaps between each statement. He was in effect thinking out loud.

'Yes,' he said, 'the ocean really does have a circulation, and to get it going, the Creator of all things needed only to promote caloric stimulation and increase the amount of salts and the number of animalcules which it contains. Heat creates variations in density, which give rise to currents and counter-currents. Evaporation, virtually non-existent in northern latitudes but very active in equatorial zones, creates a constant exchange of tropical and polar waters. Furthermore, I have found that these currents also run from surface to bottom and bottom to surface and constitute the elemental respiration of the ocean. I have established that molecules of sea-water which have been heated on the surface sink down into the depths, reach their maximum density at a temperature of 2 degrees above zero and then, as they continue to cool, become lighter and move back up. When we reach the Pole, you will see the result of this phenomenon and you will understand, thanks to this law of all-foreseeing nature, that water can freeze only on the surface of the sea!'

As Captain Nemo was completing his sentence, I thought to myself: 'The Pole? Is this presumptuous man intending to take us all the way there?'

But the captain fell silent as he gazed out at the element which was the complete and constant object of all his studies. Then he spoke.

'There are large quantities of various salts in the sea, professor, and if you were to remove all of those which are presently dissolved in it, you would be left with a mass of 4½ million cubic leagues which, if spread evenly over the entire globe, would form a layer more than 10 metres thick. But you should not think that the presence of these salts is due to a mere caprice of nature. Far from it: they inhibit the process of evaporation and thus prevent the winds from removing too much water vapour, which, when it becomes liquid once more, would submerge the temperate zones. This plays a hugely important, central role in the general economy of the globe!'

Captain Nemo stopped, straightened up, walked a few paces along the platform and returned to me.

'As to the infusoriae,' he resumed, 'those billions of animalcules of which there are millions in a single drop of water and of which it would require 800,000 to make one milligram, their role is no less crucial. They absorb the marine salts, assimilate the solids suspended in water and become the creators of calcareous continents by producing corals and madrepores! Now, when that drop of water is depleted of its mineral sustenance, it grows lighter, returns to the surface, where it absorbs salts left as a result of evaporation, becomes heavier and sinks, thus bringing fresh nutrients for the animalcules to absorb. And there is your double current, one rising the other falling, perpetual motion, inexhaustible life! And life that is more intense than on land, more exuberant, more infinite, blooming in every part of the ocean, which is an element deadly to man, as has been said, but an element which means life for myriads of animals – and for me!'

When Captain Nemo spoke like this he was transformed and aroused the most extraordinary feelings in me.

'I say to you,' he added, 'true life is there! I could conceive of cities built beneath the sea, agglomerations of underwater dwellings which, like the *Nautilus*, would return every morning to the surface of the oceans to breathe, towns freer than any that have ever been, independent cities. And yet, who can say that some despot . . .'

Captain Nemo completed his sentence with an angry gesture. Then, addressing me directly, as though to chase away some depressing thought:

'Professor Aronnax,' he asked, 'do you know how deep the ocean is?'

'Well, I know what the major soundings have revealed.'

'Would you give them to me so that I can confirm them as required?'

'Here are a few,' I said, 'which I happen to recall. If I'm not mistaken, figures for average depth are 8,200 metres in the North Atlantic and 2,500 metres in the Mediterranean. The most remarkable soundings were taken in the South Atlantic, near the 35th parallel, and they came up, at different times, with figures of 12,000 metres, 14,091 metres and 15,149 metres. It has been estimated that if the sea-bed were rolled flat, the average depth would be around 7 kilometres.'

'Well, professor,' said Captain Nemo, 'I hope we can do better than that for you. As to the average depth of this part of the Pacific, I can tell you that it is just 4,000 metres.'

And so saying, Captain Nemo headed for the hatch and disappeared down the ladder. I followed and returned to the Great Saloon. The screw immediately started turning, and the patent-log showed a speed of 20 knots.

In the days and weeks that followed, Captain Nemo was very sparing with his visits. I saw him only at rare intervals. His first mate regularly took our position, which I found marked on the chart so that I was able to plot the route of the *Nautilus* accurately.

Conseil and Ned Land spent many long hours with me. Conseil had told his friend all about our wonderful crossing of the sea-bed, and the Canadian regretted that he had not gone with us. But I hoped that the opportunity would present itself for a further excursion into the ocean's forests.

For a few hours of virtually every day, the panels in the saloon were opened. We never grew weary of discovering new mysteries of the underwater world.

The general direction of the *Nautilus* was south-east, and the vessel maintained a depth of between 100 and 150 metres. But one day, on some whim or other, diving diagonally by means of its angled steering boards, it reached depths located some 2,000 metres down. The thermometer showed a temperature of 4.25 degrees Centigrade, a figure which for water at this depth seems common to all latitudes.

On 26 November, at three in the morning, the *Nautilus* crossed the Tropic of Cancer at longitude 172°. On the 27th, we passed within sight of the Sandwich Islands, where the illustrious Cook was killed on 14 February 1779.[34] We were then 4,860 leagues from our point of departure. That morning, when I climbed out on to the platform, I saw Hawaii 2 miles to leeward, the largest of the seven islands that form the archipelago. I could clearly make out its cultivated coastal strip, the various mountain ranges running parallel to the shore and its dormant volcanoes dominated by Mauna Kea, which rises to a height of 5,000 metres above sea-level. Among other fish varieties of the region, our nets scooped up specimens of *flabellaria pavonia*, which are polyps compressed into elegant shapes and are particular to this part of the ocean.

The *Nautilus* maintained its south-easterly course. We crossed the equator on 1 December at longitude 142° and on the 4th of the same month, after a fast, uneventful passage, we sighted the Marquesas group of islands. I distinctly made out, 3 miles off, at latitude 8° 57' south and longitude 139° 32' west, Point Tikapo on the south-east edge of Nuku Hiva, the largest of this group and a French possession. All I saw of it were the wooded mountains which rose in the distance, for Captain Nemo disliked the proximity of land. There the nets caught some fine specimens of fish: coryphenes with sky-blue fins, golden tails and flesh unrivalled anywhere in the world; hologymnoses, which have almost no scales but a delicious flavour; cardinal fish, with their bony jaws; yellowish frigate tuna, which are every bit as good as bonito – all items worthy of the pantry of the ship's galley.

Leaving behind these charming islands, over which the French flag flies, the *Nautilus* covered some 2,000 miles between

4 and 11 December. This passage was made memorable by our encounter with an enormous shoal of calamari, strange molluscs, close relatives of the cuttlefish. French fishermen call them squid, and they belong to the class of *cephalopoda* and the family of *dibrachiata*, which includes cuttlefish and argonauts. These animals were closely studied by the naturalists of Antiquity and they furnished numerous metaphors for the orators of the Agora[35] as well as an excellent dish for the tables of rich citizens, if we are to believe Athenaeus, a Greek physician who lived before Galen.[36]

It was during the night of 9–10 December that the *Nautilus* came upon this army of molluscs, which are more nocturnal than most creatures. They could be counted by the million. They were travelling from temperate to warmer zones following the migration routes of herring and sardine. Through the thick glass windows we watched them swimming backwards at high speeds, propelled by their locomotive tubes, pursuing fish and molluscs, eating the small ones, being eaten by the big ones, and in a state of indescribable confusion waving the ten feet which nature has planted on their heads, like a mane of pneumatic snakes. Despite its speed, the *Nautilus* sailed through this great mass of animals for several hours, and its nets gathered up countless numbers of them. Among them I recognized the nine varieties which d'Orbigny[37] has classified as being natives to the Pacific.

It must now be clear that as we sailed, the sea produced an endless succession of the most amazing sights, in an almost infinite variety. It changed scene and setting to keep our eyes filled with delights. It was an invitation to us not only to contemplate the works of the Creator from inside the fourth element but also to try to unravel the most intractable mysteries of the ocean.

During the day of 11 December, I had my head in a book in the Great Saloon. Ned Land and Conseil were looking out at the luminous waters through the half-open viewing panels. The *Nautilus* had come to a dead stop. With its water tanks full, it was holding station at a depth of 1,000 metres, a sparsely populated area of the ocean, where only large fish made rare and ghostly appearances.

At that moment I was perusing a delightful volume by Jean Macé entitled *The Servants of the Stomach*[38] and was savouring its ingenious lessons, when Conseil interrupted my reading.

'Would monsieur be good enough to come here for a moment?' he said in a singular voice.

'What is it, Conseil?'

'If monsieur would care to look . . .'

I got to my feet and walked over to the window and, leaning on my elbows, looked out.

Caught in the full beam of our beacon light, a huge, dark mass hung without moving in the middle of the water. I observed it closely, trying to identify what this gigantic cetacean could possibly be. And then a sudden thought crossed my mind.

'A ship!' I exclaimed.

'Yes,' said the Canadian, 'a disabled ship that has sunk!'

Ned Land was right. We were in the presence of a ship whose severed shrouds were still hanging from their chain-plates. Its hull seemed to be sound, and it could not have foundered more than a few hours earlier. Three jagged stumps that stood just 2 feet above deck level showed that the vessel had been swamped and forced to sacrifice its masts. But, turned on its side, it had filled with water, and indeed it was still listing to port. It made a sorry spectacle, a carcass consigned to the deep, but even sorrier was the sight of the deck, where bodies, held fast by ropes, still lay! I counted four – four men, one still standing at the wheel – and then a woman who was half in, half out of the deadlight in the poop, holding an infant in her arms. She was young, and I could make out her features, brightly lit by the *Nautilus*'s lights and not yet decomposed by the water. With one supreme effort she had raised her child above her head, a poor little thing whose arms still clung around its mother's neck! The positions of the four sailors were horrible to behold, for they were frozen in their final throes as they made one last attempt to free themselves from the ropes which lashed them to the ship. The only exception, a picture of calmness, his face clear and serious, his greying hair plastered over his forehead and his hand still clutching the wheel, was the helmsman, who

'We were in the presence of a ship'

looked as if he were still steering his three-master through the depths of the ocean!

It was a gruesome sight! We were speechless, our hearts pounding, before this shipwreck captured in the act, as if photographed in its final moments. And already I saw a number of enormous sharks, with fire in their eyes, bearing down on it, attracted by the lure of human flesh!

In the meantime, the *Nautilus*, altering course slightly, sailed round the sunken ship, and, for one moment, I was able to read on the stern: *The Florida, Sunderland.*

19
Vanikoro

That dreadful encounter was merely the first of a series of maritime disasters which the *Nautilus* would encounter as she went on her way. After we had begun sailing the busier shipping routes, we often saw shipwrecked hulks suspended in the water, slowly rotting, and, at lower depths, cannons, cannonballs, anchors, chains and countless other iron artefacts which were being eaten away by rust.

But, ceaselessly borne along by the *Nautilus*, where we lived in virtual isolation, we sighted on 11 December the Pomotu Islands, Bougainville's old 'dangerous archipelago',[39] which spread across 500 leagues east-south-east to west-north-west between latitudes 13° 30' and 23° 50' south and longitudes 125° 30' and 151° 30' west, from Ducie Island to Lazareff Island. The archipelago covers an area of 370 square leagues and is formed of about sixty groups of atolls, among which are the Gambier Islands, which are now French protectorates. All these islands are coralligenous. They are slowly but steadily rising as a result of the activity of polyps and one day they will all be joined together. This new consolidated island will eventually be united with neighbouring archipelagos, and a fifth continent will extend from New Zealand and New Caledonia to the Marquesas.

The day I set out this theory before Captain Nemo, he gave me a cool response:

'The earth does not need new continents but new men!'

The vagaries of navigation had brought us to Clermont-Tonnerre Island, one of the most curious of the group. It was discovered in 1822 by Captain Bell, master of the *Minerva*. I was now able to study the madriporic system by which the atolls in this ocean are built up.

Madrepores, which should not be confused with corals, are composed of soft tissue enclosed by a hard, calcareous exterior, and modifications of this structure have led Mr Milne-Edwards, my illustrious teacher, to class them into five groups. The minute animalcules which secrete this polypary live by the billions in their own cells. It is their deposits of limestone which turn into rocks, reefs, atolls and islands. Here they form a circular ring enclosing a lagoon or small inner lake which is connected to the sea by breaches in the walls. There, they form into barrier reefs like those found on the coasts of New Caledonia and various others of the Pomotu Islands. In other locations, such as Réunion or Mauritius, they form fringed reefs, tall, sheer walls around which the ocean drops away to considerable depths.

When we had put a few cable-lengths between us and the edges of the reefs of Clermont-Tonnerre Island, I was well placed to admire the tremendous handiwork of these microscopic toilers. The walls were particularly the work of madrepores known as millepores, porites, astraea and brain corals. These polyps thrive near the surface in water agitated by wave action, and consequently it is at their tips that the substructures begin to form and then sink slowly along with the debris of new secretions which underpin them. Such at least is the theory of Mr Darwin, who explains the formation of atolls in this way – a theory which, to my sense, is more convincing than the argument that the foundation on which the madrepores build are the tops of mountains or volcanoes submerged a few metres below sea-level.

I was able to examine those remarkable walls at close hand for, at their most perpendicular, our sounding lead measured a depth of more than 300 metres, and our electric lights made the gleaming limestone shine.

In answer to a question from Conseil about how long it took these colossal barriers to grow, I took him rather aback by saying that experts estimate the rate of growth to be an eighth of an inch per century.

'Which means that it took how long,' he asked, 'to raise these walls?'

'One hundred and ninety-two thousand years, Conseil, which lengthens a biblical day dramatically. Actually, the formation of coal, which is the mineralization of forests drowned by floods, took considerably longer. But I would add that biblical "days" are really epochs and not intervals between two sunrises for, according to the Bible itself, the sun does not date from the first day of the creation.'

When the *Nautilus* surfaced, I got a proper sense of the full extent of Clermont-Tonnerre Island, which was low and wooded. Its madreporic rocks had obviously been made fertile by tempest and storm. One day, a seed, carried by a hurricane sweeping over from neighbouring land, was deposited on strata made of a mixture of limestone and deposits of decomposed fish and marine plants which had created vegetable tilth. A coconut driven by the waves arrived on this new shore. The nut took root. As it grew, the tree trapped the water vapour. A stream appeared. The vegetation spread slowly. A few small creatures, worms or insects, were landed by the trunks of trees which came upwind from other islands. Turtles arrived to lay their eggs, birds nested in the young trees. In this way animal life throve and, attracted by the greenery and fertility, man appeared. That was how these islands, the colossal constructions of microscopic creature, came into being.

By evening, the island of Clermont-Tonnerre was fading into the distance, and the course of the *Nautilus* changed perceptibly. Having nudged the Tropic of Capricorn at longitude 135°, we now steered west-north-west and recrossed the whole intertropical zone. Although the summer sun was generous with its strength, we did not suffer from the heat since, 30 or 40 metres beneath the surface, the temperature never went above 10 or 12 degrees.

On 15 December, we passed west of the beguiling Society Islands and graceful Tahiti, queen of the Pacific. In the morning, a few miles to leeward, I made out its uplands. Its waters supplied our dinner table with excellent fish, mackerel, bonitos, albacore tuna and a species of sea snake called *muraenophis*, or moray eel.

The *Nautilus* had now covered 8,100 miles. The log was reading 9,720 miles by the time we sailed between the island of Tongatapu, where the *Argo,* the *Port-au-Prince* and the *Duke of Portland* foundered, and the Samoan Islands, where Captain de Langle, La Pérouse's friend, was killed.[40] Then we sighted the Fijian archipelago, where the savages massacred the crew of the *Union* and Captain Bureau, of Nantes, master of the *Aimable Joséphine.*[41]

This archipelago runs 100 leagues north to south and extends over 90 leagues east to west. It is spread between latitude 6° and 2° south and longitude 174° and 179° west. It is made up of a number of islands, atolls and reefs, notable among which are the islands of Viti Levu, Vanua Levu and Kadavu.

It was discovered by Tasman in 1643, in the same year that Torricelli invented the barometer and Louis XIV became king of France. I shall leave it to others to decide which of these three events was of the greatest significance for mankind. Then came Cook in 1774, d'Entrecasteaux in 1792 and finally Dumont d'Urville,[42] who made sense of the geographical chaos of this group of islands in 1827. The *Nautilus* entered the Bay of Vaileka, scene of the terrible adventures of Captain Dillon,[43] who first solved the mystery of where La Pérouse had been shipwrecked.

This bay, which we dragged with our nets several times, supplied us with an abundance of excellent oysters. We ate large quantities of them, opening them, as Seneca recommends, as we sat at table. These molluscs belong to the species known as *ostrea lamellos*, which is very common in Corsica. The bed at Vaileka must have been very extensive, and it is certain that, in the absence of any of the many causes of their destruction, these accumulations would eventually have filled the whole bay, since each individual can produce up to 2 million eggs.

If Ned Land did not have reason to regret his greed on that occasion, it is because oysters are the only food which never causes indigestion. It is a fact that it requires at least sixteen dozen of these acephalous molluscs to provide the 315 grams of nitrogenous matter which is the required daily intake of one person.

On 25 December the *Nautilus* was sailing through the middle of the New Hebrides archipelago, which was discovered by Quiros[44] in 1606, explored by Bougainville in 1768 and was given its present name by Cook in 1773. The group consists mainly of nine large islands and forms a line 120 leagues long running north-north-west to south-south-east between latitude 15° and 2° south, and longitude 164° and 168°. We passed quite near the island of Aurou, which, when we took our noontime position, looked to me like a mass of green woods crouching under a very high mountain peak.

That day was Christmas Day, and I thought Ned Land seemed unhappy at missing the traditional celebration, a family occasion which means so much to Protestants.

I had seen nothing of Captain Nemo for a week when, on the morning of the 27th, he walked into the Great Saloon, acting as usual as if he hadn't been gone more than five minutes. I was busy trying to follow the course of the *Nautilus* on the planisphere. The captain came straight up to me, placed one finger on a spot on it and said just one word:

'Vanikoro.'

The word was talismanic. It was the name of the islands on which La Pérouse's ships had been wrecked.

'Is the *Nautilus* going to take us to Vanikoro?' I asked.

'Yes, professor,' replied the captain.

'And will I be able to land on the famous islands where the *Boussole* and the *Astrolabe* foundered?'

'If you wish, professor.'

'When will we reach Vanikoro?'

'We're there, professor.'

Followed by Captain Nemo, I climbed up to the platform and from there I scoured the horizon eagerly.

To the north-east rose two unequal-sized volcanic islands encircled by a ring of coral 40 miles in circumference. We had arrived at Vanikoro Island proper – which Dumont d'Urville named the Ile de la Recherche – and more exactly just outside the small harbour of Vanou situated at latitude 16° 4' south and longitude 164° 32' east. The place seemed to be covered with greenery from the shoreline to the highest land of the interior, which culminated in Mount Kapogo at an altitude of 476 fathoms.

After negotiating a way through the outer barrier of rocks by means of a narrow channel, the *Nautilus* arrived inside the reef, where the sea was between 30 and 40 fathoms deep. Beneath the green shade of the mangrove trees I made out a number of natives, who displayed considerable surprise on seeing us making towards them. In this long, dark shape approaching just on the surface of the water they probably saw some dangerous cetacean which they should treat with the utmost caution.

At that moment, Captain Nemo asked me what I knew of how La Pérouse's ships were wrecked.

'Only what everyone knows, captain,' I replied.

'And would you tell me what everyone knows of it?' he asked in a rather ironic tone.

'I'd be glad to.'

I told him what the most recent accounts by Dumont d'Urville had made public, of which the following is a brief summary.

In 1785, La Pérouse and his second in command, Captain de Langle, were sent by Louis XVI to complete a voyage of circumnavigation of the globe. They fitted out two corvettes, the *Boussole* and the *Astrolabe*, neither of which was ever seen again.

In 1791, the French government, rightly anxious about the fate of the two ships, equipped two large supply vessels, the *Recherche* and the *Espérance*, which sailed from Brest on 28 September under the command of Bruni d'Entrecasteaux. Two months later, he learned from information given by a Captain Bowen, master of the *Albermarle*, that debris from wrecked ships had been sighted off the coast of New Georgia. But d'Entrecasteaux, ignoring this report, which seemed rather unlikely, headed instead towards the Admiralty Islands, which had been named in a report by Captain Hunter as the location where La Pérouse's ships had foundered.

He searched but found nothing. The *Recherche* and the *Espérance* sailed close to Vanikoro without putting in, and, in short, their voyage proved to be most unfortunate since it cost the lives of d'Entrecasteaux, two of his second officers and several members of his crew.

It was an old Pacific hand, Captain Dillon, who was first to find indisputable traces of the wreck. On 15 May 1824, his ship, the *Saint Patrick*, passed close to the island of Tikopia, one of the New Hebrides. There, a lascar paddled alongside in a canoe and sold him the silver hilt of a sword on which engraved letters were still visible. Furthermore, the man claimed that six years earlier, during a visit to Vanikoro, he had seen two Europeans, survivors from ships which had come to grief years before on the island's reefs.

Dillon guessed that the wrecks must be those of La Pérouse's ships, whose disappearance had shocked the world. He decided to go to Vanikoro, where, so the lascar said, there were still various remnants of the shipwrecked vessels. But he was prevented from doing so by adverse winds and currents.

Dillon returned to Calcutta. There he succeeded in interesting the Asiatic Society and the East India Company in his discovery. A vessel, named the *Recherche*, was made available to him and he set sail on 23 January 1827, accompanied by a French agent.

After calling at various locations in the Pacific, the *Recherche* dropped anchor at Vanikoro on 7 July 1827, in the self-same natural harbour of Vanou where the *Nautilus* was now moored.

There it recovered various pieces of wreckage, iron utensils, grommets from pulley-blocks, swivel-guns, an 18-pound round shot, broken parts of astronomical instruments, part of a taffrail and a brass bell inscribed with the words: 'Bazin made me'. Bazin was the name of a foundry in the Arsenal at Brest which had been operating around 1785. This left no further room for doubt.

Still collecting evidence, Dillon remained at the site of the disaster until October. He then left Vanikoro, made for New Zealand, reached Calcutta on 7 April 1828 and returned to France, where he was warmly welcomed by Charles X.

By then, Dumont d'Urville had already left to look for the location of the wrecks in an entirely different quarter. This was because a whaling ship had reported that various medals and a Cross of Saint-Louis had been found in the hands of the natives of the Louisiade Archipelago and New Caledonia.

Dumont d'Urville, captain of the *Astrolabe*, was thus already at sea and, two months after Dillon left Vanikoro, was at anchor on the port of Hobart Town. There he was told about the discoveries made by Dillon and, in addition, learned that a certain James Hobbes, first officer of the *Union*, of Calcutta, who had landed on an island situated at latitude 8° 18' south and longitude 156° 30' east, had observed iron bars and red fabrics being used by the natives of those parts.

Dumont d'Urville was quite nonplussed. Not knowing what credence to give to these stories, which were reported in newspapers not generally considered reliable, he nevertheless decided to set off on the trail of Dillon.

On 10 February 1828, the *Astrolabe* reached Tikopia, took on board a deserter who had settled on the island as guide-cum-interpreter and set a course for Vanikoro, which was sighted on 12 February. The vessel skirted its coral collar until the 14th, and only on the 20th did she anchor inside the reef, in the harbour of Vanou.

On 23 February, a party of officers toured the island and returned with several large pieces of wreckage. The natives adopted a policy of denial and evasion and refused to take them to the exact place where the ships had gone aground. Such shifty behaviour made it look likely that they had maltreated the survivors of the wreck and indeed they appeared to fear that Dumont d'Urville had come with the sole intention of avenging La Pérouse and his unfortunate companions.

However, on the 26th, persuaded by gifts and seeing that they had no reason to fear reprisals, they led Jacquinot, the first officer, to the location of the shipwreck.

There, in 3 or 4 fathoms of water, between the reefs of Pacou and Vanou, lay anchors, cannons, iron ingots and pigs of lead, all encrusted with chalky deposits. Both the *Astrolabe*'s longboat and whaleboat were dispatched to the spot and, not without considerable labour, their crews succeeded in raising an anchor weighing 1,800 pounds, a cast-iron 8-inch cannon, a pig of lead and two copper swivel-guns.

On questioning the natives, Dumont d'Urville further discovered that, after losing both his ships to the island's reefs, La
Pérouse had built a smaller craft, only to be wrecked a second
time. Where? No one could say.

The captain of the *Astrolabe* ordered a monument to be
erected to the memory of the famous navigator and his companions, which was placed in a grove of mangle-trees. It took
the form of a plain four-sided pyramid set on a base of coral
and completely free of any metal ornamentation which might
tempt the acquisitiveness of the natives.

Dumont d'Urville was then ready to leave. But the health of
his crew had been undermined by the fevers endemic in those
unhealthy regions, and, being gravely ill himself, he was not
able to set sail until 17 March.

Meanwhile, the French government, fearing that Dumont
d'Urville might not be aware of the discoveries made by Dillon, had dispatched to Vanikoro a corvette then stationed off
the west coast of America, the *Bayonnaise*, under the command of Legoarant de Tromelin. It dropped anchor at Vanikoro
a few months after the departure of the *Astrolabe*. It found no
new evidence but reported that the natives had respected the
memorial raised in honour of La Pérouse.

Such was the substance of what I told Captain Nemo.

'So,' he said, 'it is still not known what happened to the
third vessel built by the men who were wrecked on the island
of Vanikoro?'

'That is so.'

Captain Nemo did not respond but indicated that I was to
follow him into the Great Saloon. The *Nautilus* submerged a
few metres beneath the surface, and the viewing panels slid
open.

I hurried to the window and what did I see? Encrusted with
coral and covered with coral fungi, *syphunulae*, alcyonarians,
caryophyllia, through myriads of brilliantly coloured fish –
girelles, damselfish, *pempheridae*, *diacopes* and squirrelfish – I
made out various items of wreckage which had escaped attempts
to raise them: iron stirrups, anchors, cannons, cannonballs,
the housing of a capstan, the entire stern of a boat, all objects

which had come from wrecked vessels and were now cloaked in living flowers.

As I stared at these desolate remains, Captain Nemo said gravely:

'Captain La Pérouse set sail on 7 December 1785 with his ships the *Boussole* and the *Astrolabe*. He dropped anchor first at Botany Bay, then called at the Friendly Islands, New Caledonia, made for Santa Cruz and put into Namouka, one of the islands of the Hapai Archipelago. Then his ships encountered the uncharted reefs of Vanikoro. The *Boussole*, which was leading the way, came to grief on the southern coast. The *Astrolabe* went to her aid and also foundered. The first vessel broke up almost immediately. The second, beached by the force of the wind, survived for a few days. The natives gave a tolerable reception to the survivors, who established themselves on the island and built a smaller boat using what they could salvage from the wrecks of the two larger vessels. A few sailors decided to remain on Vanikoro. The rest, weak and ill, sailed away with La Pérouse. They set a course for the Solomon Islands and perished, with all their possessions, on the western shore of the largest island of the group, between Cape Deception and Cape Satisfaction.'

'How do you know all this?' I exclaimed.

'I found this on the site where this final wreck occurred.'

Captain Nemo held out a tin box stamped with the coat of arms of France and much corroded by salt water. He opened it. Inside was a bundle of papers which had yellowed but were still legible.

They were the actual written orders given by the French Navy minister, no less, to Captain La Pérouse, with notes written in the margins in the hand of Louis XVI!

'A sailor could not wish for a better death!' said Captain Nemo. 'This tomb of coral makes a quiet grave. God grant that my companions and I shall know no other end!'

20

The Torres Strait

During the night of 27–8 December, the *Nautilus* left Vanikoro astern at a tremendous rate of knots. Our course was south-west, and in three days we covered the 750 leagues which separate the La Pérouse archipelago from the most south-easterly point of Papua.

Very early in the morning of 1 January 1868, Conseil joined me on the platform.

'Would monsieur,' the excellent fellow said, 'would monsieur allow me to wish him a happy New Year?'

'Well now, Conseil, this is exactly as if I were back in Paris, in my study in the Jardin des Plantes! I accept your good wishes and thank you for them. But may I ask what you mean by a "Happy New Year" in our present circumstances? Will this be the year that brings an end to our confinement, or a year which will see us continue our strange voyage?'

'Well, monsieur,' Conseil replied, 'I do not know what to reply. It is clear that we are seeing strange sights and that for the past two months we have not had time to be bored. The latest wonder is invariably more astonishing than the one before. If things carry on as they are, I have no idea of how it will all end. Be that as it may, my view is that we will never have an opportunity like this again.'

'Never, Conseil.'

'Especially since Captain Nemo, who is fully living up to his Latin name, is no more trouble to us than if he were non-existent.'

'Well put, Conseil.'

'If I may say so, I believe that a new year that is happy is one which will enable us to see everything there is to see.'

'Everything, Conseil? That would make it a very long year. But should we not spare a thought for Ned Land?'

'Ned Land is the exact opposite of me,' replied Conseil. 'He has a positive turn of mind and a clamouring stomach. Simply staring at fish and eating them are not enough for him. The absence of wine, bread and meat does not suit a doughty Saxon who is accustomed to steak and is not afraid of brandy or gin when taken in moderation.'

'Speaking personally, Conseil, that is not what exercises me. I have adapted very easily to our diet on board.'

'My sentiments exactly,' replied Conseil. 'As a result, I think about staying put as much as Mister Land thinks about escaping. So if the year just beginning proves to be unhappy for me, it will turn out to be happy for him, and vice-versa. In this way, one or other of us will be satisfied. To sum up, I wish for monsieur anything and everything that will make monsieur happy.'

'Thank you, Conseil. However, I must ask you to accept a postponement of the matter of a New Year's gift and to make do, for the time being, with a handshake. It is all I have with me.'

'Sir has never been more generous,' he replied.

And so saying, he left me.

By 2 January, we had travelled 11,340 miles (or 5,250 leagues) since our starting point in Japanese waters. Under the bow of the *Nautilus* lay the dangerous bed of the Coral Sea, on the north-eastern coast of Australia. Our vessel kept to a station of just a few miles off the fearsome barrier reef where Cook's ships nearly came to grief on 10 June 1770. Cook's own ship ran on to a rock, and if it did not sink it was only because a section of coral which was broken off by the impact remained embedded in the side of the holed ship.

I would very much like to have visited the reef, which is 360 leagues long and against which the sea, always rough, breaks with tremendous power and a noise like thunder. But at this juncture, the *Nautilus*'s angled direction fins took us down to a great depth, and so I was unable to see much of those high, coral ramparts. I was obliged to make do with the samples of fish caught in our nets. Among others, I found albacores, a

form of *scombridae*, but as large as tuna, having bluish sides
and transversal bands which fade when the creature dies. These
fish escorted us in shoals and supplied our table with extremely
succulent fare. We also caught large quantities of gilthead about
5 centimetres long with the taste of sea-bream; and flying pirapeds, dubbed undersea swallows, which on dark nights leave
phosphorescent trails on both air and water. Among the molluscs and zoophytes dragged up by the mesh of the nets I found
various species of alcyonarians, urchins, hammer-shells, spur
shells, solariums, ceriths and *hyalleae*. The flora yielded some
magnificent floating seaweeds, sea tangle and macrocystes kelp
which trailed strands of mucilage produced by their pores. I
picked out an admirable *nemastoma gelinaroïde* for the museum's collection of natural curiosities.

On 4 January, two days after sailing across the Coral Sea,
we sighted the coast of Papua. Captain Nemo used the opportunity to inform me that his intention was to make for the
Indian Ocean via the Torres Strait. He gave no further details.
Ned was happy when he realized that this course would bring
us nearer to European waters.

The Torres Strait is considered to be dangerous both for the
jagged reefs which line it and for the savage inhabitants who
live along its coasts. It separates New Holland from the largest
island of Papua, also known as New Guinea.

Papua is 400 leagues long and 130 wide, with a total area of
40,000 geographical leagues. It is situated between latitudes 0°
19' and 10° 2' south and between longitudes 128° 23' and 146°
15'. At noon, while the first officer was taking the height of the
sun, I saw the tops of the Arfak Mountains, which rise by stages
and culminate in pointed peaks.

The territory, discovered in 1511 by the Portuguese Francisco Serrano, was visited successively by Don José de Menesès
in 1526, Grijalva in 1527, the Spanish general Alvar de Saave-
dra in 1528, Juigo Ortez in 1545, the Dutchman Shouten in
1616, Nicolas Sruick in 1753, by Tasman, Dampier, Fumel,
Carteret, Edwards, Bougainville, Cook, Forrest and Mac
Clure, then by d'Entrecasteaux in 1792, Duperrey in 1823, and
Dumont d'Urville in 1827. According to Monsieur de Rienzi,

'It is the heartland of the swarthy races which inhabit the various parts of the Malayan Archipelago, and I was in no doubt that the vagaries of our journey would bring me into contact with the formidable Andamanese people.'[45]

The *Nautilus* approached the entrance to the most dangerous passage on the globe, one that even the boldest sailors rarely dare sail through, the strait that Luis Paz de Torres tackled[46] when returning from the Southern Sea on his way to Melanesia and where the corvettes of Dumont d'Urville ran aground in 1840 and were nearly lost with all hands and cargo goods. Even the *Nautilus*, though equal to every danger presented by the sea, would nevertheless become closely acquainted with its coral hazards.

The Torres Strait is about 34 leagues wide but is obstructed by countless islands, islets, broken water and rocks, which make it virtually impossible to navigate. Captain Nemo therefore took all the necessary precautions to find a safe passage through. The *Nautilus*, just breaking the surface, proceeded at a moderate speed. Her propeller, like a whale's tail, beat the water slowly.

Making the most of our opportunity, my two companions and I had taken up a position on the still deserted platform. In front of us rose the helmsman's glass shelter and unless I was very much mistaken, it was occupied by Captain Nemo, who was steering the *Nautilus* himself.

I had with me the excellent charts of the Torres Strait which had been mapped and drawn by the hydrographical engineer Vincendon Dumoulin and Coupvent-Desbois, then an ensign and now an admiral, who both served with Dumont d'Urville during his last voyage of circumnavigation. Along with the plans made by Captain King, they are the best charts available for finding a way through the tangled channels of this narrow strait, and I kept referring to them with the greatest attention.

All around the *Nautilus* the sea boiled furiously. The direction of the waves was south-east to north-west and they moved at 2½ miles an hour, breaking on corals which kept rising above the surface at intervals.

'A bad sea,' commented Ned Land.

'Abominable,' I agreed, 'and the route is not at all suited to a vessel like the *Nautilus*.'

'The captain must be damned sure of his course,' added the Canadian, 'because I can see clumps of coral that would rip her hull open if she gave them even the lightest nudge!'

We were indeed in considerable danger but the *Nautilus* seemed to slip as if by magic through those lethal reefs. She did not keep exactly to the route taken by the *Astrolabe* and the *Zélée* which had proved fatal to Dumont d'Urville. We steered a more northerly course, cleared Murray Island and tacked back to the south-west, heading for Cumberland Passage. I thought the captain was going to run us straight into it when, switching to a north-westerly direction, he weaved through a large number of little-known islands and islets and made for Tound Island and Bad Channel.

I wondered if Captain Nemo, reckless to the point of folly, was actually going to take his vessel into this passage where both of Dumont d'Urville's corvettes had struck rocks, when, again changing course, he cut straight to the west and made for Gueboroar Island.[47]

It was then three in the afternoon. The swell eased, the tide then being almost at the full. The *Nautilus* approached the island, which I can still see in my mind's eye with its remarkable shoreline of screw pines. We were sailing round it at a distance of 2 miles.

Suddenly, I was thrown off my feet by an almighty jolt. The *Nautilus* had just snagged a coral outcrop and came to a complete stop, listing slightly to port.

When I got up I saw that Captain Nemo and his first officer had come out on to the platform. They were inspecting the lie of the ship and discussing the position in their incomprehensible language.

This is how matters stood. Two miles off the starboard side we could see Gueboroar Island. Its coast formed a curve running north to west, like an enormous arm. To the south and east a few coral outcrops were becoming visible as they were being uncovered by the ebbing tide. We had run aground at the flood and being in one of those seas where there are only small tidal variations, this was most unfortunate, for it made our chances of refloating the *Nautilus* problematic. The ship had not been damaged, so strongly built was her hull. But although she could neither sink nor have her seams split, there was a strong possibility that she might be hooked on the reef permanently, which would mean the end of Captain Nemo's submarine vessel.

My thoughts were running along these lines, while the captain, cool, collected, as much in control of himself as ever and clearly neither concerned nor frustrated, came up to me.

'An accident?' I inquired.

'No,' he replied, 'an incident.'

'But an incident,' I said, 'which may very well force you to become once more an inhabitant of the land you abominate!'

Captain Nemo gave me a strange look and waved one hand dismissively. It was to give me clearly to understand that nothing would ever force him to set foot on any of the five continents again. Then he said:

'As it happens, professor, the *Nautilus* is in no danger. She will yet transport you through the wonders of the ocean. Our journey has only just begun and I am in no hurry to deprive myself of the pleasure of your company.'

'Still, Captain Nemo,' I went on, without picking up on the irony of these words, 'the *Nautilus* ran aground at the high point of the tide. The differences between tides in the Pacific are not large and unless you can lighten the *Nautilus*, which seems impossible to me, I cannot see how you will be able to refloat her.'

'Tidal variations are not great in the Pacific, as you say, professor,' replied Captain Nemo. 'But here in the Torres Strait it is possible to find a difference of a metre and a half between high and low tides. Today is 4 January, and in five days' time there will be a full moon. I would be very much surprised if that accommodating satellite does not raise the level of the sea sufficiently and thus render me a service for which I do not intend to look elsewhere.'

So saying, Captain Nemo, followed by his first officer, went below inside the *Nautilus*. The boat had stopped moving altogether, as though the coral polyps already held her fast in their indestructible cement.

'Well, professor?' asked Ned Land, who joined me after the captain's departure.

'Well, Ned, we are to sit quietly and wait for the high tide of the ninth. It seems that the moon is going to be obliging enough to float us off.'

'As easily as that?'

'As easily as that.'

'Why doesn't the captain drop his anchors in deeper water, use the engines to wind in the chains and winch her off?'

'Why? Because the tide will do it,' Conseil said simply.

The Canadian stared at Conseil then shrugged his shoulders. It was the sailor in him who replied:

'Believe me when I say that this lump of iron will never sail again on or under any sea. It is now only good to be sent for scrap. So I think the time has come to part company with Captain Nemo.'

'Listen, Ned,' I said, 'I haven't given up all hope for the *Nautilus* as you have. Four days from now, we will know where we stand on the question of Pacific tides. In any case, there might be something in your idea of getting away if we were in sight of the coast of England or Provence, but the shores of Papua are quite a different matter. We'll still have time to fall back on desperate measures if the *Nautilus* cannot be freed, an eventuality which I would regard as extremely serious.'

'But couldn't we at least try to see how the land lies?' Ned Land continued. 'We have here an island. On the island, there will be trees. Under the trees will be land animals, chops and steaks on legs which I would be only too glad to get my teeth into.'

'Now there Ned is right,' said Conseil, 'and I fully endorse his point of view. Could not monsieur ask his friend Captain Nemo to ferry us ashore, if only that we should not lose the habit of walking on the more solid parts of our planet?'

'I can always ask,' I said, 'but he will say no.'

'Perhaps monsieur would run that risk?' said Conseil. 'Then we would know how far we can depend on the captain's good-will towards us.'

Much to my surprise, Captain Nemo gave us the permission I asked for and moreover did so with grace and alacrity and without even extracting from me a promise that we would return to the ship. But flight through the territory of New Guinea would have been a very dangerous venture, and I would not have advised Ned Land to attempt it. Better a prisoner on board the *Nautilus* than a prisoner in the clutches of the savages of Papua.

Arrangements were made for the dinghy to be broken out for us the following morning. I did not ask if Captain Nemo would be coming with us. I even assumed that no member of the crew would be assigned to our party and that Ned Land would be placed in sole charge of the boat. In any case, the shore lay not above 2 miles away, and it would be child's play for the Canadian to steer a light craft through the lines of the reefs which were so lethal for large vessels.

The following day, which was 5 January, the boat's cover was removed and it was released from its housing and launched from the platform. Only two crewmen were needed for this manoeuvre. The oars were already in the boat, and all we had to do was get into it.

At eight o'clock, armed with guns and axes, we moved off from the *Nautilus*. The sea was quite calm. A light breeze was blowing off the land. Conseil and I, manning the oars, put our backs into it, and Ned took us through narrow channels between areas of broken water. The boat handled well, and we made good speed.

Ned Land was beside himself. He was like a prisoner who had escaped from jail, and the fact that he would have to go back was the last thing on his mind.

'Meat!' he kept repeating. 'We're going to eat meat, real meat! Right royal game! And no bread either! I'm not saying there's anything wrong with fish, but you can have too much of a good thing, and a piece of fresh venison, grilled over charcoal, will make a nice change from our usual diet!'

'Gourmand!' replied Conseil. 'You're making my mouth water.'

'But first,' I said, 'we must find out if these forests are game country and if the game here is not so big that it can hunt the hunter.'

'Agreed, Professor Aronnax,' said the Canadian, whose teeth seemed to be as sharp as the blade of an axe, 'but I could eat a tiger, sirloin of tiger, if there are no other quadrupeds on the island.'

'Ned makes me feel nervous,' said Conseil.

'Whatever it is,' said Ned Land, 'I shall greet any animal with four legs and no feathers, or two legs with feathers, with my first shot.'

'Good,' I said. 'Ned Land is up to his old tricks again!'

'Don't worry, professor,' said the Canadian, 'just keep rowing! Give me twenty-five minutes, and I'll set before you one of my very special dishes!'

At 8.30, the *Nautilus*'s dinghy slid gently on to a sandy beach, having safely negotiated the collar of coral which ringed the island of Gueboroar.

21

A Few Days on Dry Land

It felt strange to set foot on terra firma again. Ned Land tested the ground with his boot, as if he were staking a claim to it. Yet it was only two months since we had become, to use Captain Nemo's word, 'passengers' on board the *Nautilus*, or, in reality prisoners, so to speak, before the mast.

Within minutes we were within gunshot range of the shore, which proved to consist entirely of madreporic matter, though some dried-up torrent-courses were littered with granite debris showing that the island had primordial origins. The horizon was hidden by a curtain of stunning forest. Giant trees, some 200 feet tall, were woven together by garlands of liana, which formed natural hammocks rocking in the gentle breeze. There were mimosas, figs, casuarinas, teaks, hibiscus, screw pines and palm trees, all jumbled together, and in the shade of their verdant canopy, and around the base of their gigantic trunks grew orchids, ferns and leguminous plants.

However, paying no heed to the splendid specimens of Papuan flora, the Canadian sacrificed the pleasing to the useful. He saw a coconut palm, cut down a few of its fruits, broke them open, and we drank their milk and ate their white kernels with a relish which expressed our relief after the usual fare provided by the *Nautilus*.

'Excellent!' said Ned Land.

'Exquisite!' added Conseil.

'I don't think,' said the Canadian, 'that yon Nemo would say no if we wanted to take a load of coconuts on board, would he?'

'I doubt if he'd object,' I replied, 'though he wouldn't want to taste any.'

'It would be his loss,' said Conseil.

'The horizon was hidden by a curtain of stunning forest'

'And our gain!' retorted Ned Land. 'There'd be more for us!'

'Just one thing, Ned,' I said to the harpooner, who was about to strip a second tree. 'The coconut is an excellent thing, but before you fill the boat with them it would be sensible to ascertain whether or not the island produces anything even more useful. Fresh vegetables would be a welcome addition to the *Nautilus*'s larder.'

'Monsieur is quite right,' replied Conseil, 'and I propose that we allocate three spaces in the boat: one for fruit, one for vegetables and the third for the venison, of which I have yet to see the smallest sign.'

'Conseil, never rule anything out,' replied the Canadian.

'Well, let's carry on with our exploration,' I said, 'but we should keep our eyes open. Although the island seems to be uninhabited, it could conceal natives who are less finicky than we are about the kind of game they hunt.'

'Ha ha ha!' said Ned Land, and he gnashed his teeth in the most graphic manner.

'Come, come, Ned!' exclaimed Conseil.

'Hell's bells!' retorted the Canadian, 'I'm beginning to understand the attraction of cannibalism!'

'Ned! Ned! What are you saying?' replied Conseil. 'You, a cannibal? I'll never feel safe again when I'm with you – and I have to share a cabin with you! Does this mean that one day I'll wake up half eaten?'

'Conseil, I like you a lot, but not enough to want to eat you unless, of course, it becomes strictly necessary.'

'I am not entirely reassured by that,' answered Conseil. 'But let's get started on the hunt. We're going to have to bag something if we're to satisfy the cravings of this cannibal or else, one fine morning, monsieur will find only leftovers of servant to attend him.'

While this banter was going on, we were making our way into the dark canopy of the forest, which for the next couple of hours we roamed in every direction.

We had great good luck in our search for edible vegetables: one of the most useful products of the tropical zone supplied us with a foodstuff lacking on board.

I mean the bread-fruit tree, which grew profusely on Gueboroar. My attention was mainly caught by the seedless variety
which, in Malay, is called *rima*.

This tree differed from the other trees by having a straight
trunk 40 feet high, its top being elegantly rounded and made
up of large multilobate leaves. This alone told the naturalist
that here was *artocarpus*, which has been introduced very successfully into the Mascarene Islands. Its fruit hung out of the
greenery of its dense foliage. They were large, globe-shaped,
10 centimetres across and covered by a rough skin formed of
hexagon-like discs. It is a most useful vegetable, a blessing which
nature has showered on regions where wheat is unknown: the
tree needs no cultivation and bears fruit for eight months of the
year.

Ned Land was well acquainted with these fruits, having
eaten them during the course of numerous voyages, and he
knew how to prepare their edible parts. Just seeing them stim-
ulated his appetite, and he could contain himself no longer.

'Professor,' he said, 'I'll die if I don't have some of that
bread-fruit!'

'Help yourself, Ned, have as much as you like. We're here to
try things out, so let's try them.'

'It won't take long,' responded the Canadian.

He used a magnifying glass to light a fire of dead wood,
which was soon crackling merrily. Meanwhile, Conseil and I
selected the best fruits on the tree. Some were not yet ripe
enough, and inside their thick rind the flesh was white but
insufficiently fibrous. Others, of which there were many, were
yellowish and glutinous, just waiting to be picked.

These fruits had no kernels. Conseil handed a dozen of them
to Ned Land, who cut them into thick slices and put them directly on the live embers, repeating as he did so:

'You'll see, professor, just how good this bread tastes!'

'Especially when you've been deprived of it for so long,' said
Conseil.

'It's not just bread,' added the Canadian, 'it's more like a
delicate pastry. Have you never tasted it, professor?'

'No, Ned.'

'Then get ready for something really mouth-watering. If you're not delighted with it, then I'm not the king of harpooners!'

After a few minutes, the parts of the flesh exposed to the embers were charred all over. Inside was light white crumb, like soft crust bread, which tasted rather like artichoke.

This bread was excellent, it must be admitted, and I ate it with great relish.

'Unfortunately,' I remarked, 'this kind of bread pulp cannot be kept fresh, so there seems to me to be no point in collecting enough to take back and store on board.'

'Fiddlesticks, professor,' said Ned Land. 'You're talking like a naturalist, but I intend to behave like a baker. Conseil, go and pick a crop of these fruits and we'll collect this again when we get back.'

'How will you preserve them?' I asked the Canadian.

'By using the pulp to make a fermented dough, which will keep indefinitely without going bad. When I want to use it, I'll have it baked in the ship's galley. Although it will have a slightly acid taste, you will find it excellent eating.'

'In that case, Ned, I see that this bread leaves absolutely nothing to be desired.'

'Not so, professor,' replied the Canadian, 'it still needs some fruits or at least a few vegetables to go with it.'

'Then let us go looking for fruit and vegetables.'

When we had got our bread-fruit harvest in, we set out to complete our banquet on terra firma.

Our search did not go unrewarded. By about noon we had gathered in an ample supply of bananas. These delicious products of the torrid zones ripen throughout the whole year. The Malays, who call them *pisang*, eat them raw, without cooking them. As well as bananas, we picked huge jackfruit, which have a very distinctive taste, juicy mangoes and implausibly large pineapples. Our haul took a great amount of time to assemble, but we had no reason to regret it.

Conseil kept watching Ned. The harpooner led the way, and during our incursion into the forest, he used his knowledge to pick first-rate fruits to complete our supplies.

'Am I right in thinking, Ned,' asked Conseil, 'that you don't need anything else?'

'Well . . .' said the Canadian.

'What, still not satisfied?'

'All these vegetable stuffs will never amount to a proper dinner,' said Ned. 'They're only an accompaniment, or a dessert. What about the soup? Or the roast?'

'True, Ned,' I said. 'Those chops you promised us now look highly unlikely.'

'Professor,' he replied, 'the hunt is not only not finished, it hasn't even begun! Be patient. Before we're done, we will come across some animal with hair or feathers, and if it's not here then it will be somewhere else.'

'And if it doesn't happen today, it will happen tomorrow,' added Conseil. 'We mustn't go too far. I would even suggest that we go back to the boat now.'

'What, so soon?' asked Ned.

'We must be back before it gets dark,' I said.

'What time is it now?' asked the Canadian.

'It's at least past two,' said Conseil.

'How time flies on dry land!' observed Ned with a sigh of regret.

'So let's get going,' was Conseil's reply.

And so we returned through the forest and completed our harvesting operation by raiding the cabbage palms. This involved climbing to the tops of the trees and picking small beans which I recognized as being the same as what Malays call *abrou*, and also some yams of first-rate quality.

We were weighed down with provisions by the time we arrived back at the boat. But Ned Land still did not think that we had garnered a sufficient supply. However, his luck was in. Just as we were about to cast off, he spotted a number of trees, 25 or 30 feet high, a variety of palm. These trees, every whit as precious as the bread-fruit, rank among the most useful products of Malaysia.

They were sago palms. They need no cultivation and reproduce, like the mulberry, through their shoots and seeds.

Ned Land knew how to deal with these trees. He took his

axe and, setting to work with great vigour, he had in no time felled two or three sago-palms, judging that they were ripe by the white dust covering their leaves.

I watched him more with the eyes of a naturalist than with those of a hungry man. He began by removing from each trunk a ring of the inch-thick bark, revealing a network of longitudinal fibres forming knotted tangles cemented together by a kind of thick, sticky gum. This gum was sago, an edible substance whose main use is to feed the population of Melanesia.

For the time being, Ned Land merely cut the trunks into sections, as he would have chopped firewood, leaving until later the business of extracting the gum, sieving it through cloth to remove the stringy fibres, allowing it to dry off in the sun and finally to harden in moulds.

At last, at five in the afternoon, laden with all our riches, we rowed away from the shores of the island. Half an hour later we lay alongside the *Nautilus*. No one came out to greet us. The enormous iron cylinder seemed deserted. When we had transferred our cargo on board, I went below to my cabin. I found my supper waiting for me. I ate and then I slept.

The next morning, 6 January, nothing new seemed to be happening on board. There was not a sound inside the boat, no sign of life. The dinghy was still moored alongside in the same place where we had left it. We decided to return to Gueboroar Island. Ned Land was hoping to have better luck than on the previous day from a hunting point of view and was keen to explore a different part of the forest.

We were on our way by the time dawn was breaking. Our boat, borne along by the incoming waves, reached the island in next to no time.

We disembarked and, thinking it best to trust ourselves to the Canadian's instincts, we followed Ned Land, whose long stride threatened to leave us behind.

He followed the coast westwards, fording a number of water-courses, and led us to a high plain ringed by magnificent forests. Kingfishers patrolled the streams, but we could not get near them. Their caution was proof to me that these birds knew what to expect from two-legged creatures of our species. From this I concluded that if the island was not actually inhabited, it had had human visitors.

After traversing a very large area of meadow land, we reached the edge of a small wood alive with the song and flight of a vast number of birds.

'So far there seem to be only birds,' said Conseil.

'But some of them will be edible,' said the harpooner.

'I don't think so, Ned. All the ones I've seen are parrots.'

'Listen, Conseil,' said Ned soberly, 'to those who have nothing to eat, the parrot is a pheasant.'

'And I would add,' I said, 'that if it is properly prepared it earns its place on anyone's plate.'

And indeed, beneath the dense foliage of this little wood was a large population of parrots which hopped from branch to branch, needing only better training to be able to speak the language of humans. But for the time being, they merely chattered away in the company of brilliantly coloured parakeets and solemn cockatoos, which all looked as though they were pondering some deep philosophical problem, while bright crimson lories flitted like little strips of bunting blowing in the breeze, among hornbills in raucous flight, papuas dressed in the subtlest shades of blue and a motley host of feathered creatures which, though lovely to look at, were mostly inedible.

However, one bird, a native of these regions, which has never spread beyond the shores of the Aru and Papuan Islands, was absent from this assembly. But fate was keeping it back so that I might admire it at a later moment.

After passing through an area of moderately thick brush, we re-emerged on to a plain choked with bushes. I saw magnificent birds fly up, the setting of their long feathers requiring them to head into the wind. Their undulating flight, the grace of their aerial manoeuvres and their shimmering colours drew and delighted the eye. I had no difficulty in identifying them.

'Birds of paradise!' I exclaimed.

'Order of *passeriformes*,' said Conseil, 'suborder of *paradiseidae*.'

'And related to the partridge family?' asked Ned Land.

'I don't think so, Mister Land. But I'm counting on your

skill to catch us one of these delicious products of tropical nature.'

'We can but try, professor, though I'm more used to handling a harpoon than a gun.'

The Malays, who carry on a lively trade in these birds with the Chinese, have a number of different ways of catching them which were not available to us. They set snares in the tops of tall trees where birds of paradise tend to congregate. Or they take them using a very strong bird-lime, which immobilizes them. They even poison the springs where these birds go to drink. But all we were equipped to do was to shoot them out of the air, and this left us with only a slim chance of bagging any. And so it proved: we used up a good part of our ammunition without result.

At about eleven in the morning, we had crossed the first line of the mountains which form the centre of the island and we had still not shot anything. The pangs of hunger drove us on. The hunters had been reckoning on killing something and they had been wrong. Luckily, Conseil, much to his surprise, brought down two birds with one shot and thus provided us with lunch. He got a white pigeon and a ring-dove, which, promptly plucked and skewered on a spit, were put to roast over a hot fire of dead wood. While these delightful birds were cooking, Ned prepared several bread-fruits. Then the bones of the dove and the pigeon were picked clean, and both birds were pronounced excellent. The nutmeg on which they regularly graze flavoured their meat and made it delicious eating.

'Tastes as good as fowl fed on truffles,' declared Conseil.

'And now, Ned, what else do you have in mind?' I asked.

'Some kind of four-legged game, Professor Aronnax,' he replied. 'The pigeons were just for appetizers, something to start with! I'll not rest until I've bagged an animal that can provide us with chops!'

'Nor will I, Ned, not until I bag a bird of paradise!'

'So let's go on with the hunt,' said Conseil, 'but preferably on our way back to the sea. We've reached the foothills of the mountains, and I think it would be best if we headed back towards the forest.'

It was good advice, and it was accepted. After an hour's

walking we found ourselves in a regular forest of sago-palms. A number of harmless snakes fled from our advancing feet, the birds of paradise flew off at our approach, and I was giving up hope of ever shooting one down when Conseil, who was in the lead, suddenly bent down, gave a triumphant shout and returned to me holding a magnificent specimen.

'Oh, well done, Conseil!' I exclaimed.

'Monsieur is too kind,' he replied.

'Not at all. You've brought off a master-stroke. Catching one of these birds alive – and with your bare hands!'

'But if monsieur would care to look more closely, he will see that I can claim very little credit.'

'Why is that, Conseil?'

'Because the bird is as drunk as a piper!'

'Drunk?'

'Yes, monsieur, drunk on all the fallen nutmeg it was gobbling under the nutmeg tree where I found it. Look, Ned, and behold the terrible effects of intemperance!'

'Hell's teeth!' answered the Canadian, 'given the amount of gin that's passed my lips these last two months, surely you're not going to start lecturing me now!'

Meantime, I was examining this curious bird. Conseil was quite right. The bird, inebriated by the intoxicating nutmeg juice, had been reduced to a state of helplessness. It could not fly and was barely able to walk. But this was of no account to me, and I left it to sleep off the effects of the nutmeg.

That specimen belonged to the most beautiful of the eight species to be found in Papua and the neighbouring islands. It was a Great Emerald, one of the rarest. It was 30 centimetres long. Its head was relatively small, as were its eyes, which were located near the opening of the beak. But it was a stunning array of colours, having a yellow beak, brown feet and claws, hazel wings with purple tips, pale yellow on the top of its head and the back of his neck, an emerald-green throat and a chestnut belly and breast. Two stiff, downy plumes sprouted from beneath its tail, which was elongated by wonderfully fine, light feathers, completing the livery of this amazing bird for which the natives have a poetic name: 'the Sun Bird'.

I would very much like to have taken this superb example of the bird of paradise back to Paris and presented it to the Jardin des Plantes, which does not have a live specimen,

'So is it very rare?' asked the Canadian, speaking like a hunter who doesn't think much of game from the aesthetic point of view.

'Extremely rare, Ned, and extremely difficult to catch alive. But even when they are dead there is a highly profitable trade in them. So much so that the natives actually make imitation ones rather as artificial pearls or diamonds are made.'

'What!' exclaimed Conseil, 'they make fake birds of paradise?'

'Yes, Conseil.'

'And does monsieur know how they do it?'

'Of course. During the monsoon season, birds of paradise lose their magnificent tail feathers, which naturalists call sub-alary feathers. These are precisely the feathers used by those who make counterfeit copies of these birds by skilfully attaching them to some poor, suitably mangled cockatoo. They dye the stitches, apply a varnish to the birds and then send these products of their strange labours to museums and collectors in Europe.'

'So,' said Ned Land, 'they may not get the bird itself but at least they'll have the feathers. Provided the thing is not meant to be eaten, I can't see that much harm is done.'

But if my wishes had been satisfied by being able to hold a real live bird of paradise in my hand, the desires of the Canadian hunter were not. Fortunately, at about two o'clock, Ned Land brought down a splendid wild pig, the kind which the natives call *bari-outang*. Its demise was timely, for it provided us with animal meat and was most welcome. Ned Land was very proud of that particular shot. The pig, hit by the electric bullet, had died instantly.

The Canadian skinned and drew the carcass, setting aside half a dozen chops to grill for our dinner. Then the hunt resumed. It would be marked by further exploits by Ned and Conseil.

The two friends beat the bushes and roused a number of

kangaroos, which fled in leaps and bounds on their springy rear legs. But they did not move so fast that the electric capsules did not stop them in their tracks.

'Ah, professor!' cried Ned Land, gripped by hunting fever, 'now this is what I call game, especially when stewed! We'll have such a supper for the *Nautilus*! That's two ... three ... five downed. And when I think that we'll eat the whole lot ourselves and the stupid crew on board won't get any! ...'

I truly believe that the Canadian, carried away by delight, would have slaughtered all of them if he hadn't talked so much! But he settled for a mere dozen of these curious marsupials, which, Conseil pointed out, constitute the first order of pouched mammals.

They were not large, a kind of 'rabbit kangaroo' which normally lives in the hollows of trees and is known for its extreme fleetness of foot. But though only of moderate size, they give meat that is highly regarded.

We were delighted with the results of our hunt. Ned was cock-a-hoop and proposed that we should return the following day to this enchanted isle, which he would have gladly depopulated of all its edible quadrupeds. But he wasn't reckoning on what was going to happen next.

At six o'clock, we were back on the shore. We had beached the dinghy in the same place. The *Nautilus*, looking like an elongated reef, was sitting in the water 2 miles away.

Without further ado, Ned Land set about the important business of preparing our dinner. He was an old hand at this kind of cooking and knew exactly what he was doing. The *bari-outang* chops, set to grill on the fire, were soon filling the air with the most delicious aroma.

But I realize now that I was beginning to follow the Canadian's lead exactly. There I was, with my tongue hanging out at the sight of freshly grilled pork! I hope the reader will forgive me as I forgave Mister Land, and for the same reasons!

We ate an excellent dinner. A brace of pigeons completed a marvellous menu. Sago purée, bread-fruit, a few mangoes, a half-dozen pineapples and the fermented juice of certain kinds of coconuts gladdened more than our hearts. I rather think

'Ned settled for a mere dozen of these curious marsupials'

that my companions might not have been as clear-headed as they might have been.

'What if we don't go back to the *Nautilus* tonight?' said Conseil.

'What if we never went back at all?' added Ned Land.

At that very moment, a stone landed at our feet and cut short the harpooner's proposal.

22

Captain Nemo's Thunderbolt

We looked towards the forest without getting up, my hand arrested halfway to my mouth and Ned Land's reaching its destination.

'A stone does not just drop out of the sky,' said Conseil, 'or if it does it should be called a meteorite!'

A second stone, of a carefully rounded shape, which knocked a tasty pigeon leg clean out of his hand, gave added weight to his observation.

Then we were all on our feet, guns raised to our shoulders and ready to repel any attack.

'Is it monkeys?' cried Ned Land.

'More or less,' replied Conseil. 'It's savages.'

'To the boat!' I cried, turning to head for the sea.

Indeed, we had no option but to retreat, for a score of natives armed with bows and slings had emerged from a clump of trees which obscured the horizon on our right, barely a hundred paces from us.

The dinghy lay on the beach 20 metres away.

They bore down on us, not running but gesturing at us threateningly. Stones and arrows rained on us.

Ned Land refused to abandon our provisions, despite the imminence of the danger, he carried the pig over one shoulder and the kangaroos over the other and decamped with commendable speed.

Two minutes later we were at the water's edge. To load the dinghy with the provisions and our guns, push off and slide two oars into the rowlocks was but the work of a moment. We had gone no more than two cable lengths when a hundred savages, yelling and waving their arms, waded into the water up to their waists. I looked round to see whether their sudden appearance would bring members of the crew of the *Nautilus* on to the platform. But no. The huge vessel, lying out to sea, remained absolutely deserted.

Twenty minutes later, we were clambering on board. The hatchways were open. We moored the dinghy and then made our way below.

I went directly to the Great Saloon, from which I could hear strains of music. Captain Nemo was there, bent over the organ keyboard, lost in the beauty of the harmonies.

'Captain?' I said.

He did not hear me.

'Captain!' I said again, putting one hand on his shoulder.

He gave a start and turned round.

'Ah, it's you, professor,' he said. 'Well, was your hunt successful? Did you find interesting plants?'

'Yes, captain,' I replied. 'But unfortunately we have brought back a horde of bipeds whose arrival might well prove troublesome.'

'What kind of bipeds?'

'Savages.'

'Savages?' replied Captain Nemo in an ironic voice. 'And are you surprised, professor, that having set foot on one of the dry parts of the globe you should find savages there? Where are there not savages? And are these savages, as you call them, noticeably worse than all the rest?'

'But, captain . . .'

'Over the years, professor, I have found savages wherever I go.'

'But,' I replied, 'if you do not want them on board the *Nautilus*, you would be well advised to take precautions.'

'Calm down, professor, there's nothing to worry about.'

'But there are a lot of them . . .'

'How many of them would you say there are?'

'At least a hundred.'

'Professor Aronnax,' replied Captain Nemo, whose fingers were already hovering over the keys of the organ, 'if all the natives of Papua were assembled on that beach ready to attack, the *Nautilus* would still have nothing to fear.'

By now, the captain's fingers were again moving over the organ keyboard, and I noticed he was using only the black keys, which gave what he was playing an essentially Scottish feel. He quickly forgot that I was there and retreated into a dreamy mood which I did nothing further to dispel.

I went back up to the platform. Night had already fallen, for, in those latitudes, the sun sets suddenly, and there is no twilight. In the gloom I could just make out the island of Gueboroar. But the numerous fires which had been lit on the beach suggested that the natives were not proposing to leave dry land.

I remained where I was by myself for a good few hours, at times thinking about these islanders – but no longer particularly with fear, for I had caught something of the captain's unshakeable confidence – and at others forgetting all about them to admire the splendour of the tropical night. My thoughts took me back to France, seeing the constellations of the zodiac, which would be shining there in a few hours. The moon was bright in the constellations of the zenith. I reflected then that this faithful, companionable satellite would return the day after the next to raise the tide and lift the *Nautilus* off her bed of coral. Around midnight, since all was quiet on the dark surface of the sea and under the trees on the land, I returned to my cabin and slept peacefully.

The night passed uneventfully. In all likelihood, the Papuans were afraid of the very sight of this monster which had fetched up in their bay, for the hatches had been left open and offered an easy way into the *Nautilus*.

At six in the morning – 8 January – I climbed back up to the platform. The morning gloom was lifting. Soon the island emerged from the early mists: the beach at first and then the mountain tops.

The natives were still there, and more numerous than the night before: there were five or six hundred of them. Some, taking advantage of the low tide, had come out as far as the coral outcrops, less than two cables' lengths from the *Nautilus*. I could make them out clearly. They were authentic Papuans, athletically built, a handsome breed of men, with high, wide foreheads, large but not flat noses and white teeth. Their woolly hair, dyed red, formed a contrast with their black bodies, which gleamed like those of Nubians. From the lobes of their ears, which had been pierced and stretched, hung strings of bones. They were, for the most part, naked. Among them I saw a few women. They were dressed from hip to knee in crinoline skirts made of grasses and held up by belts of straw. Some of the chiefs had crescent-shaped collars round their throats plus necklaces of red and white glass beads. Almost all were armed with bows, arrows and shields. From their shoulders hung a kind of net filled with round pebbles, which they shoot with great accuracy using a sling.

One of these chiefs, who had come quite close, was carefully examining the *Nautilus*. He was almost certainly a *mado* of high degree, for he had draped himself in a woven mat of banana leaves which was spiky round the edges and painted in dazzling colours.

I could have easily shot him at that close range. But I thought it wiser to wait and see if there would be any genuinely hostile intent. In any contest between Europeans and natives, it is only right that Europeans should always defend themselves and never attack first.

As long as the tide was low, these natives kept prowling round the *Nautilus* but made no trouble. I often heard them repeating the word *assai*, and by the gestures I understood that they were inviting me to go ashore, an invitation which I felt obliged to decline.

So that day, the dinghy did not leave the ship, much to the frustration of Ned Land, who was prevented from completing his stock of provisions. Instead, this resourceful Canadian used his time preserving the meat and farinaceous products he had brought back from Gueboroar Island. Meanwhile the natives all returned to land around eleven in the morning, as soon as the tops of the coral began disappearing under the swell of the rising tide. But I saw that their numbers on the beach were increasing rapidly. It was likely that they were coming from neighbouring islands or from Papua itself. Even so, I had not yet seen one native canoe.

Having nothing better to do, I thought about dragging a net through these crystal-clear waters, in which a profusion of shells, zoophytes and marine plants were clearly visible. For it was the last day the *Nautilus* would spend in this location, provided, of course, that she was refloated at high tide the following day according to the assurances Captain Nemo had given.

So I called Conseil, who brought me a small, light dragnet rather like those which are used for gathering oysters.

'What about the savages?' asked Conseil. 'If monsieur won't mind my remarking, they don't look very hostile.'

'Nevertheless, cannibals is what they are.'

'It is surely possible to be a cannibal and a gentleman,' replied Conseil, 'in the same way that a man may be a glutton and perfectly civilized. The one does not exclude the other.'

'Fair enough, Conseil. I'll concede that these are gentlemanly cannibals who eat their prisoners in the most civilized way. But as I have no wish to be eaten at all, even by gentlemen, I shall remain on my guard, for the master of the *Nautilus* seems to have no intention of taking any safety precautions. And now to work!'

For two hours, we fished with a will but without catching any rare specimens. Our net filled with trumpet shells, harp snails, elongated melanians and in particular the finest examples of hammer shells I had seen to date. We also scooped up sea cucumbers, pearl oysters and a dozen small turtles, which we set aside for the ship's larder.

But just as I was least expecting it, I got my hands on a wonder, or I should say an extremely rare natural malformation. Conseil had just plied his net and was hauling it to the surface filled with various kinds of very ordinary shells when all of a sudden he observed me thrust my hand into it, retrieve a shell and give a conchologist's whoop, which must be the most ear-splitting sound produced by the human larynx!

'What is it?' asked Conseil, somewhat taken aback. 'Has monsieur been bitten?'

'No, Conseil, though I would gladly have lost a finger to make such a find!'

'What find?'

'This shell,' I said, holding up the object in triumph.

'But it's only a porphyry olive, family *olividae*, order of *pectinibranchiata*, class of gastropods, branch of molluscs.'

'True, Conseil, but instead of turning right to left, this one winds left to right!'

'That can't be so!' exclaimed Conseil.

'But it is! It's an anti-clockwise shell!'

'An anti-clockwise shell!' repeated Conseil, his heart racing.

'Look at the spiral.'

'I can assure monsieur,' said Conseil, taking the precious shell in a trembling hand, 'that I have never ever felt so thrilled!'

And indeed there was plenty to be thrilled about. It is well known, as naturalists have pointed out, that right-handedness is a law of nature. The stars and their satellites in their transits and orbits move from right to left. Man uses his right hand more than his left, and as a result all his instruments and artefacts such as staircases, locks, watch movements and so forth are designed to operate from right to left. Most of the time, nature obeys this law for the way shells grow. With rare exceptions, they are all right-handed, and when by chance their whorl is left-turning, then collectors will pay a fortune for them.

Conseil and I were totally absorbed, fascinated by our precious find, and I was promising myself that I would add it to the Museum's collection, when alas a stone from a native sling smashed the irreplaceable specimen into pieces in Conseil's hand.

I let out a wail of despair! Conseil seized his gun and took aim at a native who was swinging his sling not 10 metres away. I tried to stop him, but the gun went off and shattered the bracelet of charms dangling from the man's arm.

'Conseil, oh, Conseil!' I cried.

'What? Does monsieur not agree that it was the cannibal who attacked first?'

'A shell does not have the same value as a man's life!'

'The wretch!' cried Conseil. 'I would rather he had broken my shoulder!'

Conseil was absolutely serious, but I did not agree with him. However, the situation had changed in just a few moments without our noticing. The *Nautilus* was now surrounded by a score of canoes made out of dug-out tree-trunks. They were long, narrow and skilfully designed for speed. Balance was achieved by means of two bamboo floats, attached to transversal poles, which sat on the water on each side. The canoes were expertly manoeuvred by half-naked paddlers. I watched them getting nearer and nearer with growing alarm.

It was obvious that these Papuans had already had some contact with Europeans and that they were familiar with their ships. But this long, metal cylinder aground in the bay had no masts and no funnels: what did they think of it? Nothing good for sure, because hitherto they had maintained a respectful distance. But when they saw that it did not move, they gradually took heart and decided to familiarize themselves with it. It was just this familiarity that had to be prevented. Our air guns, which were silent when fired, would not have much effect on these natives, who only respect noisy weapons. Lightning without thunder does not frighten men, even though the danger is in the lightning and not in the noise.

At this juncture, the canoes were getting nearer the *Nautilus* at every moment, and a shower of arrows clattered on to her hull.

'Damn! It's like hail!' cried Conseil. 'Only these hailstones might be poisoned!'

'We must warn Captain Nemo!' I said, scuttling inside through the hatchway.

I went down to the Great Saloon. It was deserted. I took a chance and knocked on the door of the captain's cabin.

I was answered by a 'Come!' I went in and found Captain Nemo bent over a mathematical calculation where 'x' and other algebraic signs were present in large numbers.

'I hope I'm not disturbing you,' I said politely.

'You are, as a matter of fact,' replied the captain. 'But I assume that you must have some good reason for this visit.'

'Very good. We are surrounded by native canoes and within minutes we shall be under attack by several hundred savages!'

'Come in their canoes, have they?' the captain said calmly.

'Yes, sir.'

'Well, professor, all we need do is close the hatches.'

'Exactly, and I came to say . . .'

'Nothing could be simpler,' said Captain Nemo.

He pressed an electric button and transmitted an order to the crew in their quarters.

'There, professor, it's done,' he said after a few moments. 'The dinghy is locked down, and the hatches are closed. I don't imagine that you're afraid that these people will smash their way through walls that the shells of your frigate were unable to dent?'

'No, captain, but there is still a danger.'

'And what might that be?'

'This time tomorrow we shall have to open the hatches to replace the air inside the *Nautilus*.'

'Absolutely true, given that our boat breathes exactly the way cetaceans do.'

'Now if at that moment the Papuans are occupying the platform, I do not see how you can stop them getting in.'

'So you think that they will board us?'

'I'm sure of it.'

'Let them try. I see no reason for stopping them. You know, the Papuans are poor devils, and I would not want my visit to Gueboroar Island to cost the life of a single one of these unfortunates.'

He had spoken, and I was about to withdraw. But the captain detained me and invited me to sit down. He asked me with obvious interest about our forays on dry land and about our hunt. He did not seem able to understand the Canadian's visceral craving for meat. The conversation then touched on other matters and, although he became no more forthcoming, Captain Nemo showed himself in a more amiable light.

Among these other topics, we spoke of the plight of the *Nautilus*, then stranded in this narrow strait where Dumont d'Urville had nearly come to grief. In this context, he went on:

'D'Urville was one of the great sailors, one of the world's most intelligent navigators. He was France's Captain Cook. He was a learned man but most unfortunate. To have braved the ice of the South Pole, the coral reefs of Oceania, the cannibals of the Pacific, and then to die a miserable death in a banal train accident! If, during the last moments of his life, this enterprising man was at all capable of reflection, just imagine what his final thoughts must have been!'

As he spoke these words, Captain Nemo seemed moved, and I decided his feelings did him credit.

Then, map in hand, we reviewed the labours of the indefatigable Frenchman, his voyages of circumnavigation, his two attempts on the South Pole, which led to the discovery of Adélie Land and Louis-Philippe Land, ending with his hydrographic record of the principal islands of Oceania..

'What d'Urville did on the surface of the oceans,' Captain Nemo told me, 'I have done beneath them, and more easily and more comprehensively. The *Astrolabe* and the *Zélée*, constantly battered by hurricanes, could never compete with the *Nautilus,* which is a peaceful, undisturbed place to work in under the world's seas.'

'That may well be, captain,' I said, 'yet in one respect there is a similarity between Dumont d'Urville's corvettes and the *Nautilus.*'

'And what is that?'

'The fact that the *Nautilus* has run aground just as they did.'

'The *Nautilus* has not run aground, professor,' Captain Nemo replied coldly. 'The *Nautilus* was so constructed that she can settle on the sea-bed, so that I shall not have to undertake the hard work and intricate manoeuvres forced upon d'Urville in his efforts to refloat his corvettes. The *Astrolabe* and the *Zélée* were almost lost, but my *Nautilus* is in no such danger. Tomorrow, on the appointed day, at the stated time, the tide will lift her and she will resume her journey through the seas.'

'Captain,' I said, 'I do not doubt it for a moment . . .'

'Tomorrow,' said Captain Nemo, getting to his feet, 'tomorrow, at 2.40 p.m., the *Nautilus* will be afloat and will sail out of the Torres Strait undamaged.'

Having made this brief, curt statement, Captain Nemo inclined his head slightly, thus intimating that I should now leave. I returned to my cabin.

There, I found Conseil who was eager to know the outcome of my conference with the captain.

'Well,' I said, 'when I pretended to think that the *Nautilus* was under threat from the natives of Papua, the captain gave me a rather sarcastic reply. So I have only one thing to say: trust in him and sleep soundly.'

'Monsieur has no further need of my services?'

'No, Conseil. What is Ned Land doing?'

'Monsieur may wish to know that at this moment Ned is making a kangaroo pâté, which will be a wonder of the universe!'

Left to myself, I went to bed but slept very badly. I kept hearing the sound of natives walking about on the platform, uttering deafening cries. And so the night dragged on. The crew never emerged from their customary inertia. They were no more worried by the presence of the cannibals than soldiers inside a stoutly defended fort would be concerned by ants crawling up its fortifications.

I got up at six. The hatches had not been opened, which meant that the air had not been replaced. But the tanks, kept topped up against all eventualities, were doing what they were supposed to by releasing several cubic metres of oxygen into the depleted atmosphere of the *Nautilus*.

I worked in my cabin until noon. During that time I never set eyes, however briefly, on Captain Nemo. No one on board seemed to be making any preparations whatsoever for our departure.

I waited a little while longer then went along to the Great Saloon. According to the chronometer, it was now 2.30 p.m. Another ten minutes and the tide would reach its highest point, and unless Captain Nemo had made a very rash promise, the *Nautilus* would be instantly released. Otherwise, many months would pass before she could be free of her bed of coral.

But several preliminary shudders were soon felt all through the hull of the boat. I heard her metal sheath grinding against the jagged chalky growths of her coral resting place.

At 2.35, Captain Nemo walked into the saloon.

'Ah!' I exclaimed.

'I have ordered the hatches to be opened.'

'What about the Papuans?'

'The Papuans?' Captain Nemo said with a slight shrug of his shoulders.

'Won't they get inside the *Nautilus*?'

'And how would they do that?'

'By coming in through the hatches which you've opened.'

'Professor Aronnax,' Captain Nemo replied calmly, 'no one can just step through the hatches of the *Nautilus*, even when they are wide open.'

I stared at him.

'Don't you understand?'

'Not at all.'

'Follow me, and you can see for yourself.'

I made my way to the central stairwell. There, Conseil and Ned Land, looking highly intrigued, were already watching members of the crew opening the hatches while yells of rage and blood-curdling screams could be heard outside.

The hatch covers opened outwards, and immediately a score of ghastly faces appeared, looking down. But the first of these natives to grab the handrail of the staircase recoiled, repulsed by some inexplicable, invisible force, then turned and fled uttering ear-splitting howls and hopping like a scalded cat.

Ten of his companions followed his example, and they all suffered the same fate.

Conseil was ecstatic. Ned Land, carried away by his combustible temperament, started up the stairs. But as he gripped the rail with both hands, he too was knocked backwards.

'Hell's teeth!' he cried. 'I've been struck by lightning!'

That word made the whole thing clear to me. The handrail was not an ordinary handrail but a metal cable connected to the vessel's electricity supply which ran all the way up to the platform. Whoever touched it got a terrible shock which would have been lethal if Captain Nemo had put the full power produced by his generators through it. It was literally the case that between his assailants and him he had erected an electric net that could not be crossed painlessly.

Meanwhile, the stricken Papuans had retreated, crazed with

'Ten of his companions suffered the same fate'

terror. We, half laughing, consoled and massaged poor Ned's hands, while he swore like a trooper.

But at that moment, the *Nautilus*, raised by the latest swell of the risen water, slipped off her ledge of coral at exactly the fortieth minute of the hour predicted by Captain Nemo. Her propeller turned in the water with a majestic slowness. Slowly she increased her speed and, advancing over the surface of the water, she sailed through the dangerous channels of the Torres Strait, safe and sound.

23

Aegri Somnia – Unpleasant Dreams

The next day, 10 January, the *Nautilus* resumed her progress, sailing beneath the waves, and at a remarkable rate which I reckoned to be not less than 35 knots. The speed of her propeller was such that I was able neither to see it turn nor count the revolutions.

When I reflected that this marvellous electric power, after providing the *Nautilus* with propulsion, heat and light, also protected her against attacks from outside and transformed her into a sacred vessel which no profane hand could touch without being struck down by lightning, my admiration knew no bounds. And from the invention, my admiration extended to the inventor who had made it.

We were proceeding due west and on 11 January we sailed round Cape Wessel, the eastern point of the Gulf of Carpentaria located at longitude 135° and latitude 10° north. The reefs were still very numerous but more scattered and were marked on the chart with great accuracy. The *Nautilus* had no trouble avoiding the broken water of Money to port and the Victoria reefs on our starboard side at longitude 130° and on the 10th parallel, along to which we were keeping most strictly.

On 13 January, we reached the Timor Sea, and Captain Nemo sighted the island of that name at longitude 122°. This island, which has an area of 1,625 square leagues, is governed by rajahs. These princes reckon themselves to be the sons of crocodiles, which is to say that they are descended from the noblest origins any man can lay claim to. Furthermore, these scaly forebears exist in large numbers in the island's rivers and are the object of special veneration. They are protected, pampered, worshipped and fed. Maidens are left out for them to graze on, and woe to the stranger who raises his hand against these sacred lizards.

But the *Nautilus* was to have no dealings with these fearsome brutes, for Timor was sighted only briefly, at midday, when the first officer took our position. In the same way, I got only a glimpse of tiny Rote Island, part of the same archipelago, whose women have a longstanding reputation in the markets of Malaya for beauty.

From this point on, the *Nautilus* began steering a new course, bearing south-west, towards the Indian Ocean. Where would the whims of Captain Nemo take us next? Would he turn north to the coasts of Asia? Was he intending to make for the shores of Europe? Neither option seemed likely for a man who kept well away from inhabited continents. So would he turn and go south? Would he sail round the Cape of Good Hope, then Cape Horn and push on to the Antarctic Pole? Would he return to the seas of the Pacific, where the *Nautilus* could move freely and without interference? Only the future would tell.

On 14 January, after sailing past the reefs of the atolls of Cartier, Hibernia, Seringapatam and Scott, the last battle-grounds of the struggle between solid ground and water, we lost all contact with land. Curiously, the speed of the *Nautilus* dropped considerably, and now, capricious in her progress, she cruised sometimes under the water and at other times on the surface.

During this phase of the voyage, Captain Nemo carried out a number of interesting experiments on the different temperatures of the ocean at different depths. In normal conditions, such readings are taken using very complicated equipment, which give results that are at best unreliable, such as thermometric sounding leads, whose glass has a tendency to shatter under the pressure of the water, or instruments based on variations in the resistance of metals to electric currents. Figures obtained by these means cannot be properly verified. Captain Nemo, on the other hand, was able to go down into the depths to record temperatures for himself, and his thermometer, being exposed directly to various levels of the sea, gave him the required readings instantly and accurately.

Thus, either by filling her tanks or descending obliquely by means of her angled fins, the *Nautilus* reached depths of three, four, five, seven, nine and ten thousand metres, and the unarguable conclusion of these experiments was that at a depth of 1,000 metres the sea remains at a permanent temperature of 4½ degrees, irrespective of latitude.

I followed his experiments with the keenest interest. Captain Nemo approached them with genuine passion. I often wondered for what purpose he conducted them. Was it for the benefit of mankind? That was hardly likely, since his work was fated to die with him at any moment in some unknown sea! Unless he was intending to pass the results of his experiments to me? But that would mean a limit had been placed on the length of my strange odyssey, though I was not yet aware of any such limit.

Be that as it may, Captain Nemo also showed me various readings he had obtained which established a connection between the relative densities of water in the world's major seas. In the process, I learned a personal lesson which had nothing to do with science.

As we strolled on the platform on the morning of 15 January, Captain Nemo asked me if I knew the various densities of sea-water. I said I didn't, adding that science lacked objectively reliable observations on that question.

'I have myself made such observations,' he said, 'and I can vouch for their accuracy.'

'No doubt,' I replied. 'But the *Nautilus* is a world apart, and the discoveries of its learned men do not reach as far as dry land.'

'You are right, professor,' he said after a few moments of silence. 'It really is another world. It is as alien to Earth as the planets which accompany our globe as they orbit the sun. No one would ever know of the work of scientists on Saturn or on Jupiter. And yet, since chance has chosen to link our two existences, I shall inform you of the results of my observations.'

'I'm listening, captain.'

'You will know, professor, that sea-water is denser than fresh water, but the level of density is not uniform. If I give the value 1 to the density of fresh water, then 1.028 is the figure for waters of the Atlantic Ocean, 1.026 for the Pacific, 1.030 for the Mediterranean . . .'

'Aha!' I thought. 'So he ventures into the Mediterranean!'

'. . . 1.018 for the Ionian Sea, and 1.029 for the Adriatic.'

So the *Nautilus* made no particular effort to avoid the busy seas of Europe, and I concluded that he would really take us back – and sooner rather than later, perhaps – to more civilized parts of the world. I thought Ned Land would receive the news with understandable satisfaction.

For several days, our time was spent on various experiments which dealt with the degree of salinity of water at different depths, its electrical charge, coloration and transparency, and in every case Captain Nemo showed a degree of inventiveness equalled only by his good grace towards me. Then I did not see him for several days and was again left in virtual isolation on his vessel.

On 16 January, the *Nautilus* appeared to come to a complete stop just a few metres below the surface of the waves. Her electric machinery was not operating, and with her propeller immobilized she drifted wherever the current took her. I assumed the crew were engaged on repair-work needed perhaps as a result of the stresses caused by the powerful movements of the engines.

And then my companions and I witnessed a curious sight. The panels in the Great Saloon were open, and as the *Nautilus*'s searchlight was not turned on, the water was plunged into semi-darkness. The stormy skies above were blanketed by thick clouds, giving the upper levels of water no more than a feeble glow.

I was observing the sea in these conditions, in which even the largest fish were no more than barely perceptible shadows, when without warning the *Nautilus* was lit by a brilliant illumination. I thought for a moment that the searchlight had been turned back on and that it was projecting its electric light into the mass of water. I was wrong, and a quick glance was enough to convince me of my error.

The *Nautilus* was sitting in the middle of an area of phosphorescence which in this murk was dazzling. It was produced by myriads of luminous microscopic organisms and increased in intensity as they came into contact with the hull of the vessel. I saw trails in the luminosity reminiscent of the flows of molten lead in a fiery furnace or metal when it becomes white hot. On the other hand, some bright areas looked like shadows in such igneous company from which anything resembling shadow was excluded. No, this was nothing like the steady radiance of our regular lighting! This light had a strange vigour and movement to it. It felt alive!

We were dealing with a numberless agglomeration of marine infusoria, of miliary noctiluca, in effect diaphanous jellies each having thread-like tentacles of which some 25,000 have been found in 30 cubic centimetres of water. The intensity of the light they give off is doubled by the luminosity of jellyfish, starfish, aurelias, piddocks and other phosphorescent zoophytes all impregnated with the residuum of organic matter decomposed by the sea, and perhaps also the mucus secreted by fish.

For several hours, the *Nautilus* floated in the midst of this brilliance, and our wonder grew on seeing large marine creatures playing in it like salamanders. In that fire which did not burn I saw elegant, fast-moving porpoises, those tireless clowns of the oceans, and sailfish 3 metres long, intelligent heralds of hurricanes whose fearsome bills rattled the saloon windows on occasion. After them came smaller fish, various strains of trigger-fish, leaping bonitos, unicorn fish and many others which left trails as they streaked through the luminous zone.

The entire dazzling spectacle was spellbinding! Perhaps some particular atmospheric condition enhanced the intensity of the phenomenon. Perhaps a storm was being unleashed on the surface of the water. But at this depth of just a few metres, the *Nautilus* felt nothing of its fury, and she continued to rock gently in the peaceful water.

And so we travelled on, perpetually delighted by new wonders. Conseil observed and classified his zoophytes, articulates, molluscs and fish. The days passed quickly, and I stopped counting them. Ned followed his custom of looking for ways of varying the shipboard diet. We were like snails: we grew accustomed to being snug in our shell. I can confirm that it is all too easy to turn into a snail!

The life we led seemed to us undemanding and quite natural, so that we stopped imagining that a very different kind of existence continued to persist on the surface of the terrestrial globe. But then an event occurred which reminded us of the strangeness of our situation.

On 18 January, the *Nautilus* was at longitude 105° and latitude 15° south. The weather had turned threatening. The sea was rough, and there was a heavy swell. The wind was in the east and blowing hard. The barometer had been falling for days and was predicting an imminent battle of the elements.

I had climbed up on to the platform just as the first officer was measuring the angle of the sun. I waited as usual for him to make his daily pronouncement. But that day, it was replaced by another, which was no less incomprehensible. Almost immediately I saw Captain Nemo appear. His eye, pressed to a telescope, surveyed the horizon.

He stood stock still for a few moments, his gaze fixed on the point at the centre of the telescope's field. Then he lowered his glass and exchanged a few words with his first officer, who seemed in the grip of emotions he vainly strove to contain. Captain Nemo, much more in control of himself, remained cool and collected. He appeared to be raising objections to which his subordinate replied with categorical assurances. At least, going by the differences between their tone of voice and gestures, that was how I understood matters.

For my part, I had peered carefully in the same direction but saw nothing. Sky and sea merged into the perfectly clear line of the horizon.

However, Captain Nemo was pacing up and down on the platform without looking at me and perhaps without even seeing me. His tread was confident but less regular than usual. He stopped from time to time and, with his arms folded across his chest, he scrutinized the sea. What could he be looking for in that vast emptiness? The *Nautilus* was then a few hundred miles from the nearest land!

The first officer had taken back his telescope and was stubbornly raking the horizon, walking up and down, stamping his feet, his anxiety and agitation making a sharp contrast with his captain's cool behaviour.

But the mystery would have to be cleared up, of necessity, and before long, for at an order from Captain Nemo, the engine power was increased, and the propeller began to rotate more quickly.

At that moment, the first officer again attracted the attention of the captain, who stopped his pacing and pointed the telescope in the direction indicated. He maintained his gaze for some time. Meanwhile, becoming increasingly intrigued, I went below to the Great Saloon and returned with the excellent telescope I normally used. Resting it on the searchlight housing which projected over the forward-end of the platform, I readied myself to scan the entire line where the sea met the sky.

But my eye was not yet at the eyepiece when the instrument was snatched from my hands.

I turned. Captain Nemo stood in front of me, but I did not recognize him. His face was transfigured. His eyes, ablaze with dark fire, had shrunk beneath his beetling brows. His teeth were partly bared. His rigid posture, clenched fists and head sunk on his shoulders bore witness to of the bitter hatred filling his entire body. He did not move. My telescope, which he had dropped, rolled at his feet.

Was I the unwitting cause of his look of fury? Did this unfathomable man imagine that I had stumbled across some secret or other which was forbidden to the passengers of the *Nautilus*?

But it was not so! I was not the focus of his hatred, for he was not looking at me. His eyes remained obstinately fixed on that mysterious point on the horizon.

Eventually, Captain Nemo regained control of himself, and his features, so profoundly altered, resumed their habitual calm. He spoke a few words to his first officer in that strange tongue of theirs, then turned to me.

'Professor Aronnax,' he said in a rather commanding way,

'I must now ask you to observe one of the conditions of our agreement.'

'Which one, captain?'

'You must allow yourself and your companions to be kept under lock and key until such time as I see fit to restore your liberty.'

'You are the master here,' I replied, looking him in the eye. 'But may I ask one question?'

'No, professor.'

After that, I was in no position to argue, only to obey, since resistance was out of the question.

I went below to the cabin occupied by Ned Land and Conseil and informed them of the captain's decision. It may be imagined how this news went down with the Canadian. But there was no time for further explanations. Four crew members were waiting outside the door and they led us to the same cell in which we had spent our first night on board the *Nautilus*.

Ned Land tried to protest, but the slamming of the cell door was all the response he got.

'Perhaps monsieur will tell me what this means?' asked Conseil.

I told my companions about what had happened. They were both as surprised as I was, and just as perplexed.

Meanwhile, my head filled up with conjectures, and I could not get the memory of the fear in Captain Nemo's face out of my mind. I found I was unable to string my thoughts together and wandered into the wildest surmises until I was roused from my quarrelling thoughts by these words spoken by Ned Land:

'Hello! Lunch is served!'

For the table was laid. It was clear that Captain Nemo had arranged it at the same time as he was giving orders for the *Nautilus* to increase her speed.

'Would monsieur allow me to make a suggestion?' asked Conseil.

'Please do,' I said.

'Then perhaps monsieur would like to have lunch now? It would be wise, for we do not know what might happen.'

'You are right, Conseil.'

'Unfortunately,' said Ned Land, 'they've only given us the usual ship's fare.'

'True, Ned,' replied Conseil, 'but what would you have said if there'd been no fare at all?'

This thought put an end to the harpooner's complaining.

We sat round the table. The meal passed more or less in silence. I ate little. Conseil 'forced himself', as a precaution, while Ned Land, despite his reservations, did not leave a mouthful. Once lunch was finished, each of us sat back in his chair.

At that moment, the luminous globe which lit the cell went out, and we were left in complete and utter darkness. It was not long before Ned Land was asleep, and I was surprised that Conseil too had fallen into a heavy slumber. I was beginning to wonder what could have caused this overpowering need to sleep when I felt my own brain growing sluggish and torpid. I tried to keep my eyes open but they kept closing of their own accord. A painful thought entered my mind. Surely some soporific substance had been added to the lunch we had just eaten! So prison was not enough to prevent us knowing what Captain Nemo was up to! We had to be rendered unconscious as well!

I heard the hatches close. I felt the swell of the sea, which had caused the vessel to roll slightly, cease. Did this mean we were no longer on the surface? Had the *Nautilus* dived and was it now in the still water below the waves?

I tried to fight off sleep. It was impossible. My breathing grew shallow. I felt icy cold, and the feeling spread to all my limbs, which were heavy and virtually paralysed. My eyelids, like lead shutters, came down over my eyes. I could not raise them. A deadly sleep filled with wild hallucinations took possession of my entire being. Then the visions vanished, leaving me in a pit of nothingness.

24

In the Realm of Coral

The next day I woke feeling unexpectedly clear-headed. To my great surprise, I was in my own cabin. No doubt my companions had also been returned to theirs without being any more aware of the how of it than I was. They did not know what had happened in the night any better than I did, and to resolve the mystery I could only look to whatever the future might bring.

Then I thought I would try to leave my cabin. Was I once again free or still a prisoner? I was absolutely free. I opened my door, headed along the walkways until I reached the central staircase and climbed up. The hatches, which had been closed the previous day, were now open. I emerged on to the platform.

I found Ned Land and Conseil waiting for me. I plied them with questions. They knew nothing. They had fallen into a heavy sleep and remembered nothing. They had been very surprised to wake up in their own cabin.

The *Nautilus* seemed as silent and mysterious as ever. She had surfaced and was moving at a moderate speed. Nothing on board appeared to have changed.

Ned Land was scouring the sea with those keen eyes of his. It was an empty expanse. He sighted nothing new on the horizon, not a sail to be seen, and no land. A moderate westerly wind was blowing gustily, and long waves, combed white by the breeze, made the vessel roll heavily.

Having replaced the air inside, the *Nautilus* dived, then maintained an average depth of 15 metres so that she could resurface quickly, a manoeuvre which, against her normal practice, was repeated several times during that day, which was 19 January. The first officer would then go out on to the platform, and his customary declaration would sound throughout the ship.

Captain Nemo did not reappear. Of the crew on board I saw only the stony-faced steward, who served me with his usual meticulous – and silent – efficiency.

Around two in the afternoon, I was in the Great Saloon, busily putting my notes in order, when the captain opened the door and walked in. I bade him good day. He returned the greeting with an imperceptible nod but did not say a word. I went back to my work, hoping he might throw light on the events of the previous night. But he did not. I thought he looked tired: his red-rimmed eyes had not been refreshed by sleep, and his face wore an expression of infinite sadness, of profound dejection. He paced up and down, sat then stood up again, taking a book from a random shelf then replacing it, checked the readings of his instruments without writing them down as he always did and generally seemed incapable of settling in any one place.

Eventually, he joined me and said:

'Are you a medical man, professor?'

I was not expecting the question and looked at him for a moment or two without replying.

'Are you a doctor?' he repeated. 'A number of your colleagues studied medicine, Gratiolet, Moquin-Tandon and various others.'

'As a matter of fact,' I said, 'I am a doctor and have worked as a resident hospital physician. I practised for several years before moving to the Museum.'

'Good.'

My answer had evidently satisfied Captain Nemo. But not knowing what he was driving at, I waited for him to follow up with further questions, determined that I would answer them as required by circumstances.

'Professor Aronnax,' said the captain, 'would you agree to treat one of my men?'

'One of your crew is ill?'

'Yes.'

'I shall follow you.'

'This way.'

I will confess that my heart was racing. I did not know why but I felt there was a connection between this man's illness and the previous day's events. It was a mystery which occupied me as least as much as the illness.

Captain Nemo led me to the stern of the *Nautilus* and showed me into a cabin situated close to the crew's quarters.

On a bed lay a man of about forty, with energetic features, a true Anglo-Saxon type. I leaned over him. He was not just ill, he had been wounded. His head, wrapped in blood-soaked bandages, was propped up on two pillows. I undid the bandage while the patient, looking at me with large, staring eyes, let me get on with it without a murmur of complaint.

It was a ghastly wound. His skull had been broken open by a blunt instrument, leaving part of the brain exposed and the cerebral matter badly damaged. Clots of blood had formed in the diffluent swelling, which had turned browny-red. The brain had been both bruised and concussed. The man's breathing was slow, and at intervals muscular spasms made his face twitch. The cerebral phlegmasia was massive. He had lost all feeling, and all his movements were paralysed.

I felt his pulse, which was intermittent. The extremities of his limbs were already growing cold. I saw that death was not far away, and that there seemed nothing I could do to halt it. After applying a fresh dressing, I rebandaged his head and turned to Captain Nemo.

'How did this man come by such an injury?' I asked.

'That is of no importance,' replied the captain evasively. 'The *Nautilus* was involved in a collision during which a lever on the engine flew off and struck him. My first officer was standing next to him, and this man threw himself forward and took the blow instead of his brother. It's very simple: a man laid down his life for his friend. That is our law on the *Nautilus*. But what is your opinion of his condition?'

I hesitated before I spoke.

'You may speak freely,' said the captain. 'He does not speak French.'

I gave the injured sailor one last look then said:

'This man will be dead within two hours.'

'Can nothing be done to save him?'

'Nothing.'

Captain Nemo's knuckles turned white, and tears glistened in eyes which I never thought were capable of weeping.

I stood for a few minutes longer, looking down at the injured man, whose life was gradually slipping away. His pallor was further accentuated by the electric glare bathing his death bed. I gazed at his intelligent face, furrowed by premature lines which had been drawn on it long ago by misfortune and perhaps poverty. I lingered, hoping to unlock the secret of his life in the last words that escaped his lips!

'There is no further need for you to stay, Professor Aronnax,' said Captain Nemo.

I left Captain Nemo in the dying man's cabin and returned to mine, deeply moved by what had happened. All day I was troubled by sinister presentiments. That night I slept badly and between frequently interrupted dreams I seemed to hear a distant moaning, which sounded like a funeral chant. Was it the prayer for the dead being murmured in their tongue, which I did not understand?

The following morning, I went up on deck. Captain Nemo was already there. The moment he saw me, he came over.

'Professor Aronnax,' he said, 'would you care to go exploring under water today?'

'With my companions?' I asked.

'If they so wish.'

'We await your orders, captain.'

'In that case, please get into your diving suits.'

Nothing more was said about the dying, or rather dead, man. I rejoined Ned Land and Conseil. I told them about Captain Nemo's proposal. Conseil accepted with alacrity, and this time the Canadian seemed very eager to come too.

It was eight o'clock in the morning. At 8.30, we were suited up for this new expedition, each carrying lighting and breathing equipment. The double doors opened and, accompanied by Captain Nemo and a dozen members of the crew, we set foot on the sea-bed where the *Nautilus* had come to rest at a depth of 10 metres.

A shallow incline led down to an uneven plateau some 15 fathoms down. This terrain was completely different from the one I had explored on the first expedition I had made under the waters of the Pacific. Here, there was no fine sand, no underwater meadows, no marine forest. But the wonderful place to which Captain Nemo led us that day was immediately familiar to me. It was the Realm of Coral!

In the branch of zoophytes and the class of *alcyonacea* is to be found the order of *gorgonidae* formed by the three groups: gorgonians, isididae and corallidae. It is to the last that coral belongs. It is a curious substance which has been variously classified as part of all three kingdoms, animal, mineral and vegetable. Believed to have medicinal properties in the ancient world, used as jewelry in modern times, it was not until 1694 that Peysonnel,[48] of Marseille, placed it definitively in the animal kingdom.

Coral consists of colonies of tiny animals living on a polypary, which is brittle and stony by nature. Polyps have a single parent, which produces them by budding. All have their own separate existence while at the same time being part of the collective life around them: a kind of natural socialism, as it were. I was familiar with the latest work published on this strange zoophyte, which develops tree-like forms and becomes mineralized, as naturalists have rightly shown. Nothing could have fascinated me more than to be able to examine one of these petrified forests planted by nature at the bottom of the ocean.

The Ruhmkorff lamps were turned on, and we followed a bank of coral which was still growing and will in time close off this part of the Indian Ocean. The way was lined with intricate bush-like growths formed by tangled shrubberies covered in masses of small star-shaped flowers with white stripes. But unlike land-based plants, these structures, which anchored themselves to the rocks of the sea-bed, all grow top down.

Our lamps produced countless delightful effects as they played on the vividly coloured branches. I thought I saw the jelly-like, cylindrical tubes wave in the current. I was tempted to pick their fresh corolla with their delicate tentacles, some fully open and others only just emerging, while small, quick-finned fish brushed past them like flights of birds. But if my hand strayed anywhere near those living flowers, which were so sensitive, the whole colony was immediately alerted. The white corolla withdrew into their red calyx, the flowers vanished before my eyes, and the whole structure turned into a solid mass of small stony excrescences.

Chance had brought me close to the most precious specimens of this zoophyte. This coral was at least the equal of that which is collected in the Mediterranean, off the coasts of France, Italy and North Africa. Its colours fully justified the poetic names – *fleur de sang* and *écume de sang* – which the coral trade has given to the finest examples. Coral fetches up to 500 francs a kilo, and the seas here conceal enough booty to make any number of coral fishers very rich. This valuable material, often combined with other polyparies, had formed compact, matted aggregations called *macciota*, on which I saw admirable specimens of pink coral.

Soon the bush-like structures grew closer together, and the branched forms became taller. Petrified forests and long architectural spans of the most fanciful kind opened before us. Captain Nemo led us into a dark arcade, which sloped down gently until we were at a depth of 100 metres. At times, the light of our Ruhmkorff coils produced magical effects, catching the scalloped edges of the natural arches and the pendentives hanging down like chandeliers, which sparkled with flashes of brilliance. Between the coral structures I noticed other, no less strange polyps: melites and irises with jointed branches, then a few tufts of coralline, some green, others red, which looked like algae preserved in calcareous salts. After much debate, naturalists have definitively put these in the vegetable kingdom. But as a scientist once observed: 'this is perhaps the defining point at which life springs mysteriously from the sleep of stone without quite snapping the thread that links it to its primitive origins'.[49]

In due course, after walking for two hours, we were about 300 metres down, the extreme limit at which coral begins to grow. But at that depth, there were no isolated bushes or modest thickets of low undergrowth, nothing but an immense forest, huge forms of mineral vegetation and enormous petrified trees connected by elegant garlands of feather coral, the liana of the sea, all clad in colours and reflecting light. We passed unimpeded beneath their high branches, which disappeared into the watery gloom above, while under our feet pipe coral, meandrines, astreas, fungoid corals and caryophilli formed a carpet of flowers strewn with dazzling gems.

It was an indescribable sight! Oh, if only we had been able to communicate what we felt! Why had we to be imprisoned inside masks of metal and glass? Why were we prevented from speaking to each other! Ah, if only we were able to live like the fish that swam in the water – or rather, more like the amphibians, which are able for long periods to wander at will through the dual domains of land and sea!

Then we saw that Captain Nemo had halted. My two companions and I came to a standstill, and as I turned I saw that his men had formed a semicircle around him. Looking more closely, I noticed that four of them were carrying something oblong in shape on their shoulders.

We had reached the middle of a large clearing ringed by the tall coral branches of the underwater forest. Our lamps cast something close to twilight over the area and lengthened the shadows on the sea-bed considerably. On the fringes of the clearing, the gloom became complete again, broken only by occasional flashes where the light reflected off the sharp bony surfaces of the coral.

Ned Land and Conseil were standing next to me. As we watched, it crossed my mind that I was about to witness something very strange. Glancing down at the sea-floor, I noticed that it was marked here and there by slight swellings encrusted with calcareous deposits and arranged in an orderly fashion, indicating the work of human hands.

At the centre of the clearing, on a cairn of crudely heaped stones, was a coral cross, the two long arms of which looked as if they might have been made of petrified blood.

At a sign from Captain Nemo, one of the men stepped

forward, halted a few feet short of the cross and began digging
a hole with a pick-axe which he took from his belt.

Then I understood! The clearing was a cemetery, the hole
was a grave, and the oblong object was the body of the man
who had died during the night. Captain Nemo and his crew
had come to bury their comrade in this common resting place
at the bottom of this inaccessible ocean.

Never had my mind been so deeply stirred! Never had such
startling thoughts taken over my brain so completely! I did not
wish to look at what my eyes were seeing!

Meanwhile the grave was slowly being dug. Fish fled in all
directions from their disturbed habitat. I heard the calcareous
sea-bed ring as the iron pickaxe struck. It gave off occasional
sparks when it encountered a stray flint which had found its
way to the bottom of the sea. The hole became longer and
wider, and soon it was deep enough to receive the body.

The bearers then approached. The corpse, wrapped in a
shroud made of white byssus, was lowered into its watery
tomb. Captain Nemo, his arms folded across his chest, together
with all the friends who had been loved by the dead man, knelt
in prayer . . . My two companions and I held our heads rever-
ently bowed.

The grave was then filled with the spoil dug from the ground
and left as a low mound.

When it was all over, Captain Nemo and his men got to their
feet, then each stepped forward close to the tomb, knelt again
and held out one hand as a gesture of eternal farewell . . .

After this the funeral party set off back to the *Nautilus*,
marching under the canopy of the forest, though the thickets,
past coral bushes and climbing all the way.

Finally we made out the lights of the vessel, its searchlight
beam guiding us to the *Nautilus*. By one o'clock we were back.

As soon as I had changed, I went up on to the platform and,
haunted by the most oppressive thoughts, I sat down next to
the searchlight.

Captain Nemo joined me. I stood up saying:

'Am I right in thinking that the man died during the night,
as I predicted?'

'Yes, professor,' said Captain Nemo.

'And he is now resting near his companions in that coral cemetery?'

'Yes, forgotten by all, but not by us! We dig the grave and leave it to the polyps to seal up it for eternity!'

And abruptly he covered his face in his clenched fists, vainly trying to choke back a sob. Then he went on:

'It's our resting place, a place of peace, several hundred feet below the surface of the water!'

'There at least, captain, your dead sleep beyond the reach of sharks.'

'Indeed, professor,' Captain Nemo replied solemnly, 'beyond the reach of sharks – and men!'

PART TWO

VINGT MILLE LIEUES

SOUS

LES MERS

DEUXIEME PARTIE

I
The Indian Ocean

Here begins the second part of our voyage under the sea. The first ended with the moving scene in the coral cemetery which made such an indelible impression on my mind. It was now clear that the entire life of Captain Nemo was lived in the depths of the vast ocean, and that everything, even his final resting place, had been prepared in its most inaccessible heart. The final sleep of those sailors of the *Nautilus*, friends as closely bound to each other in death as they had been in life, would not be disturbed by any monster of the deep – 'nor by any man,' the captain had added.

Always the same fierce, implacable mistrust of human society!

For my part, I was no longer prepared to accept the theories which satisfied Conseil. That worthy fellow persisted in seeing the Master of the *Nautilus* as one of those unsung scientists who respond with contempt to humanity's indifference to them. He saw him as a misunderstood genius who had fled the disappointments of society and found refuge in inaccessible regions where he could be free to follow his nature. But to my mind, this hypothesis explained only one facet of the captain's character.

For the mystery of the previous night, when we had been neutralized by both prison and drugs, the forceful way the captain wrenched my telescope away just as I was raising it to scan the horizon, the crewman's fatal injury, which was caused by some unexplained accident involving the *Nautilus*, all of this directed me along a natural train of thought. No! Captain Nemo was not just running away from people! His magnificent vessel did not just serve his freedom-loving instincts but also perhaps some terrible need for revenge!

At that point, nothing was clear in my mind. I still could see no more than a few gleams in the dark. But now this account must proceed by following, as it were, the dictates of events.

We had no reason to be loyal to Captain Nemo. He knew that we could not escape from the *Nautilus*. We had not even given our word not to try. We were not honour-bound to remain incarcerated. We were plain captives, prisoners euphemistically given the courtesy title of 'passengers'. Even so, Ned Land had not given up all hope of recovering his freedom, and it was clear that he would take the very first opportunity that came along to escape. I would unquestionably have done likewise. Yet it was not without a pang of regret that I would go, taking with me all that the captain's generosity had allowed us to see of the mysteries of the *Nautilus*. Should we have hated or admired him? Was he oppressor or oppressed? And to be frank, before parting company with him for ever, I would have liked to complete our journey around the world under the sea which had begun so magnificently. I wanted to see what no other man had yet seen, even if my insatiable thirst for knowledge were to cost me my life! What had I learned thus far? Nothing, or almost nothing, for we had covered only 6,000 leagues of the Pacific!

Yet at the same time I knew that the *Nautilus* would eventually approach inhabited land and that if any chance of escape presented itself, it would be cruel to sacrifice my companions to my passion for discovery. I would have to follow them, even lead them perhaps. But would the opportunity ever arise? As a man divested of his freedom to act, I hoped it would. But as a scientist, a man of curiosity, I feared it too.

At noon on that day, 21 January 1868, the first officer went up to measure the height of the sun. I climbed out on to the platform, lit a cigar and watched while he carried out his duties. It was obvious that he did not understand French, for several times I made remarks out loud which should have produced some involuntary reaction if he had understood them, but he remained unresponsive and silent.

While he took his readings with the sextant, one of the

sailors – the powerfully built one who had been with us on our first outing under the sea to Crespo Island – came to clean the glass of the searchlight. This led me to examine its mechanism more closely, for its power was increased a hundredfold by circular lenses similar to those found in lighthouses, which kept the beam focused as required. The lamp itself was designed to maximize its luminous power. Its light was generated in a vacuum, which regulated its steadiness and intensity. The vacuum also prolonged the life of the graphite points between which the luminous arc was produced. This was an important consideration, for Captain Nemo could not have replaced them easily. But by this arrangement, the wear and tear on them was negligible.

While the *Nautilus* was preparing to resume her progress under water, I went below to the Great Saloon. The hatches were closed, and our course was set due west.

We were then travelling through the waters of the Indian Ocean, a vast expanse of empty sea with an area of 550 million hectares and water so clear that anyone looking down on its surface would become dizzy. The *Nautilus* generally sailed between 100 and 200 metres under the water and could maintain that depth for a good few days. To anyone without my boundless love of the sea, the hours must have seemed very long and monotonous indeed. But my daily visits to the platform to refill my lungs with the health-giving air of the sea, the wonders of those rich waters seen through the glass viewing panels in the Great Saloon, the time spent reading books in the library and writing up these memoirs, all filled each and every hour and left me no time to feel weary or bored.

Our health remained in a most satisfactory state. The ship's fare suited us very well, and, speaking personally, I could have done without the variations which Ned Land, in a spirit of rebellion, found ways of introducing. Since the temperature remained constant, there were no colds to catch. In any case, the madrepore, *dendrophillia ramea*, known in Provence as sea fennel, a supply of which was carried on board, would have yielded tender polyps from which we could have prepared an effective remedy for coughs.

Over a period of some days, we saw large numbers of aquatic

birds: palmipeds, gulls and sea mews. Some were shot by skilled marksmen and, when prepared in different ways for the pot, served as flavoursome waterfowl. Among the large long-haul birds which are carried on the wind far from land and settle on the water to recover from the fatigue of flying, I saw magnificent albatrosses, which are members of the family of longipennates and whose raucous cry resembles the braying of an ass. The family of totipalmates was represented by fleet-winged frigate birds, which swooped down and caught fish on the surface, and by numerous tropic birds (or boatswain birds), some with red bills and as large as pigeons, whose white plumage is tinged with a pink that contrasts vividly with the dark colour of their wings.

The *Nautilus*'s nets landed several species of marine turtles of the hawkbill family, with dome-shaped shells that are much sought after. These reptiles, which are good divers, can remain for long periods under water by closing fleshy valves situated at the front end of their nostrils. When they were caught, some of these hawkbills were asleep in their shells, safe from marine animals. The meat of these turtles is of indifferent quality, but their eggs make an excellent meal.

As to fish, they never ceased to fill us with admiration when we watched them through the open glass panels and could observe the secrets of their aquatic life. I noticed several species which I had not been able to observe until then.

I will give a special mention to the *ostraciidae* or box-fish, native to the Red Sea, the Indian Ocean and the part of the ocean off Central America. Like turtles, armadillos, sea urchins and crustaceans, these fish are protected by a shell which is neither cretaceous nor lapideous but in fact bony. Some take the form of a solid triangle, while others are quadrangular in shape. Among the triangular variety I saw some which were 5 centimetres long, wholesome to eat and exquisitely flavoured, with brown tails and yellow fins. I would recommend that they be acclimatized to fresh water, where, in fact, a number of saltwater fish can thrive happily. I will also mention the quadrangular box-fish, which have four large dorsal tubercles; speckled box-fish, with white spots on the underside of its body, which can be kept in captivity, like birds; trigonias, which have spines formed by excrescences of their bony exoskeletons and emit the strange grunts which have earned them the name of 'sea-pig'; and dromedaries, with distinctive cone-shaped protuberances, which make hard, tough eating.

Also from the daily notes taken by Conseil, I can add certain puffers of the tetrodon family native to those seas: *tetrodon spengleri*, with red backs and white chests and three character-istic longitudinal rows of filaments; electric fish, 7 inches long, all with vivid liveries. Then, as examples of other families: ovals, which are egg-shaped, dark brown with white bands and no tails; *diodontidae*, rightly called porcupinefish, which have quills and can puff themselves up so that they look like balloons bristling with spines; sea-horses, which are found in oceans everywhere; pegasus seamoths, with elongated snouts and enlarged, wing-shaped pectoral fins that allow them, if not to fly, at least to glide through the air; spatulate pigeons, with tails covered with scaly rings; long-jawed spiny eels, an excellent food fish, 25 centimetres long and brightly coloured; pale-yellow dragonets with heads like rasps; myriads of black-striped flying blennies, with long pectoral fins by means of which they skip over the surface of the sea at amazing speeds; delicious velifers, which are able to raise their fins like sails to take advantage of favourable currents; magnificent kurtus, on which nature has lavished yellow, cerulean blue, silver and gold; trichoptera, with wings made of filaments; *cottidae*, mud-coloured and emitting a rustling sound; sea robins, whose liver is supposedly poisonous; bodians which have moveable flaps over their eyes; and not least banded bellows fish, with a long tubular snout, the flycatchers of the ocean, armed with a firing mechanism undreamed of by Chassepot and Remington with which they shoot insects by hit-ting them with a small drop of water

In the eighty-ninth genus of Lacépède's classification of fish, which belongs to the second sub-class of bony fish, which are characterized by opercula and bronchial membranes, I noticed the scorpion fish, which has 'stings' in the form of spines on its head and only one dorsal fin: these animals are or are not covered with scales, according to which sub-class they belong to. This second sub-genus also supplied us with examples of didactyls 15 or 20 centimetres long, having yellow stripes and spectacularly misshapen heads. The first sub-genus provided several examples of a bizarre fish aptly named the 'sea-toad'. It has a large head, which may have a cavity of deep sinuses, or else it is bloated with protuberances. Bristling with spines and dotted with nodules, it also has malformed, very ugly horns. Its whole body and tail are graced with calluses. Its sting is dangerous. It is altogether repulsive and quite disgusting.

Between 21 and 23 January the *Nautilus* proceeded at a rate of up to 250 leagues every twenty-four hours, or 540 miles a day at an average speed of 22 knots. We were able to identify all these varieties of fish as we passed because they were attracted by our electric lights and tried to swim along with us. Most were unable to keep up with our speed and dropped behind. But a few succeeded in staying with the *Nautilus* for some time.

On the morning of the 24th, at latitude 12° 5' south and longitude 94° 33' east, we sighted Keeling Island, a madreporian atoll with admirable coconut groves which was visited by Charles Darwin and Captain Fitzroy. The *Nautilus* sailed past the shores of this desert island at no great distance. Her nets dragged up numerous specimens of polyps and echinoderms plus curious shells from the branch of molluscs. A few examples of varieties of smaller dolphins helped swell Captain Nemo's precious store of treasures, to which I further added a punctiferous astraea, a kind of parasitic polypary attached to a shell.

Soon Keeling Island dropped below the horizon, and a north-westerly course was set towards the tip of the Indian peninsula.

'Ah! Civilized countries!' Ned Land said to me that day. 'Much better than those Papuan islands, where a man comes across more savages than deer. On the Indian sub-continent, professor, there are roads, railways and English, French and Hindu towns. You can't go 5 miles without meeting a fellow countryman. Look, hasn't the moment come to forget all about being polite to Captain Nemo and jump ship?'

'No, Ned,' I said very firmly. 'Let's run before the wind, as you sailors say. The *Nautilus* is heading back towards inhabited land. She's making for Europe, so let her take us there. Once in home waters, we'll see then what is best and safe to do. Besides, I don't expect Captain Nemo will let us go hunting on the shores of Malabar or Coromandel as we did in the forests of New Guinea.'

'But couldn't we do it without asking his permission?'

I did not answer the Canadian. I did not want an argument. Basically, I was committed to the idea of exhausting the vagaries of the fate which had brought me on board the *Nautilus*.

After we passed Keeling Island, our overall speed dropped. Our progress also became less predictable, and on occasions we descended to very great depths. Several times we used the directional fins, which were operated from the inside by levers that set them at oblique angles to the water line. We maintained the dive for up to 2 or 3 kilometres but never once ascertained the exact depth of the Indian Ocean, which soundings of 13,000 metres have not plumbed. As for the temperature at such levels, the thermometer gave a constant reading of 4 degrees above zero. I also noted that the water nearer the surface was invariably colder in shallow waters than on the high seas.

On 25 January, the sea being absolutely empty, the *Nautilus* remained on the surface all day, churning the water with her powerful propeller and sending spray up into the air to a great height. How, in these conditions, could she not have been mistaken for some large cetacean? I spent three-quarters of the day on the platform, just watching the sea. There was nothing on the horizon except, at around four in the afternoon, a long steamship sailing west on an opposite tack. Its masts were visible for a moment, but the vessel could not have seen the *Nautilus*, too low in the water. I thought the steamer must belong to the Peninsular and Orient Line, which runs a regular service between Ceylon and Sydney, calling in at King George Sound and Melbourne.

At five o'clock, just before the brief twilight that connects day and night in the tropics, Conseil and I were amazed by a curious sight.

Now, according to the Ancients, there is a fascinating creature which brings luck to anyone who encounters it. Aristotle,

Athenaeus, Pliny and Oppian all studied its habits and combed the poetics of the most learned men of Greece and Italy for references to it. They called it variously *Nautilus* and *Pompylius*. But modern science has not adopted their terminology, and this mollusc is now known as the argonaut.

Anyone who had asked Conseil would have learned from him that the branch of molluscs is divided into five classes; that the first class – the cephalopods – contains individuals which may or may not have shells, and comprises two families, the *dibranchiata* and the *tetrabranchiata*, which differ in the number of their gills; and that the family of *dibranchiata* is made up of three types, argonaut, squid and cuttlefish, while the *tetrabranchiata* has only one, the nautilus. And if, in the light of this nomenclature, some argumentative person were to confuse the argonaut, which is acetabuliferous and has suckers, with the nautilus, which is tentaculiferous and has tentacles – he would have had no excuse whatsoever.

Be that as it may, there was now a flotilla of these argonauts proceeding over the surface of the ocean. We counted several hundred of them. They belonged to the species of tuberculate argonauts unique to the seas of India.

These graceful molluscs travel backwards by means of a locomotive tube which expels water they have taken in. Of their eight tentacles, six, which are long and thin, float on the water, while the remaining two, curved and palmate, are hoisted into the wind to form a light sail. I had a clear view of their spiral, ribbed shells, which Cuvier rightly likens to the shape of an elegant shallop or launch – and a boat it undoubtedly is. Its shell transports the animal which secreted it, though the animal itself is not attached to it.

'The argonaut is free to leave its shell,' I said to Conseil, 'but never does.'

'Then it's just like Captain Nemo,' he observed wryly. 'And for that reason, he would have been better advised to name his ship the *Argonaut*.'

For about an hour the *Nautilus* sailed through this shoal of molluscs. Then for some reason they suddenly took fright. As if a signal had been given, all the sails were quickly furled; the

twin arms were folded, the bodies contracted as the shells
turned upside down and shifted their centre of gravity, and the
entire flotilla sank beneath the waves. It was instantaneous,
and no ships in a naval squadron ever manoeuvred with such
precision.

At that same moment, night fell abruptly, and the waves,
barely ruffled by the breeze, passed gently under the wales of
the *Nautilus*.

The following day, 26 January, we crossed the equator at
the 82nd meridian and entered the northern hemisphere.

During the day, a fearsome cohort of sharks formed an
escort for us. These terrible animals abound in these waters
and make them dangerous. They were Phillipian sharks, brown
on the back and whitish underneath and equipped with eleven
rows of teeth; 'one-eyed' sharks, with a neck that is marked by
a large patch of black ringed with white that looks like an
eye; and Isabella sharks, which have rounded snouts peppered
with dark dots. These powerful creatures often hurled themselves against the glass panels of the Great Saloon with rather
alarming violence. When this happened, Ned Land was beside
himself. He wanted to go up to the surface and harpoon these
monsters, in particular certain gummy sharks, whose jaws are
lined with teeth laid out as in a mosaic, and large tiger sharks
5 metres long which provoked him with unusual persistence.
But soon the *Nautilus* increased her speed and quickly outdis-
tanced even the fastest of these sharks.

On 27 January, at the entrance to the vast Bay of Bengal, we
met more than once with a sinister sight: dead bodies floating on the sea. They were corpses from Indian cities, brought
by the Ganges down to the sea, which vultures, the only
grave-diggers in those parts, had not been able to eat up. But
there was no shortage of sharks to help them with their funeral
labours.

Around seven in the evening, the half-submerged *Nautilus*
sailed into a milky sea. As far as the eye could see, the ocean
appeared to have been turned into milk. Was it an effect of the
moon's light? No, because the moon was new, hardly two days
old, and hung below the horizon, where it still caught the rays

of the sun. The whole sky, though lit by the stars, seemed black in contrast with the whiteness of the water.

Conseil could hardly believe his eyes and asked me about the causes of this inexplicable phenomenon. Fortunately I was able to give him an answer.

'This is what is called a "milk sea",' I said, 'a wide expanse of white water frequently occurring off the coasts of Amboyna and in this part of the world.'

'But,' asked Conseil, 'is monsieur able to enlighten me as to the cause which produces this effect? I don't imagine the water has really been changed to milk?'

'No it has not. This whiteness which so amazes you is due merely to the presence of myriads of infusoria, which are in fact a kind of tiny glow worm, gelatinous, colourless, no thicker than a hair and less than a fifth of a millimetre long. These creatures can combine and then they may cover an area of several leagues.'

'Several leagues?' said Conseil.

'Absolutely – and don't even try to estimate the number of these infusoria! You couldn't do it. Because, unless I am very much mistaken, some ships have sailed across these "milk seas" for more than 40 miles.'

I have no idea if Conseil heeded my advice, but he seemed to surrender to deep thoughts, probably in an attempt to calculate how many fifths of one millimetre there are in 40 square miles. Meanwhile, I continued to observe the phenomenon. For several hours, the *Nautilus*'s prow continued to slice through the whitish waves, and I noticed that she made no noise as she moved over this soapy water, as though she were skimming over the swathes of spume in bays which are caused by the action of currents and counter-currents.

Around midnight, the sea suddenly resumed its normal appearance. But behind us, clear to the horizon, the sky reflected the whiteness of the water and seemed for some time to shimmer with the promise of an aurora borealis.

2

A Fresh Invitation from Captain Nemo

At noon on 28 February, when the *Nautilus* resurfaced at latitude 9° 4' north, she was in sight of land 8 miles to the west. All I saw at first was a range of mountains about 2,000 feet high, their outline being very irregular. When our position had been taken, I returned to the Great Saloon and checked it against the entries on the planisphere. I realized that we were within closing distance of Ceylon, that pearl which hangs from the lower ear lobe of the Indian peninsula.

I turned to the library's shelves in search of a book about the island, one of the most fertile on the earth's surface. I came across a volume by H. C. Sirr, Esq., entitled *Ceylon and the Cingalese*.[1] Returning to the Great Saloon, I noted some basic facts about Ceylon, to which Antiquity gave so many names. It is situated between latitude 5° 55' and 9° 49' north and longitude 79° 42' and 82° 4' east of the Greenwich meridian; it is 175,000 miles long and 150 miles broad at its widest point; its circumference is 900 miles; its surface area is 24,448 square miles, making it slightly smaller than Ireland.

At this point, Captain Nemo and his first officer walked in. The captain glanced at the planisphere, then turned to me.

'The island of Ceylon,' he observed, 'is a land famous for its pearl fishing. Professor Aronnax, would you care to see one of its pearl-fishing beds?'

'I should indeed, captain!'

'Good. It will not be difficult. We will see the fishing beds, but we will not see any pearl fishers. The annual harvest has not yet started. But that does not signify. I shall give the order to stand in to the Gulf of Manaar. We shall reach it sometime during the night.'

The captain spoke a few words to his first officer, who left the room at once. Soon the *Nautilus* returned into its liquid element, and the gauge indicated that she was holding a depth of 30 feet.

I tried to locate this Gulf of Manaar on the map and found it at the 9th parallel, on the north-west coast of Ceylon. It was formed by a long arm extending from the small Island of Manaar. To get there meant travelling up the entire west coast of Ceylon.

'Professor,' said Captain Nemo, 'pearls are fished in the Bay of Bengal, in the seas of India, China and Japan, in the waters of South America, the Gulf of Panama and the Gulf of California. But the finest pearls are those obtained from the oyster beds of Ceylon. We shall be arriving a little too early, however. The pearl-fishers foregather in the Gulf of Manaar only in the month of March. There, for thirty days, 300 boats are busy making the most of the lucrative treasures of the sea. There are ten oarsmen in each boat and ten divers. The latter, divided into two groups, take turns diving and go down to a depth of 12 metres using a heavy stone gripped between their feet, which is attached to the boat by a length of rope.'

'So the same primitive technique is still in use?'

'It is indeed,' answered Captain Nemo, 'although these fishing grounds belong to the most industrious people on the globe, I mean the English, to whom they were granted by the Treaty of Amiens in 1802.'

'But it seems to me that the diving suit of the kind you have here on board would be very useful to them for their work.'

'True, for these unfortunate pearl-divers cannot remain under water for long. An Englishman named Percival,[2] in his account of his journey to Ceylon, mentions one *kafir* who could stay down for five minutes without coming up for air, but that seems hardly credible. Still, I know that some divers can stay down for fifty-seven seconds and the most skilful up to eighty-seven, but they are very exceptional, and once they are back in the boat the poor devils have water tinged with blood coming out of their ears and nose. I gather that the average time that divers can last is thirty seconds, during which they scuttle about filling a small net with all the oysters they can prise loose. But most of them do not live to any great age. Their sight goes, ulcers form around their eyes, they get sores on their bodies, and it is not rare for them to die of heart attacks on the sea-bed.'

'Yes,' I said, 'it's a hard life, and one that serves only the whims of the few. But tell me, captain, how many oysters can a boat collect in one day?'

'In the region of forty or fifty thousand. It is even said that in 1814, over a period of twenty days, the British government managed to harvest 76 million oysters using its own divers.'

'But at least,' I asked, 'I imagine that these divers are reasonably well paid?'

'Far from it, professor. In Panama, they earn just one dollar a week. More often than not they get one cent for every oyster with a pearl in it, and how many do they bring up that do not have pearls in them?'

'One cent for these poor people who make their masters rich! It's odious!'

'Quite, professor,' said Captain Nemo. 'But you and your companions shall visit the Manaar oyster beds, and if we are lucky and a few divers are already there, we shall be able to see them at work.'

'Very well, captain.'

'By the by, Professor Aronnax, you're not afraid of sharks, are you?'

'Sharks?' I exclaimed.

I couldn't see the point of the question.

'Well?' said Captain Nemo.

'I will confess, captain, that I have as yet only been on rather distant terms with that particular fish.'

'Every man on board the *Nautilus* is used to them,' replied Captain Nemo, 'and in time you will be too. Besides, we shall be armed and on our way there we might even get a chance to hunt a dogfish. They make very good hunting. Until tomorrow, then, professor, very early tomorrow morning.'

It was said in a relaxed tone of voice. Captain Nemo left the Great Saloon.

If you were invited to hunt bears in the Swiss mountains, you would say: 'Fine! Tomorrow we'll go hunting bears!' If you were invited to hunt lions on the plains of the Atlas Mountains or tigers in the jungles of India, you would say: 'Right oh! It looks like we're off tomorrow to take pot shots at lions or tigers!' But if somebody asks you to go hunting sharks in their natural element, you might perhaps feel inclined to think twice about it before accepting.

I confess I passed a hand over my brow and felt it break out in a cold sweat.

'Let's stop and consider for a moment,' said I to myself. 'Hunting otters in forests under water, as we did in the forest of Crespo Island, is one thing. But to go roaming around the ocean floor, when there is every chance of coming face to face with a shark, is another. I realize that in some countries, notably the Andaman Islands, the natives will not hesitate to go after a shark with just a knife in one hand and a noose in the other. But I also know many of those who confront those fearsome creatures do not come back alive! Besides, I am not a native and I think that, in this matter, a slight hesitation on my part would not be out of place.'

So there I was, dreaming of sharks with my head full of enormous jaws armed with multiple rows of teeth capable of cutting a man in two. I thought I could already feel the pain in my back. I found it hard to take, the casual manner in which the captain had issued his dire invitation! Anyone would have thought that we would be tracking down some harmless fox or other!

'At least,' said I to myself, 'Conseil won't want to go, and that will be my excuse for not accompanying the captain.'

As for Ned, I confess I did not feel as sure of his prudence. Danger, however great, always had attractions for his combative nature.

I went back to reading Sirr's book but found myself just turning the pages mechanically. Between the lines I kept seeing malevolently opened jaws.

Just then, Conseil and the Canadian came in, looking

relaxed, even delighted. They had no idea of what was in store for them.

'Well now, professor,' said Ned Land, 'your Captain Nemo, devil take the man, has just made us a very friendly proposal.'

'Oh!' I said. 'So you know!'

'Begging monsieur's pardon,' said Conseil, 'but the master of the *Nautilus* has asked us, along with monsieur, to visit the magnificent pearl-fishing grounds of Ceylon tomorrow. He issued the invitation in the friendliest spirit and behaved like a true gentleman.

'Did he say anything more?'

'No, professor,' replied the Canadian, 'except that he had already spoken to you about this little excursion.'

'So he has,' I said. 'But did he give you any details about . . .'

'No. But you will be coming with us, won't you, professor?'

'Me? Why, of course! I see that the idea appeals to you, Ned.'

'It does. It sounds interesting, very interesting.'

'And may be dangerous too,' I said insinuatingly.

'Dangerous?' said Ned Land. 'A straightforward stroll through a bed of oysters?'

Evidently Captain Nemo had not thought it necessary to put the idea of sharks into my companions' minds. I looked at them, feeling somewhat uncomfortable, as if one or both of them had already lost an arm or a leg. Should I tell them? Yes, of course. But I had no idea of where to begin.

'Would monsieur,' said Conseil, 'be so good as to give us some facts about pearl fishing?'

'You mean pearl fishing itself,' I asked, 'or about the conditions which . . .'

'About pearl fishing,' said the Canadian. 'Before going into the field, it is always a good idea to know how the land lies.'

'Very well. Sit down, friends, and I will tell you everything the Englishman Sirr has just taught me.'

Ned and Conseil both sat down on a divan, and immediately the Canadian asked me:

'Professor, what exactly is a pearl?'

'Well Ned,' I began, 'for poets, it is a tear shed by the ocean. For Orientals, it is a crystallized dewdrop; for ladies, it is an oblong-shaped jewel, with a hyaline lustre, made of mother-of-pearl, which they wear on their fingers, around their necks or in their ears; for the chemist, it is a mixture of phosphate and carbonate of lime with a small quantity of gelatine; and lastly, for the naturalist, it is merely a defective secretion from the organ which produces mother-of-pearl in certain bivalves.'

'Branch of molluscs,' said Conseil, 'class of acephalans, order of testacaeans.'

'Quite right! How clever you are, Conseil! Anyway, among these testacaeans, pearls are produced by the haliotis, the irises, the turbos, the tridacnae, the marine pinnae, in short by all the varieties which secrete mother-of-pearl, that is, the blue, bluish, purple and white material that lines the inside of their valves.'

'Does that go for mussels too?' asked the Canadian.

'Yes. Mussels in certain water courses in Scotland, Wales, Ireland, Saxony, Bohemia and France.'

'That's good!' said the Canadian. 'From now on, I'll watch out for them.'

'But,' I resumed, 'the mollusc which produces the best pearls by far is the pearl oyster, *meleagrina margaritifera*, otherwise known as the valuable pinctada. The pearl itself is simply a concretion of mother-of-pearl which accumulates in orbicular form. Either it is deposited on the shell of the oyster or it grows independently in the folds of the oyster's flesh. If deposited on the shell, it sticks fast to it; if it grows in the flesh, it is free to move. But inside every pearl there is a kernel of some hard material which may be a sterile ovule or a grain of sand, around which the nacreous matter accrues over a period of several years in a series of thin, concentric layers.'

'Are there sometimes several pearls in the same oyster?' asked Conseil.

'Yes indeed. There are some pearl oysters which are virtual pearl cases. It is even said that there was an oyster, though I am not inclined to believe it, which contained no fewer than 150 sharks.'

'Did you say 150 sharks?' cried Ned Land.

'Did I say sharks?' I exclaimed. 'I meant 150 pearls. Sharks would make no sense.'

'No indeed,' said Conseil. 'But perhaps monsieur would now tell us how pearls are extracted.'

'There are various techniques. Often, when the pearls stick to the valves, divers just remove them with their teeth. But most times, the pinctadas are spread out on mats made of the esparto grass which grows at the water's edge. In the air they die and after ten days they reach the required stage of putrefaction. They are then immersed in huge tanks of sea-water, after which they are opened and washed. Now begins the double task of cleaning and extraction. First the lamellas of mother-of-pearl are removed. These are known in the trade as "pure silvers", "mixed whites" and "mixed blacks" and are sold in 125 and 150 kilogramme boxes. Then the oyster's parenchyma is cut away, boiled and then sieved so that even the smallest pearls are recovered.'

'Does the price of pearls depend on their size?' asked Conseil.

'Not only on the size but also on their shape, *water*, or colour, and their *orient*, the silky, dappled lustre which makes them so delightful to the eye. The finest pearls are called virgin pearls or paragons. They are the ones which grow in the tissue of the molluscs. They are white, often pellucid, but sometimes have an opaline transparency, and are most often spherical or pear-shaped, like dewdrops, and these, being the most valuable, are sold individually. The pearls which stick to the oyster shells are less regular in size and shape and are sold by the pound. Lastly, lower-grade pearls are classed as small, go by the name of *seed pearls*, are sold by the load and are used mainly for embroidery work on church vestments and the like.'

'But all this work of separating the pearls according to size must be long and difficult,' said the Canadian.

'Not really. The task is done by means of eleven sieves or riddles, each having a different number of holes. Pearls that remain in sieves having between twenty and eighty holes, are the finest grade. Those which do not fall through sieves with 100 to 800 holes are second grade. Lastly the pearls which are riddled in sieves with 900 to 1,000 holes are all classed as *seeds*.'

'Ingenious,' said Conseil. 'So the separation and classification of pearls is done mechanically. And could monsieur also tell us how much the farming of pearl oyster beds is worth?'

'Going by Sirr's book,' I replied, 'the pearl-fishing grounds of Ceylon are leased for an annual sum of 3 million sharks.'

'Francs,' Conseil corrected me.

'Francs, of course! Three million francs,' I said. 'But I believe the beds do not bring in as much as they used to. The same is true of oyster fisheries in the Americas. During the reign of Charles V they generated 4 million francs, which has now fallen to two-thirds of that figure. All in all, the overall value of pearl fishing can be put at 9 million francs.'

'But is it not a fact that there are famous pearls which are worth a very great deal of money?'

'Quite true. It is said that Caesar gave Servilia a pearl valued at 120,000 francs in today's money.'

'I have even heard,' said the Canadian, 'that a certain lady in ancient times used to drink pearls dissolved in vinegar.'

'That was Cleopatra,' said Conseil.

'Must have tasted foul,' said Ned Land.

'Ghastly, Ned,' replied Conseil. 'Still, a tot of vinegar costing 1,500,000 francs is not to be sneezed at.'

'I'm sorry I was never that lady's husband,' said Ned Land, raising one arm in a threatening sort of way.

'Ned Land! Cleopatra's husband!' cried Conseil.

'Actually, Conseil, I was about to get married,' the Canadian answered earnestly, 'and it wasn't my fault if the whole thing fell through. I'd even bought my fiancée, Kat Tender, a pearl necklace, but she went and married somebody else. Well, that necklace didn't set me back more than a dollar fifty, even though – you can take it from me, professor – the pearls it was made of wouldn't have gone through the sieve with twenty holes!'

'But Ned,' I said with a laugh, 'they must have been artificial pearls, just hollow glass beads coated on the inside with essence of orient.'

'This essence of orient,' said the Canadian, 'can't come cheap.'

'Actually it hardly costs anything at all! It's just the silver material on the scales of a fish called a bleak, or ablet, which is collected in the water and preserved in ammonia. It has virtually no value.'

'Maybe that's why Kat Tender married somebody else,' replied Ned Land with a philosophical sigh.

'But returning to the subject of high-value pearls, I don't think any monarch ever possessed one that was finer than Captain Nemo's.'

'Monsieur means this one,' said Conseil, pointing to a magnificent pearl which was kept in its own case.

'Yes, that's the one, and I wouldn't be far wrong in valuing it at 2 million . . .'

'. . . francs!' said Conseil quickly.

'Quite,' I said, '2 million francs. And I'd wager that all it ever cost the captain was the trouble of picking it up.'

'Yes, and who is to say,' cried Ned, 'that when we're out strolling tomorrow we won't come across another one just like it!'

'Bosh!' said Conseil.

'And why not?'

'What use would millions of francs be to us on board the *Nautilus*?'

'On board ship, not much,' said Ned Land, 'but . . . elsewhere.'

'Oh, elsewhere!' said Conseil, shaking his head.

'No, Ned is right,' I said. 'For if one day we were to return to Europe or America with a pearl worth millions, it would put the seal of authenticity, not to mention a high value, on the story of our adventures.'

'I think so,' said the Canadian.

'But,' said Conseil, who invariably returned to the educational aspect of things, 'is pearl fishing dangerous?'

'No,' I said quickly, 'not if certain precautions are taken.'

'What's dangerous about it?' said Ned Land. 'Swallowing a few mouthfuls of salt water?'

'You're right, Ned. But by the way,' I went on, trying to catch Captain Nemo's off-hand tone, 'are you afraid of sharks?'

'Me? A harpooner by profession? I get paid to laugh at them!'

'Ah yes, but we won't be fishing for them with a swivel hook, hauling them on to the deck of a boat, cutting their tails off with an axe, slicing them open, ripping their hearts out and tossing them back into the sea!'

'You don't mean . . .'

'That's exactly right.'

'Under water?'

'Under water.'

'But with my trusty harpoon! Look, professor, a shark is not very well designed. A shark has to turn belly-up so that it can crunch you in its jaws and while it's doing that . . .'

Ned Land had a way of pronouncing the word 'crunch' that made the blood run cold.

'Well, and what about you, Conseil? What do you feel about sharks?'

'If I may speak frankly to monsieur . . .'

'Please do.'

'If monsieur is prepared to confront sharks,' he said, 'I don't see why his faithful servant cannot confront them with him!'

3

A Ten Million Franc Pearl

Night fell. I went to bed but slept badly. Sharks figured prominently in my dreams, and I concluded that the etymology which derives *requin* (the word for shark) from *requiem*, was as accurate as it was unhelpful.

At four in the morning, I was woken by the steward who had been specially allocated to me by Captain Nemo. I got up immediately, dressed and went directly to the Great Saloon.

Captain Nemo was waiting for me there.

'Professor Aronnax,' he said, 'are you ready to start?'

'Quite ready.'

'If you would follow me . . .'

'What about my two companions, captain?'

'They have been called and are waiting for us.'

'Are we not going to wear diving suits?' I asked.

'Not yet. I have not taken the *Nautilus* close in to the coast, and we are standing some way off the Manaar beds. But I have ordered the dinghy to be broken out. We will use it to reach our disembarkation point and spare ourselves a long trek. It will carry our diving apparatus, which we shall don before we begin our underwater exploration.'

I followed Captain Nemo to the central staircase and climbed the stairs which led up to the platform. Ned and Conseil were already there, delighted at the prospect of our 'day out'. Five sailors from the *Nautilus* were waiting for us, oars at the ready, in the dinghy, which had been tied up alongside.

It was still dark. Layers of cloud covered the sky and allowed only a few stars to be seen. I looked landwards but could only make out a fuzzy line that filled three-quarters of the horizon from south-west to north-west. During the night, the *Nautilus* had moved up the west coast of Ceylon and was now hove to west of the bay, or, more accurately, the gulf formed by the territory and the island of Manaar. There, beneath the dark waters, were the pinctada beds, the inexhaustible field of pearls, which extended over 20 miles.

Captain Nemo, Conseil, Ned Land and I got into the stern of the dinghy. The first mate took the helm, his four companions leaned on their oars, the line was cast off, and we pulled away.

The dinghy headed south. The oarsmen did not hurry. I noted that their strokes, plied vigorously in the water, kept to the ten-second rhythm which was the general practice followed by the crews of men o' war. In the intervals between strokes, water streamed off the oars and pattered on to the black surface, sizzling like splashes of molten lead. A light swell from seawards made the dinghy roll gently, and now and then the tops of waves slapped against our bow.

No one spoke. What was Captain Nemo thinking? Perhaps about the land he was approaching and maybe found too close for comfort? This was in stark contrast with the view of the Canadian, for whom it probably still seemed too far away. As for Conseil, he was just an interested bystander.

At about 5.30 a.m., the first rosy glimmers on the horizon showed the upper line of the coast more clearly. More or less flat in the east, it began to rise towards the south. We were still 5 miles from it, and the shoreline was hard to distinguish from the mist on the water. Between it and us the sea was empty. Not one boat, not a single diver. Complete and utter solitude filled this place where the pearl-fishers would soon congregate. As Captain Nemo had told me, we had come a month too early.

At six, it was suddenly day, with the abruptness peculiar to the tropics, where there is neither dawn worth the name nor twilight. The sun's rays broke through the clouds massed on the eastern horizon, and the golden orb rose quickly.

I could now clearly make out the land, with trees scattered here and there.

The dinghy pulled closer to Manaar Island, which formed a

round shape at its southern end. Captain Nemo stood up in the boat and was staring down into the sea.

At his signal, the anchor was dropped, but hardly any chain ran out because the water was not much more than a metre deep, for the bottom here was one of the highest points of the entire submerged pinctada grounds. But the mooring enabled the dinghy to ride the ebbing tide, which would have taken us out to sea.

'Well, here we are, Professor Aronnax,' said Captain Nemo. 'You see this narrow bay? It is to this place that within the month the pearl-fishing boats will come in large numbers, and in these waters that the brave divers will scour the beds. Fortunately, the bay is ideally suited to this kind of fishing. It is sheltered from the strongest winds, and the sea never gets angry, conditions which greatly favour the labours of the divers. We shall now put on our suits and then we can begin our visit.'

I did not respond but kept my eyes fixed nervously on these suspect waters. Assisted by the crew of the dinghy, I began to get into my heavy underwater suit. Captain Nemo and my two companions did likewise. None of the sailors from the *Nautilus* would be coming with us on our new undersea foray.

Soon we were imprisoned up to our necks in our rubber suits, with our breathing apparatus strapped on our backs. There were no Ruhmkorff lamps. Just before inserting my head into the copper helmet, I mentioned this to the captain.

'They would be of no use to us,' he replied. 'We shan't be going down to any great depth, and the sun's rays will be enough to light our way. Besides, it would not be prudent to take electric lanterns down into these waters. The light might attract unwanted attention from some dangerous denizen of these seas.'

As Captain Nemo was telling me this, I turned towards Conseil and Ned Land. But both friends had already donned their metal helmets and could neither hear me nor respond.

There was one final question I needed to put to the captain. 'Are we to be armed? Will we have guns?'

'Guns? What for? Do not mountain men attack bears armed only with a knife, and is not steel more dependable than lead? Here, take this strong blade. Slot it through your belt, and we'll be off.'

I looked at my companions. They were armed as we were, but Ned Land was also brandishing an enormous harpoon, which he had stowed aboard the dinghy before we left the *Nautilus*.

Then, following the captain's example, I allowed my head to be encased in the heavy copper sphere, and our air tanks were immediately turned on.

A moment later, the sailors helped us over the side of the dinghy one by one, and our feet were soon planted on smooth sand in a metre and a half of water. Captain Nemo gave a sign with one hand and, following his lead, we shuffled down a gentle incline and soon disappeared beneath the waves.

There, the ideas which had filled my mind faded completely. I became amazingly calm. The ease with which I moved only increased my confidence, and the strangeness of what I saw captured my imagination.

The sun's rays shining through the water were already giving us adequate light to see by. The smallest objects were clearly visible. After walking for ten minutes, we were 5 metres beneath the surface, and the sea-floor was more or less flat.

Following closely on our heels, like flocks of snipe on the wing, rose companies of inquisitive fish of the monopteral species, which have only a single tail fin. I recognized Javanese eels, virtual serpents with white bellies and 80 centimetres long, which could easily be mistaken for the conger but for their lateral gold lines. In the genus *stromateidae*, characterized by compressed, oval body shapes, I observed brilliantly coloured harvest fish with scythe-like dorsal fins, an edible fish which when dried and marinated makes an excellent dish called *karawade*; then there were tranquebars of the genus *apsiphoroides*, which have bodies sheathed in scaly armour made of eight longitudinal panels.

Meantime, the steady, gradually ascending sun lit the water more and more brightly. The sea-bed changed imperceptibly as we proceeded. Fine sand was succeeded by a causeway formed of smoothly rounded rocks covered with a carpet of molluscs and zoophytes. Among the specimens of these two branches, I observed windowpane oysters with delicate, asymmetrical valves which are a variety of *ostreidae* particular to the Red

Sea and the Indian Ocean; orange *lucunidae* with orbicular shells; subulate terebellums; a few Persian purpurae, which supplied the *Nautilus* with an excellent dye; spiky rock snails 15 centimetres long, which stand tall in the water like hands ready to grab you; cornigerous chanks bristling with spines; violet-hued *lingulidae*; duck bills, which are edible shellfish sold in large numbers in the markets of Hindustan; faintly luminescent pelagic clams; and, lastly, flabelliform oculinas, those splendid fan corals which form one of the richest of all kinds of marine afforestations.

In the midst of all these living plants and under the bowers of hydrophytes scurried ungainly legions of articulates, particularly toothed frogfish, whose carapace forms a slightly rounded triangle; a kind of robber crab found only in these parts; and hideous parthenope crabs, which so offend the eye. A no less repulsive creature I noticed several times was a huge crab observed by Charles Darwin, which nature has endowed with the instinct and strength to feed on coconuts: it climbs the palms growing on the shore, knocks down the coconuts so they fall and crack and then prises them open with its powerful claws. Here, in the clear water, it moved with incredible speed, while green turtles, of the kind frequently encountered off the coasts of Malabar, meandered quietly through the litter of rocks.

By seven o'clock, we were at last striding over the pinctada beds on which the pearl oysters reproduce by the million. These valuable molluscs clung to the stones, attaching themselves by the brown byssus which prevents them moving from their anchor point. This makes oysters inferior to mussels, which nature has permitted to have some freedom of movement.

The pinctada *meleagrina*, known as 'mother-of-pearl' oyster, with valves more or less equal in size, has a rounded shell made of thick, rough-surfaced chalky material. Some of them were laminated and furrowed with greenish bands which radiated out from the top. These were the shells of young oysters. The rest, with rough, black shells, were over ten years old and measured up to 15 centimetres across.

Captain Nemo pointed to this prodigious accumulation of pinctadas, and I realized I was looking at an inexhaustible mine, for nature's creative powers are greater than man's destructive instincts. Ned Land, faithfully following this instinct, wasted no time in collecting the finest specimens and put them in a net which he carried at his side.

But we could not linger. We had to follow the captain, who seemed to keep to paths known only to him. The sea-bed began to rise more steeply, and sometimes when I raised my arm it broke the surface of the water. Then the level of the beds fell away again unpredictably. Frequently we skirted rocks tapered like pyramidions. In their dark crannies, large crustaceans, craning up on their long legs like war machines, watched us with beady eyes, while under our feet crawled worms – syllids, glyceras, aricias and annelids – which reached out with their preposterously long antennae and probing barbels.

And then before us we saw the gaping mouth of a huge grotto formed by a picturesque jumble of rocks carpeted with long streamers of marine flora. At first, I thought the grotto was completely dark. Inside, the sun's rays seemed to be extinguished by degrees; the murky transparency was nothing more than drowned light.

Captain Nemo walked straight in. We followed. My eyes quickly adjusted to the relative gloom. I made out the whimsically contorted springings of the vault, which was supported by natural pillars solidly set on granite plinths, rather like the heavy columns of Tuscan architecture. Why was our enigmatic guide leading us to the back of this submarine crypt? I was soon to find out.

We reached the bottom of a pretty steep slope, where our feet encountered the floor of a circular well of sorts. There, Captain Nemo halted and pointed to an object I had not noticed.

It was an oyster of monstrous size, a giant tridacna, shaped like a stoop which could have held a whole lake of holy water, a basin more than 2 metres in diameter and thus larger than the one in the Great Saloon on board the *Nautilus*.

I stood close to this phenomenal mollusc. It was attached to a granite table by its byssus, and there it had grown in the isolation of the grotto's still waters. I judged its weight to be around 300 kilograms. An oyster this size would contain 15

'I stood close to this phenomenal mollusc'

kilos of meat, and it would take a gargantuan stomach to eat a dozen like this one!

Captain Nemo evidently knew of the existence of this bivalve. It was not the first time he had come to see it, and I thought that by bringing us to this spot he simply wanted to show us a curiosity of nature. I was wrong. Captain Nemo had a particular reason for checking on the present condition of this tridacna.

Both valves of the mollusc were partly open. Captain Nemo went up to it and thrust a knife between the shell halves to prop them open and prevent them from closing. Then with the other hand he lifted the fringed membrane which protected the creature.

There, between the layers of tissue, I saw a free pearl the size of a coconut. Its globular shape, its perfect translucence and admirable nacreous lustre made it a jewel beyond price. Impelled by curiosity, I reached out to take it in my hand and test its weight, to feel it! But the captain stopped me, gave a negative shake of the head and with a rapid movement of his hand retrieved the knife and allowed the two valves to snap shut.

Then I understood Captain Nemo's plan. By leaving the pearl buried in the tridacna's flesh, he was allowing it to continue to go on increasing in size. With every passing year, the mollusc's secretions added new concentric layers. Only he knew of this grotto where this wonderful 'fruit' of nature was 'ripening'; only he was, as it were, 'growing' it so that one day he could take it away and place it in his priceless museum. Perhaps, following the example of the Chinese and Indians, he had engineered the production of the pearl by inserting between the folds of the mollusc a piece of glass or metal which had slowly been covered in nacreous layers. Be that as it may, if I compared this pearl with all those I had previously seen and with those which glowed in the captain's collection, I concluded that it was worth a minimum of 10 million francs. It was a magnificent curiosity of nature, not a fabulously costly jewel, for I have yet to see a feminine ear capable of bearing its weight.

Our visit to the opulent tridacne was now at an end. Captain Nemo left the grotto, and we climbed back up to the oyster bed in that limpid water which was as yet undisturbed by pearl-fishers.

We were now strolling separately like ramblers, each of us pausing or straying as the fancy took him. I no longer had any fears about the dangers which my imagination had so ludicrously exaggerated. The sea-floor rose markedly towards the surface, and soon my head projected a full metre out of the water. Conseil came up to me and, leaning his large helmet against mine, gave me a friendly greeting with his eyes. But the raised plateau measured only a few metres, and soon we were once more in our adopted element: I believe I now have the right to call it that.

Ten minutes later Captain Nemo came to a sudden stop. I thought he had called a halt so that he could return the way he had come, but no. He signalled that we were to crouch round him in a wide fissure. With one hand he pointed into the water, and I stared hard in the direction indicated.

Not 5 metres away a shadow appeared which floated down to the sea-bed. Alarming thoughts of sharks came into my head. But I was wrong, and once again we were not dealing with those monsters of the deep.

It was a man, a living man, an Indian, a Black, a diver, a pearl-fisher, a poor devil no doubt who had come early in the season to fill his net. I could see the bottom of his boat, which was moored a few feet above his head. He dived and resurfaced repeatedly. He carried a stone carved in the shape of a sugar loaf, which he gripped between his feet and was attached to his boat by a rope. It enabled him to reach the bottom more quickly. It was the only tool he used. When he was on the sea-bed in about 5 metres of water, he quickly got on to his knees and filled his net with pinctadas grubbed up at random. Then he returned to the surface, emptied his net, hauled up his stone and recommenced the operation, which lasted no more than thirty seconds.

He did not see us, for the shadow of the rock concealed us. Anyway, how could this poor Indian have ever imagined that there were men, creatures like him, under the water, watching his every movement, missing no detail of his efforts?

Several times he resurfaced and dived again. Each time, he managed to bring up no more than a dozen oysters, because he had to prise them from the rocks to which they were attached by their strong byssus. And how many of those oysters for which he was risking his life contained no pearls at all?

I watched him with enthralled attention. He repeated his manoeuvre regularly, and for over a half an hour no danger threatened. I was beginning to get used to the sight of that fascinating fishing technique when suddenly, as the Indian was kneeling on the sea-floor, I saw him give a start of fear, get up quickly and prepare to return to the surface.

I understood why he was afraid. A huge shadow had appeared above the head of the wretched diver. A very large shark was bearing down on him at an angle, eyes blazing and jaws wide open!

I was struck dumb with horror, unable to move.

With a powerful thrust of its fin, the ravening creature swooped down on the man, who leaped to one side and avoided the shark's teeth, but not its tail, which caught him in the chest and laid him out on the sandy floor.

The scene had lasted scarcely a few seconds. The shark returned and, swimming on its back, was about to cut the Indian in two when I felt Captain Nemo, who was standing next to me, suddenly get to his feet and, knife in hand, make straight for the monster, ready to fight him at close quarters.

Just as it was about pounce on the wretched diver, the shark caught sight of a new enemy, righted itself and went for it.

I can still see the captain standing there. Bracing himself, he stood his ground with wonderful coolness and waited for the fearsome shark to come to him. When it launched itself at him, he sprang to one side with astounding agility, avoiding the impact, and buried his knife in its underbelly. But that was not the end of it, and a terrible battle ensued.

The shark had so to speak roared. Blood streamed out of its wounds. The sea grew tinged with red until I could see nothing through the clouded water.

Nothing at all ... until the moment when, as it thinned momentarily, I saw the doughty captain clinging to one of the animal's fins, fighting the monster at close quarters, raking its belly with his knife but without striking the mortal blow,

'*A terrible battle ensued*'

without reaching the creature's heart. It writhed, stirring the mass of water with such fury that the turbulence almost knocked me off my feet.

I wanted to go to the captain's assistance. But I was rooted to the spot with horror and could not move a muscle.

I looked on through eyes filled with dismay, and as I did so saw the struggle move into a new phase. The captain fell to the ground, knocked off balance by the sheer bulk which hovered over him. Then the shark's jaws opened as wide as the maw of an industrial metal grinder, and the captain's fate would have been sealed if Ned Land, as quick as a thought, harpoon in hand, had not rushed at the creature and impaled the monster on the end of his weapon.

Immediately the water was filled with streams of blood. It was thrashed into a turmoil by the writhing of the shark, which churned it with indescribable fury. Ned Land had not missed: we were watching the death throes of the monster. Struck clean through the heart, it twisted, it flailed, and its terrifying paroxysms lifted Conseil clear off his feet.

Meanwhile, Ned Land had helped Captain Nemo back on to his feet. Seemingly unharmed, the captain immediately bent over the Indian, quickly cut the rope attaching him to the stone, lifted him in his arms and with one mighty spring rose to the surface of the sea.

All three of us followed, and a few moments later, saved by a miracle, we were in the diver's boat.

Captain Nemo's first thought was to revive the wretched man. I was not sure he could. I certainly hoped so, for the poor devil had not been under water very long. On the other hand, the blow struck by the shark's tail might well have killed him.

Happily, as a result of vigorous kneading and massaging by Conseil and the captain, I saw the man slowly regain consciousness. He opened his eyes. Who could imagine just how shocked, even frightened, he must have been to see four large copper helmets peering down at him?

But what in particular must he have thought when Captain Nemo took a small bag of pearls from the pocket of his diving suit and put it in his hand? This magnificent gesture of charity offered by this man from the sea to the impoverished Ceylon Indian was received by trembling hands. His bewildered eyes showed only too clearly that he had no idea who these super-human being were to whom he owed both his fortune and his life.

At a sign from the captain, we went back down to the oyster beds, and, retracing the route by which we had come, a half hour's march brought us back to the anchor that moored the dinghy of the *Nautilus*.

On the dinghy, each of us, with the help of the sailors, was divested of his hard copper helmets.

The first words spoken by Captain Nemo were for Ned Land.

'Thank you, Mister Land,' he said.

'Just returning the favour, captain,' replied the Canadian, 'only repaying a debt.'

A faint smile flickered on the captain's lips, and nothing more was said.

'Back to the *Nautilus*,' he ordered.

The dinghy skimmed over the waves. A minute or so later, we saw the dead body of the shark floating on the water.

By the black markings on the ends of its fins, I identified it as the terrible melanopter of the Indian Ocean, which in strict scientific terms belongs to the genus *squali*. It was more than 25 feet long; its enormous mouth made up one-third of its body. It was an adult, as was indicated by the six rows of teeth, arranged on the upper jaw in a series of isosceles triangles.

Conseil inspected it in a true scientific spirit, and I felt sure that he was placing it – correctly, no doubt – in the class of car-tilaginous fish, of the order of fixed-gilled chondropterygians and the family of selachians, in the genus *squali*.

While I was watching its inert remains, a dozen of the same voracious melanopters appeared out of nowhere and sur-rounded the dinghy. But paying no attention to us, they threw themselves on to the carcass and fought for every scrap of flesh.

At 8.30 p.m., we were once more on board the *Nautilus*.

There, I began to reflect upon the events of our visit to the oyster beds of Manaar. Two observations sprang inevitably to mind. One concerned the incredible bravery of Captain Nemo, and the other centred on his devotion to another human being, a representative of the hated race he had taken to the sea to escape. Despite what he said, this strange man had not yet succeeded in killing his heart entirely.

When I told him as much he replied with a hint of emotion:

'That Indian, professor, lives in a country where people are oppressed, and I am still, and shall be until my dying day, a part of that country!'[3]

4
The Red Sea

During the day of 29 January, the island of Ceylon disappeared below the horizon, and the *Nautilus*, maintaining a speed of 20 knots, slipped through the labyrinth of channels which separate the Maldives from the Laccadives. She skirted Kiltan, a coral island discovered by Vasco da Gama in 1499, one of the nineteen principal islands of the Lakshadweep archipelago, which lies between latitude 10° and 14° 30' north and longitude 69° and 50° 72' east.

We had by then covered 16,220 miles – 7,500 leagues – since our starting point in the seas of Japan.

The next day – 30 January – when the *Nautilus* resurfaced there was no land in sight. We were then heading north-north-west, making for the Gulf of Oman, which is situated between Arabia and the Indian peninsula and forms an outlet from the Persian Gulf.

It was clearly a dead end, for there was no other way out of it. So where was Captain Nemo taking us now? I could not have said. This state of affairs did not satisfy the Canadian, who on that day asked me where we were going.

'We are going, Ned, wherever the captain's fancy takes us.'

'Well, his fancy is not going to take us very far,' replied the Canadian. 'The Persian Gulf does not have an outlet, and if we sail into it, it won't be long before we sail out of it again.'

'Well, Ned, we'll just have to sail back out of it. And if, after the Persian Gulf, the *Nautilus* fancies a trip up the Red Sea, the Strait of Bab el-Mandeb is always there to provide a way through.'

'I don't need to inform you, professor,' said Ned, 'that the Red Sea is no less closed than the Gulf, since the Suez isthmus has not been cut through. Even if it were open, a mystery ship like this one could not dare venture into a canal which has locks. It follows that the Red Sea cannot yet be the route which will take us back to Europe.'

'That is why I did not say that we were returning to Europe.'

'So where do you imagine we're going?'

'I imagine that after visiting these interesting regions of Arabia and Egypt, the *Nautilus* will sail back down through the Indian Ocean, maybe by way of the Mozambique Channel or perhaps the sea route round the Mascarene Islands, and then travel on to the Cape of Good Hope.'

'And when we get to the Cape of Good Hope, where then?' asked the Canadian with particular insistence.

'I expect we'll sail into the Atlantic, which we have not yet been to. What's the matter, Ned? Are you getting tired of our voyage under the seas? Is the never-endingly varied spectacle of marvels of the ocean beginning to pall on you? Personally, I shall be extremely sorry to reach the end of a journey which few men are privileged to undertake.'

'Do you realize, Professor Aronnax,' replied the Canadian, 'that soon we will have been held prisoner on the *Nautilus* for three months?'

'No, and I do not wish to be reminded of the fact. I am not counting the days, or the hours.'

'But when's it all to end?'

'It will end in the fullness of time. Besides, there is nothing we can do about it, and we will be wasting our time if we argue about it needlessly. If you came to me and said: "A chance to escape has just come up", I'd gladly discuss it with you. But no such opportunity has arisen, and, to be frank, I don't think Captain Nemo ever goes anywhere near European waters.'

From this brief exchange of views, it will be patently obvious that in not being prepared to hear a word spoken against the *Nautilus* I was now seeing things from her master's standpoint.

As for Ned Land, he ended our conversation with these words, which did not call for a reply: 'That's all very well, but in my opinion wherever there is constraint there can be no pleasure.'

For four days, until 3 February, the *Nautilus* cruised round the Gulf of Oman at different speeds and different depths. She

seemed to be cruising aimlessly, as if there were some hesitation about setting her a course, though she never crossed the
Tropic of Cancer.

As we sailed out of the Sea of Oman, we passed close to Muscat, the largest city in the whole of the territory of Oman. I was
much taken with its exotic appearance: its white houses and
forts standing out dramatically against the black rocks which
surround it. I made out the rounded domes of its mosques, the
elegant spears of its minarets and its fresh green terraces. But it
was only a distant prospect, and soon the *Nautilus* sank beneath
the surface of the surrounding sea.

Then we coasted at a distance of 6 miles along the Arabian
shores of Al Mahrah and Hadramaut and their undulating line
of mountains, broken only by occasional ancient ruins. On 5
February we reached the Gulf of Aden, a sort of a funnel in the
neck of the bottle that is the Strait of Bab el-Mandeb, through
which the waters of the Indian Ocean are funnelled into the
Red Sea.

On 6 February, the *Nautilus* came within sight of Aden,
which stands on a promontory linked to the mainland by a
narrow isthmus, a kind of inaccessible Gibraltar. Its fortifications were rebuilt by the British, who captured it in 1839. I had
a view of the octagonal minarets of the town, which was once,
according to the historian Idrisi, the richest and busiest trading
post on the entire coast.

I thought it most likely that, having reached this point, Captain Nemo would now turn back. But I was wrong, for to my
great surprise he did nothing of the sort.

The next day, 7 February, we entered the Strait of Bab
el-Mandeb, which means in Arabic 'Gateway of Tears'. Though
20 miles wide, it is just 52 kilometres long, and it took the *Nautilus*, moving at full speed, not quite an hour to pass through it.
I saw nothing of it, not even the island of Perim, which the British government uses to reinforce the position of Aden. Too many
English or French steamers on their runs from Suez to Bombay,
Calcutta, Melbourne, Réunion and Mauritius use this narrow
waterway for the *Nautilus* to show herself. Instead, she remained
at a prudent depth beneath the surface.

Finally, at noon, we were sailing on the Red Sea.

The Red Sea, the famous lake of biblical tradition, on which fresh rain rarely falls, is fed by no large river. It is subject to such high rates of evaporation that each year its water level drops by a metre and a half! This most curious gulf would most probably have dried up completely if it had really been an enclosed inland lake. It is less fortunate in this than its neighbours, the Dead Sea and the Caspian Sea, where levels have fallen only to the point where their loss through evaporation is exactly equal to the water which flows into them.

The Red Sea is 2,600 kilometres long and has an average width of 240 kilometres. In the days of the Pharaohs and the Roman Emperors, it was the most important commercial artery in the world, and cutting a canal through the isthmus will give it back its ancient importance, which the Suez railways have already partially restored.[4]

I did not try to understand this latest whim of Captain Nemo nor see what could have persuaded him to take us into this dead-end gulf. But I fully endorsed the decision to sail up it. He set a moderate speed, sometimes remaining on the surface and occasionally diving to avoid by some ship or other, so I was thus able to observe at close quarters both what was under and what was on the surface of this most curious sea.

On 8 February, more or less at first light, we sighted Mocha, now a ruined city with walls that fall down at the mere sound of cannon fire and now are home to green-fronded date palms. Once an important city with six public markets and twenty-six mosques, it had ramparts studded with fourteen forts that ran round it in a circumference of 3 kilometres.

Then the *Nautilus* drew nearer to the shores of Africa, where the water is very much deeper. There, at an intermediate depth of crystal-clear water, we crowded round the glass viewing panels and were able to see wonderful gardens of brilliantly coloured corals and immense walls of rock clothed in a fur of green algae and brown fucus. There are no words to describe it! Such variety of sites and seascapes where the reefs and volcanic islands of the Libyan coast[5] fall away under water! But of all the places where these shrub-like forms appeared in full glory, the eastern shores were the most dazzling, and it was there that the *Nautilus* was soon patrolling, especially along the coast of Tihama. For not only did displays of zoophytes flourish there beneath the waves but they also formed lacey skeins which spread out for up to 20 metres over the surface of the water. The latter were more freakish in shape but less highly coloured than the former, which were kept bright by the vivifying water of their habitat.

I passed many fascinating hours glued to the viewing panels in the Great Saloon. How many new forms of marine flora and fauna did I admire as they were picked out by the beam of our electric searchlight: mushroom-shaped fungus coral; slate-coloured sea anemones, among them the thalassianthus aster; organ-pipe corals looking like flutes waiting only for the breath of the god Pan to play; shells unique to this sea which establish themselves inside crevices in madreporian structures and whose base has the form of a short spiral; plus innumerable specimens of a polypary which I had not seen before, the common sponge.

The class of *spongiae* (*porifera*), the first in the group of polyps, was specifically created by this curious organism, which has so many practical uses. Sponge is not a plant, though some naturalists think it so, but an animal of the lowest order, a polypary which is inferior to that of coral. Its animal nature is indisputable, and there are no grounds for clinging to the opinion of the Ancients, who considered it to be an intermediate stage between plant and animal. I must say, however, that naturalists do not all agree about the way the sponge is structured. For some, it is a polypary and for others, like Henri Milne-Edwards,[6] it is in a separate, distinct category.

The class of *spongiae* contains around 300 species, which abound in many seas and even in freshwater courses, where they have been given the name of 'fluviatiles'. But their preferred habitats are the Mediterranean, the Greek Archipelago and the coast of Syria and the Red Sea. The sponges that reproduce and grow there are soft and fine and can sell for up to 150 francs each: the yellow sponge from Syria, the North African Barbary sponge, etc. But since I could not hope to study these zoophytes in the commercial ports of the Levant from which we were separated by the impassable isthmus of Suez, I had to settle for observing them in the Red Sea.

So I summoned Conseil to my side while the *Nautilus*, at an average depth of 8 or 9 metres, slowly sailed close to the impressive rocks of the eastern coast.

Sponges grew there in all shapes and sizes, pediculate, foliaceous, globular, digitate . . . They fully lived up to the names (basket, chalice, cat's tail, bulrush, elkhorn, lion's paw, peacock tail, Neptune's glove) that have been given to them by fishermen, who have a more poetic imagination than naturalists do. From their fibrous tissue, coated with a semi-fluid gelatinous substance, issues a steady flow of minute trickles of water which, after bringing life to each of the creature's cells, is expelled by contractile movement. This gelatinous material disappears after the death of the polyp and releases ammonia as it rots. All that remains are the horny or gelatinous fibres of which domestic sponge is made. It takes on a reddish colour and has a range of uses according to the degree of elasticity, permeability and resistance to immersion in water.

These polyparies attached themselves to rocks, the shells of molluscs and even the stems of hydrophytes. They lined the smallest nooks and crannies, some fanning out and others standing straight or hanging like coralligenous growths. As I explained to Conseil, sponges are collected in two ways, either by dragnet or by hand. This last method requires the use of divers and is preferable, for it does less damage to the tissue of the polypary and thus gives it a higher value.

The other zoophytes which teemed around the *spongiae* were made up mainly of jellyfish of a very elegant kind. The molluscs were represented by varieties of squid which d'Orbigny says are peculiar to the Red Sea, and reptiles by virgata turtles which belong to the genus *chelonia* and supplied our table with a wholesome, delicate meat.

As for fish, they were numerous and frequently quite remarkable. I list those caught most often in the nets of the *Nautilus*: rays, including the oval brick-red ribbon-tails, splashed with irregular blue spots and identifiable by their two

serrated stings; silver-backed arnacks; whip-tailed sting rays
with spotted tails; mantas like huge cloaks 2 metres long, rippling
through the water; toothless aodons, a kind of cartilaginous fish
related to squali; dromedary ostracea, whose hump ends in a
curved sting a foot and a half long; squamate reptiles, resembling moray eels, with silvery tails, blue backs and brown
pectoral fins edged with grey; butterfish, *stromateus fiatole*,
with narrow gold stripes and adorned in the three colours of the
French tricolour; perciform blennies 40 centimetres long;
wonderful examples of caranx decorated with seven black
transversal bands, blue and yellow fins and scales of gold and
silver; *centropomidae*; gold-flamed mullets with yellow heads;
parrot-fish; wrasse; trigger-fish; delicious scampi; etc.; not forgetting thousands of other fish common to the oceans through
which we had passed.

On 9 February, the *Nautilus* was cruising through the widest part of the Red Sea situated between Sawakin on its west
coast and Al Qunfudhah, which lies 190 sea-miles east.

That day at noon, after our bearings had been taken, Captain Nemo appeared on the platform, where I was already
standing. I promised myself that I would not allow him to go
below again without having at least sounded him out about his
future plans. When he saw me, he approached, graciously
offered me a cigar and said:

'Well, now, professor! Are you pleased with the Red Sea?
Have you seen enough of the wonders it conceals, its fish and
its zoophytes, its gardens of sponges and its forests of coral?
Have you noticed any of the towns lining its shores?'

'Indeed I have, Captain Nemo,' I replied, 'and the *Nautilus* has lent herself wonderfully well to my observations. Oh,
this is such an intelligent boat!'

'Yes, professor, intelligent, bold and invulnerable. She fears
not the terrifying storms of the Red Sea nor its currents nor its
reefs.'

'And these waters are regularly quoted as being among the
worst in the world. If I am not very much mistaken, its reputation in ancient times was abominable.'

'Abominable is the right word, Professor Aronnax. Greek

and Roman historians had nothing to say in its favour, and Strabo reported that it was particularly bad both when the Etesian winds blew and in the rainy season. The Arab Edrisi, who referred to it as the Sea of Colzoum, tells of how many ships foundered on its sandbanks and that no one dared sail on it by night. It was, he said, prone to terrible storms, was studded with inhospitable islands and "was no good to anyone either below or on its surface". Similar views were expressed by Arrian, Agatharchides and Artemidorus.'

'Obviously,' I answered, 'those historians never sailed on the *Nautilus*!'

'True,' smiled the captain, 'and in that respect the Moderns are not much more advanced than the Ancients. It took many centuries to discover the mechanical possibilities of steam! Who knows if it might not take a hundred years before there will be a second *Nautilus*? Progress is such a slow business, Professor Aronnax.'

'That is so,' I replied. 'Your vessel is a century, perhaps several, ahead of its time. It would be a tremendous shame if such an invention were to die with its inventor!'

Captain Nemo did not respond. Then after a few minutes' silence:

'You were speaking, I believe,' he said, 'about the views expressed by ancient historians about the dangers of sailing in the Red Sea.'

'Quite so,' I replied, 'but surely their opinions were somewhat exaggerated?'

'Yes and no, Professor Aronnax,' said Captain Nemo, who, I thought, seemed to be completely knowledgeable in all matters concerning 'his' Red Sea. 'What is no longer dangerous for modern ships, which are fully rigged, solidly built and responsive to the wheel thanks to the convenience of steam, presented the vessels of ancient mariners with all sorts of perils. We must imagine those early sailors venturing forth in boats made of planks lashed together with palm ropes, caulked with crushed resin and waterproofed with the fat of dogfish. They did not even have instruments to help them know their position and were reduced to sailing by dead reckoning through currents of which they knew almost nothing. In such conditions, ship-wrecks were, and could not be other than, frequent. But these days steamers that ply between Suez and the southern oceans have nothing to fear from the moods of this sea, despite con-trary winds. Their captains and passengers do not prepare themselves for departure by making propitiatory sacrifices, nor on returning do they don garlands and chaplets of gold and rush off to give thanks to the gods in the nearest temple.'

'I agree,' said I. 'Steam seems to have made gratitude redun-dant in the hearts of sailors. But, captain, since you appear to have made a special study of the Red Sea, can you tell me where it got its name?'

'There are, Professor Aronnax, a number of answers to your question. Do you wish to hear the opinion of a fourteenth-century chronicler?'

'Gladly.'

'He was a fanciful scribbler and claimed that the name was given to it after the passage of the Israelites, when Pharaoh drowned in the waters which closed up when Moses gave the command:

> To mark the miracle of the flood
> The sea became the colour of blood
> No one knew what its name should be
> So perforce they called it the Red Sea

'A poet's explanation, Captain Nemo,' I replied, 'but one which does not satisfy me. So I ask you what your own opinion is.'

'It is this. I believe, Professor Aronnax, that we should see in the name Red Sea a translation of the Hebrew word "Edrom".[7] If the Ancients called this sea "red", it must have been because of the particular colour of its water.'

'Thus far I personally have seen only water that is crystal clear, without any colour of any kind.'

'Quite, but as we travel further towards the end of the gulf you will observe that it acquires a strange appearance. I recall once seeing the Bay of Tor when it was completely red, like a lake of blood.'

'And would you attribute this colour to the presence of some microscopic algae?'

'Yes. There is a mucilaginous purple-hued substance which is produced by a humble, tiny plantlet, known to naturalists as *trichodesmium erythraeum*. It would take 40,000 of them to fill a space one millimetre square. Maybe you will see them when we reach Tor.'

'I take it then, captain, that this is not the first time you have sailed the Red Sea in the *Nautilus*?'

'No indeed.'

'Well, since earlier you mentioned the passage of the Israelites and the destruction of the Egyptians, may I ask if you have ever come across any trace of that great historical event on the sea-bed?'

'No, professor, and for that there is an excellent reason.'

'Which is?'

'The exact spot where Moses led his people across is now so clogged by sand that even camels can scarcely find enough water to cool their legs in. So obviously there would not be anywhere deep enough for the *Nautilus*.'

'And this place . . . ?' I asked.

'It is situated a short way north of Suez, in the branch which once was a deep estuary in the days when the Red Sea extended as far as the salt lakes. Now, whether their passage was miraculous or not, the Israelites must have crossed there to reach the Promised Land, and Pharaoh's army therefore perished at the spot. So I think that excavating those sands would turn up a large quantity of weapons and implements of Egyptian origin.'

'Most certainly,' I replied, 'and we must hope for the sake of archaeologists that such excavations will be undertaken at some point when new cities will be built on the isthmus after the completion of the Suez Canal. Though it is a canal which will not be of any use to a vessel like the *Nautilus*!'

'True, but very useful for the rest of the world,' said Captain Nemo. 'The Ancients understood how important it would have been for trade and commerce if a practical link could be established between the Red Sea and the Mediterranean. They never actually considered the possibility of digging a direct canal and instead used the Nile to connect the two. The canal linking the Nile to the Red Sea was probably begun under Sesostris, if tradition is to be believed. What is certain is that in 615 BC Necos started work on a canal, drawing water from the Nile, which crossed the plain of Egypt facing Arabia. It took four days to pass through it, and it was wide enough for two triremes to pass each other. It was continued by Darius, son of Hystaspes, and finished probably by Ptolemy II. Strabo saw it used for navigation. But the shallowness of its gradient between its starting point near Bubastis and the Red Sea made it accessible for only a few months of the year. It was used by commercial traffic until the century of the Antonines. Abandoned, it became silted up but was restored by order of the Caliph Omar before finally being filled in around 761 or 762 by Caliph Al-Mansour to cut the supply line of Mohammad ben Adallah, who had risen up against him. During the Egyptian expedition, your fellow countryman General Bonaparte found traces of these works in the desert of Suez. He was surprised there by the tide and almost perished only hours before returning to Hadjaroth, the very spot where Moses had camped 3,300 years before.'

'Well, captain, what the Ancients did not dare to undertake, a means of linking two seas which would shorten the route from Cadiz to the Indies by 9,000 kilometres, Monsieur de Lesseps[8] has undertaken, and before long he will have turned Africa into one immense island.'

'Quite so, Professor Aronnax, and you have every reason to be proud of your compatriot. He is a man who does more honour to his country than the greatest generals! Like many others, he had first to contend with hardship and rejection but he won through because his is the triumph of will! It is sad to think that this work, which should have been an international effort and a feather in the cap of any nation, would never have been brought to fruition but for the energy of one man. I take my hat off to Monsieur de Lesseps!'

'Hear, hear, all honour to this great civic-minded man,' I said, somewhat taken aback by the strength of feeling with which Captain Nemo had spoken.

'Unfortunately,' he resumed, 'I cannot take you through the canal, but you shall see the wharves of Port Said the day after tomorrow, when we shall be in the Mediterranean.'

'In the Mediterranean?' I exclaimed.

'Of course. You sound surprised.'

'What surprises me is the thought that we will be there the day after tomorrow.'

'Really?'

'Yes, captain, though by rights I should be used by now to not being surprised by anything since I came aboard the *Nautilus*!'

'But what exactly are you surprised by?'

'By the terrifying speed you will need to reach in the *Nautilus* if she is to sail round the whole of Africa, doubling the Cape of Good Hope, and be in the middle of the Mediterranean the day after tomorrow!'

'Who said anything about circumnavigating Africa, Professor Aronnax, or sailing round the Cape of Good Hope?'

'But unless the *Nautilus* can sail overland and pass over the isthmus . . .'

'Or under it.'

'Under it?'

'Why not?' replied Captain Nemo coolly. 'A very long time ago, nature did beneath this tongue of land what men have only just got round to doing on the surface.'

'You mean there's a way through?'

'Yes, an underground passage which I have named the Arabian Tunnel. It starts under Suez and comes out in the Bay of Pelusium.'

'But isn't the isthmus made of shifting sand?'

'It is, down to a certain depth. But just 50 metres down is solid rock.'

'Was it by chance that you discovered this passage?' I asked, lurching from one surprise to the next.

'A mixture of chance and logic, professor, though in fact with more logic than chance.'

'Captain, I'm listening carefully, but my ears are not taking in what they are hearing.'

'Oh, professor! *Aures habent et non audient*[9] is a dictum which never goes out of date. Not only does this passage exist but I have used it several times. Otherwise, I would not have ventured into the Red Sea since it is a dead end.'

'Would it be indiscreet of me to ask how you discovered the tunnel?'

'Professor,' said Captain Nemo, 'there can be no secrets between people who will never again part company.'

I did not respond to the implication of the remark but waited for Captain Nemo to go on with his tale.

'Actually,' he said, 'it was simply by thinking like a naturalist that I was led to find the tunnel, whose existence is known only to me. I had noticed that in both the Red Sea and the Mediterranean there were a number of species of fish which were absolutely identical – ophidians, butterfish, small wrasse, sea perch, jack mackerel and flying fish. Starting from this fact, I began to wonder if there might be some connection between the two seas. If there was, then the underground flow had to be from the Red Sea to the Mediterranean because of the difference in their levels. So I hauled up a large number of fish from the sea near Suez. I fixed a copper ring round their tails and threw them back into the water. A few months later, off the coast of Syria, I caught a few of the fish I had ringed. That there was some form of communication was therefore proved beyond doubt. Using the *Nautilus* I looked for it, located it, ventured into it and very soon now, professor, you too will have passed through my Arabian Tunnel!'

5

The Arabian Tunnel

The same day I informed Conseil and Ned Land about the part of my recent conversation which directly concerned them. When I told them that within two days we would be in the Mediterranean, Conseil clapped his hands gleefully, but the Canadian shrugged his shoulders dubiously.

'An underwater tunnel!' he cried. 'A passage between the two seas? Who ever heard of such a thing?'

'Ned,' said Conseil, 'you'd never heard of the *Nautilus* either, but it exists. So don't be so eager to shrug your shoulders and deny that things exist just because you have never heard of them before.'

'We'll see,' retorted Ned Land with a shake of his head. 'After all, nothing would please me more than to believe in the captain's tunnel. God grant that it does take us to the Mediterranean.'

That evening, our position being latitude 21° 30' north, the *Nautilus*, cruising on the surface, approached the Arabian coast. I saw Jeddah, an important trading port which serves Egypt, Syria, Turkey and the Indies. I had a clear view of its buildings, the boats which were moored along the wharves and those whose draught obliged them to anchor in the roads. The sun was low on the horizon and fell squarely on the town's houses, emphasizing their whiteness. On the outskirts a few huts made of wood or reeds marked the Bedouin quarter.

Jeddah soon disappeared into the evening mist, and the *Nautilus* dived into the faintly phosphorescent sea.

The next day, 10 February, several ships hove into view, sailing on an opposite tack to us. The *Nautilus* resumed her progress

'*A few huts made of wood or reeds*'

under water, but at noon, when our position was always taken, she resurfaced and remained level on her water line.

Accompanied by Ned and Conseil, I went out and sat on the platform. The line of the eastern coast formed a solid mass whose contours were only lightly shrouded in damp gloom.

Leaning with our backs against the dinghy, we were talking of this and that when Ned Land held out one hand towards a point on the sea and said:

'Can you see something over there, professor?'

'No, Ned,' I replied. 'But you know that my eyes are not as good as yours.'

'Look harder,' Ned went on, 'there, ahead on the starboard beam about the height of the searchlight. Can you make out some sort of large disturbance?'

'Why yes!' I said, after looking more closely. 'I can see a kind of long blackish body breaking the surface.'

'Is it another *Nautilus*?' asked Conseil.

'No,' said the Canadian, 'but unless I'm very much mistaken it's some sort of marine creature.'

'Are there whales in the Red Sea?' asked Conseil.

'Yes, there are,' I replied. 'They are sighted occasionally.'

'It's no whale,' said Ned Land, who was not taking his eyes off the object in question. 'Whales and I are old acquaintances. I could never make a mistake about the way they move.'

'Just wait,' said Conseil. 'We are heading in that direction and we'll soon know what we're dealing with.'

In no time, the blackish shape was less than a mile from us. It looked like a large reef stranded on the high sea. What was it? For the time being I could not say for sure.

'Ah! It's on the move! It's diving!' cried Ned Land. 'Hell's teeth! What sort of animal is it? Its tail is not forked like a whale's or a cachalot's, and its fins look like shortened limbs.'

'So what could it possibly . . .' I said.

'Look,' the Canadian went on, 'it's turned on its back and is poking its dugs in the air!'

'Then it's a siren,' cried Conseil, 'a real-life siren, if monsieur would kindly spare my blushes.'

The word 'siren' set me on the right track, and I realized

that the creature belonged to the class of marine animals which inspired what in fables are called mermaids, which are half woman, half fish.

'No,' I said, turning to Conseil. 'It's not a siren or a mermaid but a curious creature of which there are only a few individuals left in the Red Sea. It is a dugong, a sea-cow.'

'Order of *sirenia*, group of pisciforms, sub-class of *monodelphia*, a class of mammalia, branch of vertebrates.'

And Conseil having pronounced, there was no more to be said.

But Ned Land was still gazing at the creature. His hunter's eyes blazed at the sight of the animal. His hand looked as if it was ready to launch his harpoon. It was as if he was only waiting for the right moment to jump into the sea and attack it in its own element.

'Ah, professor!' he said to me in a voice bristling with excitement. 'I never killed me one of those creatures!'

Those words summed up Ned Land the harpooner.

At that point, Captain Nemo came out on to the platform. He saw the dugong, realized what the Canadian was thinking, turned to him and said:

'If you had a harpoon in your hand at this moment, Mister Land, wouldn't you be just burning to use it?'

'I would, sir.'

'And would it displease you to resume your trade of fisherman for one day and add this cetacean to the tally of those you have already caught?'

'It would not displease me in the least!'

'In that case, you'd better try.'

'Oh, thank you, sir!' replied Ned, his eyes already shining.

'But,' the captain went on, 'you'd better not miss, for your own good.'

'Are dugongs dangerous to attack?' I asked, though the Canadian merely shrugged his shoulders.

'Sometimes,' said Captain Nemo. 'The animal can turn on its attackers and upset their boats. But Mister Land does not have that particular danger to watch out for. His eyes are sharp, and his aim is sure. If I suggested that he take care not to miss the dugong it is because it is highly regarded for being excellent eating, and I am quite aware that Mister Land is not a man to turn up his nose at a good steak.'

'Ah!' exclaimed the Canadian. 'So these creatures afford the added luxury of being good to eat?'

'Correct, Mister Land. Its flesh is real meat and so greatly prized in Malaysia that it is reserved for the table of princes. As a result, this excellent animal is hunted with such persistence that, like the manatee, to which it is closely related, it is becoming increasingly rare.'

'Perhaps, captain,' said Conseil earnestly, 'this particular dugong is the last of its kind, so would it be as well to spare it, in the interests of science?'

'Perhaps,' said the Canadian. 'But how much better to give chase, in the interests of cooking!'

'Go ahead, Mister Land,' said Captain Nemo.

At this juncture, seven crew members, as silent and as expressionless as ever, climbed out on to the platform. One was carrying a harpoon and a line similar to the kind that is used by whale hunters. The dinghy was broken out of its housing and set on the water. Six oarsmen took their places, and the mate grasped the helm. Ned, Conseil and I sat in the stern.

'Aren't you coming, captain?' I asked.

'No, professor, but I wish you good hunting!'

The dinghy put off and, propelled by six oars, bore down quickly on the dugong, which was then basking 2 miles from the Nautilus.

When we were a few cable lengths from the cetacean, we slowed, and the oars dipped soundlessly into the placid water. Ned Land, harpoon in hand, stood in the bow of the dinghy. The harpoon used in whaling is attached to a very long line which plays out rapidly when the wounded animal flees, dragging it with him. But in our case, the line was not more than 60 feet long, and its end was secured to a small barrel which would float on the surface and show the movements of the dugong under the water.

I was standing and had a clear view of the Canadian's opponent. The dugong, which is sometimes called halicore, is very similar in appearance to the manatee. Its oblong body ends in an elongated caudal fin, and its lateral fins resemble real fingers. Where it differs from the manatee is in the way its upper jaw is armed with two elongated, pointed teeth which project on both sides of it as two divergent tusks.

The dugong which Ned Land was lining up was huge. It was at least 7 metres long. It was motionless and appeared to be asleep in the water. This would make its capture much easier.

The dinghy approached warily to within about 6 metres of the creature. The oars ceased to move in their thole pins. I half rose. Ned Land, body arched slightly back, gently swung his harpoon backwards and forwards with a practised action.

Suddenly there was a hiss, and the dugong disappeared. The harpoon, launched with considerable power, had hit only water.

'Hell's teeth!' cried the Canadian in a fury. 'Missed!'

'No,' I said, 'you wounded it, you can see the blood. But the harpoon did not stay in its body.'

'My harpoon, my harpoon!' cried Ned.

The sailors began rowing again, and the mate guided the dinghy towards the floating barrel. When the harpoon was retrieved, the dinghy set off in pursuit of the animal.

The dugong returned to the surface from time to time to breathe. Its wound had evidently not weakened it, for it moved very fast. The dinghy, propelled by lusty arms, went after it. Several times it came within a few metres, and the Canadian prepared to strike. But the dugong would escape by diving suddenly so that it was impossible to hit it.

It is easy to imagine the fury which filled the impatient Ned Land. He bawled the choicest epithets in the English language at the unfortunate animal. I was less enraged, merely frustrated, as I saw the dugong repeatedly eluding all our efforts.

We hunted it relentlessly for an hour, and I was beginning to think that it would be difficult to land it when the animal unwisely decided to take its revenge, an idea it would regret: determined to go on the attack, it turned on the boat.

This change of tack was not lost on the Canadian.

'Look out!' he cried.

The mate said something in his strange language, doubtless to warn his men to be on their guard.

The dugong came to within 20 feet of the dinghy, stopped, sharply sniffed the air with its enormous nostrils, which were located not on the end but on the upper part of its snout. Then, gathering itself for action, it hurled itself on us.

The dinghy could not avoid the impact. Half keeled over, it shipped a ton, maybe two tons, of sea-water, which we had to bail out. But thanks to the quick thinking of the mate, it hit us at an angle, not full on. Ned Land, crouching in the bow, kept stabbing his harpoon into the huge animal, which, with its tusks hooked in the gunwhale, was lifting the dinghy clear out of the water as a lion tosses a buck. The rest of us had collapsed on top of each other, and I don't know how the battle would have ended if the Canadian, still fiercely attacking the creature, had not struck it clean through the heart.

I heard a grating of teeth on the metal gunwhale, and the dugong disappeared, taking the harpoon with it. Moments later, the barrel popped up on the surface, followed by the body of the animal floating on its back. The dinghy secured it and then towed it back to the *Nautilus*.

We had to use our strongest block and tackle hoist to lift the body up on to the platform. It weighed 5,000 kilos. It was quartered while the Canadian, keen to follow the details of the operation, looked on. That evening, the steward served a dinner featuring choice cuts which had been skilfully prepared by the chef. I found it excellent, better than veal but not beef.

The next day, 11 February, the *Nautilus*'s larder was further enriched by more delicate game. A flock of terns came to rest on the *Nautilus*. They were a species of *sterna nilotica* peculiar to Egypt, with black beak, grey spotted head, eyes surrounded by flecks of white, greyish back, wings and tail, white belly and throat and red feet. We also caught several dozen Nile ducks, a very gamey-tasting wildfowl. Their necks and the tops of their heads are white and speckled with black.

The *Nautilus* was holding a moderate speed. She moved in a sauntering sort of way, if I may express it so. I observed that the water of the Red Sea grew less salty the closer we got to Suez.

Around five in the afternoon we sighted the Cape of Ras

Mohammed to the north. It marks the limit of Arabia Petraea, the area between the Gulf of Suez and the Gulf of Aqaba.

The *Nautilus* entered the Jubal Strait at the mouth of the Gulf of Suez. There, I had a clear sight of a high mountain which looked down on the Ras Mohammed between the two Gulfs. It was Horeb, or Sinai, where Moses came face to face with God and whose summit one always imagined crowned with a blaze of lightning.

At six the *Nautilus*, sometimes keeping to the surface and sometimes beneath it, cruised past Tor, which is located at the end of a bay whose waters look as though they are tinged with red, a phenomenon already pointed out by Captain Nemo. Then night fell, and we were surrounded by a heavy silence which was occasionally broken by the cries of pelicans and various night birds, the surge of the surf breaking on the rocks and the distant thrum of a steamer threshing the water with its paddle wheels.

Between eight and nine o'clock the *Nautilus* maintained a depth of a few metres. By my calculations, we must now be very near Suez. Through the viewing panels in the Great Saloon, the sea-floor seemed to grow increasingly rocky in the brilliant illumination of our searchlight. It also appeared that the channel was growing narrower.

At 9.15 we resurfaced, and I went up on to the platform. Being impatient to be through Captain Nemo's tunnel, I was restless and felt the need to breathe the cool night air.

Soon, in the gloom, I saw a faint light, dimmed by the mist, shining a mile away.

'A floating beacon,' a voice said close to me.

I turned and saw the captain.

'It's Suez's floating beacon,' he continued. 'It won't be long now before we're at the entrance to the tunnel.'

'I don't imagine entering it is easy?'

'Correct, and that is why I always take the wheel and man-oeuvre the ship myself. But now, perhaps you would go below, professor. The *Nautilus* is about to dive and will not surface again until we are through the Arabian Tunnel.'

I followed Captain Nemo. The hatch closed behind us, the

water tanks started to fill, and the vessel sank 10 metres or so in the water.

Just as I was about to go back down to my cabin, the captain caught me by the arm:

'Professor Aronnax,' he said, 'would you care to come with me into the pilot's cockpit?'

'I didn't dare ask,' I replied.

'Come along, then. You'll be in a position to see everything there is to see of our passage, which is both underground and under water.'

Captain Nemo led me to the central stairwell. When we were halfway down, he opened a door, proceeded along the upper walkways and reached the pilot's cockpit, which, it will be remembered, formed a kind of bubble at the end of the platform.

It was a room 6 feet square reminiscent of those occupied by helmsmen on paddle boats on the Mississippi and the Hudson. At the centre was a steering wheel set vertically which was connected to the cables controlling the rudder in the stern of the *Nautilus*. Four round lenticular panes of glass set into the walls enabled the helmsman to see in all directions.

It was dark inside, but soon my eyes became accustomed to the gloom, and I saw the pilot, a powerfully built man, with his hands firmly grasping the spoke handles of the ship's wheel. Outside, the water was brightly lit by the searchlight placed aft of the cockpit, at the stern end of the platform.

'Now,' said Captain Nemo, 'let's look for this tunnel.'

Electric wires connected the pilot's cockpit to the engine room, so from there the captain could direct both the speed and direction of the *Nautilus*. He pressed a metal button, and immediately the propeller began turning more slowly.

I stared in silence at the high, sheer wall as it glided past, the unshakeable foundation of the entire sandy mass of the coast above. We proceeded thus for an hour, never more than a few metres from it. Captain Nemo never took his eyes off the two concentric rings of the compass which hung in the cockpit. On a nod from the captain, the helmsman would make small changes in the direction of the *Nautilus*.

I was standing by the port window and had an uninter-
rupted view of the magnificent substructures of corals,
zoophytes, algae and the crustaceans which from the fissures
in the rocks reached out with their enormous claws.

At 10.15 Captain Nemo took the wheel himself. A wide,
black, deep gallery opened before us. The *Nautilus* headed
boldly into it. An unaccustomed whooshing sound was heard
on both her sides. It was water from the Red Sea rushing down
the slope of the tunnel towards the Mediterranean. The *Nautilus* was being taken by the current, moving with the speed of
an arrow even though the engine reversed the direction of the
propeller to slow our progress.

All I could see of the walls of this narrow tunnel were
streaks of bright colours and straight fiery lines, blazing fur-
rows lit by our electric light. I clasped my hand to my heart,
which was racing.

At 10.35 Captain Nemo surrendered the wheel and, turning
to me, announced:

'The Mediterranean!'

In less than twenty minutes, the *Nautilus*, riding the torrent, had crossed the isthmus of Suez.

6

The Greek Archipelago

The next day, 12 February, at dawn, the *Nautilus* surfaced. I rushed up to the platform. Three miles to the south the misty contours of Pelusium were visible. The rushing torrent had carried us from one sea to another. But if the tunnel had been easy to sail down, there seemed little prospect that the return journey would be feasible.

At about seven I was joined by Conseil and Ned. My two inseparable companions had slept peacefully, without giving a second thought to the exploits of the *Nautilus*.

'So where, professor,' the Canadian asked, with more than a touch of sarcasm, 'is this famous Mediterranean you told us about?'

'We're sitting on it.'

'What?' said Conseil. 'We got here overnight?'

'Yes, last night, in a matter of minutes, we crossed the uncrossable isthmus.'

'I don't believe it,' said the Canadian.

'You are wrong, Mister Land,' I said. 'That low, curving coastline you see to the south is Egypt.'

'Pull the other one, professor,' said the mule-headed Canadian.

'If monsieur says it is true,' Conseil told him, 'we should believe him.'

'Actually, Ned, Captain Nemo was good enough to show me his tunnel. I was there in the helmsman's cockpit while he took the controls and took us through the narrow passage.'

'Did you hear that, Ned?' asked Conseil.

'And since you have such exceptional eyesight, Ned,' I

added, 'you can see for yourself: those are the wharves of Port Said reaching out into the sea.'

The Canadian stared hard.

'You're right, professor. Your captain certainly is a master mariner. So we are in the Mediterranean. Fine. Now, if it's all right with you, let's put our heads together and discuss our little problem – where we can't be overheard.'

I knew what the Canadian had in mind. Still, I thought it best to have it out in the open, since that was what he wanted. So all three of us went and sat down next to the searchlight, where we would be less exposed to the spray blowing off the waves.

'Well, Ned,' I said, 'we're listening. Tell us what you have to say.'

'What I have to say is very simple,' replied the Canadian. 'We're in Europe now, and before the whims of Captain Nemo whisk us away to the depths of the polar seas or take us back to Oceania, I want to leave the *Nautilus*.'

I will admit that this discussion with the Canadian still left me in two minds. I had absolutely no wish to deprive my companions of their freedom, but nor did I want to leave Captain Nemo. Thanks to him, thanks to his ship, I was adding to my knowledge of marine life and rewriting my book on the lower depths while actually travelling through them. Would another such opportunity of observing the wonders of the ocean ever come my way again? Absolutely not! So I could not reconcile myself to the idea of leaving the *Nautilus* until our tour of explorations was completed.

'Tell me, Ned,' I said, 'and please feel free to speak. Are you bored here? Are you ready to rebel against the fate which delivered you into the hands of Captain Nemo?'

The Canadian hesitated for a few moments before replying. Then he folded his arms and said:

'To be frank, I don't regret having been part of this journey under the sea and I will always be glad I did it. But before I can be glad I did it, it has to be over and done with. That's what I think.'

'It will end, Ned.'

'Where and when?'

'Where? I have no idea. When? I cannot say, or rather I assume that it will end when the seas have nothing more to tell us. Everything in this world which has a beginning must necessarily have an end.'

'I share monsieur's view,' said Conseil. 'It is quite likely that after travelling through all the seas in the world, Captain Nemo will just show us the door.'

'Show us the door?' exclaimed Ned Land. 'I suppose you mean with the toe of his boot?'

'Don't exaggerate, Ned,' I said. 'We have nothing to fear from the captain, though I don't share Conseil's opinion. We know everything about the *Nautilus*, and I can't see that to restore our freedom he would easily resign himself to letting his secrets walk off out into the world with us.'

'Well, what hope do you have?' asked the Canadian.

'That circumstances will arise, perhaps in six months, perhaps today, which we can and must turn to our advantage.'

'Oh yes,' said Ned Land, 'and would you please say where we will be in six months, professor?'

'Perhaps here, or maybe China. As you know, the *Nautilus* covers great distances quickly. She sails through oceans the way swallows fly through the air or express trains cross continents. She does not have to steer clear of busy shipping lanes. Who is to say she might not sail along the coast of France, England or America, where an escape might be attempted just as easily as here?'

'Professor Aronnax,' replied the Canadian, 'what you say is based on a false supposition. You speak in the future tense: "We will be there! We shall be here!" But I'm talking of the here and now: "We are here and we must make the most of the chance!"'

I was hard pressed by Ned Land's logic and I knew I was beaten on that terrain. I did not know what arguments I could produce to make my case.

'But,' said Ned, 'suppose, though it's hardly likely, suppose Captain Nemo came up to you today and offered to restore your freedom. Would you accept?'

'I don't know,' I said.

'And if he added that this offer he was making now would not be made again at some later date: would you accept then?'

I did not reply.

'And what does my good friend Conseil think?' asked Ned Land.

'Your good friend Conseil,' my worthy servant replied calmly, 'has nothing to say. He has no interest whatsoever in the question. Like his employer and his good comrade Ned, he is unmarried. No wife, no parents, no children are waiting for him to come home. He is in the service of monsieur, he thinks like monsieur, he speaks like monsieur, and, though he much regrets it, you must not count on him to cast the deciding vote. There are only two people here: monsieur on one side and Ned Land on the other. Conseil is here to listen and he is ready to keep the score.'

I could not help but smile at seeing Conseil erase his own personality so completely. Deep down, the Canadian must have been really glad not to have him as an opponent.

'Well, professor,' said Ned Land, 'seeing that Conseil does not exist, let's keep the discussion between you and me. I have said my piece, and you listened to me. What do you have to say in reply?'

I saw that we needed to reach a conclusion and I despised shilly-shallying.

'Very well, Ned, here is my answer. You are quite right, and my arguments do not stand up against yours. We cannot count on Captain Nemo's continuing goodwill. The most basic prudence prevents him from letting us go free. But equally, prudence also demands that we should take the first opportunity that comes along to escape from the *Nautilus*.'

'Good, Professor Aronnax, you have spoken wisely.'

'However,' I observed, 'I would add one thought, just one. It must be a real opportunity. We must succeed at the first attempt, because if it fails we will not get another chance, and Captain Nemo will not forgive us.'

'All that is very true,' replied the Canadian, 'but what you say applies to any attempt to escape whether it happens in two years from now or in two days. So the question remains: if a favourable opportunity crops up, we must take it.'

'Agreed. But now, Ned, tell me what you mean by a "favourable" opportunity.'

'One that on a dark night brings the *Nautilus* close to a European coast.'

'And you'd swim for it?'

'Yes, if we were close enough to the shore and if the vessel was on the surface. No, if it was too far and the boat was submerged.'

'And in those circumstances?'

'I would try to break out the dinghy. I know how it's done. We'd climb into it, and once the bolts were removed, we'd float up with it to the surface. The helmsman's cockpit is situated forward, and he wouldn't see us getting away.'

'Very well, Ned. Keep watching for the right moment – but remember: if it goes wrong we'll all be in deep trouble.'

'I won't forget, professor.'

'But now, Ned, do you want to know what I think about your plan?'

'I'm all ears, Professor Aronnax.'

'I think – I'm not saying I hope – I think that this favourable opportunity won't ever arise.'

'Why not?'

'Because Captain Nemo won't have forgotten that we have not abandoned all hope of recovering our freedom. He will keep his guard up, especially when we are sailing through waters which are in sight of European coasts.'

'I share monsieur's view,' said Conseil.

'We shall see soon enough,' replied Ned Land, shaking his head in a very confident manner.

'And now, Ned, let's leave it there. Not another word on the subject. The day you are ready, let us know, and we will follow you. I place myself completely in your hands.'

This conversation, which was later to have such dire consequences, ended on this note. I must say now, with hindsight, that my predictions were borne out by events, much to the chagrin of the Canadian. Either Captain Nemo did not trust us in these busy waters, or else he was simply keeping out of sight of the many ships of all nations which sailed through the Mediterranean; I could not tell which. But most of the time he remained submerged and kept well clear of land. At times, the *Nautilus* would emerge with only the helmsman's cockpit exposed; at others we dived to great depths, for between the Greek Archipelago and Asia Minor we could dive down to 2,000 metres and still not reach the bottom.

I would not have known we were anywhere near the island of Karpathos, one of the Sporades, if Captain Nemo had not quoted these lines of Virgil as he placed his finger on a spot on the planisphere:

> Est in Carpathio Neptuni gurgite vates
> Caeruleus Proteus . . .[10]

It was in fact the ancient dwelling-place of Proteus, the old shepherd of Neptune's flocks, but now the island of Scarpanto, which is situated between Rhodes and Crete. I saw only the granite foundations on which it stood through the viewing panels in the Great Saloon.

The following day, 14 February, I decided to devote a few hours to studying the fish of the archipelago, but for some reason the panels stayed hermetically shut. When I noted down the *Nautilus*'s course, I saw that she was heading towards Candia, the old name for Crete. When I boarded the *Abraham Lincoln*, the whole island had just risen up against the despotism of the Turks. But I had no idea of how the insurrection had fared since that time. And Captain Nemo, cut off entirely from all contact with humankind, was not in any position to enlighten me.

So I did not mention the uprising when I found myself alone with him that evening in the Great Saloon. Besides, he seemed preoccupied and in no mood for talk. Then, very much against his normal custom, he ordered the viewing panels to be opened and, moving from one to the other, stared intently into the water outside. What was he looking for? I could not fathom it and instead used my time observing the fish which swam into my line of vision.

Among many others, I noticed a species of goby mentioned by Aristotle and commonly known as rockling, which are found especially in the salt reaches of the Nile Delta. Nearby swam semi-phosphorescent sea bream, a kind of spar, which the Egyptians ranked as sacred. When they arrived in the waters of their great river, heralding the fertile floods to come, they were greeted by religious ceremonies. I also observed shoals of cheilinus, a kind of wrasse, 30 centimetres long, a bony fish with transparent scales whose pale bodies are splashed with patches of red; they eat mainly marine vegetation, which gives them an exquisite flavour and also explains why they were in great demand by the connoisseurs of ancient Rome. Their entrails, stewed with the milt of moray eels, peacock brains and the tongues of flamingos, made a dish fit for the gods and delighted the emperor Vitellius.

Another denizen of these deeps drew my eye and reminded me of all my memories of Antiquity. It was the remora, or sucker fish, which travels by attaching itself to the bellies of sharks. According to the Ancients, this small fish could cling to the keel of a ship and bring it to a halt. One of them slowed Mark Antony's boat during the battle of Actium and thus helped Augustus to win the day. On such trifles hang the destinies of nations! I also observed admirable anthias, or snappers, belonging to the order of *lutjanidae*, which the Greeks regarded as sacred: it was believed they had the power to chase away sea monsters from the seas they swam in. Their name means 'flower', and they truly lived up to it with their shimmering colours, including every possible shade of red from blushing pink to the most brilliant ruby, and the fleeting glitter of their dorsal fins. I could not take my eyes off these wonders of the sea. But then I was struck by a totally unexpected sight.

A man appeared in the water outside the viewing panels. At his waist was a leather bag. It was not a corpse which had been thrown into the sea but a living man who was swimming strongly, vanishing at moments to breathe on the surface and diving back down again immediately.

I turned to Captain Nemo and said with some surprise:

'A man! He's been involved in a shipwreck!' I cried. 'We must save him whatever the cost!'

The captain did not answer but leaned close to the pane.

The man came nearer and stared at us with his face pressed against the glass.

To my great astonishment, Captain Nemo made a sign to him. The diver replied with a gesture of the hand, swam directly to the surface of the sea and did not reappear.

'There's no need for you to worry,' said the captain. 'It's Nicolas, from Cape Matapan. They call him "the Fish", and he is famous throughout the Cyclades. He's a bold diver! Water is his element, and he spends more time in it than on land, moving from one island to another all the way at times to Crete.'

'Do you know him, captain?'

'Of course I know him, Professor Aronnax.'

Having given me an answer, Captain Nemo moved to a cabinet which stood by the left-hand panel. Next to this cabinet was an iron-bound chest. On the lid was a brass plate with the name of the *Nautilus* and its motto: *Mobilis in mobile*.

Then Captain Nemo, paying no attention to my presence, opened the cabinet, which was in fact a safe and contained a large number of ingots.

Gold ingots! Where had all this precious metal come from? It was worth a vast sum of money. Where had the captain acquired this gold and what was he going to do with it?

I did not speak. I watched. Captain Nemo took the ingots out of the cabinet one by one and stacked them neatly in the chest, filling it completely. I estimated that it must have contained around 1,000 kilograms of gold, worth close to 5 million francs.

The chest was then closed and locked, and on the lid the captain wrote an address which looked as though it was written in modern Greek.

When he had finished, he pressed a button which communicated with the crew room. Four men appeared and with considerable difficulty hauled the chest out of the Great Saloon. Then I heard them hoisting in up the iron stairs by means of pulleys.

Captain Nemo turned to me.

'You were saying, professor?'

'Nothing of importance, captain.'

'In that case, perhaps you would allow me to bid you good night.'

And so saying, Captain Nemo left the room.

I returned to my cabin greatly intrigued, as may be imagined. I tried in vain to sleep. I lay racking my brains trying to find a connection between the appearance of the diver and the chest full of gold. It was not long before I felt the vessel begin to pitch and roll slightly and realized that the *Nautilus* was rising from deep water and was about to surface.

I heard footsteps on the platform. I sensed that the dinghy was being broken out and lowered on to the sea. It bumped against the hull of the *Nautilus*, and then all sounds ceased.

Two hours later I heard the same noises, the same comings and goings. The dinghy, hauled on board, was bolted once more in its recess and the *Nautilus* dived beneath the waves.

So those millions had been ferried to their destination. But where on the mainland? And who had Captain Nemo sent them to?

The next morning, I told Conseil and the Canadian about the things which had happened during the night and had so roused my curiosity. My companions were no less astonished than I was.

'Where does he get all these millions?' asked Ned Land.

It was a question I could not answer. After lunch I went to the Great Saloon and settled down to work. I wrote up my notes until five in the afternoon. And then – should I attribute it to a constitutional weakness? – I suddenly felt extremely hot and was obliged to take off my byssus jacket. I could not understand it, for we were not in tropical latitudes and in any case once she was under the water the *Nautilus* should not be affected by any rise in the external temperature. I looked at the depth gauge. It showed a reading of 60 feet, deep enough to be beyond the reach of surface air temperatures.

I continued working, but it grew hotter until it was almost intolerable.

'Is there fire on board?' I wondered.

I was just about to leave the Great Saloon to investigate when Captain Nemo walked in. He strode up to the thermometer, noted the reading then turned to me.

'Forty-two degrees,' he said.

'I am all too aware of it, captain,' I replied, 'and if it gets any worse it will be unbearable.'

'No fear of that, professor. It will get hotter only if we want it to.'

'You can change it whenever you want?'

'No, but I can move us away from the source of the heat.'

'So it's coming from outside?'

'Certainly. We are cruising through a current of boiling water.'

'Surely that cannot be?'

'Look.'

The viewing panels opened and I saw that the sea all around the *Nautilus* had turned white. The bubbling smoke of sulphurous fumes was billowing through the sea, which was boiling like water in a kettle. I leaned one hand against the glass, but it was so hot I was obliged to take it away again.

'Where are we?' I asked.

'Near the island of Santorini,' replied the captain, 'or, more accurately, we are in the channel between Nea Kameni and Palea Kameni. I wanted to show you the fascinating spectacle of an undersea eruption.'

'I thought,' I said, 'that the formation of new islands was finished.'

'Nothing is ever finished in volcanic regions,' replied Captain Nemo. 'The entire planet is constantly being reshaped by subterranean fires. As early as 19 AD, according to Cassiodorus and Pliny, a new island, Thira the Divine, appeared in the place where those two islands were formed only recently. Then Thira sank beneath the surface only to resurface in 69 AD but again it disappeared at a later date. Between then and now, Pluto has stayed his hand. But on 3 February 1866 a new extrusion, called George Island, emerged in a cloud of sulphurous fumes near Nea Kameni and fused with it on the sixth of the same month. A week later, on 13 February, the islet of Afroessa appeared, leaving a channel between it and Nea Kameni just 10 metres wide. I was here, in these waters, when it happened and I was able to follow every phase. The islet of Afroessa was rounded in shape, 10 metres high with a diameter of 100 metres. It was composed of black, vitreous lava containing fragments of feldspathic material. Then on 10 March, a smaller island, named Reka, came up near Nea Kameni. Ever since, these three islands, have remained joined together and now they form just one.'

'Which channel are we in at this moment?' I asked.

'It's here,' said Captain Nemo, showing me a map of the archipelago. 'As you see, I have marked the new islands on it.'

'And will the channel get filled in some day?'

'It's very likely, Professor Aronnax, because since 1866, eight small islands have appeared opposite the port of Saint Nicolas on Palea Kameni. So it's certain that Nea and Palea will also be joined sooner rather than later. If in the Pacific continents are made by infusoria, here it is the result of volcanic activity. So gaze, professor, gaze on the activity which never ceases here on this sea-floor.'

I went back to the observation panel. The *Nautilus* was at a standstill. The heat was becoming intolerable. The sea had been white; it was now red, thanks to the presence of a compound of iron. Despite the hermetic insulation of the Great Saloon, a sickening sulphurous odour was everywhere, and outside I saw crimson flames so dazzling that they overpowered the brightness of our own electric lights.

I was bathed in sweat, I couldn't breathe, I felt that I was being roasted alive!

'We can't stay any longer in this boiling water,' I gasped to the captain.

'No, it would not be wise,' replied the impassive Nemo.

He gave the order. The *Nautilus* turned and began moving away from that hellish furnace which she could not defy any longer without coming to grief. A quarter of an hour later, we were breathing fresh air on the surface of the sea.

I suddenly had the thought that if Ned had chosen this spot for us to make our escape, we would not have emerged from this devil's kitchen and lived to tell the tale.

The next day, 16 February, we sailed away from the trench that lies between Rhodes and Alexandria, where the water can reach depths of 3,000 metres. The *Nautilus* stood off Cerigo and, after doubling Cape Matapan, left the Greek Archipelago behind.

7

Around the Mediterranean in Forty-eight Hours

The Mediterranean, the peerless Big Blue, called the Great Sea by the Hebrews and simply The Sea by the Greeks, the Mare Nostrum of the Romans, fringed by orange groves, aloes, cactus and sea-pine, perfumed by the scent of myrtle, framed by rugged mountains, permanently steeped in pure, limpid air and constantly fashioned by the great subterranean fire, is a battlefield where Neptune and Pluto still fight for mastery of the world. It is there, around its shores and on its waters, says Michelet,[11] that man's soul is continually restored in one of the most stimulating climates in the world.

But, however beautiful it may be, all I managed to get was the briefest glimpse of this enclosed sea, which covers an area of 2 million square kilometres. Even Captain Nemo's extensive personal knowledge of it was not available to me, because that enigmatic person was not seen once during our rapid crossing. I put a figure of around 600 leagues on the distance covered by the *Nautilus* as she cruised beneath the waves. She completed the voyage in twice twenty-four hours. Leaving the coast of Greece on the morning of 16 February, we were through the Straits of Gibraltar by the time the sun was rising on the 18th.

It was clear to me that the Mediterranean, squeezed between two great land masses from which it sought to escape, brought no pleasure to Captain Nemo. Its waves and sea breezes brought back too many memories, and perhaps too many regrets. Here he did not have the freedom of movement, the independence of action which the open ocean gave him, and the *Nautilus* felt as though she were constrained between the proximate shores of Africa and Europe.

Our speed was maintained at 25 miles an hour, or 12 four-kilometre leagues. It goes without saying that Ned Land, much to his chagrin, was forced to abandon his plans for escape. He could not use the dinghy because it was moving through the water at a rate of 12 or 13 metres a second. Attempting to leave the *Nautilus* in those conditions would have been the equivalent of jumping off a train going at the same speed, a foolhardy action if there ever was one. Besides, our vessel only surfaced at night, to replace the air inside it, and its course was dictated solely by the compass and the log's readings.

So I only saw the Mediterranean from the inside, the way a passenger on an express train sees the landscape rushing past him, that is, distant prospects and no details of the foreground as it flashes past. However, Conseil and I managed to see Mediterranean species which had sufficiently powerful fins to enable them to keep up briefly in the water around the *Nautilus*. We sat and watched through the viewing panels in the Great Saloon, and the notes I made now allow me to summarize briefly the ichthyology of that sea,

Of the various fish that live in it, I spotted some, glimpsed others, but missed all those which the speed of the *Nautilus* prevented me from seeing. Perhaps, therefore, I might be allowed to classify them according to this rather unscientific system. It will convey my rapid observations more vividly.

In those waters, brightly lit by our searchlight, snaked lampreys, a metre long, which are found virtually in all climes. The long-snouted oxyrhynchus, a species of ray 5 feet broad, with white underside and ash-grey spotted back, flapped like large shawls caught in a current. Other kinds of rays passed so quickly that I could not tell if they better deserved the name of eagle applied to them by the Greeks, or that of rat, toad or bat which modern fishermen have given them. Dogfish, 12 feet long and particularly feared by divers, strove to outrun each other. Eight-feet-long threshers, which have an acute sense of smell, loomed up like great blue shadows. Sparid dolphins, some measuring 4 feet in length, appeared in their livery of silver and blue with narrow stripes which contrasted with the dark colour of their fins. These fish, dedicated to Venus, have their eyes framed by golden brows and are highly prized. They live in all waters, fresh and salt, are found in rivers, lakes and oceans and in all climates and tolerate all temperatures: a species dating back to the geological epochs of the earth's history, which has lost none of the beauty of those far-off days. Magnificent sturgeons 9 or 10 metres in length, long-distance swimmers, beat their powerful tails against the glass of the viewing panels, displaying their backs, which are bluish and flecked with small brown spots; they resemble squali but lack their strength and are found in every sea; in the spring, they swim up large rivers, fighting the currents of the Volga, the Danube, the Po, the Rhine, the Loire and the Oder, feeding on herring, mackerel, salmon and gade; although they are officially a cartilaginous fish, their flesh is delicate; they are eaten fresh, dried, marinated or salted and in former times were carried in triumph to the table of Lucullus and his like. But of all these varied denizens of the Mediterranean, the one which I succeeded in observing most closely, when the *Nautilus* cruised nearer to the surface, belonged to the sixty-third genus of bony fish. They were common tunny, with blue-black backs, silver breastplate and dorsal rays which gleamed like gold. They have a reputation for tracking the progress of ships for the cool shade they provide against the heat of tropical suns and they lived up to it by escorting the *Nautilus* as they once accompanied the ships of La Pérouse. For many hours they would keep up with us. I never wearied of admiring these animals which were born to race: small heads, sleek, streamlined bodies (in some cases over 3 metres long), their remarkably strong pectoral fins and forked caudal fins. They swam in a triangular formation, like flocks of some kinds of birds whose speed they equalled, thus giving the Ancients grounds for saying that they must be familiar with geometry and strategy. Even so, they were not equipped to escape the toils of the fishermen of Provence, who value them no less highly than did the inhabitants of Propontis and Italy. These precious animals blindly, foolishly throw themselves into the dragnets of the men of Marseille and die.

Next I will mention, for reference only, those Mediterranean fish which either Conseil or I managed only to glimpse. They are: semi-transparent electric eels, which passed like swirls of thin smoke; conger morays, serpents 3 or 4 metres in length, sporting bright greens, blues and yellows; 3-feet long gade-hake, whose liver makes a delicately flavoured dish; cepola-tenia, drifting like flat ribbon algae; grunt fish, which poets name lyre-fish (and fishermen call whistlers), for they have snouts with two serrated triangular plates which resemble Homer's instrument; spotwing flying gurnards, which swim with the speed of swallows; a species of grouper with a red head and a dorsal fin which trails filaments; shad, prettily spotted black, grey, brown, blue, yellow and green, which respond to the silvery sound of bells; magnificent turbots, the pheasants of the sea, lozenge-shaped with yellowish fins and brown spots, whose upper left side is generally mottled with brown and yellow; and finally wonderful schools of red mullet, the marine bird of paradise, for which the Romans would pay as much as 10,000 sesterces each so that they could kill them at their dinner table and watch cruelly as the creatures changed colour from the vermillion red of life to the pallor of death.

And lastly, if I was unable to observe for myself miralets (a kind of ray), trigger-fish, globe fish, sea-horses, garfish, trumpet-fish, blennies, surmullets, wrasse, sparling, flying fish, anchovy, sea bream, boöps, sea-pike nor any of these principal representatives of the order of pleuronects: flatfish, flounders, plaice, soles and dabs, which are common to the Atlantic and the Mediterranean, then the heavy burden of blame must be laid squarely on the colossal speed with which the *Nautilus* careered through the water.

As for marine mammals, I do believe I may well have glimpsed, as we sped into the waters of the Atlantic, two or three cachelots, each with a dorsal fin of the genus *physeteridae*; a few dolphins, related to the pilot whale, specific to the Mediterranean, which have the front part of their heads scored with narrow light-coloured lines; plus a dozen white-bellied seals with black fur, which are known as monk-seals and look exactly like 3-metre-long Dominican friars.

Meanwhile, Conseil thought he caught a glimpse of a sea turtle, 6 feet wide, which had three prominent ridges running the length of its shell. I bitterly regretted having missed this reptile for, judging from Conseil's description, I do believe I could safely identify it as a luth, a quite rare species. The only turtles I noticed myself were a few loggerheads with elongated shells.

In the matter of zoophytes, I was able to admire, briefly, a quite glorious orange-coloured fan worm which clung to the panel on the port side; it was a long, thin filament which spread out into countless branches, each ending in a lace finer than any ever made by the rivals of Arachne. Unfortunately I could not lay my hands on this admirable specimen, and no other Mediterranean zoophyte would have ever offered itself for my inspection if, on the evening of the 16th, the *Nautilus* had not unexpectedly dropped her speed. It happened as follows.

At that moment, we were sailing between Sicily and the Tunisian coast. In the restricted space between Cape Bon and the Strait of Messina, the level of the sea-bed rises quite quickly. Just there, it forms a ridge which reaches to within 17 metres of the surface while on each side it falls away to a depth of 170 metres. The *Nautilus* had therefore to steer a careful course to avoid colliding with this underwater obstacle.

I showed Conseil the exact position of this long reef on a chart.

'But if monsieur would permit me to say,' he remarked, 'it is very like an isthmus linking Europe and Africa.'

'So it is,' I replied, 'it runs across the entire Sicilian Strait. Soundings taken by Smith have demonstrated that once upon a time the two continents were joined between Cape Boeo and Cape Farina.'

'I can well believe it,' said Conseil.

'I will add,' I went on, 'that there is a similar ridge between Gibraltar and Ceuta, which, sometime during the geological epochs, closed the Mediterranean entirely.'

'What if volcanic activity were to raise these two ridges above the surface some day?'

'That's hardly likely.'

'Perhaps monsieur would let me finish. If such a thing did happen, it would be a great inconvenience to Monsieur de

Lesseps, who is going to such trouble to dig his canal across the isthmus.'

'True, but I repeat, Conseil, it will never happen. The violence of subterranean forces is declining. Volcanoes, so numerous in the early aeons of the earth, are gradually dying. The internal fires are burning less fiercely, and the temperature inside the globe is falling appreciably with each passing century, much to the detriment of the planet, for its heat is its life.'

'But the sun . . .'

'The sun is not enough. Can the sun warm a corpse?'

'Not that I know of.'

'Well, the earth will one day become a cold corpse, where nothing lives, as on the Moon, which lost its life-giving heat a long, long time ago.'

'How many centuries will it take?'

'It will take hundreds of thousands of years.'

'In that case,' said Conseil, 'we'll have plenty of time to see our voyage through to the end – unless Ned Land has his way!'

Then Conseil, fully reassured, sat down again to observe the marine shallows over which the *Nautilus* passed closely at a moderate speed.

There, on the rocky, volcanic sea-bed flourished a whole range of living flora: sponges; holothurians; hyaline *cydippe*, which have reddish tendrils and emit a faint phosphorescence; forms of the genus *beroe*, commonly known as sea cucumbers, which become iridescent on exposure to the full solar spectrum; peripatetic feather stars a metre wide, whose purple colouring turned the water red; extremely handsome branched euryales; long-stemmed pavonaceous creatures; large numbers of edible sea urchins of various species; and green actinias with greyish trunk and brown oral disc, which are virtually invisible under their thatch of olive-coloured tentacles.

Conseil was particularly absorbed in his observation of molluscs and articulates, and although their nomenclature may seem to some a trifle arid, I would not wish to betray my worthy servant by omitting his personal report.

In the branch of molluscs he recorded numerous pectiniform scallops; examples of *spondylus gaedeporus* piled up in

heaps; the triangular *donax*; trident-shaped hyalines, which
have yellow fins and transparent shells; orange-coloured *pleu-
robrachia* like eggs speckled with green; huge *aplysia*, also
known as sea hares; dolabella gastropods; fleshy *turbonilla
akera*; umbrella molluscs unique to the Mediterranean; sea
ears, whose shell produces a quality of mother-of-pearl which
is most sought after; flammulated scallops; anomia, which, it
is said, the people of Languedoc prefer to oysters; cockles,
much loved in Marseille; outsize clams, white and plump, the
same clams that abound on the coast of North America and
are sold in large quantities in New York; trapdoor comb-shell
scallops in various colours; stone crabs which lurked in their
holes, whose spicy flesh was greatly to my taste; groove-backed
venericardes, whose dome-shaped shells have bulging ribs;
cynthiae bristling with scarlet tubercules; carinaria sea-snails,
rounded fore and aft like delicate gondolas; crowned giant
worm molluscs; spiral-shelled heteropod atlanta; grey tethys
flecked with white and draped in a fringed mantilla; shell-less
eolides, which resemble small slugs; *cavolinia*, which crawl
upside down; auriculas, including the forget-me-not auricula
which has an oval shell; carnivorous scalaria; winkles; *janthina janthina*; cineraria; *petricolae*; flat *lamellibranchia*, or
tube worms; cabochons; bivalves of the genus *pandora*; etc.

As for articulates, Conseil quite rightly divided them in his
notes into six classes, of which three belong to the marine
world. These are the classes of crustaceans, cirripedia and
annelida.

The crustaceans are divided into nine orders, and the first of
these orders include the decapods, that is animals in which
head and thorax are generally joined, whose mouths comprise
several pairs of jaws and which have four, five or six pairs of
thoracic or ambulatory legs. Conseil followed the methodology
of our master, Milne-Edwards, who divided decapods into
three groups: the *brachyura*, the *macrura* and the *anomura*.
These appellations are somewhat rough and ready, but they are
both accurate and exact. Among the *brachyura*, Conseil mentions *amathia*, whose foreheads are armed with two divergent
points; the *inachida* scorpions, which, for some reason,

symbolized wisdom for the Greeks; various *amanthia*, including one species of hairy crab which must have strayed into this shallow water since it normally lives at great depths; *xanthidae*; bristly *pilumni*; rhomboids; granular *calappidae* (easy to digest, according to Conseil); toothless *corystes*, the helmet crab; crabs of the genus *ebalia*; *palici*; woolly porter crabs; and so forth and so on. Among the *macrura*, which are subdivided into five families – the armoured, the burrowers, *astacidae*, *paelemon* and *ocypodinae*, or ghost crabs – he mentions crayfish, of which the female yields such highly regarded meat; *scyllaridae*, the slipper lobster; riparian squilla and all manner of edible crayfish. But, alas, he says nothing of the subdivision of the *astacidae*, which includes the lobsters, for crayfish are the only kind of lobster found in the Mediterranean. Finally, among the *anomura*, he observed drocina crabs, which live in abandoned sea shells which they appropriate; *homola barbata*, spiny-headed crabs; hermit crabs; porcelain crabs; etc.

And there end Conseil's observations. Lack of time prevented him from completing his identification of members of the class of crustaceans, the stomatopods, amphipods, homopods, isopods, trilobites, branchiopods, *ostracoda* and *entomostraca*. And to complete his observation of marine articulates, he was remiss in not including the class of cirripeds, which includes Cyclops and argulus, and the class of annelids, which he most surely would not have failed to subdivide into tubiculous and dorsibranchiate. But the *Nautilus* soon passed over the shallows covering the ridge in the Sicilian Canal and sank into deeper waters, where she resumed her cruising speed. From that point on, no more molluscs, articulates and zoophytes, and only a precious few large fish were observed passing us like ghosts.

During the night of 16–17 February we sailed into the second basin of the Mediterranean, where the water is deeper and reaches a floor of 3,000 metres. The *Nautilus*, driven forward by her propeller, slipped easily over the rise and fall of the sea-bed and dived down to the lowest depths of the sea.

There, in the absence of natural marvels, the water supplied my eyes with many moving and sometimes eerie scenes. For we

were then crossing that part of the Mediterranean renowned
for its shipwrecks. From the Algerian coast to the shores of
Provence, how many ships have come to grief, how many boats
have disappeared! The Mediterranean is only a lake compared
with the vast watery expanses of the Pacific. But it is a lake
which has moods and uncertain whims, one day well disposed
to the frail tartane which appears to drift between the double
seascape made of water and sky, and the next angry, tormented
and enraged by the winds, smashing the strongest ships with
its short, precipitate waves.

In our rapid passage through those deep waters, I saw
countless sunken wrecks lying on the sea-bed, some already
furred by coral, others covered by no more than a veneer of
rust, anchors, cannon, cannon balls, chains and rails,
propeller-blades, parts of machinery, broken cylinders, battered boilers, not to mention entire ships' hulls just hanging in
the water, some upright, others capsized.

Of all these ships, some had been sunk as a result of a collision, others because they had struck a granite reef. I saw boats
which had gone down like stones, masts intact, rigging stiff in
the water. But they all looked as though they were at anchor in
an immense sunken harbour waiting for the moment when
they would get under way again. As the Nautilus passed
between them, casting her electric glow over them, it felt as
though these ships were about to acknowledge us and transmit
their identification numbers with their signalling flags. But
they did not, and nothing disturbed the silence and the embrace
of death which enveloped this field of calamities.

I noticed that the bed of the Mediterranean grew increasingly cluttered with these sinister hulks the nearer the Nautilus
got to the Straits of Gibraltar, where the coasts of Africa and
Europe draw close together. In this narrow space encounters
became more frequent. I saw a number of metal hulls, the fantastic remnants of steamships, some lying on their sides, others
upright, but all looking like terrifying animals. One of them
was a frightening sight: her beam stove in, her funnels leaning
drunkenly and only the mountings of her paddles intact, her
rudder parted from the stern but still attached by an iron chain,

her rear escutcheon eaten away by salt water! How many lives had been destroyed by her loss? How many victims had been swallowed by the waves! Had some mariner who sailed on her survived to tell the harrowing tale or had the sea kept the secret of her fate intact? I do not know why, but I was struck by the thought that this ship, entombed by the sea, might be the *Atlas*, which had disappeared with all hands some twenty years before, and had never been heard of again![12] The dark story of the bed of the Mediterranean, that vast charnel house where so much wealth has been lost and so many victims have perished, would make a macabre chronicle!

But the *Nautilus*, heedless and swift, sped at full power through the middle of that marine graveyard. On 18 February, at around three in the morning, we arrived at the entrance to the Strait of Gibraltar.

There we found two currents: an upper current, whose existence has long been known, which carries water from the Atlantic into the basin of the Mediterranean; and a lower counter-current, whose existence has only recently been theoretically inferred. The water level of the Mediterranean, constantly swelled by inflows from the Atlantic and the rivers which pour into it, should in theory be raised with each passing year, because what it loses by evaporation is insufficient to maintain the balance. But since the level does not rise, then of course the existence of an undercurrent, moving through the Strait of Gibraltar out into the Atlantic, taking the overflow with it, must be conceded.

And the supposition is perfectly true. It was this lower counter-current which the *Nautilus* now rode. She sped rapidly through the narrow pass.

For just one moment I was able to glimpse the admirable ruins of the Temple of Hercules, which, according to Pliny and Avienus, was drowned, along with the small island on which it stood. Minutes later, we were sailing on the surface of the Atlantic.

'The admirable ruins of the Temple of Hercules'

8

The Bay of Vigo

The Atlantic! A vast expanse of water whose surface covers an area of 25 million square miles. It is 9,000 miles long and 2,700 miles wide on average. An important sea almost unknown to the Ancients, with the possible exception of the Carthaginians, those Dutchmen of classical antiquity, who in their commercial forays sailed along the west coasts of Europe and Africa. An ocean whose serpentine, parallel coasts form a vast perimeter, which is fed by the greatest rivers in the world, the Saint Lawrence, the Mississippi, the Amazon, the Plata, the Orinoco, the Niger, the Senegal, the Elbe, the Loire, the Rhine, which all bring their tribute of water from the world's most civilized countries and the most primitive! A magnificent plain, constantly ploughed by ships of all nations, shaded by all the world's flags, and bounded on each side by fearsome extremities which are every sailor's nightmare: Cape Horn and the Cape of Good Hope!

The *Nautilus* now sliced a path through its waters with her sleek cutwater, after having sailed nearly 10,000 leagues in three and a half months, a distance greater than one of the earth's great circles of longitude. Where were we going now? What did the future have in store for us?

Once the *Nautilus* was through the Strait of Gibraltar, she was in open water. We surfaced, and our daily outings up to the platform were resumed.

I went out at the first opportunity, accompanied by Ned Land and Conseil. Twelve miles off we made out the vague shape of Cape Saint Vincent, the most south-westerly point of the Iberian Peninsula. There was a stiff southerly blow. The sea was angry, with a strong swell which made the *Nautilus* roll heavily. It was well nigh impossible to remain on the platform, which was constantly swept by foaming waves, so we went below again, after filling our lungs with sea air a few times.

I returned to my cabin, Conseil to his, but the Canadian, who clearly had something on his mind, followed me. Our fast crossing of the Mediterranean had not given him an opportunity to put his plans into operation, and he did not hide his disappointment.

Once the door of my cabin was closed he sat down and looked at me in silence.

'Ned,' I said, 'I do understand your frustration, but you are not to blame. Given the conditions in which the *Nautilus* was sailing, any attempt to leave her would have been madness!'

Ned Land did not answer. His tightly closed lips and furrowed brows were a clear statement of the stubborn tenacity of his obsession.

'Come now,' I said, 'all is not yet lost. We are now sailing up the coast of Portugal. Not far away are France and England, where we would easily find a place of refuge. Now if, as she came out of the Strait of Gibraltar, the *Nautilus* had turned south, if we had been carried off to regions where there are no continents, I would share your anxiety. But as we now know, Captain Nemo does not go out of his way to avoid inhabited land, and a few days from now I believe you will be able to make your move safely.'

Ned Land glared at me even more balefully but eventually opened his lips:

'It's tonight,' he said.

I sat up with a start. I confess I was totally unprepared by what he had said. I tried to respond, but the words would not come.

'We agreed to wait for a genuine opportunity,' Ned went on. 'Well, I believe the circumstances are right. Tonight, we shall be just a few miles off the Spanish coast. It's a dark night. The wind is blowing off the sea. I have your word on this, Professor Aronnax. I am counting on you.'

As I still said nothing, the Canadian got up and stood in front of me.

'Tonight, at nine,' he said. 'I've alerted Conseil. At that time, Captain Nemo will be in his cabin and probably in bed. Neither the men in the engine room nor the rest of the crew will be able to see us. Conseil and I will go to the central stairwell. You, professor, will stay in the library close to where we'll be, waiting for my signal. The oars, mast and sail are stowed in the dinghy. I've even managed to gather some provisions. I've got hold of a spanner to undo the bolts which clamp the dinghy to the hull of the *Nautilus*. So you see, everything is ready. Until tonight . . .'

'The sea is rough,' I said.

'So it is,' said the Canadian, 'but we'll have to risk it. Freedom doesn't come cheap. Besides, the dinghy is a sturdy craft, and a few miles with a following wind aren't much of a challenge. Who knows if tomorrow we won't be 100 leagues out to sea? If things go our way, then between ten and eleven o'clock we'll be either stepping on to dry land or dead. We'll place our trust in God. Until tonight, then!'

And so saying, the Canadian left, leaving me totally bewildered. I had imagined that if it came to this I'd have time to think, to discuss it. My mule-headed companion had left me no opportunity for that. But what would I have told him? Ned Land was absolutely right. It was half a chance, and he was taking it. Could I go back on my word? Could I accept the responsibility of jeopardizing the future of both my companions for purely personal reasons? Wasn't it entirely possible that the next day Captain Nemo would whisk us away far from any land?

Just then a loud hissing told me that the water tanks were being filled, and that the *Nautilus* had begun to dive under the waters of the Atlantic.

I stayed in my cabin. I wanted to avoid the captain, so that he would not see the look in my eyes and read there the feelings which swamped me. I spent the day in a state of depression, torn between my desire to be free again and my reluctance to abandon the wonderful *Nautilus* with my marine studies unfinished. To leave this ocean, 'my' Atlantic, as I had come to think of it, without exploring its lowest depths, without wresting from it secrets comparable to those which had been revealed to me by the Indian and Pacific Oceans? What! End my great

adventure before it was halfway through? Break it off just
when it was getting truly exciting? Many unhappy hours went
by in this way. At times I saw myself in my mind's eye safe, on
land, with my companions. At others, I wished irrationally for
some unforeseen event to crop up which would prevent Ned
Land from putting his plan into practice.

Twice I went to the Great Saloon, to consult the compass. I
wanted to know if the *Nautilus*'s course was still taking us
nearer the coast or away from it. But the *Nautilus* remained in
Portuguese waters, still heading north, closely shadowing the
shoreline.

I had no choice except to bow to the inevitable, to act and
get ready to escape. I would be travelling light: I would take
only my notes.

I wondered what Captain Nemo would think of our escape,
whether it would worry him, what damage it would do him,
but also what he would do if our plans were discovered or we
did not succeed. I had certainly no grounds to complain of in
his treatment of me, the very opposite. No hospitality had ever
been more open-handed than his! But if I did escape, I could
not be accused of ingratitude. No oath of loyalty bound us to
him. He was relying on the force of circumstances to keep us
on board, not on our word. Moreover, his frankly stated insistence that he intended to keep us eternal prisoners on his ship
fully justified our action.

I had not seen the captain since our visit to the island of
Santorini. Would fate decree that I should find myself in his
presence again before we left? I hoped so, yet at the same time
I feared it. I listened hard to see if I could hear him pacing
around his cabin, which was next to mine. But I heard nothing. His cabin must have been deserted.

Then I started wondering if this strange man was even on
board. Ever since the night when the dinghy had rowed away
from the *Nautilus* on some mysterious business, my ideas
about him had been somewhat modified. I believed, despite
what he said, that Captain Nemo must have maintained some
contact, a connection of some kind with the land. Did he never
leave the *Nautilus*? Whole weeks had often gone by without

my catching sight of him. What did he do at those times? While I was imagining that he was a victim of misanthropic moods, was he not perhaps away, engaged on some secret mission of which I had no idea?

I was assailed by all these ideas, and many more besides. The field of conjecture could not be other than infinite in the strange situation in which we found ourselves. I felt unbearably uneasy. That day which I spent waiting seemed to go on for ever. The hours struck too slowly to satisfy my impatience.

As usual, my dinner was brought to me in my cabin. I toyed with my food, for my mind was elsewhere. I got up from table at seven o'clock. One hundred and twenty minutes – I counted them – still lay between me and the time when I was to join Ned Land. My agitation grew. My pulse raced. I could not stay still. I walked up and down, hoping that moving my muscles would calm my troubled mind. The idea of dying in our foolhardy enterprise was the least of my worries. But the thought that our plans would be discovered before we had left the *Nautilus*, that we would be dragged before a Captain Nemo who was angry or – worse – saddened by my betrayal, made my heart beat faster.

I wanted to see the Great Saloon one last time. I proceeded along the walkways and reached that museum where I had spent so many pleasant, useful hours. I looked round at all its riches, its treasures, like a man doomed to depart into perpetual exile, never to return. All those marvels of nature, those great artistic masterpieces among which my every waking hour had been spent, I was about to abandon for ever. I only wished I could have looked out through the viewing panels in the Great Saloon into the waters of the Atlantic, but they were hermetically sealed, and a metal plate separated me from the ocean, which I did not yet know.

As I strolled around the Great Saloon, I eventually halted outside the door in the angled wall in the corner which opened into the captain's cabin. To my astonishment, I saw that it was ajar. I took a step back instinctively. If Captain Nemo was inside, he could see me plainly. But I could not hear anything and approached: there was no one there. I pushed the door open and stepped inside. It still had the same ascetic look, like the cell of a hermit.

And then, a number of etchings hanging on the wall which I had not noticed during my first visit now caught my eye. They formed a series of portraits of great men from history whose lives had been unswervingly devoted to promoting some great human ideal: Kosciusko, the hero who died crying 'Finis Poloniae!', Botzaris, the Leonidas of modern Greece, O'Connell, Ireland's defender, Washington, the founder of the American Union, Manin, the Italian patriot, Lincoln, slain by a slaver's bullet and, lastly, the martyr of the emancipation of the black race, John Brown, hanging on the gibbet, as drawn with such terrible power by Victor Hugo.[13]

What connection was there between these heroic men and Captain Nemo? Was this group of portraits my chance at last to solve the mystery of his life? Was he the champion of oppressed peoples, the liberator of the enslaved? Had he taken part in the latest political and social upheavals of our century? Had he been one of the heroes of the terrible American Civil War, a war both tragic and everlastingly glorious?

Suddenly, the clock struck eight. The first stroke of the hammer on the bell brought me back to earth. I shuddered as if an invisible eye had looked into my innermost thoughts and I ran out of the cabin.

As I passed, I caught sight of the compass. Our course was still due north. The log showed that we were cruising at a moderate speed and the manometer a depth of approximately 60 feet. Circumstances were conspiring to favour the Canadian's plan.

I returned to my cabin. I dressed in warm clothes, sea boots, otter-skin cap, a jacket made of byssus and lined with sealskin: I was ready. I waited. The silence that filled the boat was broken only by the vibrations of the propeller. I listened. I strained my ears. Would there be sudden shouts and excited voices which would tell me that Ned Land's plan of escape had been discovered? I was seized by mortal fear. I tried in vain to keep calm.

At a few minutes to nine, I leaned with my ear pressed hard against the captain's door. Silence. I slipped out of my cabin and went back to the Great Saloon, which was in semi-darkness but deserted.

I opened the library door. The same dim light, the same solitude. I crossed to the door that opened on to the central stairwell and waited for Ned Land's signal.

And then the vibrations of the propeller decreased significantly and then stopped altogether. Why had the *Nautilus*'s speed slowed? I had no way of telling if stopped engines would help or hinder Ned's plan.

The silence now was broken only by the pumping of my heart.

Suddenly, I felt a faint jarring shock. I realized that the *Nautilus* had come to rest on the bottom of the ocean. My anxiety increased. Where was the Canadian's signal? I wanted to go in search of Ned Land and persuade him to postpone our mission. I had a feeling that the way the boat was being handled departed noticeably from normal practice.

Just then the door of the Great Saloon was flung open, and Captain Nemo emerged. He saw me and, without preliminaries, he said pleasantly:

'Ah, there you are, professor, I was looking for you. How good is your Spanish history?'

Even a man who knew the history of his own country backwards would have been no more able than I to say a single thing about it if he had been in my shoes at that moment, with his mind reeling and thoughts scattered to the four winds.

'Well?' resumed Captain Nemo. 'Did you hear the question? How much do you know about the history of Spain?'

'Not much,' I replied.

'Spoken like a scientist,' he said. 'So ignorant of history! Sit down, and I'll tell you all about a fascinating episode of Spain's past.'

The captain stretched out on a divan, and, numbly, I sat down on a chair near him, in the semi-dark.

'Listen well, professor. This story will interest you from a certain point of view, for it will answer a question to which you have probably not found the answer.'

'I'm listening, captain,' I said, not knowing what was on his mind and wondering if this turn of events had anything to do with our escape plans.

'If you will allow me, professor,' the captain went on, 'I shall turn the clock back to 1702. You will, of course, recall that at that time your King Louis XIV, believing that with a wave of his royal hand he could make the earth open and swallow the Pyrenees,[14] had imposed his grandson, the Duke of Anjou, on the Spanish people. As King Philip V, he ruled more or less badly and followed a foreign policy which met with strong opposition.

'Now, the previous year the royal houses of Holland, Austria and England had met at The Hague and signed a treaty of alliance the aim of which was to remove the Spanish crown from the head of Philip V and place it on that of an archduke whom they – prematurely – called Charles III.

'Spain was forced to oppose the coalition. But she had precious few soldiers and sailors. However, she was not short of money, always assuming that her galleons continued to reach her ports laden with gold and silver from America. Towards the end of 1702 Spain was awaiting the arrival of a rich convoy for which France supplied an escort consisting of a fleet of twenty-three ships under the command of Admiral de Château-Renault, because the coalition's navies were patrolling the Atlantic.

'The convoy was heading for Cadiz, but on learning that the English fleet was cruising those waters the admiral decided instead to make towards a French port.

'The captains of the galleons in the Spanish convoy protested against his decision. They insisted on being escorted to a Spanish port which, if it could not be Cadiz, should be the Bay of Vigo on the north-west coast of Spain, where there was no blockade.

'Admiral de Château-Renault gave way weakly and granted what they demanded. The galleons duly sailed into the Bay of Vigo.

'Unfortunately, the bay is an open harbour which cannot be defended. So the galleons had to be unloaded quickly before the coalition fleet arrived. There would have been more than

enough time to complete the operation if a sordid conflict of
rivalry had not suddenly flared up.

'Are you following this series of events?' asked Captain
Nemo.

'Perfectly,' I replied, still not knowing why I was being given
this history lesson.

'Good. I'll carry on. This is what happened next. The Cadiz
merchants had been awarded sole rights to handle all goods
arriving from the West Indies. Unloading the ingots carried by
the galleons in the port of Vigo was thus an infringement of
their monopoly. So they complained to Madrid and obtained a
ruling from the ineffectual Philip V, stating that the convoy
was not to be unloaded but would remain in quarantine in the
Vigo roadstead until the enemy fleet had sailed away.

'While this ruling was being decided on, English vessels
arrived in the Bay of Vigo on 22 October 1702. Admiral de
Château-Renault, despite commanding an inferior force, fought
with courage. But when he saw that the riches carried by the
convoy were in danger of falling into the enemy's hands, he
burned and scuttled the galleons along with their immense
treasure.'

Captain Nemo stopped. I confess I still did not see how this
tale could possibly concern me.

'Well?' I asked.

'Well, Professor Aronnax,' said Captain Nemo, 'we are
now, at this moment, in the Bay of Vigo. You have only to say
the word and you shall solve its mysteries.'

The captain got to his feet and asked me to follow him. I
had had time to recover and did what he asked. The Great Saloon was in darkness, but through the glass panels the sparkling
waves of the sea were visible. I stared out.

Around the *Nautilus*, over a radius of half a mile, the water
was bright with the illumination of our electric searchlight.
The sandy bottom was clean and clear. Members of the crew
in diving suits were retrieving half-rotted barrels and disem-
bowelled chests from the blackened wreckage. From the chests
and barrels spilled ingots of gold and silver, cascades of piasters
and jewels. The sand was littered with them. Laden with their

'*From the chests and barrels spilled ingots of gold and silver*'

precious booty, they returned to the *Nautilus*, set down their burdens, then returned to the task of harvesting more of this inexhaustible haul of silver and gold.

Now I understood! We were in the middle of the scene of the sea battle of 22 October 1702. Here, on this very spot, had been sunk the galleons loaded with a cargo intended for the Spanish government. Here Captain Nemo came whenever he needed money and simply carried off the millions with which he kept the *Nautilus* afloat. It was to him and him alone that the Americas had ultimately delivered their precious metals. He was the direct and sole heir of the treasures taken from the Incas and the peoples who had been vanquished by Hernán Cortez!

'Professor,' he asked with a smile, 'did you ever realize the sea contained such wealth?'

'I know,' I replied, 'that it has been estimated that some 2 million tons of silver are held in suspension in its waters.'

'Quite true, but in order to raise them, the cost of extracting that sliver would be greater than the profit. Whereas here, I only have to pick up what other men have mislaid, not only in the Bay of Vigo but at the site of thousands of shipwrecks which I have carefully marked on my submarine charts. Now do you understand why I am a multi-billionaire?'

'I do, captain. But allow me to observe that, by plundering the Bay of Vigo, all you have done is to anticipate the activities of a rival company.'

'And what company would that be?'

'A company to which the Spanish government has given sole rights to search for sunken galleons. Investors are tempted by the bait of huge profits, because it has been estimated that the total value of such sunken treasure is around 500 million francs.'

'Five hundred million!' said Captain Nemo. 'That may have been the figure, but it is no longer.'

'As you say,' I replied. 'Therefore a word of advice to investors would be a gesture of kindness. But who can say if it would be welcome? What gamblers always regret most is not so much the money they lose as the money their wild hopes led them to believe they would acquire. Still, I am less sorry for them than I am for the thousands of unfortunates whose lot would have been eased if such wealth had been charitably distributed. As things are, these riches will never do them any good at all.'

I had no sooner expressed this regret than I sensed that I must have touched on a sore point with Captain Nemo.

'Do them no good!' he said, bridling. 'So you think this wealth is lost because you see me salvaging it? Do you believe that I go to the trouble of recovering treasure solely for my own benefit? How do you know that I don't put it to good use? Do you really think that I am unaware that there are people who suffer, whole races on the globe which are oppressed, needy people who must be helped, victims who must be avenged? Do you not understand . . .'

Captain Nemo broke off there, regretting perhaps that he might have said too much. But I had sensed the rest. Whatever the reasons which had driven him to seek independence beneath the seas, he had remained a man! His heart still beat in time to the sufferings of humanity, and his charitable impulses extended to enslaved races as well to individuals.

At that moment, I knew exactly to whom the millions Captain Nemo had sent when the *Nautilus* had sailed through the waters of insurgent Crete were destined!

9

A Drowned Continent

The next morning, 19 February, the Canadian strode into my cabin. I had been expecting him. He looked a disappointed man.

'Well, professor?' he said.

'Well, Ned, luck was against us yesterday.'

'It certainly was. Why did the damned captain have to stop at the very moment we were about to escape from his boat?'

'Actually, Ned, he had an appointment with his banker.'

'Banker?'

'Or rather, his bank. I mean by that the ocean, where his money is safer than it would be in the coffers of any state.'

I told the Canadian about what had happened the previous evening, secretly hoping to bring him round to the idea of not abandoning the captain. But my account of events had no other result than to make him express strong regret at not having had the chance himself to go out for a tour of the site of the battle of Vigo Bay, for his own benefit.

'But we're not finished yet!' he said. 'It's just one harpoon off target. Next time, we'll succeed, maybe even tonight!'

'What's the *Nautilus*'s course?'

'No idea,' said Ned.

'No matter. We'll get the bearing at noon.'

The Canadian went back to Conseil. As soon as I was dressed, I strolled to the Great Saloon. The compass was not reassuring. The *Nautilus*'s course was south-south-west. We had turned our backs on Europe.

I waited with some impatience for our position to be marked on the map. At about 11.30 the tanks were emptied, and the vessel returned to the surface. I climbed up to the platform. Ned Land had beaten me to it.

There was no land in sight, only empty sea. A few sails on the horizon. They probably belonged to boats which make for Cape Saint Roch, where they can pick up favourable winds to take them to and round the Cape of Good Hope. The sky was grey with cloud. Soon the wind would be blowing hard.

Ned, fuming, tried to see through the misty horizon, still hoping that behind the fog was land, which he was burning to see.

At noon the sun appeared briefly. The first officer took advantage of the break in the cloud to measure its height. Then, when the sea began to develop a swell, we went below again, and the hatch was closed behind us.

When I looked at the map an hour later, I saw that the position of the *Nautilus* was given as longitude 16° 17' and latitude 33° 22', which put us at 150 leagues from the nearest land. There was no point in thinking of escape now, and, as will be easily imagined, the Canadian became incandescent with rage when I told him where we were.

Personally, I was not overly put out. Actually, I felt that a weight had been taken off my mind, and I was able to resume my usual labours in a mood of relative calm.

Around eleven in the evening I received an unexpected visit from Captain Nemo. He inquired most considerately if I felt tired after staying up so late the previous night. I said I did not.

'In that case, Professor Aronnax, I would like to suggest an interesting expedition.'

'What do you propose?'

'Thus far you have inspected the sea-floor only during the day, by the light of the sun. Would you be interested in seeing what it's like in total darkness?'

'I would indeed.'

'I must warn you that you will find the experience taxing. We shall have to walk a long way and climb a mountain. The paths are not at all well maintained.'

'What you say, Captain, makes me doubly curious. So lead on. I am ready.'

'In that case, come with me. We shall go and put on our diving suits.'

When we reached the locker room, I saw that neither of my companions nor any members of the crew would be going with us on our expedition. Captain Nemo had not even suggested that we should take Ned Land and Conseil along with us.

Within minutes, we had donned our suits. Fully filled cylinders of air were fastened to our backs, but the electric lamps had not been got ready for us. I remarked upon this to the captain.

'We won't need them,' he replied.

I thought I must not have heard him properly but I could not ask him again because his head had already disappeared inside his metal helmet. I finished strapping myself into my suit. Someone handed me a metal-tipped hiking stick, and soon, after the usual exit drill, we were treading the floor of the Atlantic Ocean, at a depth of 300 metres!

It was getting near to midnight. The water was pitch-black, but Captain Nemo pointed into the distance, towards a reddish glimmer, a kind of spreading glow, which was visible about 2 miles from the *Nautilus*. What this fire was, what materials fuelled it, why and how it kept on burning when surrounded by water were things I could not explain. Be that as it may, it gave us light, a dim light it's true, but I soon grew accustomed to the eerie gloom and now saw why there was no need for Ruhmkorff lamps.

Captain Nemo and I walked abreast by the straightest route towards the fiery light. The flat ground began to rise gradually. We took great strides, aided by our sticks, yet our progress was slow, because our feet kept sinking into a kind of mud mixed with seaweed which was full of small, flat stones.

As we advanced, I began to hear a kind of sizzling sound above my head. At times, it got louder and became a continuous pattering. I soon realized what was causing it. It was rain beating noisily on the waves on the surface. Instinctively I thought I would get wet! Made wet by water when I was immersed in water! I could not help laughing at this weird idea. Still, it must be remembered that inside the thick diving suit, we were not aware of any effects of being surrounded by water, only of being in an atmosphere that was only slightly denser than the atmosphere on land.

After we had been walking for half an hour, the terrain became rocky. Jellyfish, microscopic crustaceans and sea pens and sea pansies of the order *pennatulacea* lit our way dimly with a phosphorescent glow. In the gloom, I made out heaps of stones covered with millions of zoophytes and tangled marine algae. Our boots kept slipping on these carpets of seaweed, and without the help of my stick I would have fallen more than once. When I turned round, I could still see the whitish searchlight of the *Nautilus*, which grew fainter the further we got from it.

The heaps of stones I mentioned were spread out over the ocean bed in a regular pattern which I could not explain. I saw wide channels which ran away into the dark distance and defied my attempts to estimate their length. Other oddities appeared which I could not account for. I had a feeling that my heavy lead soles were crushing a litter of bones that made sharp snapping sounds. What on earth was this vast plain which I was now traversing? I wished I could have asked Captain Nemo. But he communicated by means of signs if he wished to speak with his members of the crew when they accompanied him on these underwater forays, and I had yet to understand them.

Meanwhile, the reddish glow which guided us grew stronger and soon filled the entire horizon. The presence of this source of fire under the water puzzled me greatly. Was it a manifestation of some sort of electrical discharge? Was I walking towards some kind of natural phenomenon as yet unknown to science? Or even – the thought did cross my mind – was the hand of man to some degree involved in this blazing inferno? Was it fanning the flames? Was I about to meet, in these lower depths, companions or friends of Captain Nemo, leading the same strange style of life as he, whom he was about to visit? Would I find, here below, a whole colony of exiles who, tired of the miseries of life on land, had sought and found independence deep below the surface of the ocean? These wild, extravagant ideas went round and round in my head. Given my state of mind, a turmoil constantly fuelled by the succession of wonders

which unfolded before me, I should not have been at all surprised to discover, at the bottom of the sea, one of those
undersea cities which Captain Nemo dreamed of!

Our way got lighter the further we went. A whitish light
shone from the top of a mountain which must have been 800
feet high. But what I was seeing was simply an optical effect
produced by the crystal clarity of the water. The seat of the
fire, which was the source of this inexplicable brilliance, was
located on the further side of the mountain.

Captain Nemo strode surefootedly through the labyrinth of
rocks which scarred the floor of the Atlantic Ocean. He knew
his way in the dark. He had probably come this way often and
would not get lost. I followed him with total confidence. To
me, he seemed like one of those spirits of the sea, and as he
walked on ahead of me I admired his tall figure outlined in
black against the luminous backdrop of the ocean.

It was now one in the morning. We had reached the lower
slopes of the mountain. To climb them we would first have to
make our way through the tangled paths of an extensive grove
of marine trees.

Yes, a grove of dead trees, without leaves, without sap, carbonized by the action of sea-water, dominated here and there
by gigantic pines. It was as if it had turned to coal while still
standing, a vertical rather than horizontal seam, its roots still
clinging to the sunken soil, its branches as though cut out of
black paper standing out crisply against the sky of the waves
above. Picture a forest in the Bavarian Hartz clinging to the
side of a mountain, only completed submerged. The pathways
were clogged with green and brown algae among which was a
teeming world of crustaceans. On I went, scrambling over
rocks, stepping over fallen trunks, snapping the trailing marine
lianas that hung between one tree and the next, scaring the
fish, which flew from branch to branch. I felt no fatigue and
kept up with my indefatigable guide.

What a sight it was! How can I convey the scene? What
words can I use to describe the way the woods and the rocks
looked in that watery world, dark and grim low down but coloured in shades of red on their upper branches when lit by the

light which was intensified by the reflective powers of water?
We clambered up crumbling rocks. Whole blocks broke away
and rolled down with the muffled roar of an avalanche. To
right and left gaped the mouths of shadowy caverns whose
depths defied the keenest eye. But here too were wide, open
glades which seemed to have been cleared by human hands,
and I began to wonder if some citizen of this watery place
would not suddenly jump up out of nowhere.

But Captain Nemo continued his ascent. I had no wish to be
left behind and followed boldly. My stick proved invaluable.
One wrong step would have been very dangerous on these narrow paths scooped out of the sides of precipices, but I pressed
on with a firm step, quite unaffected by vertigo. One moment
I would leap across a crevasse, whose depth would have made
me flinch had I been confronted by it on a land-bound glacier,
and the next I was venturing on to the unstable trunk of a tree
which bridged an abyss, without looking down, having eyes
only for admiring the wild grandeur of the place. There monu-
mental blocks of stone teetering on uneven foundations seemed
to defy the laws of equilibrium. From the crevices in the stone,
trees sprouted like jets as if they had been squeezed out by
some colossal pressure, and they supported other trees which
in turn supported them. There were also natural towers and
mighty rock faces sheer as castle walls that leaned at angles
which would not have been tolerated on land by the laws of
gravity.

Was not I myself also being subjected to that same difference due to the powerful effect of the density of the water? For
despite my heavy suit, copper helmet and lead soles, I found I
was able to scale impossibly steep slopes, skipping as lightly as
a Pyrenean goat or a chamois, so to speak!

As I pen this account of our underwater expedition, I know
how unbelievable it must sound. I am the chronicler of things
which seem to be impossible but are true and incontestably
real. It was not a dream! I saw and felt it all!

Two hours after leaving the *Nautilus* we emerged above the
tree-line. A hundred feet above us towered the summit of the
mountain, which loomed over us in such a way as to blot out

the source of the intense light coming from the other side of it. A few petrified bushes sprouted here and there in ragged, irregular clumps. Fish rose in shoals from under our feet like birds startled in tall grass. The rocky mountain side was fissured with impenetrable caves, deep grottos and bottomless pits, from which I heard fearsome stirrings. My heart almost stopped whenever I saw an enormous feeler barring my path or some terrible claw snapping shut inside a shadowy cavern! Thousands of small lights gleamed in the dark. They were the eyes of giant crustaceans lurking in their dens, huge lobsters standing to attention like halberdiers, waving their claws to an accompaniment of dry, metallic rattles, massive crabs primed like cannon on their carriages, and terrifying octopi writhing like living bushes with serpents for branches.

What sort of outrageous world was this about which I knew so little? In what marine order could these articulates, for whom the living rock was a second shell, be placed? Where had nature discovered the secret of their vegetative life? For how many centuries had they been living like this in the darkest depths of the ocean?

But I could not afford to loiter. Captain Nemo, well accustomed to these terrifying creatures, paid them no attention. By now we were on a level ledge where even greater surprises awaited me. Here were picturesque ruins which bore the mark, not of the Creator, but of human hands, vast heaps of stones which resembled the vague outlines of castles and temples draped in robes of flowering zoophytes over which, instead of ivy, a vegetable cloak of green and brown marine plants had grown.

What was this place on the globe which had clearly been swallowed up by some natural disaster? Who had laid out these rocks and stones which looked like dolmens from prehistoric times? Where was I? Where had Captain Nemo's whim brought me?

I wanted to ask him. But since this was not possible, I stopped him and gripped his arm. But he shook his head negatively and pointed to the final summit of the mountain. He seemed to be saying:

'Huge lobsters, massive crabs'

'Come on! Keep going! Don't stop now!'

I followed him for one last effort and within minutes I was standing on top of the mountain which rose about ten metres or so above the rocky escarpment.

I turned and looked down over the slope we had just climbed. On that side, the summit was no more than seven or eight hundred feet above the plain below. But on the other side, the mountain towered over its foot, which was located on the bed of the Atlantic at more than twice that depth. Then I raised my eyes and looked into a vast space lit by a dazzling blaze. For the mountain was in fact a volcano. Some 50 feet below the summit, under a rain of stones and scoria, a wide crater was spewing torrents of lava which flowed like a cascade of fire into the surrounding water. Placed where it was, the volcano stood like an immense beacon which lit up the plain below all the way to the horizon.

As I said, the submarine crater produced molten lava but no flames. Flames require oxygen derived from the air and they cannot live in water. But flows of lava, which contain the principle of their combustion within them, can remain white hot and overcome water, which they vaporize on contact. Fast-running currents carried away all the gases which were released, and the lava flowed to the foot of the mountain exactly as molten rock from Vesuvius runs down towards Torre del Greco.

For there at my feet, in ruins, devastated, toppled, lay a mass of rubble which had once been a city. Its roofs were stove in, its temples fallen, its arches broken, its columns lying on the ground, but over it all hung the faint echoes of the solid proportions of what might have been Tuscan architecture. Further along stood the remnants of a gigantic aqueduct, the furred-up remains of an acropolis, with the blurred outlines of a Parthenon; then the vestiges of a wharf, as if some ancient port had once sat by a vanished sea where trading boats and war triremes had once berthed; still further off, long lines of broken-down walls, wide deserted streets, another Pompeii beneath the water. This was what Captain Nemo had brought me here to see and by seeing it, to bring it to life once more.

Where was I? I felt I had to know whatever the cost, I needed

'There at my feet, in ruins, devastated, toppled, lay a mass of rubble which had once been a city'

to ask, I wanted to tear off the metal sphere in which my head
was encased.

But Captain Nemo came to me and stopped me with a sign.
Then picking up a piece of chalky stone he stood in front of a
block of black basalt and on it wrote a single word:

ATLANTIS

Illumination flooded my brain! Atlantis – as the ancient Mer-
opis of Theopompus of Chios and the Atlantis of Plato, the
continent whose existence was denied by Origen, Porphyry,
Iamblichus, d'Anville, Malte-Brun and Humboldt, who believed
that its disappearance belonged to the realm of legend, but
accepted by Posidonius, Pliny, Ammianus Marcellinus, Tertul-
lian, Engel, Sherer, Tournefort, Buffon and d'Avezac – Atlantis
was there, before my very eyes, still bearing the irrefutable
marks of its destruction! So it was here in this submerged region
located outside Europe, Asia and Libya, 'beyond the Pillars of
Hercules', that the powerful Atlanteans, against whom ancient
Greece had waged its first wars, had lived!

The historian who first put on paper the major achievements
of those heroic times was Plato himself. His dialogues *Timaeus*
and *Critias* were written, so to speak, under the direct inspiration of Solon, who was both poet and lawmaker.

One day Solon was in conversation with venerable priests of
Sais, an Egyptian city already 800 years old, as is attested by
the civic annals engraved on the holy walls of its temples. One
of the sages told the story of another city, which was 1,000
years older. This first Athenian city, 900 centuries old, had
been invaded and partly destroyed by the Atlanteans. These
Atlanteans, he said, came from a vast continent, far greater
than Africa and Asia put together, which was situated between
the twelfth and the fortieth degrees of latitude north. Their
empire reached as far as Egypt, and they sought to impose
their power on Greece. But they were obliged to withdraw
when faced by the unconquerable resistance of the Hellenes.
Centuries passed. Then a cataclysm occurred which led to
floods and earthquakes. A night and a day sufficed for the

whole continent of Atlantis to be engulfed by the sea. Only its
tallest mountains, Madeira, the Azores, the Canaries and the
Islands of Cape Verde, were left showing above the water.

Such were the historical memories stirred in my mind by the
inscription Captain Nemo showed me. It had come about that,
propelled by my strange destiny, I was able to set foot on one
of the mountain peaks of that drowned continent. I could
reach out and touch ruins which were thousands of centuries
old and dated back to the great geological epochs. I walked
where once had walked the contemporaries of the first men!
Beneath my heavy boots I trampled on the skeletons of animals
which had lived in the age of fables and had once upon a time
sought the shade of leafy trees now turned to carbon![15]

Oh why did I have so little time there? I would have liked to
climb down the steep-sided mountain, travel across the whole
of that immense continent, which had clearly once joined
Africa to America, and visit its antediluvian cities. There, perhaps as I gazed down, lay bellicose Machimos and god-fearing
Eusebes, whose gigantic inhabitants lived for centuries and
whose strength was more than equal to the task of lifting the
blocks of stone that still resisted the destructive action of the
sea. Some day, perhaps, a new eruptive event would bring these
submerged ruins back to the surface. A number of subterranean volcanoes have been detected under this part of the
ocean, and many ships have detected unexplained tremors as
they sailed over these troubled depths. Some have heard muffled sounds which they reckoned were made by the clash of
warring elements; others have picked up volcanic ash cast up
from under the sea. The entire sea-bed as far as the Equator is
still subject to the active forces of Pluto. Who knows if, at some
distant date in the future, volcanic dejecta will not build up on
successive layers of lava and bring the tops of new ignivomous
mountains into existence on the surface of the Atlantic?

While I was musing along these lines and forcing myself to
fix in my memory every detail of this grandiose seascape, Captain Nemo, leaning on his elbows on a mossy stele, remained
perfectly still, as if petrified, lost in silent wonder. Was he
thinking about those vanished generations? Was he asking

them if they knew the secret of human destiny? Was it here
that this enigmatic man returned to reconnect with his knowledge of the past and live for a while the life of this ancient
city – for was he not a man who refused to have anything to do
with modern living? What would I not have given to know his
innermost thoughts, so that I could share them and understand
them?

We remained in this place for a whole hour, contemplating
the immense plain lit by the molten lava which at times glowed
with astonishing intensity. The earth's internal convulsions
sent sudden tremors running up the outer surface of the mountain. The sound of deep explosions, swiftly transmitted in that
liquid medium, reverberated with majestic fullness.

Just then, the moon appeared, shining briefly through the
water above us, and cast a short-lived pale light over that
drowned continent. It was a brief interlude, but its effect was
indescribable. Captain Nemo straightened up, cast one final
look over the vast plain and then raised one hand. It was the
signal for me to follow him.

We turned and went back down the mountain in short
order. Once we had passed though the mineralized forest, I
caught sight of the *Nautilus*'s searchlight twinkling like a star.
The captain headed straight for it, and we were back on board
ship just as the first glimmerings of dawn began to blanch the
surface of the ocean.

10

Neptune's Coalfields

The next day, 20 February, I woke late. The exertions of the previous night made me sleep on until eleven o'clock. I dressed quickly for I was most anxious to know what course the *Nautilus* was following. The instruments told me that we were still heading south at a speed of 20 knots and a depth of 100 metres.

Conseil entered the room. I told him all about our nocturnal expedition, and through the viewing panels, which were open, he was able to see something of that submerged continent.

For the *Nautilus* was skimming over the Atlantean plain not more than 10 metres above the ocean floor. She was moving like a balloon blown by wind over flat land, though it would be more accurate to say that we were more like passengers in an express train. The foreground passing before us contained detached outcrops of stone carved into fantastic shapes, forests of trees which had ceased to belong to the vegetable kingdom and had graduated to the animal realm. Their stark, unmoving outlines looked grim beneath the waves. There were also heaps of stones buried under a covering of marine exidia and sea anemones bristling with tall, vertical hydrophytes. We also saw strangely contorted blocks of lava, which bore vivid witness to the fury of Pluto's convulsions.

While watching these bizarre sites resplendent in the electric light which we shed all around us, I told Conseil the history of the Atlanteans who, in terms of pure imagination, had inspired Bailly to devote such delightful pages to them. I told him about the wars fought by those heroic people. I discussed Atlantis as a man who had no cause now to doubt its existence. But Conseil's mind was on other things, and he did not listen very closely. His reluctance to show interest in the historical point of view was soon explained.

For his eye was continually drawn to numerous kinds of fish. Whenever they swam past, Conseil, transported to the blissful realms of classification, ceased to live in the real world. When that happened, there was nothing for it but to follow his lead and resume my ichthyological studies.

In the event, it turned out that the fish of the Atlantic were not noticeably different to the fish we had observed up to this point. There were rays of monstrous size, 5 metres long and endowed with tremendous muscular power which allowed them to leap quite out of the water; squali of various kinds including one 15-foot *isurus glaucus* with triangular, razor-sharp teeth, its semi-transparency making it virtually invisible in the water; brown sea-bream; dogfish shaped like prisms and armour-plated with tuberculous skin; sturgeons not very dissimilar to their near relatives in the Mediterranean; *syngnathidae*, yellowish-brown, 18 inches long, with small grey fins but neither teeth nor tongue, which sped by like thin, lithe serpents.

Among the bony fish Conseil noted blackish blue marlin 3 metres long with the upper jaw forming a sharp sword; brightly coloured weever fish, known in Aristotle's time as sea dragons, which have stinging dorsal spines that make them very dangerous to handle; *coryphaena*, with brown backs striped with thin blue flashes trimmed with gold border; fine specimens of dorados; moonfish, disc-shaped with light-blue bands which when reflecting the rays of the sun, look for all the world like flashes of silver; and lastly swordfish 8 metres long, operating in groups, with yellowish scythe-shaped fins and swords measuring 6 feet, intrepid animals, more herbivorous than piscivorous, which obey the smallest command of their females, like well-trained husbands.

But while observing these various specimens of marine fauna, I did not pass up this chance to scrutinize the wider plains of Atlantis. From time to time, random irregularities in the terrain forced the *Nautilus* to reduce speed. At such times, she would glide, agile as any crustacean, through narrow clefts between ragged hills. If the way grew too labyrinthine, she

simply rose, like an air balloon, and once safely over the obstacle, she went swiftly on her way just metres above the ocean
floor. It was a splendid, delightful way to travel, not unlike a
balloon flight, except that the *Nautilus* automatically responded
to the directing hand of the helmsman.

Around four in the afternoon, the nature of the terrain,
which for the most part had consisted of thick mud bristling
with mineralized branches, changed imperceptibly. It became
rockier, with more conglomerates and basaltic tuff, with an
admixture of lava and sulphurous obsidian. I assumed that this
mountainous region would soon give way to long, rolling
plains. But at various phases of the *Nautilus*'s progress, I did in
fact see that the southern horizon was barred by a wall, which
seemed to have no way through. Its highest point obviously
reached well above sea-level. It had to be the start of a continent, or at the very least an island, perhaps one of the Canaries,
or the Cape Verde Islands. No noon reading had been made –
perhaps deliberately – so I did not know our position. Either
way, I thought that a cliff wall like that must signal the extreme
limit of the Atlantean plain, of which we had sailed over only a
tiny part.

The coming of night did not interrupt my observations. I
was now alone, for Conseil had returned to his cabin. The
Nautilus, reducing speed, was weaving through the anfractu-
osities of the terrain, at times almost grazing the bottom as
though it were about to set down on it, at others returning
unpredictably to the surface. I was then able to catch sight
through the crystal-clear water of bright constellations or – to
be precise – of five or six of the stars in the Zodiac which cling
to Orion's tail.

I would have remained at my post for much longer, admiring the beauties of sea and sky, but the viewing panels suddenly
closed. At that moment the *Nautilus* had fetched up against
the foot of the high rock face. How she proposed to navigate
thereafter I could not even guess. I returned to my cabin. The
Nautilus had come to a dead stop. I fell asleep quite determined to wake after snatching a few hours' sleep.

But it was already eight o'clock the next morning when I

returned to the Great Saloon. I glanced at the depth gauge and saw that the *Nautilus* was now on the surface. I could hear the sound of feet on the platform. I was also aware that the ship was not rolling, which did not suggest the action of waves.

I climbed up and paused by the hatch, which was open. But instead of full daylight, as I had expected, I found myself staring into pitch blackness. Where were we? Had I made some mistake? Was it still night-time? No! No stars twinkled overhead and night is never as completely dark as this!

I did not know what to think. Then a voice spoke:

'Is that you, professor?'

'Ah, Captain Nemo!' I said. 'Where on earth are we?'

'Under it.'

'Under the earth?' I cried. 'Is the *Nautilus* still afloat?'

'Still afloat.'

'I don't understand.'

'Wait a moment. Our searchlight is about to be turned on, and if you prefer well-lit conditions, I think you'll like what you see.'

I stepped out on to the platform and waited. The darkness was so intense that I could not even see Captain Nemo. But if I looked up, straight above my head, I thought I could make out an uncertain glimmer, a sort of half-light which filled a circular shape. At that moment, the searchlight suddenly came on, and its brightness swamped the faint glow.

For a few moments I was too dazzled to see anything. When I opened my eyes I saw that the *Nautilus* was stationary, berthed beside a spit of land which served as a natural jetty. The sea on which she had come to rest was a lake locked inside a ring of walls 2 miles in diameter, with a circumference of 6. Its level, as had been shown by the depth gauge, had to be the same as that of the ocean outside, since there must be a channel or some other link between this lake and the sea. The high walls sloped out over their base then curved inwards to form a vaulted roof, so that the whole resembled an inverted funnel five or six hundred metres high. At the top was an opening through which I had seen that faint glimmer which evidently came from the daylight outside.

Before taking a closer look at the interior of this huge cavern, and before trying to determine whether it was the handiwork of nature or of man, I turned to Captain Nemo:

'Where is this place?' I asked.

'In the centre of an extinct volcano,' replied Captain Nemo, 'a volcano which was flooded by the sea after some underground convulsion. While you were asleep, professor, the *Nautilus* entered this lagoon through a natural tunnel 10 metres below the surface of the ocean. It is our home base, a safe port, convenient, secret, a refuge against the worst that the winds can do. Could you name me a place on the coast of any continent or island which could offer any such shelter against the fury of the elements?'

'I can see, captain,' I replied, 'that you are very safe here. Who could get to you in the middle of a volcano? But is that not an opening I see up there?'

'Yes, it's the crater, which was once full of lava, fumes and flames but now allows in the life-giving air which you are breathing.'

'So what or where is this volcanic mountain?'

'It is situated on one of the many small islands which are scattered all over this part of the ocean. For ships it is just another reef. For us, it is a huge cave. I discovered it purely by chance, and, for once, chance has served me well.'

'But wouldn't it be possible to come down through the opening which used to be the crater?'

'No more possible than for me to climb up through it. To a height of 100 feet, the inside walls of the cavern are climbable. But above that, the walls form an overhang and cannot be scaled.'

'I see, captain, that nature is constantly on your side. You are quite safe here on this lake, and no one else can sail into these waters. But why do you need a refuge? The *Nautilus* does not need a home port.'

'She does not, professor, but she does need electricity to power her and materials to produce the electricity, sodium to produce the materials, coal to produce the sodium and mines to produce the coal. Here, in this place, the sea covers whole

forests which were engulfed by the sea in geological times.
Carbonized now and changed into coal, they give me an inexhaustible supply of fuel.'

'So your sailors become miners here?'

'Exactly. The coalfields extend under the sea just as they do
at Newcastle. Here, my men dig out coal in diving suits, armed
with pick and mattock. I have never had to beg coal from any
mine on land. When I burn it to make sodium, the smoke which
escapes through the top of this mountain gives the impression
that it is a still active volcano.

'And shall we see your men at work?'

'No, not this time, because I am anxious to press on with
our underwater tour of the world. So I shall just use the reserves
of sodium which I have built up here. Give us time to load it on
board – one day will be enough – and we shall be on our way.
So if you would like to explore the cavern and walk around the
lake, make the most of today, Professor Aronnax.'

I thanked the captain and went in search of my companions, who had still not emerged from their cabin. I invited them
to come with me without telling them where they were.

They went out on to the platform. Conseil, always imperturbable, considered it perfectly natural to wake up inside a
mountain, having gone to bed the night before under the sea.
But Ned Land had only one thought: to find out if there was
some way out of this domed cavern.

After breakfast, around ten in the morning, we stepped out
on to the jetty.

'So here we are, back on dry land again,' said Conseil.

'I don't call this "land",' replied the Canadian. 'Anyway,
we're not on it. We're under it.'

Between the foot of the rocky walls and the water's edge
was a stretch of sand 500 feet wide at its broadest point. It was
possible to walk all the way round the lake using this beach.
But at the base of the high walls the ground was very uneven,
strewn with picturesque accumulations of volcanic blocks and
huge slabs of pumice stone. All these broken rocks, enamelled
to a polished shine by the action of the subterranean fires,
gleamed as they caught the electric beam of the searchlight.

The micaceous dust disturbed by our feet rose in sparkling clouds.

The ground rose steeply the further we got from the shoreline. We soon reached long, winding ledges which formed steps, and we climbed them steadily, though we had to tread warily across the shale and gravel, as it had nothing to cement it together, and our feet kept slipping on vitreous trachytes made of crystals of feldspar and quartz.

The volcanic origin of this huge, scooped-out space was clear everywhere we looked. I pointed this out to my companions.

'Can you imagine,' said I, 'what this funnel must have been like when it was full of boiling lava and the level of incandescent sludge rose all the way up to the opening in the mountain, the way molten iron fills a blast furnace?'

'I have no difficulty imagining it,' said Conseil. 'But perhaps monsieur would explain why this great foundry ceased operations and how it came about that the fiery furnace has been replaced by the tranquil waters of a lake?'

'It was most probably, Conseil, because there was some sort of eruption on the ocean bed which opened up the channel which the *Nautilus* uses to come and go. When that happened, water from the Atlantic rushed inside the mountain. There followed the most almighty struggle between the two elements, resulting in victory for Neptune. But many centuries have passed since then, and during that time the drowned volcano turned into a peaceful grotto.'

'That's clear,' said Ned Land, 'and I accept your explanation. But from our point of view, I regret that the tunnel you mentioned, professor, was not located above sea-level.'

'But Ned,' replied Conseil, 'if the tunnel hadn't been under the sea, the *Nautilus* would not have been able to use it.'

'And I would add, Ned, that neither would the sea have rushed into the mountain in the first place and that the volcano would have gone on being a volcano. Your regrets are therefore wide of the mark.'

We pressed on with our ascent. The way grew steeper and narrower. At times, it was interrupted by deep fissures, which we had to jump over. Huge overhangs had to be negotiated. We were forced on to our hands and knees. We crawled on our bellies. But with the help of Conseil's agility and the Canadian's strength, we overcame all these obstacles.

When we had reached a height of about 30 metres, the nature of the terrain changed, though it became no easier. After the shale and the trachytes came black basalt. Sometimes there were rough, gritty stretches of it. Elsewhere, it had formed into regularly shaped prisms which rose in colonnades and supported the arching of the enormous roof, a wonderful example of natural architecture. Between the basalt colonnades wound long flows of cooled lava encrusted with seams of bituminous coal and, in places, with wide swathes of sulphur. Though the light entering through the crater above us was stronger here, it cast a still uncertain illumination over all these volcanic dejections entombed inside this extinct mountain.

But our upward progress was halted when we were about 250 feet high by an unsurpassable obstacle. The arching of the roof turned into a permanent overhang, and our vertical climb had to be changed to a circular trek. At this height the vegetable kingdom began to challenge the mineral. A few shrubs, even one or two trees sprouted from the crevices in the walls. I identified a few euphorbias, which oozed caustic sap. There were the half-faded colours and stale scent of heliotropes, though they failed miserably to live up to their name, since the rays of the sun never reached them here. Here and there a handful of chrysanthemums grew shyly under aloes, whose long leaves looked sad and sickly. But between the flows of solidified lava I noticed small violets which managed a faint perfume, which, I confess, delighted me. The scent of a flower is its very soul, and the flowers that grow in the sea – I refer to those splendid hydrophytes – are lacking in that department!

We had reached a clump of robust dragon trees, which had split the rocks with their powerful roots, when Ned Land cried:

'Look, professor! A hive!'

'A hive?' I exclaimed, waving a dismissive hand in total disbelief.

'Yes, a hive,' repeated the Canadian, 'with real bees buzzing all around it.'

I looked more closely and was forced to concede. There, crowding round the mouth of a hole made in the trunk of a dragon tree, were several thousands of these ingenious insects which are found throughout the Canaries, where the fruits of their labours are particularly valued.

Ned's first thought, of course, was to acquire a share of the honey, and it would have been ungracious of me to object. With his flint, he lit a handful of dried leaves, to which he added a little sulphur, and with it began to smoke out the bees. Gradually the buzzing subsided, and when the hive was opened up it yielded several pounds of fragrant honey. Ned transferred the entire comb to his haversack.

'I'll mix this honey with the inside of a bread-fruit and bake you a very tasty cake!'

'Excellent!' said Conseil. 'Gingerbread!'

'Let's forget the gingerbread for now,' I said, 'and carry on with our fascinating ramble.'

From certain points on the path we were following we had a full view of the lake. The searchlight was bright enough to illuminate its entire surface, which was free of ripples and waves. The *Nautilus* was absolutely still. On the platform and on the jetty crewmen were busy, moving like black shadows under the bright lights of the ship.

By this time we were making our way round the highest part of the ring of lower rocks which held up the roof. There I saw that bees were not the only representatives of the animal kingdom inside the volcano. Birds of prey hovered and glided here and there in the shadows or fled from nests clinging to rocky crags. There were sparrowhawks with white breasts, and shrieking kestrels. Sleek, plump bustards scurried over these lower slopes as fast as their long legs would carry them. It will come as no surprise that the Canadian's instincts were roused by the sight of such tasty game. Since he had no gun with him, he set about replacing lead with stones. After several unsuccessful attempts, he managed to hit one of those magnificent birds. To say that he risked his life a score of times trying to catch it is only the honest truth. But he persisted until the animal was safe in his knapsack along with the honeycomb.

Shortly after this, we were forced to climb back down to the lake, for the high circular trail had become impassable. Above us, the gaping crater looked like the opening of a wide-necked well. Through it, from our position, we had a pretty clear view of the sky, and I glimpsed dishevelled clouds being chivvied along by the west wind which left remnants of them clinging like wisps of mist to the top of the mountain. It was proof that the clouds were at no great height since the volcano did not rise much above 800 feet above sea-level.

Half an hour after Ned's latest exploit, we were back down on the inland beach. Here the flora were represented by a carpet of samphire, a small umbelliferous plant used for pickling and preserving, which is also known as sandfire, saxifrage and sea fennel. Conseil gathered a few bunches of it. Among the fauna there were thousands of crustaceans of every kind, lobsters, *cancer pagura*, *palaemon*, brine shrimp, *chaurus* and squat lobsters together with a prodigious number of shellfish, including cowries, rock snails and barnacles.

Just there we found the entrance to a magnificent grotto. I and both my companions lay down on its soft sand, where we were very comfortable. Volcanic flames had polished its smooth, gleaming sides, which were covered with a dusting of mica particles. Ned Land prodded the walls, trying to work out how thick they were. I could not help smiling. The conversation then got back to his eternal plans to escape. I thought I could, without over-committing myself, offer him a glimmer of hope: Captain Nemo had come south only because he wanted to replenish his stock of sodium. So I hoped that now he would turn back to the coasts of Europe or America. This might well present the Canadian with an opportunity to have another attempt to execute his plan, which had been thwarted once.

We had been lying in that delightful grotto for an hour. The conversation, animated at the outset, had grown desultory. We were slowly becoming quite drowsy. Since I could see no reason why we should not doze off, I allowed myself to fall into a heavy sleep. I dreamed – we have no control over what we dream – that my existence was being whittled down to the vegetative life of a common mollusc. I just knew that the grotto was the double valve of my shell . . .

Suddenly, I was jerked back to consciousness by a shout from Conseil.

'Wake up! Wake up!' he was yelling.

'What is it?' I cried propping myself up on one elbow.

'There's water! It's rising!'

I stood up. The sea was rushing into our hideaway like a torrent. Since we weren't molluscs, we would have to get out of there.

It took us a matter of moments to climb out to safety above the grotto.

'What's happening?' asked Conseil. 'Is it the start of a new eruption?'

'No,' I answered, 'it's just the tide, which almost caught us unawares, like the hero of that novel by Walter Scott. The ocean outside surges, and by the natural law of equilibrium the level of the lake rises too. We are lucky to have got away with only wet feet. Let's go back to the *Nautilus* and get changed.'

Three-quarters of an hour later, we had completed our walk round the lake and were back on board. The sailors were just finishing loading the supplies of sodium, and the *Nautilus* was ready to put to sea again.

However, Captain Nemo did not give the order. Was it because he wanted to wait for nightfall before leaving secretly through his underwater channel? Perhaps.

Be that as it may, by the next morning the *Nautilus* had left her home port and was soon sailing into the high seas, well away from land and a few metres below the surface of the Atlantic Ocean.

11
The Sargasso Sea

The *Nautilus*'s course had not changed. All hope of returning to the coasts of Europe had therefore to be abandoned for the time being. Captain Nemo kept heading south. Where was he taking us? I dared not imagine.

That day, the *Nautilus* passed through a very strange part of the Atlantic. Everyone has heard of the existence of the great current of warm water called the Gulf Stream. After leaving the channels of Florida, it flows in the direction of Spitzbergen. But before it enters the Gulf of Mexico, on or near the forty-second degree of latitude north, the current divides into two: the main arm flows towards the coasts of Ireland and Norway while the second turns south on a level with the Azores. It reaches the shores of Africa and returns to the West Indies in a trajectory shaped like an elongated oval.

Now this second arm – though perhaps more collar than arm – traps inside its warm circular current a part of the ocean which, cold, windless and stationary, is known as the Sargasso Sea. It is virtually a lake in the middle of the Atlantic, and the water of the great current takes no less than three years to travel all around it.

Strictly speaking, the Sargasso Sea covers the whole of the submerged area of Atlantis. Some authorities have gone so far as to say that the many marine plants scattered over its surface are plants uprooted from the fields of that ancient continent. It is more likely, however, that these weeds, green algae and brown fucus, originate on the coasts of Europe and America and float into this zone on the Gulf Stream. This was one of the reasons which led Columbus to predict the existence of a New

World. When the vessels of that bold explorer sailed into the
Sargasso Sea, they found their progress impeded by these floating plants, which could even bring them to a complete stop,
much to the alarm of the crew: it took them three weeks to pass
through it.

This was the area through which the *Nautilus* was passing
now, almost literally meadowland, a tightly woven mat of
green and brown algae and bladder-wrack, so thick and dense
that the prow of a sizeable vessel would not have cut a way
through it without great difficulty. For this reason, Captain
Nemo, not wishing to foul his propeller in this mass of vegetation, remained a few metres below the surface.

The name 'Sargasso' comes from the Spanish word *sargazzo*
and means 'kelp'. This enormous floating mat is formed mainly
of kelp, also known as sea-wrack. The reason why these hydrophytes collect in this calm part of the Atlantic is given by the
learned Maury, author of *The Physical Geography of the
Globe*:[16]

The best explanation that can be given for it, he writes, is
illustrated by a phenomenon which is universally familiar:
'Now, if bits of cork or chaff, or any floating substance, be put
into a basin, and a circular motion be given to the water, all
the light substances will be found crowding together near the
centre of the pool, where there is least motion. Just such a
basin is the Atlantic Ocean to the Gulf Stream; and the Sargasso Sea is the centre of the whirl.'[17]

I fully share Maury's opinion and I was able to study the
phenomenon *in situ*, in that very area into which ships rarely
venture. Above us were floating bodies of every provenance
which had ended up in the middle of the mass of brownish
vegetation: tree-trunks washed down from the Andes or the
Rocky Mountains on the Amazon or the Mississippi, wreckage
of various sorts, the keels and hulls of boats, broken planking
all so weighed down with shells and barnacles that they could
not stay on the surface of the water. And one day time will
surely endorse another of Maury's opinions: that these materials, accumulated over the centuries, will be mineralized by the
action of the sea and thus form an inexhaustible supply of coal.

It thus constitutes a vital reserve foreseen by nature for such time as men shall have worked out all the mines on dry land.[18]

In the middle of this inextricable tangle of algae and fucus I noticed specimens of delightful pink-coloured, starred alcyonaria; actinias trailing long, thread-like tentacles; green, red, blue jellyfish and – not least – large examples of Cuvier's barrel jellyfish, which has a bluish swimming-bell edged with a violet frill.

The whole of that day, 22 February, was spent in the Sargasso Sea, where fish that live on marine plants and crustaceans find food in abundance. The following day the sea had resumed its normal appearance.

From that moment, for nineteen consecutive days, from 23 February to 12 March, the *Nautilus* kept to the middle of the Atlantic, travelling at a steady speed of 100 leagues every twenty-four hours. It was clear that Captain Nemo was anxious to get to the end of his underwater voyage, and I was in no doubt that after sailing round Cape Horn he would return towards the southern seas of the Pacific.

Ned Land thus had every reason to fear the worst. In those wide seas, where there were no islands, there was no point even in thinking about escaping from the vessel. Nor was there any way of objecting to Captain Nemo's plans. All we could do was to submit to the inevitable. Still, what we could not expect to achieve through force or ruse I liked to think we could obtain through persuasion. Once we had reached the end of our voyage, would he not agree to restore our freedom if we swore never to reveal his existence? An oath which we would swear on our honour and keep? This delicate question would have to be discussed with the captain. But would I be in any position to ask for our freedom? Had he himself not declared from the start and in the most categorical fashion that his absolute need to keep his life secret required our permanent imprisonment aboard the *Nautilus*? For the past four months, surely my silence must have come to appear a tacit acceptance of the situation? Raising the subject again would very likely create suspicions which might harm our plans at a later date if a favourable opportunity of implementing them should ever present itself. I weighed these considerations, I mulled them over and then put them to Conseil, who was no less undecided than I was. In short, although I was not a man to give up easily, I understood that our chances of ever seeing our friends and families again grew fainter with every passing day – especially just then when Captain Nemo was sailing boldly into the South Atlantic.

The nineteen days I mentioned earlier passed without incident. I saw little of the captain. He was working. In the library I often found volumes left half open, especially works of natural history. My own book about the ocean depths had been perused by him, for there were marginal notes everywhere which often took issue with my theories and classification tables. But the captain seemed happy merely to amend my work, for he rarely discussed it with me. Occasionally I would hear melancholy chords from the great organ, which he played with great feeling, but only at night, surrounded by pitch blackness, when the *Nautilus* slept in the deserts of the ocean.

During this phase of the voyage, we cruised on the surface for days on end. The seas there were empty, apart from a few sailing vessels, with cargoes for the Indies, which were making for the Cape of Good Hope. On one occasion we were chased by a whaler's longboats, which doubtless mistook us for a very large, very valuable whale. But Captain Nemo had no wish to waste those brave men's time and efforts and he ended the pursuit by diving. This encounter seemed to interest Ned Land greatly. I don't think I am wrong when I say that he must have been sorry that our metal cetacean could not be struck through the heart by the harpoons of those fishermen.

The fish Conseil and I saw during this time were not very different from those which we had already observed in other latitudes. The main ones were a few sightings of that fearsome genus of cartilaginous fish, which is divided into three subgenera and no fewer than thirty-two species: galloon squali, 5 metres long, flattened head wider than the body, with rounded caudal fins and long, parallel, longitudinal black stripes running all along its back; also silver grey sharpnose sevengill sharks which have seven gill slits and a single dorsal fin set halfway along their body.

There were also dogfish, a voracious animal if there ever was one. No one is obliged to believe the tales told by fishermen, but this is what they say. In the stomach of one of these creatures a buffalo's head and a whole calf were found; in another, a couple of tunas and a sailor in uniform; in a third, a soldier still holding his sabre; and finally, in another, a horse and rider. None of this, to be perfectly frank, can be taken as the plain, unvarnished truth. Even so, the fact remains that none of these creatures ever allowed themselves to be caught in the *Nautilus*'s nets, so I was never able to discover how voracious they really are.

Elegant, playful schools of dolphins kept us company for days on end. They swam in groups of five or six, hunting in packs like wolves in open country. In fact, they are not any less voracious than the dogfish, if I am to believe the claim by a professor from Copenhagen who removed from the stomach of a single dolphin thirteen porpoises and fifteen seals. To be fair, it was actually a grampus, which belongs to the largest species known and can grow more than 20 feet long. This family of *delphinidae* has ten genera. Those I saw belonged with the genus *delphinorhyncus*, which have a distinctive, excessively narrow snout which is four times as long as their skull. Their bodies measure 3 metres in length and are black on top and pinkish white underneath with occasional freckles.

From these waters I should also mention curious specimens of fish of the order of *acanthopterigii* and also of the family *sciaenidae*. Some authors (more fanciful poets than true naturalists) claim that these fish sing melodiously and that their combined voices make a sound which no human choir could ever equal. I do not deny it, but these 'croakers' or 'drumheads' failed to supply any sort of serenade as we passed by, a fact I much regretted.

In conclusion, Conseil classified a large number of flying fish. There was no more curious a sight than to see dolphins hunting them with such wonderful deftness. However far they flew, whatever their trajectory, even if it took them clean over the *Nautilus*, the unfortunate fish invariably ended up in mouths which the dolphin opened ready to catch them. They were either pirapeds or flying gurnards, with luminous mouths which at night leave streaks of light in the air before diving back into the dark water like shooting stars.

Until 13 March, we journeyed on in this way. On that day, the *Nautilus* was involved in an experiment in taking soundings which interested me greatly.

By then, we had travelled almost 13,000 leagues since setting out from the waters of the central Pacific. Our position was given out as latitude 45° 37' south and longitude 37° 53' west. These were the waters in which Captain Denham, commanding the *Herald*, had let down 14,000 metres of line and did not find bottom. Here also, Lieutenant Parker, of the American frigate, *Congress*, did not reach the sea-bed at a depth of 15,140 metres.

Captain Nemo decided to take the *Nautilus* down to extreme levels in order to check on these different soundings. I got ready to keep a full record of the experiment. The viewing panels in the Great Saloon were opened, and the manoeuvre began which would see us descend to prodigiously remote depths.

As will be imagined, simply filling our reservoirs would not have enabled us to dive that far. They might not have increased the specific weight of the *Nautilus* sufficiently. Moreover, in order to return to the surface, we would need to discharge this water, and the pumps might not have been powerful enough to overcome the pressure of the water outside.

Captain Nemo resolved to reach the ocean floor by travelling on a suitably calibrated diagonal path using his lateral fins set at an angle of 45 degrees to the vessel's water line. Then the propeller was brought up to maximum revolutions, and its four blades began to churn the water with tremendous power.

Impelled by this colossal thrust, the hull of the *Nautilus* vibrated like a sounding cord and ploughed its way steadily down through the water. From our station in the Great Saloon, the captain and I watched the rapidly falling needle of the pressure gauge. Soon we were past the limits of the habitat of most fish. If some fish can only live near the surface of sea or river, a much smaller number remain at very deep levels. Among these, I observed the hexanchus, a species of dogfish with six gill slits; the telescope fish, which has huge eyes; the peristedion, or armoured sea-robin, with grey thoracic fins and black pectorals and its plastron protected by pale-red bony plates; lastly, whiptails, living at a depth of 1,200 metres and capable of withstanding 120 atmospheres.

I asked Captain Nemo if he had seen fish at even greater depths.

'Fish? Rarely,' he answered. 'But given the current limits of scientific knowledge, what hypotheses can we formulate? What do we really know?'

'We know certain things. We know as we descend into the depths vegetable life disappears sooner than animal life. We know that where animal life is still found, there are no hydrophytes. We know that some scallops and oysters can live in 2,000 metres of water and that McClintock, the hero of polar seas, brought up a living starfish from a depth of 2,500 metres. We know that the crew of the Royal Navy vessel *Bulldog* fished up an asteria from 2,620 fathoms, a depth of more than a league. So how, Captain Nemo, can you tell me that we know nothing?'

'No, professor, I would not dream of being so discourteous. Still, I will ask you to explain how it is that such forms of life are able to live at such depths.'

'I will give you two reasons. Firstly, because vertical currents, caused by differences in the salinity and density in the water, produce enough movement to support the rudimentary life of crinoidea and asterias.'

'That is true.'

'Secondly, because oxygen is necessary for life, and we know that the amount of oxygen dissolved in sea water rises with depth instead of falling, and that the greater pressures of water at the lower depths helps to compress it.'

'Ah, so that is known to science?' asked Captain Nemo, with a faint air of surprise. 'Well, professor, there is every reason for believing it, because it is quite true. Let me add that the swim bladders of fish contain more nitrogen than oxygen when they are caught on the surface, but more oxygen than nitrogen when they are taken in deep water. This supports your argument. But let us continue with our observations.'

I glanced at the depth gauge, which was now registering a depth of 6,000 metres. We had been diving steadily for an hour. The *Nautilus*, using her angled fins, was still descending. The water here was wonderfully clear and diaphanous in ways no brush could paint. An hour later, we were at 13,000 metres – about 3¼ leagues – and still there was no sign that we were nearing the bottom.

However, at 14,000 metres I saw blackish peaks rising in the water. But these summits might belong to mountains as high as the Himalayas or Mont Blanc, or even higher, so that the ultimate depths of the ocean had still not yet been ascertained.

The *Nautilus* dived even lower despite the enormous pressures now acting on it. I felt her steel plates quiver as the bolts took the strain; her iron stays began to warp; her bulkheads groaned; the glass in the viewing panels seemed to bulge inwards under the pressure of the water. And, however solidly built, the boat would have been crushed if she had not been capable, as her captain had said, of resisting as well as solid rock.

As we sailed over to these rocky slopes of mountains that had been buried under the water, I could still see a number of shellfish: serpulid tubeworms, living spirorbes and some kinds of asterias.

But soon, these last representatives of animal life disappeared completely, and, at the 3 league mark, the *Nautilus* passed the lowest limits of marine life, just as a balloon reaches altitudes where the air is no longer breathable. We had now reached a depth of 16,000 metres – 4 leagues – and the hull of the *Nautilus* was then exposed to a pressure of 1,600 atmospheres, that is, 1,600 kilos per square centimetre of its entire surface!

'This is a truly astonishing experience!' I exclaimed. 'To go through these virgin waters where no man has gone before! Look, captain! Look at those magnificent rocks, the uninhabited caves. They are the ultimate refuge of the globe, where life has become impossible. These are magnificent sights! Why is it that all we can take away with us is the memory of them?'

'Would you like,' asked Captain Nemo, 'to take back something more than just a memory?'

'What do you mean?'

'I mean that nothing would be easier than to take a photographic view of this area beneath the sea.'

I had not even had time to express my surprise at this new proposal when the captain ordered a camera to be brought to where we were. Through the viewing panels which were opened to their widest setting, the water outside was illuminated by our searchlight with perfect clarity. No shadow, no dimming of the brilliance of our artificial light. Direct sunlight would not have been any more effective for what we were about to attempt. The *Nautilus*, maintained by the power of her propeller and held in position by the angle of her fins, remained perfectly stationary. The lens was pointed at the submerged seascape, and within seconds we had obtained a negative of stunning clarity.

It survives as incontrovertible proof of what I have written. It shows primordial rocks which have never seen the light of day, the lower strata of the granite which forms the bedrock of our planet, the deep caverns excavated from the porous mass, the outlines of shapes which are rendered with incomparable clarity and their extremities edged with black, as though the scene were the work of certain Flemish artists. Beyond was a horizon of mountains, an admirably undulating line which establishes the background to these seascapes. I have no words to describe the grandeur of those smooth, black, polished rocky walls on which there is no trace of moss, no blemish, their shapes so strangely delineated and so solidly planted on the carpet of sand which sparkled in the play of our electric light.

But after taking the photograph, Captain Nemo said:

'We should return to the surface, professor. We must not outstay our welcome here nor expose the *Nautilus* to these pressures for too long.'

'Let us go up, then!' I replied.

'Steady yourself!'

I had not had time to understand why the captain gave me this warning when I was thrown on to the floor.

At a signal from the captain, the engine engaged the propeller, and the lateral fins were set to vertical. The *Nautilus* shot up, like a balloon released into the air, and continued to rise at

a dizzying rate. She sliced through the weight of water with a
shriek of protesting metal. Through the viewing panels, everything was a blur. In four minutes, we had covered the 4 leagues
which had separated us from the surface of the ocean, and,
rising out of the water like a flying fish, the *Nautilus* fell back
with a great splash which sent water up into the air to a prodigious height.

12

Cachalots and Whales

During the night of 13 to 14 March, the *Nautilus* resumed her southerly course. I assumed that when we were level with Cape Horn we would turn west, enter the Pacific and thus complete our journey round the world. This did not happen, and we continued to make towards the austral regions. Where were we heading? To the Pole? There was no sense in it, and I really began to think that Captain Nemo's impetuous whims fully justified Ned Land's fears.

For some time past the Canadian had stopped talking about his escape plans. He had grown less communicative, almost mute. I could see how much this prolonged detention weighed on him. I sensed the anger building in him. Whenever he encountered the captain his eyes smouldered darkly, and I went in dread lest his natural tendency to violence should make him do something regrettable.

That day, 14 March, he and Conseil came to see me in my cabin. I asked them why they were there.

'I just wanted to ask you a simple question,' said the Canadian.

'Yes, Ned. What is it?'

'How many men do you reckon are on board the *Nautilus*?'

'I couldn't say.'

'I get the impression,' Ned went on, 'that it doesn't take a large crew to run the boat.'

'You're right,' I replied. 'Given the present state of things, ten men at most would be enough to handle her.'

'If that's the case,' said the Canadian, 'why would there be more than that?'

'Why do you ask?' I replied.

I looked Ned Land straight in the eye: his intentions were only too clear.

'Because,' I went on, 'if I can trust my instinct, if I have correctly interpreted the captain's life and character, the *Nautilus* is not just a boat. It is a place of refuge for men who, like their commanding officer, have severed all ties with the land.'

'Perhaps that's so,' said Conseil, 'but the *Nautilus* is physically capable of holding only a certain number of men. Is monsieur able to estimate what the maximum might be?'

'And how might I do that?'

'Mathematically. Given the capacity of the vessel, which monsieur knows, and consequently the volume of air it can hold, and knowing also the amount that each man uses in breathing; and, by setting the results against the need of the *Nautilus* to surface every twenty-four hours, could not monsieur . . .'

Conseil did not finish his sentence, but I saw what he was driving at.

'I understand,' I replied. 'But the calculation, which would be easy enough to do, could only give a very approximate figure.'

'It doesn't matter,' insisted Ned Land.

'Well, let's try it,' I said. 'Each man uses up all the oxygen in 100 litres of air every hour, or all the oxygen in 2,400 litres every twenty-four hours. So we need to work out how many times 2,400 goes into the total air contained in the *Nautilus*.

'Correct,' said Conseil.

'Now,' I went on, 'the capacity of the *Nautilus* is 1,500 tons, and one ton is the equivalent of 1,000 litres. The *Nautilus* therefore contains 1,500,000 litres of air, which, divided by 2,400 . . .'

I jotted down the calculation with a pencil.

'. . . gives 625. In other words, the air inside the *Nautilus* could, mathematically, be enough for 625 men over a period of twenty-four hours.'

'Six hundred and twenty-five!' repeated Ned.

'But be assured,' I added, 'that the combined number of passengers, crew and officers does not come to one-tenth of that figure.'

'But that's still too many for three men to tackle,' muttered Conseil.

'So all I can do, Ned, is to advise you to be patient.'

'Not so much patient,' said Conseil, 'as resigned.'

Conseil had used the right word.

'Still,' he went on, 'Captain Nemo cannot go on steering south for ever! He's going to have to stop at some point, if only because he can't sail through the ice cap, and he'll return to more civilized seas! Then would be the time to think about trying Ned Land's plan again!'

The Canadian shook his head, wiped his forehead with one hand, offered no comment and left the cabin.

'If monsieur will allow me to make an observation?' said Conseil. 'The fact is that Ned keeps thinking about the things he cannot have. His old life keeps coming back to haunt him. He regrets all the things we are prevented from doing. Old memories depress him, and his heart is heavy. We must try to understand him. What is there for him to do here? Nothing. He is not a scientist, like monsieur, and he cannot be expected to take the same interest as we do in the wonders of the sea. He would do anything to be able just to walk into a tavern back home!'

It was perfectly true that the Canadian, accustomed as he was to a free and active outdoor existence, must be finding the monotony of life on board intolerable. Incidents capable of catching his interest were few and far between. However, on that very same day, something happened which reminded him of old triumphs as a harpooner.

Around eleven in the morning the *Nautilus* was on the surface and suddenly found herself in the midst of a school of whales. Such an eventuality came as no surprise to me, for I knew that these animals, hunted without quarter, have retreated to the safer waters of the high latitudes.

The role of the whale in the marine world and its part in geographical discovery have both been very great. It was the whale which lured first the Basques, then the Asturians, English and Dutch, taught them to be less afraid of the dangers of the sea and led them from one end of the earth to the other.

Whales are at home in both southern and northern seas. Ancient legend has it that these cetaceans brought fishermen to within just 7 leagues of the North Pole. If this is not factually true, it will be one day, and it is likely that it is through hunting whales in the Arctic and Antarctic regions that men will eventually reach those unknown points on the globe.

We were sitting out on the platform. The sea was calm. What in these latitudes was the equivalent of October gave us some glorious autumn days. It was the Canadian – who could not have been mistaken – who first sighted a whale on the eastern horizon. By looking carefully, we could make out its blackish back rising and falling alternately on the waves, 5 miles from the *Nautilus*.

'Ah,' sighed Ned Land, 'if I were now on a whaler, how I'd relish this moment! It's a big one! See how powerfully its spiracles blow out columns of air and vapour! Hell's teeth! Why am I kept locked up on this tin tub!'

'What, Ned?' I said. 'Haven't you got over your old notions of fishing?'

'How can a whaling man forget his old trade, professor? How can anyone get tired of the thrill of a chase like that?'

'Have you ever fished in these seas, Ned?'

'Never, professor. Only in northern waters, in both the Bering Strait and the Davis Strait.'

'I see you know nothing about these Antarctic whales. What you've hunted until now is the southern right whale, which never ventures to pass through the warm waters of the equator.'

'What are you saying, professor,' said Ned in a tone of frank disbelief.

'I'm telling you the facts!'

'Hell's teeth! And I'm telling you that in '65, just two and a half years ago, I was standing on a whale near Greenland which still had in its side a harpoon that carried the mark of a whaler from the Bering Sea. Well, tell me this: how, having been speared west of America, could that animal have ended up getting itself killed east of it if it hadn't swum round either Cape Horn or the Cape of Good Hope and done it by crossing the equator?'

'The Nautilus *suddenly found herself in the midst*
of a school of whales'

'I share Ned's view,' said Conseil, 'and I await monsieur's reply with interest.'

'Monsieur will reply, friends, that whales are territorial, with different species being particular to certain seas from which they never stray. If one of these animals found its way from the Bering Strait to the Davis Strait, it's simply because there must be a passage leading from one sea to the other, either from the American coast or the Asian side.'

'Thousands wouldn't believe you,' said the Canadian with a wink.

'We must believe monsieur,' said Conseil.

'In other words,' said the Canadian, 'since I have never fished these waters, I don't know the first thing about the whales that live hereabouts?'

'That's what I meant, Ned.'

'All the more reason for wanting to make their acquaintance,' said Conseil.

'Look! Over there!' cried the Canadian excitedly. 'It's coming nearer! It's coming straight for us! It's cocking a snook at me! It knows there's not a damn thing I can do about it!'

Ned stamped his foot. His hand twitched as he brandished an imaginary harpoon.

'Are these cetaceans,' he asked, 'as big as those in the northern seas?'

'Pretty much, Ned.'

'Well, I've seen some big baleen whales in my time, professor, some 100 feet long! I've even been told that around the Aleutian Islands, rorquals, known locally as hullamochs and umgallicks, can grow to 150 feet.'

'That sounds exaggerated to me,' I replied. 'Those particular whales are only *balaenoptera*. They have dorsal fins and, like cachalots, are generally smaller than right whales.'

'Look!' cried the Canadian without taking his eyes off the ocean. 'It's coming nearer, it's invading our water!'

Then resuming the conversation:

'You talk,' he said, 'as if cachalots, sperm whales, are small animals. But people say that there are giant cachalots. They are intelligent cetaceans. It's said that some of them cover themselves with algae and fucus. Boats have mistaken them for islands, and sailors have set up camp on them, settled in, lit fires . . .'

'And built houses too?' asked Conseil.

'I suppose you must have your little joke,' said Ned Land. 'Then, one fine day, the animal dives, taking the entire boarding party with it deep down in the sea.'

'Like in the stories of the travels of Sindbad the sailor!' I laughed. 'Oh, Ned! I see you have a taste for extraordinary voyages! Your cachalots are wonderful! I do hope you don't really believe all these stories?'

'Professor, you are a scientist,' the Canadian replied seriously, 'but anything is possible with whales. Just look at this one! See how fast it moves! How quickly it turns and weaves! I've heard people say that these creatures can swim round the globe in two weeks!'

'I don't deny it.'

'But what you probably don't know, Professor Aronnax, is that in the beginning of the world, they could swim even faster than they do now.'

'Really, Ned? And why is that?'

'Because in those days their tails went side to side, like fish, that is, their tails were set vertically and beat the water from left to right and right to left. But the Good Lord, noticing that they were swimming too fast, twisted their tails round, and ever since they have beaten the water up and down and with consequent loss of speed.'

'I see, Ned,' I said and then added one of the Canadian's own expressions: 'But thousands wouldn't believe you!'

'No more they would,' answered Ned Land, 'than if I said that there are whales 300 feet long that weigh 100,000 pounds.'

'That certainly sounds a lot,' I said, 'Even so, we must admit that some cetaceans grow very large because I've heard that they can supply up to 120 barrels of oil.'

'I agree. I've seen that with my own eyes.'

'I believe it, Ned, just as I believe that some whales grow as big as 100 elephants. Can you imagine the damage that can be done by something that big moving very fast?'

'Is it true,' asked Conseil, 'that whales can sink ships?'

'Ships I don't believe,' I said. 'Still, there is a story that in 1820, in these southern waters actually, a whale launched itself at the *Essex* and drove it backwards at a speed of 4 metres a second. She took in seas by the stern and sank almost immediately.'

Ned gave me an artful look.

'Speaking personally,' he said, 'I once got hit by a whale's tail – or rather my longboat did. I and my companions were tossed 6 metres up into the air. But next to your whale, professor, mine was just a tiddler.'

'Do these animals live a long time?' asked Conseil.

'A thousand years,' replied the Canadian without hesitation.

'How do you know, Ned?'

'Because everybody says so.'

'And why do they say it?'

'Because they know.'

'No, Ned, they don't know. They only think they do and they think they do for this reason. Around 400 years ago, when men first went whale-hunting, whales were larger than they are today. It is widely believed, and the idea is quite logical, that whales today are smaller because they do not have time to grow to maturity. Which is why Buffon observed that these cetaceans could and once did live 1,000 years. Do you follow me?'

But Ned Land was not following me. He was no longer listening. The whale kept coming nearer and nearer. He couldn't take his eyes off it.

'Hey!' he exclaimed. 'There's not just one whale, there are ten, no, twenty of them, a whole school! And there's nothing I can do about it! Imagine being here and tied hand and foot!'

'But Ned,' said Conseil, 'why don't you ask Captain Nemo for permission to hunt them?'

Conseil had hardly finished his sentence when Ned Land leaped through the hatch and sped off to find the captain. A few minutes later, both of them emerged on to the platform.

Captain Nemo stared hard at the school of cetaceans which were playing in the waves a mile from the *Nautilus*.

'They are Antarctic whales,' he said. 'They'd be worth a fortune to a whole fleet of whaling-ships.'

'True, captain,' said the Canadian, 'so why couldn't I go after them, if only to keep my hand in as a harpooner?'

'What's the point,' asked Captain Nemo, 'of hunting just to destroy? We don't use whale oil on board the *Nautilus*.'

'But when we were in the Red Sea,' countered Ned Land, 'you gave us permission to go after a dugong!'

'That was because we needed fresh meat for the crew. Here it would be killing for killing's sake. I know that this is a privilege given only to humans, but I do not approve of pastimes which involve the taking of life. By killing Antarctic whales and right whales, which are gentle and harmless creatures, Mister Land, you and your fellow fishermen pursue a course of wanton destruction. That was how you have already depopulated Baffin Bay and in the end you will hunt a class of very useful animals to extinction. Let these unfortunate cetaceans alone. They already have to cope with dealing with their natural enemies, the cachalots, swordfish and sawfish, without having to contend with you as well.'

I don't think I need to describe the look on the Canadian's face while he heard this moralistic lecture. Talking like this to a hunting man was a waste of breath. Ned Land glared at Captain Nemo and obviously had no idea of what he was getting at. But of course, the captain was right. The barbarous, unthinking ferocity of whalers will one day obliterate the last whale from the oceans.

Ned Land whistled *Yankee Doodle* through gritted teeth, thrust his hands into his pockets and turned his back on us.

All this while, Captain Nemo continued to look out at the school of cetaceans. Then he spoke to me:

'I was quite right when I said that, leaving man out of it, whales have enough natural enemies. These are going to have a fight on their hands at any moment. Professor Aronnax. Have you spotted those black dots making this way, there, 8 miles to leeward?'

'Yes, captain,' I replied.

'Cachalots. They are savage creatures. I've sometimes come across them in packs of two or three hundred! As far as I'm concerned, there'd be nothing wrong with exterminating such cruel, vicious creatures.'

At these last words, the Canadian turned quickly.

'There's still time, captain,' I said. 'And it would be in the best interest of the whales.'

'There is no need to risk it, professor. The *Nautilus* will be enough to disperse the cachalots. She is armed with a steel cutwater, which will be every bit as effective as Mister Land's harpoon.'

The Canadian did not even try to hide the shrug of his shoulders, which plainly said: 'Attack cachalots with the sharp end of a boat! Who ever heard of such a thing?'

'Wait, Professor Aronnax,' said Captain Nemo. 'You shall observe a kind of hunt which you never saw before. We shall show no quarter for those ferocious cachalots. Mouth and teeth is all they are!'

All mouth and teeth! There was no more graphic way of describing the macrocephalous cachalot, which can reach a length of 25 metres. The huge head of this cetacean accounts for about one-third of its body. Better armed than the right whale, whose upper jaw is equipped only with fine baleen filters, it has twenty-five large teeth, which are 20 centimetres long, cylindrical in shape, end in sharp points and weigh 2 pounds each. In the upper part of their enormous head, cavities separated by cartilage contain the three or four hundred kilograms of the precious wax known as 'spermaceti'. The cachalot is an ungainly animal, 'more tadpole than fish', as Frédol puts it.[19] It is badly designed, a botched creation, you might say, defective in the whole of the left-hand side of its skeleton and having poor vision – and that only in the right eye.

Meanwhile, the monstrous shoal kept coming nearer all the time. They had seen the whales and were getting ready to attack. A victory for the cachalots was all too predictable, not just because they were better equipped for attacking their inoffensive opponents but also because they can remain submerged for much longer without having to come to the surface to breathe.

It was high time to go to the aid of the whales. The *Nautilus* dived just below the surface. Conseil, Ned and I took up our positions by the viewing panels in the Great Saloon. Captain Nemo went off to the helmsman's cockpit so that he could put the ship through her paces as an engine of destruction. Soon I felt the revolutions of the propeller accelerate, and our speed increased.

Battle was already raging between the cachalots and the whales when the *Nautilus* arrived among them. She manoeuvred in such a way as to split the large group of macrocephalous attackers. At first they barely reacted to the sight of this new monster which had joined the fray. But soon they were having to stay out of its path.

What a battle it proved to be! Even Ned Land was enjoying it hugely and by the finish was clapping his hands excitedly. The *Nautilus* had become a redoubtable harpoon in the hands of her captain. The boat launched itself against those vast slabs of meat and smashed clean through them, leaving in its wake two writhing halves. Its hull was struck tremendous blows by lashing tails, but we scarcely felt them. The impacts produced by collisions made almost as little impression. When one cachalot had been exterminated, the *Nautilus* went looking for the next, turning smartly on her axis so as not to miss her prey, rushing forwards, backwards, responsive to the helm, diving when her target fled into deep water, rising with it when it returned to the surface, hitting it square on or at an angle, slicing it in two or ripping it apart, and in all directions, at every speed, thrusting with its fearsome cutwater.

It was a scene of utter carnage! The din on the surface was deafening. The air was full of the shrill screams and low-pitched boomings, which are peculiar to those panicking animals. Beneath the surface, where the water is ordinarily calm and peaceful, their tails threshed so wildly that they created a surging swell.

This Homeric struggle, from which the macrocephalous attackers could not extricate themselves, went on for an hour. Several times, ten or twelve of them joined forces and tried to crush the *Nautilus* by using their combined bulk. Through the glass we could see their huge jaws paved with teeth and their fearsome eyes. Ned Land, who was almost beside himself, threatened and swore at them. We felt them clinging to the boat the way a pack of dogs worry a boar which has gone to ground in a thicket. But the *Nautilus* increased the revolutions of her propeller and carried them off, dragged them down or brought them back to the surface, indifferent to their weight and the power of those jaws.

Gradually the numbers of cachalots began to thin. The surface of the ocean became calm once more. I felt us resurface. The hatch opened, and we all rushed out on to the platform.

The sea was covered with mutilated bodies. Even the largest explosion would not have split, sundered and shredded that mass of flesh and bones with such violence. We were sitting in the midst of gigantic bodies, with bluish backs and whitish bellies and covered all over with enormous protuberances. A few demoralized cachalots were speeding off towards the horizon. The sea was tinged with red over an area of several miles. The *Nautilus* had come to rest on a sea of blood.

We were rejoined by Captain Nemo.

'What did you think of it, Mister Land?' he asked.

'Well, captain,' said the Canadian, whose excitement had cooled, 'I think it was awe-inspiring to watch. But I am no butcher, I'm a hunter, and this was plain butchery.'

'It was a cull of malevolent animals,' replied the captain. 'The *Nautilus* is not a butcher's knife.'

'I'll stick to my harpoon,' was the Canadian's reply.

'Each to his own,' said the captain, looking levelly at Ned Land.

I was afraid that Ned might get carried away and commit some act of violence which would have serious consequences. But his anger was diverted by the sight of a whale drifting towards us.

It obviously had not escaped the jaws of the cachalots. It was, I saw, an Antarctic whale, which has a flattened head and is black all over. Anatomically, it is distinct from the right whale and the North Cape whale by the fact that its seven cervical vertebrae are joined and that it has two ribs more than its northern cousin. This unfortunate cetacean was floating on its side, with its belly punctured by teeth marks. It was dead. From the end of its ravaged fin still hung a small calf which it had not been able to save from the massacre. Water washed in and out of its open mouth with the muffled sound of a distant reef as it passed back and forth through its baleen filters.

Captain Nemo brought the *Nautilus* alongside the animal's remains. Two of his men climbed on to the whale's side, and I saw them, to my great surprise, proceed to draw off all the milk from its breasts. It filled around two or three barrels.

Captain Nemo handed me a cup of this milk, which was still warm. I could not help letting my lack of enthusiasm for this drink show. He assured me that the milk was excellent and in no respect any different from cow's milk.

I tasted it and agreed. It was a welcome addition to our larder, for in the form of salted butter or cheese it would make a pleasant variation on our normal ship's fare.

From that day forwards I noted with some misgiving that Ned Land's attitude to Captain Nemo was becoming increasingly sour. I resolved to keep a very close eye on the behaviour of the Canadian.

13
Under the Ice

The *Nautilus* had resumed her relentless progress south. We followed the 50th meridian at an impressive speed. Was she aiming to reach the Pole? I did not think so, for all previous attempts to reach that point on the globe had failed. Moreover, the season was well advanced, for 13 March in Antarctic regions corresponds to 13 September in the northern hemisphere, which is the beginning of the period of the equinox.

On 14 March I sighted floating ice at latitude 55°, isolated, pallid floes 20 or 25 feet long, which acted as small reefs over which waves broke. The *Nautilus* remained on the ocean surface. Ned Land had experience of whaling in the Arctic and was accustomed to the sight of these icebergs. But Conseil and I admired them for the very first time.

A dazzling white line stretched along the entire width of the sky above the southern horizon. English whaling men have christened the phenomenon 'iceblink'. Clouds, however dense, do not obscure it. It heralds the proximity of pack ice or an ice-shelf.

And indeed, there soon appeared much larger blocks of ice whose brightness varied with the whims of the mist. Some of these large bergs were striated with green veins, as if copper sulphate had left wavy lines inside them. Others, looking like vast amethysts, allowed light to shine into them. The first kind reflected the sun's rays via the myriad facets of their crystal formation. The second sort gleamed like limestone and looked like large marble blocks which could have been used to build an entire city.

The further south we went, the bigger and more numerous

these floating islands became. Polar birds nested on them by the thousand. Petrels, black-and-white mews and puffins deafened us with their cries. Some, mistaking the *Nautilus* for a dead whale, landed on her hull and could be heard pecking at her resonant metal plates.

During the time we cruised through the ice, Captain Nemo often went out on to the platform, scanning the empty seascape. At times, I saw his eye quicken. Was he thinking that in these polar seas, so hostile to man, he was at home, master of these remote wastes? Perhaps. But if he was, he did not speak of it. He stood motionless and became himself again only when his instinctive seamanship took control. Then he steered the *Nautilus* with consummate skill, avoiding collisions with those massive ice floes, some of which were several miles long and between 70 and 80 metres high, At times our horizon was completely blocked. At 60 degrees of latitude, every open passage had disappeared. But Captain Nemo, watching carefully, would soon find some narrow gap through which he glided boldly, knowing full well that it would close up again behind us.

In this way, the *Nautilus*, guided by his steady hand, sailed through the ice. Ice is classified by shape or size with an exactness which delighted Conseil: icebergs or mountains of ice; ice-fields, which are level, endless plains; drift ice made of floating ice; and pack ice, which is made up of broken expanses called *palchs* when circular and *streams* when long and narrow.

The temperature had dropped considerably. The outside thermometer registered 2 or 3 degrees below zero. But we were warmly dressed in furs for which seals and polar bears had given their lives. The inside of the *Nautilus* was kept constantly warm by electric heaters and easily met the challenge of the fiercest cold. In any case, we only had to dive to a few metres under the surface to find the temperature tolerable.

Two months earlier, in these latitudes, we would have had perpetual daylight. But already there were three or four hours of darkness, and soon night would wrap these circumpolar regions in permanent shadow for six months.

On 15 March we passed the latitude of the New Shetland Islands and the South Orkneys. The captain told me that in the past vast communities of seals had inhabited these regions but that English and American whalers, launched on their orgy of destruction, had massacred males and pregnant females, leaving behind them a wasteland of silence and death where once all had been bustle and teeming life.

On 16 March, around eight in the morning, the *Nautilus*, following the 55th meridian, crossed the Antarctic Circle. The ice was now all around us, totally obscuring the horizon. Yet the captain went on through pass after pass and kept on heading south.

'Where on earth is he going?' I wondered.

'Dead ahead,' said Conseil. 'Still, when he can't go any further, he'll stop.'

'I wouldn't swear to it,' I replied.

And to be frank, I'll admit that I was not in the least displeased to be part of his bold adventuring. I cannot express how truly amazing an experience it was to see the wonders of this strange part of the world. The floes and great blocks of ice were moulded into the most stunning shapes. Here was a Middle Eastern city, complete with minarets and mosques, there a ruined town, looking as if it had been reduced to rubble by an earthquake. The views changed incessantly in the slanting rays of the sun or disappeared from sight in grey mist and snowstorms. And from all sides came the booming sound of ice slippages and great floes rolling over, which constantly changed the scene, as in a diorama.[20]

If the *Nautilus* happened to be submerged when these major upheavals occurred, the noise was transmitted through the water with terrifying intensity. The collapse of huge masses of ice started strong after-shocks, which travelled all the way to the ocean bed. At these moments, the *Nautilus* pitched and rolled like a ship abandoned to the fury of the elements.

Often, when I could see no way through, I thought that we were trapped once and for all. But, guided by instinct, Captain Nemo seized on the smallest fissure to open new channels. He was unerring in picking out the trickles of bluish water which criss-crossed the ice-fields. As a result, I felt absolutely sure that this was not the first time he had taken the *Nautilus* deep into the waters of Antarctica.

Even so, during that same day of 16 March, the ice-field finally blocked our way. It was not yet the ice cap proper, just vast fields of pack ice fused together by the cold. But this was not an obstacle that could stop Captain Nemo, and he launched himself against the ice with terrifying power. The *Nautilus* drove like a wedge into the brittle ice wall, splitting it with awesome grindings and crackings. She was like some ancient battering ram propelled by titanic strength. Great chunks of ice, thrown high into the air, fell around us like hail. Using only its forward thrust, our vessel dug a channel for itself. Sometimes, carried by her own momentum, she mounted the ice, which disintegrated beneath her weight. At other times, when forced beneath it, she would pitch mightily until she had broken through and created cracks of open water.

During these days we were subjected to violent squalls. When conditions were particularly foggy we could not see from one end of the platform to the other. The wind gusted at us from all points of the compass, and snow collected in layers so hard that they had to be cleared with picks. When the temperature dropped to a mere 5 degrees below zero, it was enough for all the outer parts of the *Nautilus* to become completely iced over. A rigged ship would have been unable to manoeuvre, for the falls would not have run through the score of the pulleys. Only a vessel with no sails and powered by an electric motor rather than coal furnaces could brave these high latitudes.

In these conditions, the barometer remained more often than not stubbornly low. It even fell to a low of 73.5 centimetres. Compass readings became unreliable. The pointers swung crazily, showing contradictory directions as we approached the south magnetic pole, which is not to be confused with the geographic pole. Indeed, according to Hansten, the magnetic pole is situated at about latitude 70° and longitude 130°, while Duperrey's observations put it at longitude 135° and latitude 70° 30'. It therefore became necessary to take numerous readings on moveable compasses in different parts of the vessel and then use the average. But we were often reduced to guesswork in determining the route we had followed, hardly a very satisfactory method in those winding passages, where fixed references points did not remain fixed for long.

And then, on 18 March, after a score of unsuccessful manoeuvres, the *Nautilus* became fast in the ice. Here were not streams and *palchs* and ice-fields, but an interminable, immovable, continuous barrier formed of ice mountains welded together.

'The ice cap!' breathed the Canadian.

I realized that for Ned Land, as for all the navigators who had gone before us, this bulwark was an insuperable obstacle. The sun had appeared briefly around noon, and the captain was able to take a fairly accurate bearing, which put us at longitude 51° 30' and latitude 67° 39' south. We were deep in Antarctica.

Of the sea, meaning unfrozen water, we could see nothing. In front of the bow of the *Nautilus* extended a vast, broken plain, a litter of jumbled ice blocks looking for all the world – but on a stupendously massive scale – like the freakishly messy course of a river just before the ice thaws and breaks up. Here and there were pointed peaks like slender needles rising 200 feet into the air; while further off a series of sheer cliffs, darkened by areas of grey, acted like enormous mirrors reflecting back the few rays of the sun which pierced the mist. And over this scene of desolate nature hung a fierce silence occasionally broken by the flapping wings of petrels and puffins. Everything was frozen solid, even sound!

The bold foray of the *Nautilus* into those ice-fields was thus brought to a full stop.

'Professor,' Ned Land said to me on that day, 'if your Captain Nemo decides to venture any further . . .'

'Well?'

'. . . he's a better man than any man I ever met!'

'Why is that?'

'Because no one can cross the ice-cap. Your captain is a powerful man, I grant. But hell's teeth, he isn't more powerful than nature! And where nature has set limits, man has to toe the line, like it or not.'

'True, Ned. Still I would have liked to know what's behind

' "The ice cap!" breathed the Canadian'

that ice barrier. There's nothing more galling than to be stopped by a wall!'

'Monsieur is right,' said Conseil. 'Walls were invented to annoy scientists. Walls shouldn't be allowed anywhere!'

'Nonsense,' said the Canadian. 'We all know exactly what there is on the other side of that wall.'

'And what's there?' I asked.

'Ice. More and more ice.'

'You may be certain of that, Ned,' I replied, 'but I'm not. That's why I would like to go and see for myself.'

'Well, professor,' replied the Canadian, 'you can forget it. You've got as far as the ice-cap itself, and that should be enough, for you're not going to get any further, nor will your Captain Nemo, nor his *Nautilus*. Whether he wants to or not, we'll have to turn and head back north, by which I mean to lands where men who are not mad live.'

I was forced to agree that Ned Land was right. Until boats are built to sail across ice-fields, they will have no choice but to stop when faced by the ice-cap.

And so it proved. Despite all his manoeuvring, despite the mighty efforts employed to dislodge us from the ice, the *Nautilus* was reduced to immobility. Normally, when you cannot go any further forwards, you are obliged to go back the way you've come. But here, it was as impossible to retreat as it was to advance, for the passages in the ice had closed behind us, and if our vessel remained stationary for very long it would soon find itself permanently trapped. This is precisely what happened around two in the afternoon. Fresh ice formed all over the hull with amazing speed. I must say that Captain Nemo had been more than imprudent.

I was at that time out on the platform. The captain, who had been there taking stock of the situation, turned to me after a few moments and said:

'Well now, Professor Aronnax, and what do you make of our predicament?'

'I think that we are stuck fast, captain.'

'Stuck fast? What do you mean?'

'I mean that we can go neither forwards nor back nor to

one side or the other. I think that meets the requirements for the word "stuck", at least that is its meaning on dry, inhabited land.'

'So you don't think the *Nautilus* can free herself?'

'Only with great difficulty, captain, for the season is already too far advanced for you to be able to count on the ice breaking up.'

'Oh, professor,' said Captain Nemo ironically, 'you never change! You only see impediments and obstacles! I tell you now: not only will the *Nautilus* free herself but she will go on her way!'

'Further south?' I asked, staring at the captain.

'Oh yes. All the way to the Pole.'

'The Pole?' I exclaimed, unable to contain a start of disbelief.

'Of course,' the captain replied coolly, 'to the South Pole, that point never seen by human eyes, where all the globe's meridians meet. With the *Nautilus* at my command, I can do whatever I like, as I think you know!'

Indeed I did know! I also knew this man whose audacity spilled over into recklessness! But planning to overcome the obstacles presented by the South Pole – even more inaccessible than the North Pole, which the boldest explorers have yet to reach – was an absolutely insane idea which only a madman could have conceived!

It then struck me that I should ask Captain Nemo if he had already found the South Pole, on which no human being had ever set foot.

'No, professor,' he replied. 'We shall discover it together. Where others have failed, I shall succeed. I have never taken my *Nautilus* so far under these southern seas. But I say again: she will go further yet!'

'I'd like to believe it, captain,' I went on with a certain irony in my voice. 'Let's say I do, so best foot forward! There are no obstacles we cannot overcome! Let's smash the ice-cap! Let's blow it to smithereens if it resists us! Let's give wings to the *Nautilus* so that she can fly over it!'

'Over it, professor?' replied Captain Nemo coolly. 'Not over: *under*!'

'Under?' I cried.

A sudden revelation of the captain's plans had illuminated my thoughts. I knew now what he meant to do. And once more he would use the incredible capabilities of the *Nautilus* for this superhuman undertaking!

'I see that we are beginning to understand each other, professor,' said the captain with a faint smile. 'You are now thinking that my plan is workable, though I would say certain to succeed. What would not be feasible for an ordinary ship is a straightforward matter for the *Nautilus*. If a land mass materializes at the Pole, we shall stop when we reach it. But if, on the contrary, it is sitting in open sea, we shall go all the way to the Pole itself!'

'Of course!' I said, my mind reeling at the captain's train of thought. 'Even if the surface of the sea is frozen solid, all ice, its lower levels are not, for there is a providential law of physics which states that when the density of sea-water is greatest, it is always one degree warmer than the temperature at which water freezes. And unless I am mistaken, is not the part of the ice-cap which is under water four times the size of the part which appears above the surface?'

'More or less, professor. For every foot of iceberg above the surface of the sea, there are three under it. Since icebergs never exceed 100 metres in height, their base can never extend more than 300. And what is a depth of 300 metres for the *Nautilus*?'

'A trifle.'

'She could dive deeper and still find the same, uniform temperature of sea-water everywhere. At that depth we would have nothing to fear from surface temperatures of thirty or forty below zero.'

'True,' said I, excitedly, 'very true!'

'Our only problem,' continued Captain Nemo, 'will be having to stay submerged for several days running, which means we won't be able to replenish our air supply.'

'Is that all?' I said. 'But the *Nautilus* has vast tanks. Fill them and they'll provide us with all the oxygen we need!'

'It's a good idea, Professor Aronnax,' replied the captain. 'But since I do not want to have you accuse me of recklessness,

I am merely setting out all my reservations before we get to that stage.'

'You have other misgivings?'

'Just one. If the Pole does consist of open water, it is possible that it will be entirely frozen over and that consequently we shall not be able to return to the surface.'

'That may be the case, captain. But you're forgetting that the *Nautilus* has a formidable prow, so could we not drive her diagonally up through the ice, cracking it open by the impact?'

'Professor, you are full of ideas today!'

'Moreover, captain,' I added, warming to my theme, 'why shouldn't there be open water at the South Pole just as at the North Pole? The magnetic and geographic poles are different in the southern hemisphere, as they are in the northern hemisphere. So until there is proof to the contrary, we may continue to suppose that there is either land or sea at both these points on the globe.'

'I share your view, Professor Aronnax,' replied Captain Nemo. 'I would simply observe that, having raised so many objections to my plan, you now seem to be bending over backwards to come up with arguments in its favour.'

What Captain Nemo said was true. It had reached the point where I was bolder than he! I was now the one who was pushing him on to the Pole! I was racing ahead, leaving him behind! But it wouldn't do, really it wouldn't. Captain Nemo knew far more about the pros and cons of the matter and he was just enjoying seeing me carried away by wild fancies.

Meanwhile he had not wasted a moment. He gave a signal, and his first officer appeared. The two of them spoke quickly in their incomprehensible language. Either the first officer had been previously put in the picture or he found the plan eminently workable, because he showed no surprise.

But however imperturbable he appeared, he could not match the unflappability of Conseil when I told him of our intention to press on all the way to the South Pole. The information was greeted by a 'as monsieur wishes', and with that I had to be content. As to Ned Land, shoulders were never shrugged higher than those of the Canadian.

'Really, professor,' he said, 'I feel sorry for you, and for Captain Nemo!'

'But we're going to the Pole, Ned!'

'Maybe, but you won't come back!'

And Ned returned to his cabin, 'so as not to do something I might be sorry for', he said.

Meanwhile all was made ready for our bold venture. The *Nautilus*'s powerful pumps forced air into the tanks, where it was kept under high pressure. Around four in the afternoon Captain Nemo informed us that the platform hatch was about to be closed. I took one last look at the immense ice-cap which we were about to cross. The weather was clear, the air pure and the cold biting: it was twelve below. But the wind had died down, and this temperature was by no means unbearable.

Ten men or so went out on to the sides of the *Nautilus* armed with picks. They broke the ice around the hull, which was soon free. The operation did not take long, for the ice, being new, had formed only a thin layer. Then we all retreated below. The tanks were filled as usual, with the free water we were floating on. Then without further ado, the *Nautilus* dived.

I had gone to the Great Saloon with Conseil. Through the viewing panels we looked out into the lower depths of the southern ocean. The thermometer rose. The pointer swung on the dial of the depth gauge.

When we were about 300 metres down, it was exactly as Captain Nemo had predicted: we were sailing directly below the ridged underside of the ice cap. But the *Nautilus* went even deeper until we were at a depth of 800 metres. The temperature of the water, which had been −12 on the surface, was now −11, which meant that it had risen by 2 degrees.[21] Of course, the temperature inside the *Nautilus*, which was kept warm by its electric heaters, was much higher. Each of these manoeuvres was carried out with extraordinary precision.

'If monsieur will pardon the boldness,' said Conseil, 'I do believe that we're going to get through.'

'I am sure we will!' I replied, with complete conviction.

In this sea under the ice, the *Nautilus* had set a direct course for the Pole, without deviating from the 52nd meridian. From our position at latitude 67° 30' to 90° was 22½ degrees, a distance of about 500 leagues. The *Nautilus* adopted an average speed of 26 miles an hour, the same as an express train. If we kept up that rate of progress, forty-eight hours would be enough to see us to the Pole.

For the first part of the night, the novelty of what we were seeing held Conseil and me glued to the viewing panels. The sea around us was permanently lit by the electric beams of our searchlight. There were no fish living in these imprisoned waters. They merely used them as a conduit to travel from the Antarctic Ocean to the open sea of the Pole. We travelled quickly, as we could tell by the vibration of the long steel hull.

Around two in the morning, I left the saloon to get a few hours' sleep, and Conseil followed my example. As I proceeded along the walkways, I did not meet Captain Nemo. I assumed that he was in the helmsman's cockpit.

The next day, 19 March, at five in the morning, I returned to my post in the Great Saloon. I saw from the electric log that the *Nautilus* had slowed down and was rising to the surface, carefully, emptying her tanks slowly as she went.

My heart began to beat faster. Were we going to break surface and find ourselves in the open polar air once more?

The answer was no. A jolt indicated that the *Nautilus* had struck the underside of the ice cap, which was still very thick if the dull sound of the impact was anything to go by. In fact, we had, as sailors would say, 'nudged', but from below, at a depth of 1,000 feet. That meant that we had 2,000 feet of ice above us, of which 1.000 emerged above water. This meant that the ice cap was much higher here than it was when we had measured it at its edge. This was hardly encouraging news.

All that day, the *Nautilus* repeated the same manoeuvre several times and each time continued to come up against the ceiling of ice above. At moments, she was halted at a depth of 900 metres, which meant that there the ice was 1,200 metres thick, of which some 200 rose above the surface of the ocean. This was double the height it had been when the *Nautilus* had dived.

I made careful notes of these various depths and in this way was able to plot a linear graph of the shape of the underside of the great ice cap deep under the water.

That evening, our situation remained unaltered. We continued to find ice extending down to four or five hundred metres. This marked a clear reduction, but there was still a very great thickness between us and the surface of the sea.

It was then eight o'clock. The air inside the *Nautilus* should already have been replaced four hours earlier according to the daily routine on board ship. But I was not unduly incommoded, although Captain Nemo had not yet used his air tanks to supplement our oxygen.

But that night I slept badly. Hope battled in my mind with fear. I got up several times. The *Nautilus* went on feeling her way. At about three in the morning I became aware that the bottom of the ice mass was now located at a depth of just 50 metres. So just 150 feet still separated us from the surface. The ice cap was reverting to ice-field; mountain was turning into plain.

My eyes remained fixed on the depth gauge. We were still on an ascending gradient with, above us, the surface gleaming as it caught the beams of our electric light. The ice cap above us was losing height and under water it was thinning in a long, tapering upward slope.

Finally, at six o'clock, on that memorable 19 March, the door of the Great Saloon opened and Captain Nemo appeared:

'We have open sea,' he said.

'*Captain Nemo appeared*'

14

The South Pole

I hurried up to the platform. Yes! Open sea! Barely a handful of floes and floating ice-blocks; in the distance a wide expanse of sea; a world full of birds flying through the air and myriads of fish in water which, according to depth, ran the gamut from intense blue to olive green. The thermometer read 3° centigrade. It was comparatively spring-like enclosed here behind this ice cap, whose distant bulk loomed on the horizon to the north.

'Are we at the Pole?' I asked the captain. My heart was racing.

'I don't know,' he replied. 'We shall take a bearing at noon.'

'But surely the sun will not be visible through all this mist?' I said, peering up at the greyish sky.

'However brief its appearance, it will be enough for me,' replied the captain.

Ten miles south of the *Nautilus*, a solitary island rose to a height of 200 metres. We made for it, taking every precaution, for these waters could be treacherous with hidden reefs.

An hour later we had reached it and two hours after that we had sailed all round it. It was 4 or 5 miles in circumference. A narrow channel separated it from a sizeable expanse of land, perhaps a whole continent, whose extent we had no way of knowing. The existence of this land seemed to vindicate the hypotheses of Maury. Indeed, the ingenious American had observed that between the South Pole and the 60th parallel the sea is covered by floating ice formations of enormous size the like of which is not encountered in the North Atlantic. From this he concluded that there must be a very large land mass inside the Antarctic Circle, because icebergs cannot form in open sea, only on coasts. According to his calculations, the volume of ice encasing the South Pole forms an immense cap which must be at least 4,000 kilometres wide.

However, the *Nautilus*, not wanting to run aground, was hove to about three cable lengths from a sort of beach overhung by a magnificent jumble of huge rocks. The dinghy was launched. The captain, two of his men carrying instruments, plus Conseil and myself got into it. It was now ten in the morning. I had seen nothing of Ned Land. No doubt he did not wish to confess that he was wrong now that he was actually at the South Pole.

A few strokes of the oars brought the dinghy to the shore and on to the sand. Conseil was about to jump out but I restrained him.

I turned to Captain Nemo and said: 'Captain, the honour of being the first to set foot on this land should be yours.'

'Indeed, professor,' the captain replied. 'And if I have no hesitation about stepping on to this polar ground, it is only because no human being has ever done so before now.'

And so saying, he jumped lightly on to the sand. His heart was visibly full. He climbed to the top of an overhanging rock which was the tip of a modest promontory and there he stood, arms folded across his chest, eyes shining, motionless and silent. In this way did he seem to lay claim to this southern land. After five minutes of this trance-like rapture, he turned and came back to us.

'Whenever you're ready, professor,' he called to me.

I got out of the boat, followed by Conseil, leaving the two men in the dinghy.

The strip of land where we had disembarked looked, as far as we could see, to be tuff, reddish in colour, as if it were composed of crushed brick. It was covered by scree, solidified lava flows and pumice. It was impossible not to recognize its volcanic origin. In places, occasional fumaroles released a smell of sulphur and demonstrated that the power of the internal fires was undiminished. But after we had climbed to the top of a steep escarpment, I saw no sign of any volcano within a radius of miles. But it is generally known that when James Ross came to the Antarctic, he found that the craters of Mount Erebus and Mount Terror, on the 167th meridian at latitude 77° 32' south, were fully active.

The vegetation of this desolate land was poor and sparse. A few lichens of the species *usmea melanoxantha* which had spread over the black rocks; a small number of rudimentary diatoma, microscopic plantlets which consist of cells grouped between two quartzous shells; and long purple and red fucus, buoyed up by small natatory bladders, which had been deposited on to the beach by the surf, these pretty much exhausted the meagre range of flora in this region.

The foreshore was littered with molluscs, small mussels, barnacles, smooth cockles shaped like hearts, and particularly with clios, which have oblong, membranous bodies and heads formed of two round lobes. I also saw huge quantities of arctic clios, 3 centimetres long, of which a whale can engulf an entire shoal with every mouthful. The open water at the shore's edge was literally alive with these delightful pteropods, which are the marine version of butterflies.

Among other zoophytes in the shallows were a few shrub-like coralligenous growths like the ones which James Ross reckoned live in Antarctic waters down to a depth of 1,000 metres; small alcyonarians of the species *procellaria pelagica* along with large numbers of asterias peculiar to those climes; and starfish strewn all over the ground.

But for abundance of life, I had only to look to the air. By the thousand, birds of various kinds flew and swooped, deafening us with their shrieking. Others crowded together all over the rocks and watched us pass without fear, and indeed some were so friendly that they got under our feet. They were penguins, which are as awkward and clumsy on land as they are agile and supple in water, where they are sometimes mistaken for the fleetest bonitos. They emitted raucous cries and formed large colonies, moved little but made huge amounts of noise.

Among other birds, I noticed grallatores, a kind of wader, as big as pigeons, all white, with a short cone-shaped beak and eyes ringed with red. Conseil managed to catch some, for these fowl, when properly cooked, make a very acceptable meal.

Overhead glided sinister albatrosses, which, with their wing-span of 4 metres, are rightly called the vultures of the ocean; gigantic petrels, including *quebrante-huesos*, with arc-shaped wings, which prey on seals; parti-coloured mews, like small ducks, with black and white backs; and, finally, more petrels, a whole series of them, some whitish with wings edged with brown, others blue and unique to Antarctic waters, and yet others which, as I said to Conseil, are 'so oily that the Faroe islanders just fit them with a wick and light them'.

'If only nature had given them wicks,' he replied, 'they would have had everything to make them perfect, ready-made lamps!'

After we had gone half a mile, the ground became riddled with the nests of penguins, shallow burrows in which eggs were laid. From them, numerous birds emerged. Some time later, Captain Nemo ordered a cull of several hundred, for their dark flesh makes good eating. They honked, a sound like the braying of donkeys. They were about the size of a goose, with slate-coloured bodies, white below and a yellow collar, and were easily killed with stones, for they made no attempt to run away.

Meanwhile, the mist had not lifted, and by eleven o'clock the sun had yet to show its face. Its absence was worrying. Without the sun, it would not be possible to take a bearing. So how would we know if we had really reached the Pole?

When I caught up with Captain Nemo, I found him leaning in silence on a block of stone, staring up at the sky. He seemed impatient, frustrated. But what could he do? This bold, powerful spirit could not command the sun the way he commanded the sea.

Noon came and went without a single break in the clouds. We could not even guess the place where the sun should be behind that curtain of fog. And soon the fog turned to snow.

'We'll try again tomorrow,' was all the captain said, and we went back to the *Nautilus* through the swirling snowflakes.

In our absence, the nets had been laid, and I was very interested to see what fish had been brought on board. The seas of Antarctica provide a refuge for a large number of migrating fish fleeing the storms of lower latitudes, only to fall, it is true, into the jaws of porpoises and seals. I noticed southern-sea bullheads, 10 centimetres long, a variety of cartilaginous fish, whitish with bright stripes and armed with spikelets; 3-foot-long Antarctic chimaeras, long in the body, skin a smooth, silvery-white, round head, with three dorsal fins and a snout ending in a proboscis turned down towards the mouth. I tasted their flesh but found it insipid, though Conseil found it very much to his liking.

The blizzard lasted until the next day. It was not possible to remain standing on the platform. From the Great Saloon, where I went to write up my record of our foray on to the polar continent, I could hear the cries of petrels and albatrosses which were playfully riding the storm. The *Nautilus* did not stay still but cruised along the coast a further 10 miles south into the half-light emitted by the sun as it just skimmed the horizon.

By the following day, 20 March, the snow had stopped. The cold was a little keener. The thermometer registered 2 degrees below zero. The mist was lifting, and I had hopes that on this day our position would be accurately established.

Captain Nemo did not put in an appearance, so the dinghy took Conseil and me and deposited us on the shore. The nature of the ground was still the same volcanic tuff. Everywhere there were debris of lava, scree and basalt, but I still saw no sign of the crater which had ejected them. Here, as at our earlier landing place, countless birds filled this part of the polar continent with life. But they also shared the place with huge colonies of marine mammals, which turned their gentle eyes on us and stared. They were seals of various species. Some lay on the ground and others sprawled on drifting ice-floes, emerging from the water or diving into it. They did not run away when we approached, for they had never had any contact with human beings. I estimate that what I saw would have been enough to provision several hundred ships.

'By Jove,' exclaimed Conseil, 'it's a good thing that Ned Land didn't come with us!'

'Why is that, Conseil?'

'Because he's a fanatical hunter and would have slaughtered the whole lot!'

'Well, perhaps not quite all, though I do agree that we would not have been able to stop our Canadian friend harpooning a good few of these magnificent cetaceans. I don't think Captain Nemo would have been best pleased, given his views on the indiscriminate shedding of the blood of these inoffensive creatures.'

'He is quite right.'

'Of course, Conseil. But tell me, Conseil, have you not already classified these superb marine fauna?'

'Monsieur knows very well,' he replied, 'that I am not well versed in visual identification. But if monsieur were to tell me the names of these animals . . .'

'There are seals and walruses.'

'Two genera belonging to the family of pinnipeds,' intoned the learned Conseil, 'order of carnivora, group of unguiculates, sub-class of monodelphians, class of mammals, branch of vertebrates.'

'Absolutely correct, Conseil,' I said. 'But both these genera, seals and walruses, can be divided into species, and, unless I am very much mistaken, I suspect that we will have an opportunity to see specimens of both. Come along.'

It was eight in the morning. We had four hours to ourselves before the sun could be usefully observed. I led the way towards a wide bay which had been scooped out of the granite cliffs lining the shore.

There, I can report, all around us, as far as the eye could see, land and floating ice teemed with marine mammals, and I instinctively looked round for old Proteus, the mythological shepherd who watched over the immense flocks of Neptune. They were, in the main, seals. They formed distinct groups, male and female, fathers standing guard over their families, females suckling their young, while occasionally older juveniles, finding their feet, took a few venturesome steps away from the group. When these mammals wished to move, they advanced in a series of jerks produced by contracting their bodies and helped the process somewhat by awkwardly shuffling on their inadequate fins which, in their cousin the manatee, are effectively forearms. I would add that in the water, their natural element, these animals are splendid swimmers, having a flexible spine, narrow pelvis, a thick, close-cut coat and web-bed feet. At rest and on land, they adopt extremely graceful postures. Which is why the Ancients, when first they saw their gentle faces and those expressions, more winning than any woman's, their velvety, clear eyes and delightful poses, poeti-cized them after their fashion, transforming the males into tritons and the females into sirens.

I mentioned to Conseil that the cerebral lobes of these intel-ligent cetaceans are unusually well developed. No other mammal, with the exception of man, has a larger brain. Accord-ingly, seals can be trained to a certain extent. They are easily tamed, and I believe, along with some other naturalists, that if properly schooled they would be very useful as, so to speak, 'fishing dogs'.

Most of the seals were sleeping on rocks or on the sand. Among these specimens, which were seals in the strict sense, having no external ears – unlike the sea-lion which has visible ear flaps – I picked out several kinds of *stenorhynchus*, 3 metres long with white fur, bulldog heads, which have ten teeth, four incisors in the upper jaw and four in the lower, plus two large canines in the shape of a fleur-de-lis. Among them mingled a number of sea elephants, a kind of seal but having a short, mobile trunk. They are the largest form of the species, measure 20 feet in girth, and can reach a length of 10 metres. They did not stir as we approached.

'Aren't these animals dangerous?' asked Conseil.

'No,' I replied, 'unless they are attacked. When seals defend their young, their fury is awesome, and it is not rare for them to smash a fishing boat to matchwood.'

'Quite right too,' said Conseil.

'I wouldn't disagree.'

Two miles further on, we were halted by the promontory which sheltered the bay against winds from the south. It fell sheer to the sea, and the breakers foamed white over the rocks at its base. From beyond it came the sound of bellowing, which might have been made by a herd of cattle.

'Hello!' said Conseil. 'Sounds like a choir of bulls!'

'No,' I said. 'It's the sound of walruses.'

'Are they fighting?'

'Either fighting or playing.'

'If monsieur agrees,' said Conseil, 'we must see this!'

'We must indeed, Conseil.'

The next moment, we were scrambling over blackish boulders, which moved unpredictably as we stepped on them, hampering our way across stones already made slippery by a coating of ice. More than once, I took a tumble and hurt my back. Conseil, either because he was more careful or more sure-footed, remained cool and would help me to my feet, saying:

'If monsieur would be good enough to walk with his legs further apart, monsieur would be able to keep his balance better.'

When we reached the crest of the promontory, I saw an immense white plain entirely covered with walruses. They were playing together. They were bellowing with pleasure, not anger.

Walruses resemble seals both in the shape of their bodies and the arrangement of their limbs. But their lower jaw has neither canines nor incisors, and the upper canines take the form of two tusks 80 centimetres long, with a circumference of 30 at the base. These tusks, made of dense ivory which has no grooves or ridges, is harder than elephant ivory and is less liable to yellowing, are much sought after. Accordingly, walruses are the subject of senseless hunting which will finally eradicate every last one of them: the hunters, who indiscriminately massacre pregnant females and juveniles, kill 4,000 of them each year.

As we passed by these curious creatures, I had plenty of time to observe them closely, for they took no notice of us. Their hide is thick and rough, a sort of fawn tinged with red, and their coats are short and sparse. Some were 4 metres long. More placid and less timid than their northern cousins, they did not rely on sentries to patrol the boundaries of their colonies.

After spending some time inspecting the walruses, I decided we should return the way we had come. It was now eleven o'clock, and if Captain Nemo found the conditions suitable for taking a position, I wanted to be there when he did so. But I held out little hope that the sun would be visible that day. Clouds low on the horizon hid it from sight. It seemed that it was being selfish and did not want to shed any of its light on this inaccessible point on the globe for human eyes to see.

Even so, I thought it best to head back to the *Nautilus*. We walked along a narrow ridge which ran round the top of the cliffs. By 11.30 we were back at the spot where we had landed. The dinghy had now brought the captain ashore. I saw him standing on a block of basalt. He had his instruments with him. His eyes were fixed on the northern horizon, on which, behind the cloud, the sun was inscribing an elongated arc.

I stood at his elbow and waited without speaking. Midday came round as it had the previous day, but the sun did not appear.

It was a severe blow dealt by fate. The bearing still had not been taken. If it was not done on the next day, we would have to give up all thought of establishing our exact position.

For it was then 20 March. If the next day, the 21st, the equinox, we failed again, the sun would sink below the horizon for six months. With its disappearance the long polar night would begin. Since the September equinox, it had had re-emerged above the northern horizon, rising steadily in long spirals until 21 December. After that date, which marks the summer solstice in these southerly latitudes, it had started to decline again. Now, on the very next day, it would emit its last rays on this part of the globe.

I conveyed my calculations and fears to Captain Nemo.

'You are right, Professor Aronnax,' he said. 'If I cannot measure the height of the sun tomorrow, I won't be able to try again for six months. But of course, since the vagaries of my journey happen to have put me in these seas on 21 March, if the sun does in fact show its face, it will be a simple matter to take our position.'

'Could you explain why, captain?'

'If the sun follows such elongated spirals, it is difficult to measure its height above the horizon accurately, and instruments are always liable to give seriously incorrect readings.'

'So what will you do?'

'I shall use only my chronometer,' said Captain Nemo. 'If tomorrow at noon on 21 March, the sun's disk, after due allowance is made for refraction, is cut exactly into two by the northern horizon, it will mean that I am at the South Pole.'

'True,' said I. 'But what you say is not mathematically accurate, because the equinox is not necessarily reached exactly at noon.'

'That also is true, professor, but the margin of error will be no more than 100 metres, and that is as accurate as we need to be. So, until tomorrow.'

Captain Nemo returned to the *Nautilus*, while Conseil and I stayed on until five o'clock, walking up and down the beach, observing and studying. I encountered no interesting objects, except a penguin's egg of unusual size for which a collector would have paid more than 1,000 francs. With its cream colour and the stripes and decorative markings which looked like hieroglyphics, it was a rare curio. I gave it to Conseil to look after. Being very careful and sure-footed, he hung on to it as though it were a piece of valuable China ware and brought it back intact to the *Nautilus*.

Back on board, I placed the egg in one of the glass cases in the museum. I dined with relish on a piece of seal's liver, which to me tasted like pork. Then I went to bed, but not before invoking the favours of the radiant daystar, like some Hindu.

The next day, 21 March, at five in the morning, I was standing on the platform. Captain Nemo was already there.

'The weather is clearing a little,' he said. 'I am hopeful. After breakfast, we'll go ashore and select an observation post.'

When this was settled, I went in search of Ned Land. I would have liked to have him come with me. But the stubborn Canadian refused. It was clear that his taciturnity was growing worse daily, as was his unfortunate ill humour. Still, I did not entirely regret his mulish obstinacy at this juncture. The fact was there were too many seals on land, and it would not have been wise to put such temptation in the way of so impetuous a hunter.

When breakfast was over, I was rowed ashore. The *Nautilus* had moved a few miles further south during the night. She was now standing a good league off a coast dominated by a mountain peak four or five hundred metres high. In the dinghy with me were Captain Nemo and two crew members with the instruments, by which I mean the chronometer, a telescope and a barometer.

During the crossing I observed a number of whales which belonged to all three species native to the southern seas: the right whale (the English name for them), with no dorsal fin; the humpback, a rorqual with a furrowed underside and huge whitish fins, which, despite the name, *baleinoptère*, given to it by the French, do not amount to wings; and thirdly the brownish-grey razorback, the most active of all these cetaceans. This powerful animal can be heard over great distances when it blows columns of air and vapour resembling great swirls of smoke to considerable heights. These different mammals played in groups in these peaceful waters, and it was clear to me that this polar basin was being used as a safe haven by these cetaceans after over-hunting by whaling ships.

I also caught sight of long strings of salpae, a kind of aggregated mollusc, and extremely large jellyfish, which swayed in the undulating movement of the waves.

We went ashore at nine. The sky was getting lighter. Clouds were being blown rapidly southwards. The mist was disappearing from the cold surface of the water. Captain Nemo made straight for the mountain, which he had obviously selected as the point he would use for his observation. It was not easy scrambling up over jagged outcrops of lava and pumice in an atmosphere saturated with the sulphurous fumes from the volcanic vents. For a man so unaccustomed to moving about on land, he climbed the steepest slopes with an ease and agility which I could not equal and would have been the envy of many a hunter of Alpine goats.

It took us two hours to reach the summit of the peak, which consisted of equal amounts of porphyry and basalt. From there our eyes took in an immense sea, which, to the north, ended only where it met the line of the sky. Below us lay fields of dazzling white. Above us, the sky was clear blue and free of mist. To the north, the sun's disk, like a ball of fire, was already being clipped by the edge of the horizon. Over the surface of the sea rose hundreds of magnificent jets of water, like floral sprays. In the distance, the *Nautilus* lay like some sleeping cetacean.

Behind us, to the south and east, was a vast tract of land, a chaos of jumbled rocks and ice which extended as far as the eye could see.

When Captain Nemo reached the top of the mountain, he carefully measured its height using the barometer, as he needed to take it into account when making his calculation.

At 11.45, the sun, now visible only by refraction, was like a golden disk, and it spread its last rays over the deserted continent where no foot had stepped and the sea on which no man had yet sailed.

Looking through a reticular telescope – one which uses a mirror to correct refraction – Captain Nemo observed the sun as it dropped slowly below the horizon in a very wide arc. I held the chronometer. My heart was racing. If the disappearance of the half-disk occurred at the same instant that noon showed on the chronometer, then we were indeed at the Pole.

'Noon!' I cried.

'The South Pole!' replied Captain Nemo in a solemn voice as he passed me the telescope, which showed me the daystar cut exactly in two equal parts by the horizon.

I watched as its last rays wreathed the mountain top and shadows slowly climbed up its slopes.

At that moment, Captain Nemo laid one hand on my shoulder and said:

'Professor Aronnax, in 1600 the Dutchman Gherik, driven by currents and storms, reached latitude 60 degrees south and discovered New Shetland. On 17 January 1773 the illustrious Cook, following the 38th meridian, reached latitude 67 degrees 30 minutes south, and on 30 January 1774, following the 109th meridian, he recorded his position as latitude 71 degrees 15 minutes. In 1819 the Russian Bellinghausen arrived at the 69th parallel, and in 1821, the 66th' at longitude 111 degrees west. In 1820, the Englishman Brunsfield was halted at the 65th degree. The same year, the American Morel, though his account is unreliable, sailing south along the 42nd meridian, found open water at latitude 70 degrees 14 minutes. In 1825 the Englishman Powell was unable to proceed beyond the 62nd degree. The same year an ordinary seal-hunter, an Englishman named Weddell got as far as latitude 72 degrees 14 minutes on the 35th meridian and 74 degrees 15 minutes on the 36th. In 1829 the Englishman Forster, master of the *Chanticleer*, took possession of the Antarctic continent at latitude 63 degrees 26 minutes south and longitude 66 degrees 26 minutes west. On 1 February 1831, the Englishman Biscoe discovered Enderby Land at latitude 68 degrees 50 minutes, on 5 February 1832, Adelaide Land at latitude 67 degrees, and on 21 February Graham Land at latitude 64 degrees 45 minutes. In 1838, the Frenchman Dumont d'Urville, his progress stopped by the ice cap at latitude 62 degrees 57 minutes, sighted Louis-Philippe Land; two years later, in a new foray south, he named Adélie Land at 66 degrees 30 minutes on 21 January, and Clarie Coast eight days later at 64 degrees 40 minutes. In 1838 the Englishman Wilkes pushed on as far as the 69th parallel on the 100th meridian. In 1839 the Englishman Balleny discovered Sabrina Coast on the very edge of the Antarctic Circle. Finally, in 1842 the Englishman James Ross took the *Erebus* and the *Terror* to latitude 76 degrees 56 minutes south and longitude 171 degrees 7 minutes east and discovered Victoria Land on 12 January; on the 23rd of the same month, he was at the 74th parallel, the furthest point that had been reached until then; on the 27th, he reached 76 degrees 8 minutes; on the 28th, 77 degrees 32 minutes; and on 2 February, 78 degrees 4 minutes. In 1842 he returned to the 71st degree but could go no further. And now I, Captain Nemo, on this day, 21 March 1868, have reached the South Pole and the 90th degree and I lay claim to this part of the globe, which, in extent, is as large as one-sixth all the known continents combined!'

'In whose name, captain?'

'Mine, professor!'

And so saying, Captain Nemo unfurled a black flag on which was emblazoned a golden 'N'. Then, turning to the sinking orb, whose dying rays still just kissed the horizon:

'Farewell, sun!' he cried. 'Depart, bright star! Go to your rest beneath this open sea and let a night of six months spread her shadows across my new domain!'

15
Accident or Incident?

The next morning, 22 March, at six o'clock, preparations for our departure got under way. The last glimmer of twilight vanished into the darkness of night. The cold was intense. The stars shone with amazing brightness. Directly above us was the brilliant Southern Cross, the pole star of the Antarctic regions.

The thermometer registered 12 degrees below zero, and when the wind freshened our faces smarted and stung. Ice floes multiplied on the open water. The sea began to congeal everywhere. Blackish patches on its surface indicated the imminent formation of new ice. It was obvious that this southern basin, frozen over for six months in the year, would become totally inaccessible. What would become of the whales during this period? Most likely, they would pass under the ice cap and go in search of more congenial waters. As for the seals and walruses, accustomed to surviving the most hostile habitats, they would remain in this frozen environment. These animals dig holes in the ice which they ensure remain open, for they come to them to breathe. When the birds, driven out by the cold, migrate north, both kinds of marine mammal are left in sole charge of the polar continent.

With her tanks slowly filling with water, the *Nautilus* went into a shallow dive, stopping at a depth of 1,000 metres. Her propeller turned in the water, and the vessel moved forwards at a speed of 15 miles an hour. By evening, she was cruising beneath the immense frozen shell of the ice cap.

The viewing panels in the Great Saloon had been kept closed as a precaution, for fear that the hull of the *Nautilus* should collide with some submerged ledge or overhang of ice. Consequently I spent the day putting my notes in order. My mind was full of memories of the Pole. We had reached that inaccessible point on the globe without fatigue or danger, as if our floating carriage had been running along the track of a railway. And now, the return journey was beginning in earnest. Was I in for further surprises of the same kind? I thought it likely, since there is no end to the succession of underwater wonders! But for the last five and a half months, ever since chance had cast us up on board the *Nautilus*, we had travelled 14,000 leagues, and during our voyage over a distance greater than the Earth's equator so many happenings, some curious, others terrifying, had punctuated our travels: the hunt in the forests of Crespo, running aground in the Torres Strait, the coral cemetery, the pearl-fisheries of Ceylon, the Arabian tunnel, the fires of Santorini, the sunken millions in the Bay of Vigo, Atlantis, the South Pole ... All that night these memories filled a succession of dreams which prevented my brain from finding a moment's rest.

At three in the morning, I was awoken by a violent jolt. I was sitting up in bed, ears pricked in the dark, when I was suddenly tipped out into the middle of my cabin. It was obvious: the *Nautilus* had collided with something and was now listing badly.

I groped my way using the walls and dragged myself along the walkways to the Great Saloon, which was lit by its luminous ceiling. Tables and chairs had been overturned. Fortunately, the glass showcases, solidly bolted to the floor, had not moved. The paintings on the starboard side, given the degree of list, now lay flat against the wall coverings while the bottoms of the frames of those on the port side hung out by a good foot. The *Nautilus* was therefore lying on her right side and, moreover, had stopped moving.

From where I was, I could hear the confused sound of footsteps and voices. But Captain Nemo did not appear. I was on the point of leaving the Great Saloon, when Ned Land and Conseil clambered in.

'What's going on?' I said.

'I was just about to ask monsieur the same thing,' replied Conseil.

'Hell's teeth!' cried the Canadian, 'I know exactly what's happened! The *Nautilus* has gone aground, and, judging by the way she's lying, I don't think she'll get off as easily this time as in the Torres Strait.'

'But at least,' I asked, 'we have returned to the surface?'

'That we don't know,' said Conseil.

'It's easy enough to find out,' I said.

I looked at the depth gauge. To my great astonishment, it showed a depth of 360 metres.

'What does it mean?' I exclaimed.

'We'll have to ask Captain Nemo,' said Conseil.

'But where can we find him?' asked Ned Land.

'Follow me,' I said to my two companions.

We left the Great Saloon. There was nobody in the library, and nobody around the central stairwell, near the crew's quarters. I assumed that Captain Nemo must be in the cockpit with the helmsman. The best thing would be to wait, so all three of us returned to the saloon.

I will pass quickly over the recriminations voiced by the Canadian. He made the most of this opportunity to express his feelings. I gave him plenty of scope to give vent to his anger but did not react.

We had been there for twenty minutes, straining our ears to catch the faintest sounds of activity inside the *Nautilus*, when Captain Nemo walked in. He appeared not to see us. His face, normally so inscrutable, expressed signs of anxiety. He stared at the compass without saying a word, then the depth gauge, and eventually placed one finger on a point of the planisphere, somewhere in the section representing the southern seas.

I had no wish to interrupt him. But when he turned to me a few moments later, I recalled the word he had used in the Torres Strait and lobbed it back at him:

'Another incident, captain?'

'No, professor,' he replied. 'This time it's an accident.'

'Is it serious?'

'Perhaps.'

'Are we in any immediate danger?'

'No.'

'Has the *Nautilus* run aground?'

'Yes.'

'How did it happen?'

'By a freak of nature, not human incompetence. No mistakes have been made in any of our procedures. But there is no way of overcoming the power of equilibrium. We can defy the laws of men but not the laws of nature.'

It was an odd moment for the captain to choose to make this philosophical observation. Moreover, his answer did not tell me anything.

'May I know, captain,' I asked, 'what caused the accident?'

'A huge block of ice, a large iceberg, rolled over,' he replied. 'When icebergs are undermined by the melting of their base by warmer water or repeated collisions, their centre of gravity rises. They then roll over; they topple. That is what has happened. As one of them turned over, it struck the *Nautilus* as she cruised under water. It then slid under our hull, raised us with irresistible power and hoisted us on to a high ledge, where we are now lying on our side.'

'But can't we free the *Nautilus* by emptying the tanks in such a way that we get back on an even keel?'

'That's exactly what we are doing now, professor. You can hear the pumps working. Look at the depth gauge. It shows that the *Nautilus* is rising, but the iceberg is rising with us, and until some obstacle appears to stop its upward movement our position will not change.'

It was true. The *Nautilus* was still listing to starboard at the same angle. She would obviously right herself when the iceberg stopped rising. But for the moment, who could say if we would not come up against the underside of the ice cap and be horribly squeezed between two masses of ice?

I was thinking about the implications of our predicament. Captain Nemo did not take his eyes off the depth gauge. Since the iceberg had rolled over, the *Nautilus* had risen by about 150 feet, but the angle by which she diverged from the perpendicular remained stubbornly the same.

Suddenly, a faint tremor ran through the hull. Evidently, the *Nautilus* had straightened up a little. The objects in the Great

Saloon gradually resumed their usual position. The walls started to revert to the vertical. None of us spoke. Our hearts racing, we observed, we felt the vessel righting itself. The floor under our feet became horizontal once more. Ten minutes ticked by.

'At last!' I cried. 'Righted!'

'Quite so,' said Captain Nemo as he made for the door of the Great Saloon.

'But will we be able to float?' I asked.

'Of course,' he replied, 'because the tanks are not empty yet. Once they are, the *Nautilus* will rise to the surface.'

The captain left us and soon I realized that he had given orders that the *Nautilus* should stop rising. This was necessary because otherwise we would soon have hit the underside of the ice cap. The wisest thing was to remain at a modest depth.

'That was a close-run thing!' said Conseil.

'Very close! We could have been crushed between two masses of ice, or at best held fast by them. And if that had happened, our inability to replenish the air supply ... Yes, a narrow squeak!'

'Let's hope it's all over,' said Ned Land.

I had no wish to start a pointless discussion with the Canadian and did not respond. In any case, the viewing panels opened at that moment, and light from outside flooded in through the glass.

We were submerged, as I have said, in clear water. But not 10 metres from both sides of the *Nautilus* rose dazzling walls of ice. Above and below us was more of the same: above us because the bottom of the ice cap acted like an immense ceiling, and below because the iceberg which had rolled over had slowly stopped moving when it found support on two points of the side walls which were now holding it in position. The *Nautilus* was imprisoned in what was in effect a tunnel of ice some 20 metres wide, which was filled with still water. It would thus be an easy matter to escape by going either forwards or backwards and then, after a few hundred metres, taking an unimpeded exit beneath the ice cap.

The overhead ceiling illumination in the Great Saloon had been turned off, and yet the room was filled with brilliant light. This was because of the way the beams from our search-light were being blindingly reflected by the ice walls. I have no words to describe the impact of that brilliant, voltaically generated light on those erratically sculpted masses of frozen water. Every angle, every chamfer, every facet was lit with its own colour according to the nature of the faults running through the ice. It was like a dazzling hoard of gems, and particularly of sapphires, which set their blue flames against the green fires of emeralds. Here and there subtle tones of opals of infinite delicacy ran through those sparkling fields like so many blazing diamonds too bright to be looked on by the human eye. The luminosity of the searchlight was increased a hundredfold, the way the light from the lamp does after it passes through the lenses of the tallest lighthouse.

'It's so beautiful! So beautiful!' Conseil exclaimed.

'Yes,' I said, 'a truly wonderful sight. Don't you agree, Ned?'

'Hell's teeth!' he enthused. 'It's fantastic, though I hate to admit it! No one ever saw anything like this before. But it's a sight that could cost us dear. If I'm frank, I'd say that we are seeing things which God wished to keep hidden from the eyes of men!'

Ned was right. It was *too* beautiful. Suddenly a cry from Conseil made me turn round.

'What is it?' I asked.

'Monsieur should shut his eyes! Monsieur must not look!'

As he spoke, Conseil brought his hands up smartly and covered both his eyes.

'What's wrong?' I cried.

'I'm dazzled! I've gone blind!'

I glanced up automatically at the viewing panel but was unable to bear the glare that filled it.

I understood what had happened. The *Nautilus* had suddenly accelerated and was now travelling at high speed. The individual reflections in the ice walls had all merged and become a single dazzling, flashing explosion of light. The myriad glints of sparkling diamonds had become one. Driven on by her propeller, the *Nautilus* was sailing through the inside of a streak of lightning!

At this point, the viewing panels closed again. We kept our hands over our eyes, which still had the same concentric rings of light imprinted on their retinas as are left when they have been exposed too directly to the rays of the sun. We needed some time before our vision returned to normal.

Eventually, we were able to lower our hands.

'Gracious! I would never have believed it,' said Conseil.

'I still don't believe it!' replied the Canadian.

'When we eventually get back to terra firma,' added Conseil, 'surfeited by natural wonders, what will we make of all those little countries and the rest of the paltry handiwork of man? The inhabited world is no longer worthy of us!'

Such words in the mouth of the normally impassive Fleming showed the pitch of excitement we had reached. But our Canadian friend did not miss the chance to pour cold water on our enthusiasm.

'The inhabited world?' he said, shaking his head. 'You can rest assured that we will never see it again!'

It was then five in the morning. At that moment, a shock was felt in the bow of the *Nautilus*. I knew it meant that our bow had just run up against a block of ice. The collision must have resulted from a navigational error, for the underwater tunnel was littered with such blocks and did not offer an easy passage. I assumed that Captain Nemo would modify his route and sail round these obstacles or follow the winding course of the tunnel. In any case, there was absolutely no question that forward progress would be halted. But, contrary to my expectations, the *Nautilus* now went into reverse.

'Are we going backwards?' asked Conseil.

'Yes,' I replied. 'It must be because in this direction there is no way out of the tunnel.'

'So what now?'

'Well now,' I said, 'what we do next is very simple. We go back the way we came and leave through the exit on the southern end. That's all.'

By speaking in this way, I was trying to appear more relaxed than I really felt. Meanwhile, the speed at which the *Nautilus* was travelling backwards increased. With the propeller in reverse, we were being taken back at a high rate of knots.

'This is going to delay us,' said Ned.

'What do a few hours more or less matter as long as we get out?'

'Exactly,' said Ned, 'as long as we do get out!'

I walked the few steps necessary to take me across the saloon to the library. My companions remained seated and did not speak. I flung myself on to a divan, found myself a book and let my eyes peruse it mechanically.

A quarter of an hour later, Conseil came up to me and asked:

'Is what monsieur is reading of any interest?'

'Yes, most interesting.'

'I concur. It's the book monsieur himself wrote that monsieur is reading.'

'My own book?'

He was right. I was holding the volume *Great Ocean Depths*. I had not even noticed. I closed the tome and resumed my pacing. Ned and Conseil got to their feet and were about to return to their cabin.

'Do stay, friends,' I said, detaining them. 'Let's stay together until we're clear of this situation.'

'As monsieur wishes,' said Conseil.

Several hours went by. I frequently looked at the instruments which hung on the wall of the Great Saloon. The depth gauge indicated that the *Nautilus* was maintaining a steady depth of 300 metres; the compass showed that we were still heading south; and the log told me that we were proceeding at a speed of 20 knots, surely excessive in such a confined space. But Captain Nemo was aware that there was not a moment to waste. Every minute was worth a century.

At 8.25 we felt a second shock. This time it came from the stern. I blanched. My companions gathered round me. I gripped Conseil's hand. We looked questioningly at each other and more meaningfully than if our thoughts had been put into words.

At that instant, the captain walked into the Great Saloon. I went to meet him.

'The southern exit is blocked?' I asked.

'Yes, professor. When the iceberg rolled over, it closed every way out.'

'So we are trapped?'

'Yes.'

16
Lack of Air

And so, all around the *Nautilus*, above and below, there was an impenetrable wall of ice. We were prisoners of the polar ice cap! The Canadian thumped the table with one formidable fist. Conseil said nothing. I stared at the captain. His face had resumed its usual inscrutable expression. He had folded his arms. He was thinking. The *Nautilus* had stopped moving.

Then the captain started to speak:

'Gentlemen,' he began in a calm voice, 'in the predicament in which we find ourselves, there are two ways of dying.'

The manner of this enigmatic man was that of a professor of mathematics explaining a problem to his students.

'The first,' he began, 'is to be crushed to death and the second to suffocate to death. I shall leave aside the possibility that we will starve to death, because the provisions carried by the *Nautilus* will certainly last longer than we shall. So let us focus on our chances of being crushed or asphyxiated.'

'Asphyxiation, captain,' I said, 'is not a problem, since our air tanks are full.'

'They are indeed,' Captain Nemo went on, 'but they can give us air for only two days. And we have been under water for thirty-six hours and our depleted atmosphere already needs to be replenished. Forty-eight hours from now, our reserves will also be exhausted.'

'In that case, captain, we must make sure we get out within forty-eight hours!'

'We can at least try by cutting a way through the ice which has trapped us.'

'In which side?' I asked.

'That we shall know after we have taken soundings. I shall set the *Nautilus* down on the floor of this pocket of free water, and my men, in suits, will start tunnelling where the ice is thinnest.'

'Would it be possible to open the viewing panels?'

'There is no reason why not. We shan't be going anywhere.'

Captain Nemo left the room. Soon, the familiar hissing sound informed me that water was flowing into the reservoirs. The *Nautilus* settled slowly until she was resting on the ice 350 metres below sea-level, the depth to which the lower ice floe was submerged.

'Listen,' I said to my companions. 'The situation is very serious. But I am counting on your courage and your spirit.'

'Professor,' replied the Canadian, 'this is not the time for me to bother you with recriminations. I am prepared to do my level best in the common cause.'

'That's good to hear,' I replied, holding out my hand to the Canadian.

'I will also say,' he went on, 'that I am as handy with a pick as I am with a harpoon. So if I can be of any use to the captain, then I'm his man.'

'He won't say no to your offer of help. Come along, Ned.'

I led the Canadian to the locker room, where members of the crew of the *Nautilus* were already donning their diving suits. I repeated what Ned had said, and the captain accepted his help. The Canadian got into his suit and was ready as soon as the men he was to work with. Strapped to each man's back was the breathing apparatus, fitted with a Rouquayrol regulator, which had been filled with a good supply of pure air from the tanks. This made considerable inroads into the *Nautilus*'s reserves, but it was unavoidable. There was no need for Ruhmkorff lamps in that luminous water, which was already filled with brilliant electric illumination.

When Ned was ready to go I went back to the Great Saloon, where the viewing panels were already open. I took up a position next to Conseil and looked closely into the surrounding water, which was holding the *Nautilus* upright.

Moments later we saw a dozen crewmen move out on to the

ice floe. Among them was Ned Land, recognizable by his height. Captain Nemo was with them.

Before beginning to dig into the walls, soundings were needed in order to ascertain the best direction to work in. Long rods were inserted into the side walls. But after 15 metres they were still firmly embedded in the solid ice wall. There was no point testing the ceiling, because it was the base of the ice cap, of which there was more than 400 metres above us. Captain Nemo then decided to take a sounding of the surface on which we were grounded. There proved to be 10 metres between us and open water. That was the thickness of the ice underneath us. What was required now was to make a trench equal in area to the water line of the *Nautilus*. In order to cut this hole, through which we would drop down below the ice-field, we would have to dig out some 6,500 cubic metres.

Work began at once and was continued with indefatigable urgency. Instead of digging all around the *Nautilus*, which would have been extremely difficult, Captain Nemo took an axe and cut a shallow trench marking the outline of an excavation 8 metres from her port quarter. His men began chopping simultaneously at various points on that line. Picks were hacking urgently at the compact ice, and soon large blocks had been removed from the trench. By a curious effect of the laws of specific gravity, the blocks, being lighter than water, simply floated up and congregated under the roof of the tunnel, which thus grew downwards by the same amount that the floor was lowered. But this was of no account, given the fact that the ice underneath us was lowered in proportion.

After two hours of back-breaking work, Ned Land returned exhausted. He and his companions were replaced by new workers, Conseil and myself among them. The first officer of the *Nautilus* directed operations.

I thought the water felt extremely cold, but I soon warmed up as I swung my pick. My movements were not impeded, even though I was working in a pressure of 30 atmospheres.

When, after working for two hours, I came back on board for something to eat and to rest, I found a notable difference between the pure air fed to me by the Rouquayrol apparatus and the atmosphere inside the *Nautilus*, which now contained a high percentage of carbon dioxide. The air inside had not been changed for forty-eight hours, and its breathable quality was considerably reduced. Still, in the space of twelve hours, we had removed a layer of the designated area a metre thick, amounting to about 600 cubic metres. Assuming we could manage to do the same amount of work every twelve hours that passed, we would need another five nights and four days to see the operation through to the end.

'Five nights and four days!' I said to my companions. 'And we only have two days' worth of air in the tanks!'

'And don't forget,' replied Ned Land, 'that even when we've escaped from this hellish prison, we'll still be trapped under the ice cap and still unable to surface into the open air!'

He was quite right. Who at that moment could have put a figure on the minimum amount of time required for us to get free? Would we not have died of asphyxiation before the *Nautilus* was able to resurface? Was the vessel doomed to perish entombed in ice and everyone on board with her? The situation looked desperate. But we all had faced up to it. We were all determined to do our duty until the very end.

As my calculation had anticipated, another metre of ice was removed from the huge cavity during the night. But the next morning, as I walked in my diving suit through the water which was 6 or 7 degrees below zero, I was aware that the side walls were slowly closing in. The reason? The water furthest away from the excavation was not being warmed by the work the men were doing and the movements of their tools, and was showing signs of freezing. Given this new and dangerous development, what were our chances of getting out alive? How could we prevent the water turning solid and shattering the hull of the *Nautilus* like so much glass?

I did not make my companions aware of this new threat. What would be gained by running the risk of undermining their morale when they were giving their all to this gruelling rescue operation? But when I got back on board I pointed out this very serious development to Captain Nemo.

'I know,' he said, in that calm tone which seemed impervious

'The side walls were slowly closing in'

to the terrible situation we were in. 'It's an added danger, but I can see no way round it. Our only hope of escape is to proceed at a faster rate than the process of solidification. It's all a question of whether we win the race. There it is.'

Win the race! Still, I should have been used by now to his turns of phrase!

For several hours that day, I swung my pickaxe with a will. The work kept my spirits up. But working also meant getting out of the *Nautilus* and breathing pure air through my apparatus, which had been filled from the tanks: it meant escaping from the depleted and increasingly toxic atmosphere inside the boat.

By evening, a further metre had been dug out of the pit. When I returned to the ship, I almost choked on the amount of carbon dioxide in the air. Oh, if only we'd had some chemical means of removing this noxious gas from our atmosphere! We did not lack oxygen. The water all around us contained it in large quantities. Using our powerful batteries to extract it would have provided a new supply of the life-giving element. I had thought about this, but what was the point, since the carbon dioxide we had exhaled had filled every corner of the ship. To absorb it, we would have had to fill receptacles with caustic potash and keep them permanently agitated. But in any case, we had no potash on board and there was no substitute for it.

That evening, Captain Nemo was obliged to open the stop-cocks of the tanks and release a quantity of pure air into the atmosphere inside the boat. If he had not taken this precaution, none of us would ever have woken up again.

The next day, 26 March, I resumed my role as miner by starting work on the fifth metre. The side walls and lower surface of the ice cap were now closing in visibly. It was clear that they would soon come together before the *Nautilus* could free herself. For a moment, I was overcome by despair. My pick almost fell from my hands. What was the use of digging if the breath was to be squeezed out of me as I was crushed by water which had turned to stone, a form of torture which not even the ferocity of savages had devised? I felt as if we were being delivered into the terrifying jaws of a monster which kept drawing irresistibly nearer!

At that instant, Captain Nemo, who was directing the work and working himself, passed by. I touched him with my hand and motioned towards the walls of our prison. The wall on the starboard side had advanced to less than 4 metres from the hull of the *Nautilus*.

The captain understood my meaning and made a sign for me to follow him. We went back on board the ship. When I had removed my suit, I followed him into the Great Saloon.

'Professor Aronnax,' he said, 'we are going to have to try some bolder approach if we are not to be sealed inside solidified water as though we were being buried in cement.'

'Yes!' I cried. 'But what?'

'Say my *Nautilus* were strong enough to withstand all this pressure without being crushed?'

'What do you mean?' I asked, not understanding what he was getting at.

'Don't you see?' he went on. 'The fact that the water is turning to ice could be our salvation! Hasn't it dawned on you that the process of solidification will break up the ice which is trapping us just as it splits the hardest rocks! Don't you see that it will be a power that will be our salvation, not the power that will destroy us?'

'Yes, captain, that may well be. But however resistant to pressure the *Nautilus* might be, she could not possibly withstand the terrible pressure exerted by the encroaching ice and would end up as flat as a sheet of iron plate!'

'I know, professor. We cannot rely on nature to help us, only on ourselves. We must do all we can to resist the process of freezing. It must be impeded. Not only will the side walls close in on us, but at present there is less than 10 feet of water in front or at the stern of the *Nautilus*. The ice is moving in on all sides.'

'How much longer will the air tanks go on allowing us to breathe on board?'

The captain looked straight at me.

'The day after tomorrow,' he said, 'the tanks will be empty.'

I felt a cold sweat break out all over me. Yet why should I have been surprised by his answer? On 22 March, the *Nautilus* had dived under the surface of the open Polar Sea. It was now the 26th. For five days, we had been living on the boat's reserves. The last of the breathable air had to be kept for the workers. At this moment, as I write these words, my memory of how I felt is still so vivid that my whole being is overwhelmed by such awful terror that it seems my lungs cannot get enough air!

Meanwhile Captain Nemo was deep in thought, silent, and motionless. But I could see that he had been struck by an idea. Yet he seemed to be rejecting it, telling himself that it was not feasible. But eventually these words formed on his lips:

'Boiling water!' he muttered.

'Boiling water?' I exclaimed.

'Yes, professor. We are trapped in a relatively confined space. Would not a stream of boiling water continuously pumped by the *Nautilus* raise the outside temperature and slow the speed at which the water is freezing?'

'We must try it,' I said decisively.

'And try it we will, professor.'

The thermometer was showing the temperature outside to be 7 degrees below zero. Captain Nemo led the way to the kitchens, to the very large distillation unit which produced drinking water by a process of evaporation. It was now filled with sea-water, which, warmed by the full heat generated by the boat's electric batteries, began to course through its coils. Within minutes, the water had reached 100 degrees centigrade. It was piped to the pumps. Meanwhile, it was replaced as required in the unit by more water. The heat produced by the batteries was such that the cold water, taken directly from the sea, had only to pass through the distillation unit to arrive boiling hot at the pumps.

Pumping operations started immediately. Three hours later, the thermometer registered an outside temperature of minus 6. It was one degree gained. Two hours after that, the reading was only minus 4.

'It's going to work!' I said to the captain after we had followed and made various adjustments to the progress of the operation.

'I believe so,' he replied. 'We shall not be crushed. All we have to fear now is asphyxiation.'

During the night, the water temperature rose to 1 degree below zero. Our pumping operation was unable to raise it any more. But given that sea-water freezes only at less than minus 2, my mind was at last put at rest on the dangers of solidification.

The following day, 27 March, 6 metres of ice had been removed from the excavation. That meant only 4 remained. But they represented another forty-eight hours of toil. The air inside the *Nautilus* could not be changed. And so, on that day, the situation steadily worsened.

I was weighed down by an unbearable torpor. At about three in the afternoon, my distress became extreme. I yawned so violently I thought I should dislocate my jaws. My lungs heaved as they struggled to seek out that combustive element in air which is vital to respiration but was growing scarcer all the time. A lassitude of the spirit took hold of me. I just lay on my bed without strength and not really conscious of my surroundings. Conseil, brave fellow, suffering the same symptoms, was just as badly affected as I, but never left my side. He held my hand and said encouraging words. I can still hear him murmuring:

'What would I not give if I did not breathe so there would be more air for monsieur!'

It brought tears to my eyes to hear him speak so.

The plight of us all was intolerable inside the boat, but with what alacrity, what fervour, did we don our suits and go out to work when it was our turn! The tapping of picks rang out through the ice. Arms grew weary, and hands became raw, but what was mere fatigue, what did our calluses matter? Life-giving air was reaching our lungs! We could breathe! We could breathe!

But no one was tempted to work in the water for longer than the prescribed period. Once his task was done, each man helped his gasping companions to shoulder the breathing apparatus which would give them new life. Captain Nemo set the example and was the first to submit to this stern discipline. When the time came, he relinquished his air-supply to another man and returned to the polluted atmosphere, always calm, showing no weakness, invariably uncomplaining.

On that day, the regular work was carried out with greater enthusiasm than ever. Only 2 metres of the area of the excavation now remained to be dug out. But the tanks were almost totally empty. The small amount of air that remained had to be kept for the workers. There was none at all for the *Nautilus*.

When I came back on board, I felt half-suffocated. What a night that was! I have no words to describe it. Such suffering cannot be expressed on paper. The next day, my breathing was laboured. Headaches were accompanied by stultifying dizzy spells, which made me feel and look as if I were drunk. All my companions were afflicted with the same symptoms. Some of the crew were nearly at death's door.

That day, the sixth of our captivity, Captain Nemo decided that picks and mattocks were too slow. Instead, he resolved to smash the layer of ice which still separated us from free water below us. His energy and lucidity were undiminished. He overcame all physical hardships by sheer force of will. He continued to think, to plan, to act.

He gave orders that the boat was to be lightened, so that it would be lifted off her bed of ice, by a change in its specific gravity. When she was floating free, she was dragged by hand until she was directly above the huge pit which had been cut to accommodate her shape. Then her water tanks were filled. Slowly she sank and slotted herself into the cavity.

At this juncture, all members of the crew returned to the boat, and the double doors of the exit lock were closed. The *Nautilus* now rested on a layer of ice which was no more than a metre thick and had been drilled by sounding rods in a thousand places.

The stopcocks of the tanks were now opened fully and 100 cubic metres of water rushed into them, increasing the weight of the *Nautilus* by 100,000 kilograms.

We waited. We listened, forgetting the torments of our ordeal, and still hoping. We had staked everything on this one last throw.

After a while, despite the buzzing in my head, I felt a tremor under the hull of the *Nautilus*. The floor tilted beneath my feet. The ice gave with a strange rasping noise, like the sound of paper being torn, and then the *Nautilus* was dropping . . .

'We're going through!' Conseil murmured in my ear.

I could not speak. I seized his hand and gripped it hard.

Suddenly, pulled down by the tremendous extra weight of her overloaded tanks, the *Nautilus* began sinking with the speed of a cannonball, falling as fast as she would have done through empty space!

Immediately, full power was fed to the pumps, which began to empty the water from the tanks. After a few minutes, our rate of fall slowed. Soon, the depth gauge was showing that we had begun to rise. The propeller, turning at maximum revolutions, made every bolt in every plate of the hull vibrate as we headed north.

But for how long would we have to travel under the ice cap before we reached open sea? Another day? I would be dead by then!

Half-slumped on a couch in the library, I could hardly breathe. My face had turned purple, my lips were blue, and all my faculties were numbed. I could not see, I could not hear. The concept of time had fled from my mind. I could no longer flex my muscles.

Hours passed, but in that state I could not tell how many crawled by. I was aware that my hold on life was slipping away. I knew that I was going to die.

Suddenly, my wits returned to me. A few whiffs of air had entered my lungs. Had we surfaced? Had we sailed out from beneath the ice cap?

No! It was Ned and Conseil, my two loyal friends, who were sacrificing themselves to save me. A small amount of air remained in one of the breathing helmets. Instead of breathing it themselves, they had kept it for me. While they suffocated, they fed me new life, drop by drop! I tried to push the tube away. They got hold of my hands, and for a few moments I knew the pure sensual pleasure of being able to breathe!

I turned and looked at the clock. It was eleven in the morning. It must now be 28 March. The *Nautilus* was sailing at a fantastic speed: 40 knots! She was racing through the water!

Where was Captain Nemo? Had he succumbed? Had all his crew died with him?

At that moment, the depth gauge showed that we were only 20 feet under the surface. A thin ice-sheet was all there was between us and the earth's atmosphere. Surely we could smash though it?

Perhaps we could. In any case, the *Nautilus* was about to try, for I felt that she was lining herself up at an angle, lowering her stern and raising her bow. Filling a water tank was enough to shift her balance. Then, driven forward by her powerful propeller, she launched herself at the ice from below, like a mighty battering ram. She began breaking it up little by little, reversing and coming again at it at full speed until, with one final charge, the *Nautilus* leaped out on to the frozen surface, which shattered under her weight.

The hatch was opened, or rather torn open, and fresh air rushed in, flooding every corner of the *Nautilus*.

17

From Cape Horn to the Amazon

How I came to be on the platform I could not say. Perhaps the Canadian had dragged me out, but I was there, breathing, drinking in the reviving air of the sea. Both my companions were beside me, also gorging on clean air. Those unfortunate enough to have been deprived of food for too long cannot abandon all restraint and fling themselves on to food that is suddenly set before them. We, on the other hand, had no reason to be abstemious. We could fill our lungs with as much pure air as we wanted, for it was the breeze, the sea breeze which filled our brimming, intoxicating cup!

'Oh!' exclaimed Conseil. 'Glorious oxygen! Monsieur should not be afraid to breathe, there's enough for everyone!'

Ned Land, on the other hand, said nothing, but his jaws gaped wide enough to terrify a shark. And such powerful, deep breaths! The Canadian was 'drawing' like a fiercely burning stove.

Our strength quickly returned, and when I looked around me I saw that we were alone on the platform. There were no crew members to be seen, not even Captain Nemo. The exotic sailors of the *Nautilus* were happy to breathe the air circulating inside the boat. None had come out to drink their fill directly, out in the open.

The first words I spoke were words of thanks and gratitude to my two companions. Between them, Ned and Conseil had prolonged my life during the final hours of our long ordeal. But nothing I said could ever repay such loyalty.

'Don't mention it, professor,' replied Ned Land, 'it's hardly worth talking about. There's nothing special about what we did. It was a simple matter of arithmetic. Your life was more valuable than ours. Therefore, you had to be saved.'

'No no, Ned,' I said, 'my life is not worth more than yours. No one is better than a man who is generous and good, and you are both those things!'

'No need to go on about it,' said the Canadian, turning away with embarrassment.

'You too, Conseil. You had a hard time of it.'

'Not too hard, if monsieur pleases. I was rather short of breath but I think I could have got used to it. Besides, when I saw how monsieur was struggling, I didn't feel like breathing myself, it sort of knocked the wind out of my . . .'

Conseil, suddenly aware that he had slipped into cliché, did not finish his sentence.

'Friends,' I said, feeling quite emotional, 'we are henceforth bound together for ever. I am deeply in your debt.'

'I fully expect to be paid back,' retorted the Canadian.

'What?' said Conseil.

'Yes,' said Ned, 'my price being the right to take both of you with me when I get off this infernal boat!'

'Speaking of which,' said Conseil, 'are we going in the right direction?'

'We are,' I replied, 'since we're sailing into the sun and in these latitudes the sun is in the north.'

'True,' said Ned, 'but it remains to be seen whether we are heading for the Pacific or the Atlantic, by which I mean are we making for seas which are empty or full of shipping?'

I had no answer to that and feared that Captain Nemo was bent on taking us back to the immense ocean which laps both the coasts of Asia and America. By doing so, he would complete his journey round the world under the sea and could thus return to waters where the *Nautilus* was independent and free from outside interference. But if we were really going back to the Pacific, far from any inhabited shore, what would become of Ned Land's plans?

We would soon have our answer to this crucial question. The *Nautilus* was travelling fast. The Antarctic Circle was soon behind us, and we were on course for Cape Horn. We had reached a position off the southernmost tip of the Americas on 31 March at seven in the evening.

By then our recent sufferings had been forgotten. The memory of our captivity inside the ice was fading from our minds, which were now entirely focused on the future. We saw nothing of Captain Nemo, who never appeared either in the Great Saloon or up on the platform. The bearings marked on the planisphere each day by the first officer enabled me to determine the direction being followed by the *Nautilus*. That evening, to my great satisfaction, it became clear that we were sailing north on a course which was taking us into the Atlantic.

I told Conseil and the Canadian the results of my observations.

'Good news,' said Ned, 'but where exactly is the *Nautilus* bound for?'

'That I couldn't say, Ned.'

'Does the captain, having been to the South Pole, now propose to conquer the North Pole and return to the Pacific via the famous North-West Passage?'

'We shouldn't rule it out,' said Conseil.

'If that's what he's thinking,' said the Canadian, 'we'll have to part company with him before then.'

'Whether he is or not,' said Conseil, 'Captain Nemo is a force of nature, and we shan't ever be sorry we met him.'

'Especially after we've done our flit!' added Ned Land.

The next day, which was the first day of April, the *Nautilus* returned to the surface a few minutes before midday. We sighted land to the west. It was Tierra del Fuego, as it was christened by the first navigators when they saw much smoke rising from the huts of the native inhabitants. This 'Land of Fire' is in fact a large agglomeration of islands spread over an area 30 leagues long and 80 broad, between latitudes 53° and 56° south and longitude 67° 50' and 77° 15' west. The coast appeared to be low-lying, but in the far distance rose a chain of high mountains. I even thought I could make out Mount Sarmiento, 2,070 metres above sea-level, a pyramid-shaped mass of schist rising to a sharp peak which, according to Ned

Land, 'predicts good or bad weather', depending on whether it is clearly visible or hidden by mist.

'That, Ned, is what you might call a sizeable barometer.'

'Yes, professor, a natural barometer that never let me down in the days when I used to sail through the Strait of Magellan.'

Just at that moment, the summit happened to be standing out clearly against the sky. It was the sign of good weather. And so it proved.

The *Nautilus* submerged and sailed closer to the coast, following it for only a few miles. Through the viewing panels in the Great Saloon I saw the same long strings of seaweed, gigantic fuci and those giant kelps of which we had seen specimens in the open sea at the Pole. Including their glossy, viscous filaments, they can reach up to 300 metres in length and are natural ropes. Thicker than a man's thumb and very strong, they are often used for mooring ships. Another kind of underwater plant, velp, which has leaves four feet long, smothered various coral growths and carpeted the sea-bed. It provided a home and food for myriads of crustaceans and molluscs, for crabs and cuttlefish. There seals and sea-otters found a rich menu which allowed them to mix fish with marine vegetables the way the British do.

The *Nautilus* travelled very fast over these luxuriant fields of plenty. Towards evening she was approaching the Falkland Islands, whose rugged mountain tops I sighted the next day. The sea here is not very deep. I reckoned, therefore, reasonably enough, that both islands, surrounded by a large number of islets, must once have been part of the land now bordering the Magellan Strait. The Falklands were probably discovered by the celebrated John Davis, who named them the Davis Southern Islands. Richard Hawkins subsequently called them the Maidenland, in honour of Elizabeth I, the Virgin Queen. Later, at the start of the eighteenth century, they were renamed the Malouines by fishermen from Saint-Malo and finally the Falklands by the British, to whom they still belong.

In those waters, our nets trawled up fine specimens of seaweeds, notably a certain kind of fucus on whose roots grew the finest variety of mussels to be found anywhere. Geese and ducks landed by the dozen on the platform and were soon resting peacefully on slabs in the *Nautilus*'s larder. Among the fish, I particularly noticed a few bony varieties belonging to the goby family, especially white and yellow freckled gobies.

I also marvelled at a number of jellyfish, including the most beautiful of the species, the chrysaora, which is unique to the seas around the Falklands. Some deployed a semi-spherical swimming-bell, very smooth, with reddish-brown stripes and a fringe of twelve equidistantly spaced scallops; others looked like an upturned basket out of which wide fronds rose languidly on long red stems. They moved by flapping four foliaceous arms and allowing their opulent thatch of tentacles to trail behind them. I should have liked to keep a few samples of these delicate zoophytes. But they are just clouds, shadows, apparitions which melt and dissolve if removed from their natural element.

When the last of the heights of the Falklands had dipped below the horizon, the *Nautilus* dived to a depth of 20 or 25 metres and followed the South American coast. We saw nothing of Captain Nemo.

Until 3 April, we remained off the coast of Patagonia, cruising on and sometimes under the surface. The *Nautilus* sailed across the wide estuary formed by the mouth of the Plata and by 4 April was passing Uruguay, but now standing 50 miles out to sea. She maintained her northerly course and followed the winding coastline of South America. We had now covered 16,000 leagues since the moment we were taken on board the vessel in the seas of Japan.

Around eleven in the morning we crossed the Tropic of Capricorn on the 37th meridian, being then off Cape Frio. Much to Ned Land's disgust, Captain Nemo showed no liking for the inhabited coasts of Brazil, for he travelled so fast it made the head spin. No fish or fowl, not even the speediest of them, could keep up with us, and we were unable to observe any of the interesting life forms in those waters.

Our rapid progress continued for several days. On the evening of 9 April we sighted the most easterly point of South America: Cape San Roque. But then the *Nautilus* moved further out to sea once more, going in search of deeper water, and an underwater valley which runs from the Cape to Sierra Leone on the coast of Africa. Beginning at more or less the same latitude as the West Indies, this valley divides with the northern arm ending in a huge depression 9,000 metres deep. At this location, the geological bed of the ocean takes the form of a sheer cliff 6,000 metres high, which extends as far as the Lesser Antilles, while another cliff, just as formidable, rises more or less on a level with the Cape Verde Islands. Between these two rock walls lies the entire submerged continent of Atlantis. From the floor of this immense valley rise various mountains which offer interesting perspectives of those deep waters. What I can say of them here is based on the hand-drawn charts kept in the library of the *Nautilus*, which were self-evidently made by Captain Nemo from his personal observations.

Those empty depths were explored over two days by making full use of the *Nautilus*'s tilting rudder-fins. She descended in long diagonal dives, which took us down to all depths. But on 11 April, we suddenly began rising with the land and came up in the mouth of the Amazon, a vast estuary through which so much water flows that the sea is desalinated over a distance of several leagues.

We crossed the Equator. Twenty miles to the west were the Guyanas, French territory where we would have found a ready refuge. But the wind gusted too strongly and the waves were too rough for a frail dinghy. Ned Land obviously realized this, for it was impossible to get a word out of him on the subject. For my part I made no reference to his escape plans either, for I had no wish to push him into some wild escapade which would have inevitably failed.

Meanwhile, I put this delay to good use with some interesting observations. For two days, 11 and 12 April, the *Nautilus* remained on the surface, using her dragnet to catch a magnificent haul of zoophytes, fish and reptiles.

A quantity of zoophytes had been caught in the links of the net. They were mostly fine specimens of sea anemone, of the family of actinias, and other species included *Phyllodiscus protextus*, a native of this part of the ocean, a stubby, cylindrical body speckled red and crowned with a wonderful display of tentacles. Examples of molluscs consisted of species

I had observed elsewhere: turritella; porphyry olives with regular cross-hatching and red markings which stood out vividly against the colour of their flesh; freakish pterocera that resembled petrified scorpions; translucent hyaloea; argonauts; cuttlefish, which are very good eating; and certain kinds of squid, which the naturalists of Antiquity classed among the flying fish and are used mainly as bait in cod-fishing.

I noticed various kinds of fish in these waters which I had not yet had an opportunity to study. Among the cartilaginous fish were petromizons, or lampreys, a kind of eel, 15 inches long, greenish head, purple fins, bluish grey back, silvery brown underside speckled with bright colours, irises of the eyes ringed with gold, very strange creatures brought by the current of the Amazon down to the sea, for they are a freshwater fish; tubercled rays with pointed snouts, long, flexible tails and armed with a long-tooth-edged sting; small squali just a metre long, grey and white bodies, with teeth ranged in several rows and angled backwards, commonly known as slipper sharks; *lophie vespertilion*, reddish-brown isosceles triangles, whose pectoral fins are attached to fleshy extensions, which makes them look like bats, though a horned appendage located above their nostrils has also earned them the name of sea unicorns; and lastly, a few species of trigger-fish, notably the curassavian, which has speckled flanks that gleam like bright gold, and the *capriscus*, light violet, with iridescent hues as on a pigeon's breast.

I will close this catalogue, which may be a trifle dry but is very accurate, with the series of bony fish which I was able to observe: the black ghost knifefish, *apteronotus passan*, which has a snow-white blaze on its blunt snout, a handsome bluish-black body and a fleshy tail, which is very long and slender; spiny *odontagnathae*, which are sardines 30 centimetres long and shine like bright silver; sauries, belonging to the family *scomberesocidae*, which have two anal fins; a black-hued variety of *centronotus*, which is fished by torchlight, 2 metres long, with flesh that is fatty, white and firm and, when fresh, tastes like eel and, when dried, is reminiscent of smoked salmon; half-red wrasse, which have scales only at the base of their dorsal and anal fins; clownfish, in gold and silver inter-spersed with glints of ruby and topaz; golden-tailed spars, whose flesh is so delicately flavoured and whose phosphores-cent properties give them away in the water; bogue, a kind of sea-bream, fine-tongued with orange livery; *sciena coros*, with gold-hued caudal fins; *acanthurus nigricans*, the surgeon fish; Surinam anableps; and so on and so forth.

But that 'so on and so forth' will not stop me quoting one more fish, which Conseil had good reason to remember for a long time.

One of the nets had caught an unusually flattened variety of ray which, if its tail had been removed, would have made a perfect circle. It weighed about 20 kilos. It was white under-neath and reddish on top, with large roundels of dark-blue ringed with black. Its skin was very glossy and it had a single bilobate fin. On the platform, it was struggling to turn itself over by a series of spasms and was floundering so violently that one last effort would have flipped it back into the sea. But Con-seil, known for his liking for fish, leaped on it and before I could stop him he grasped it with both hands.

Immediately he was flung on to his back, legs in the air, with one part of his body unable to move, calling:

'My master, my master! Help me!'

It was the first time the poor fellow hadn't addressed me in the third person.

Between us, Ned Land and I picked him up and massaged him vigorously. When he was himself again, inveterate classi-fier that he was, he muttered in a still half-broken voice:

'Class of cartilageous fish; class, fixed-gill *chondrichthyes*; sub-order, *selachii*; family, rays; genus *torped*.'

'That's right, Conseil, it was a torpedo which reduced you to this deplorable state.'

'Monsieur may take it as fact,' replied Conseil, 'that I shall have my revenge on the creature.'

'How?'

'By eating it!'

And eat it he did, that same night, though only to get his own back, for in truth it was tough.

The unfortunate Conseil had taken on a torpedo, or numb fish, one of the most dangerous species, the cumaná *torped*. In water, which has excellent conductive properties, this bizarre animal can electrocute fish at a distance of several metres, such is the power of its electric organ, both surfaces of which together measure no less than 27 square feet.

The next day, 12 April, the *Nautilus* approached the coast of Dutch Guyana near the mouth of the Maroni River. There, we came across several families of manatees. Like the dugong and Steller's sea-cow, manatees belong to the order of *sirenia*. These fine animals, peaceable and inoffensive, 6 or 7 metres long, must have weighed at least 4,000 kilos. I told Ned Land and Conseil that nature in her wisdom had given these mammals a vital role to play, for, like the seals, they were directed to graze the meadows under the sea and thus keep at bay the build-up of invasive vegetation which would otherwise block the mouths of tropical rivers.

'And do you also know,' I added, 'what has happened since humans have almost wiped out these useful animals? Rotting vegetation has poisoned the air, and this bad air has brought the yellow fever which is the scourge of these magnificent lands. Poisonous plants have prospered in these warm seas, and the sickness has spread from the mouth of the Rio de la Plata all the way up to the Floridas!

'And if Toussenel is right, this pestilence is as nothing compared with what our descendants will have to face when the seas have been entirely cleared of whales and seals. They will fill up with octopi, jellyfish and squid and will become vast breeding grounds for infections, because their waters will be deprived of "those vast stomachs to which God had given the task of keeping the surface of the oceans clean".'

Without deliberately rejecting such arguments, the crew proceeded to kill half a dozen of those manatees. We badly needed to restock the steward's pantry with a supply of good meat, which proved, in the event, to be preferable to either beef or veal. The hunt was quite dull, for the manatees allowed themselves to be slaughtered and put up no resistance. Several thousand kilos of meat, for drying, were taken on board.

But on that day a most unusual form of fishing helped swell the supplies of the *Nautilus* and showed just how full of game those waters were. The drag had brought up in its nets a number of fish with skulls shaped at the top like an oval plate with fleshy rims. They were *echeneidae*, belonging to the third family of malacopterygian subbrachiales. The flattened disc on top of the head is made of mobile, transversal, cartilaginous lamellas, between which the creature can create a vacuum, so that it is able to attach itself to objects, rather as the suckers of leeches operate.

The remoras I had observed in the Mediterranean belonged to the same species. But the kind referred to here was the *remora osteochir*, of the same family of *echeneidae*, and unique to these waters. As they were taken from the nets, the sailors put them in pails of water.

When we had done with the fishing, the *Nautilus* moved closer to the coast, where a number of sea turtles were sleeping on the surface. Normally, it would have been difficult to catch any of these precious reptiles, for the smallest sounds will wake them, and then their solid shells save them from the harpoon. But the echenoids were able to manage it with amazing ease and sureness. The remora, in fact, is a living fish-hook and would delight and richly reward the most amateur angler.

The sailors of the *Nautilus* attached a ring to the tail of these fish. The ring was loose enough not to hamper them as they swam. To this ring was fastened a long line, the other end of which was secured to the boat.

The remoras were thrown into the sea and at once began doing what was expected of them: they attached themselves to the plastrons of the turtles. They stuck so fast that they would be torn apart rather than relax their grip. They were then hauled back on board and with them the turtles to which they still adhered.

We caught a number of loggerheads. They were a metre wide and weighed 200 kilos. Their carapace is made up of individual horn scutes, which are large, thin, transparent and brown, with flecks of white and yellow. It is this shell that makes them valuable. But they are also excellent from a culinary point of view – as are green turtles, which are extremely toothsome.

These fishing exploits brought our stay in the waters of the Amazon to an end, and when night descended the *Nautilus* sailed out once more to the high seas.

18

Squids

For some days, the *Nautilus* remained at a considerable distance from the coast of South America. Captain Nemo obviously had no wish to sail into the Gulf of Mexico or the seas of the Caribbean. Not that we would have lacked a reasonable draught under our keel, for the average depth of those waters is 1,800 metres. But it is probably more likely that since the whole region is studded with islands and regularly used by steamships, it held little appeal for him.

On 16 April, we sighted Martinique and Guadeloupe about 30 miles away. I managed to get a brief glimpse of the tops of their highest mountains.

The Canadian, who was reckoning on carrying out his plan in the Gulf, either by landing somewhere or by being taken on board by one of the many boats which ply between islands, was very put out. It would have been easy enough to escape if Ned Land could have managed to free the dinghy without the captain knowing. But on the high seas it was out of the question.

The Canadian, Conseil and I spoke at considerable length on this subject. We had been prisoners on board the *Nautilus* for six months. We had travelled 17,000 leagues, and, as Ned Land pointed out, there was no reason why it should ever end. He then proposed something which I was not expecting. His idea was to put the question directly to Captain Nemo: was he intending to keep us on board indefinitely?

I was reluctant to take such a step. As I saw it, nothing would come of it. There was nothing to be hoped for from the master of the *Nautilus*, and everything to be gained through our own efforts. Besides, for some time now he had become more grim, more withdrawn and less sociable. I had the impression he was avoiding me. I encountered him only at rare intervals. There had been a time when he had enjoyed explaining the wonders of the marine world to me. Now, he simply left me to my studies and never came to the Great Saloon.

What had come over him? What was the cause of this new attitude towards me? I had nothing to reproach myself with. Perhaps he found our presence on board onerous? In the meantime, I had no reason whatsoever to think that he would ever restore our freedom.

So I asked Ned to give me time to think about it before doing anything. If the direct approach proved fruitless, it could well revive the captain's suspicions, make our position more difficult and jeopardize the Canadian's plans. I should add that there was no point in trying to make our health part of our case. If we except the very real hardship we had experienced under the polar ice, neither Ned nor Conseil nor I had ever been fitter. The healthy diet, the pure air, our regular existence and the uniform temperature were singularly unsuited to making us ill. I could understand the attraction of such a life for a man who had no land-based memories to regret, someone like Captain Nemo, who was contented at sea, went wherever he wished and, by ways mysterious to others but not to him, strode directly to his goal. But we had not cut our ties with the rest of mankind. For my own part, I had no wish to be buried with my work, which was so fascinating and so new. I was now in a position to write a new book about the sea and I very much wanted that book to be published at some future date.

Here again, in the waters of the Caribbean, sailing 10 metres below the surface of the sea with the viewing panels open, there were many interesting life forms that I could write up in my daily notes! Among the zoophytes were 'men of war', also known as pelagic physalis, which are more or less swollen, oblong bladders, in mother-of-pearl colours, hoisting a membrane to the wind and allowing their blue tentacles to trail behind them like silken threads – jellyfish delightful to look at but when touched the corrosive liquid they discharge makes them feel like nettles. Among the articulates were annelida a metre and a half long, with a pink trunk and 1,700 organs of locomotion, which reflected all the colours of the rainbow as they swam snake-like through the water. In the branch of fishes were mobula rays, or squatinas, an enormous cartilaginous creature 10 feet long and weighing 600 pounds, which has triangular pectoral fins; the middle of its back is slightly humped, and its eyes are placed at the extremities of the front part of its head; it floats in the water like a piece of wreckage and occasionally adhered to the glass of our viewing panel, like opaque shutters. There were American trigger-fish, for which nature had provided a palette of only black and white; Plumier's gobies, elongated and fleshy, with yellow fins and lantern jaws; scombers a metre and a half long, which have short, sharp teeth, are encased in small scales and are related to the albacore. Then, in shoals: surmullets, with gold stripes running from head to tail, waving their gleaming fins, truly bejewelled masterpieces: they were sacred to Diana, particularly sought after by rich Romans and the original subject of the proverb which runs: 'He who catches them does not eat them.' Lastly, golden marine angel-fish, ashine with emerald flashings, clad in velvet and silks, were swimming before our eyes like the lords painted by Veronese; *sparidae* darted away on their fleet thoracic fins; 15-inch shad wrapped themselves in their own phosphorescence; mullet thrashed the water with their large fleshy tails; red whitefish seemed to scythe the water with their sharp pectorals; and silver moonfish, living up to their name, rose in the distant water like white reflections of many moons.

How many more wonderful, new specimens might I not have observed if the *Nautilus* had not slowly descended to deeper waters? With her fins set at dive, she took us down to depths of between 2,000 and 3,500 metres. There, animal life was represented only by examples of sea lilies, starfish and beautiful medusa-headed five-pointed crinoids, whose vertical stems supported a small calyx; cone-shaped shells of the superfamily of *trochoidea*; blood-red tooth shells; and keyhole limpets, which are a large kind of tidal mollusc.

On 20 April, we had come up to an average depth of 1,500

metres. The nearest land was then the islands of the Lucayan archipelago, set out like a collection of stepping stones over the surface of the water. There, under the water, were high cliffs, vertical ramparts made of rough, solidly entrenched blocks between which were gaps so black that the beams from our searchlight could not fully illuminate their dark recesses.

These rocks were carpeted with oversized marine vegetation, giant *laminaria digitata*, enormous fuci, all in all a virtual espalier arrangement of hydrophytes worthy of a world inhabited by Titans.

From discussing these colossal plants, Conseil, Ned Land and I moved on naturally to the gigantic creatures which live in the sea, given that the various seaweeds were obviously destined to feed them. However, as I watched through the viewing panels of the *Nautilus*, which was now virtually at a standstill, I saw among those long filaments only the main articulates of the infraorder of *brachyura*: the long-legged *lambre spinimane*, purple crabs, and sea butterflies peculiar to the waters of the West Indies.

It was about eleven o'clock when Ned Land drew my attention to a tremendous disturbance taking place in the massed vegetation.

'Oh,' I said, 'behind that bank of weed are caves inhabited by squid. I shouldn't be surprised to see some of those monsters.'

'What?' said Conseil, 'You mean calamari, plain calamari, class of cephalopods?'

'Not at all,' I replied. 'I mean very large squid. Ned must have been mistaken, because I can't see anything now.'

'I'm sorry to hear it,' said Conseil. 'I would very much like to see one of those squids close up. I've heard so much about them. They can drag ships down to the bottom of the sea. They're called krak . . .'

'Just say "crack" and leave it at that,' broke in Ned Land ironically.

'Krakens,' went on Conseil, finishing the word and quite missing his friend's little joke.

'You'll never convince me,' said Ned, 'that any such animals exist.'

'Why not?' asked Conseil. 'We all believed in monsieur's narwhal.'

'And we were wrong, Conseil.'

'True, but there are many people who still believe in it.'

'Very likely, Conseil,' I said, 'but as far as I'm concerned, I am determined that I shall believe in the existence of such monsters only after I have personally dissected them.'

'Does that mean,' asked Conseil, 'that monsieur does not believe that there are such things as giant squid?'

'Who the devil ever believed it anyway?' exclaimed Ned Land.

'Oh, lots of people, Ned.'

'Not fishermen. Scientists perhaps!'

'Sorry, Ned. Fisherman and scientists both!'

'And I'm telling you,' said Conseil, looking deadly serious, 'that I remember seeing a sizeable craft dragged beneath the waves by the tentacles of a cephalopod.'

'You saw that?' asked the Canadian.

'I most certainly did.'

'With your own eyes?'

'With my own eyes.'

'And where did it happen?'

'Saint-Malo,' Conseil replied imperturbably.

'In the harbour, was it?' asked Ned sarcastically.

'No. In a church,' replied Conseil.

'A church?'

'That's right, Ned. There was a painting which showed the squid I'm talking about.'

'That's a good one!' said Ned Land bursting into laughter. 'Monsieur Conseil, you've been having me on!'

'Actually, he's quite right,' I said. 'I've heard of that painting. But the subject it illustrates was based on legend, and you know how circumspect we must be in dealing with legends involving natural history. In any case, where monsters are involved, the human imagination is only too ready to go to extremes. Not only has it been claimed that these squids can drag ships down, but a certain Olaus Magnus talks of a cephalopod a mile long which looked more like an island than an animal. It is also said that the Bishop of Nidaros once erected an altar on a very large rock. When he had finished saying mass, the rock started moving and marched into the sea. The rock was a squid.'

'Is that all?' asked Ned.

'No,' I replied. 'Another bishop, Pontoppidan of Bergen, also speaks of a squid large enough to drill a whole regiment on.'[22]

'Those bishops of yore certainly had a way with words!' exclaimed Ned Land.

'But there were also naturalists in Antiquity who quote examples of monsters with jaws as large as a gulf which were unable to pass through the Straits of Gibraltar.'

'Priceless!' said the Canadian.

'But is there any truth at all in all these stories?' asked Conseil.

'Absolutely none, my friends, at least in those parts that exceed the bounds of plausibility and achieve the status of fable or legend. Still, the imagination of storytellers always needs a basis of fact or at least a pretext. We can't be certain that there are not very large species of squid and calamari, though none is larger than cetaceans. Aristotle gave the length of one measuring 5 cubits, which is 3.10 metres. Modern fishermen frequently come across specimens longer than 1.8 metres. The museums of Trieste and Montpellier display skeletons of squid measuring 2 metres. Furthermore, naturalists estimate that one of these creature measuring just 6 feet in length would have tentacles 27 feet long. Which is enough to turn it into a very authentic monster.'

'Are any caught nowadays?' asked Conseil.

'They might not be caught, but fishermen see them all the same. A friend of mine, Captain Paul Bos of Le Havre, has often told me how he encountered one such monster of colossal size in the seas off India. But the most surprising thing of all – and it means that we cannot rule out the existence of such gigantic animals – is something that happened a few years ago, in 1861.'

'What was it?' asked Ned Land.

'It was this. In 1861, off the north-east coast of Tenerife, at about the same latitude we ourselves are on at this very moment, the crew of the sloop *Alecton* sighted a monstrous squid swimming in the water. Captain Bouguer sailed close to the animal and attacked it with harpoons and guns, but to no effect, for both bullets and harpoons went clean through its unresisting body as if it was half-set jelly. After a few unsuccessful attempts the crew managed to pass a slipknot around the body of the mollusc. The knot slid down the body until it reached the caudal fins, where it stopped. They then tried to haul the monster on board, but it was so heavy that as the rope tightened it sliced through the body, its tail was torn off, and the creature vanished beneath waves.'

'At last,' said Ned Land, 'a fact to go on!'

'An undeniable fact, Ned. Which is why it was suggested the animal should be called "Bouguer's Squid".'

'How long was it?' the Canadian asked.

'Would it have been 6 metres long?' asked Conseil who, from his position at the viewing panels, was examining the cracks and crevices in the rock wall.

'Exactly 6,' I replied.

'And was its head,' Conseil continued, 'festooned with eight tentacles which writhed in the water like a nest of serpents?'

'Indeed it was.'

'And were its eyes set close against its head and very large indeed?'

'They were, Conseil.'

'And did its mouth look like the beak of a parrot, only fearsomely large?'

'It did indeed, Conseil.'

'Well then, if monsieur will allow me to say,' Conseil went on calmly, 'if what's out there is not Bouguer's Squid in person, then it must be one of its brothers.'

I stared at Conseil. Ned Land rushed to the viewing panel.

'Hell's teeth,' he exclaimed, 'what a gruesome sight!'

In turn, I also looked out and could not repress a shudder of disgust. I was looking at a horrible monster, worthy of featuring in any teratological legend.

It was a squid of colossal proportions. It was 8 metres long and was swimming backwards towards the *Nautilus* at incredible speed. It was glaring out through enormous, greenish-blue eyes. Its eight arms, or rather legs, grew out of its head – which explains why these creatures are called cephalopods – were double the length of its body and were waving wildly, like the locks of the Furies. We had a clear sight of the 250 suckers which lined the inside of each tentacle. They were semi-spherical, like cups. Sometimes the suckers clung to the glass by creating a vacuum. The monster's mouth – a beak shaped like the beak of a parrot – opened and closed vertically. Its tongue, which was of horny consistency, was itself armed with several rows of sharp teeth and flicked in and out of this pair of shears. Whatever had nature been thinking of in putting a bird's beak on a mollusc? Its spindle-shaped body, swollen in its middle section, formed a mass of flesh which must have weighed 25,000 kilos. Its colour kept changing with dazzling speed according to the state of the animal's arousal, moving in succession from livid grey to reddish-brown.

What had inflamed the mollusc's wrath? Most likely the presence of the *Nautilus*, which was more powerful and on which its suckers and mandibles had no effect. And yet what monstrous animals are these squids, with what vitality did the Creator endow them, what vigour there is in their movements, for do they not have three hearts?

Chance had brought us face to face with this animal, and I did not intend to miss the opportunity of making a careful study of this specimen of a cephalopod. I put aside the horror which the look of the creature inspired in me and, picking up a pencil, I began to draw it.

'Perhaps it's the same one as the one encountered by the *Alecton*,' said Conseil.

'No,' said the Canadian. 'This one is intact. The other one lost its tail!'

'That doesn't necessarily follow,' I replied. 'The arms and tails of these animals can be replaced by redintegration, and in the intervening seven years the tail of Bouguer's Squid has had plenty of time to grow back.'

'Well,' retorted Ned Land, 'if it isn't this one, it's perhaps one of those.'

For other squids had begun to appear in the starboard viewing panel. I counted seven. They formed a kind of ceremonial guard around the *Nautilus*. I heard the grating of their beaks against our metal hull. We were royally well served.

I went on with my drawing. The monsters stayed near us in such close formation that they hardly seemed to be moving. I could have traced their outlines on the glass, even though we were now travelling at a moderate speed.

Then the *Nautilus* stopped dead. The shock made the ribbed frame of the ship judder.

'Have we hit something?' I asked.

'If we did,' replied the Canadian, 'we must be free again because we're floating.'

The *Nautilus* was definitely afloat, but she was no longer moving. The blades of her propeller had ceased turning in the water. A minute passed, and then Captain Nemo walked into the Great Saloon. He was accompanied by his first officer.

I had not seen him for some time. He looked dejected. Without speaking to us, perhaps even without seeing us, he crossed to the viewing panels, stared out at the squids and said a few words to his second-in-command, who turned and left.

Minutes later, the panels closed. The ceiling lights lit up.

I approached the captain.

'A most interesting collection of squids,' I said, in the relaxed tone of an enthusiast standing in front of a tank in an aquarium.

'Perhaps for a naturalist, he replied, 'but we are going to have to fight it out with them, hand to hand.'

I stared at the captain. I thought I must have misheard him.

'Hand to hand?' I repeated.

'Yes, professor. The propeller has stopped. I believe that the horny mandibles of one of these squids have become wedged between the blades. It is enough to prevent us from moving.'

'What are you going to do?'

'We shall surface and exterminate these vermin.'

'A tall order.'

'True. Our electric bullets have no effect on their soft bodies, which provide insufficient resistance to make them explode. We shall attack them with axes.'

'And a harpoon, captain,' said the Canadian, 'if, that is, you'll let me help.'

'I accept your offer, Mister Land.'

'We'll come with you,' I said.

We followed Captain Nemo out to the central stairwell.

There, ten or so men armed with boarding axes stood ready for the fray. Conseil and I took an axe apiece. Ned Land grabbed a harpoon.

The *Nautilus* had now returned to the surface. One of the sailors was standing on one of the top steps, unscrewing the bolts of the hatch. The moment they were free, the hatch was lifted off with tremendous force, clearly by the suckers on an arm of one of the squids.

Immediately a long tentacle reached in through the opening like a snake, and a score of others waved about above it. With a blow of his axe, Captain Nemo cut off this awesome tentacle, which slithered down the steps, writhing as it went.

As we were all scrambling forward to get out on to the platform, two other tentacles, whipped through the air, caught the sailor standing in front of Captain Nemo and yanked him out with overwhelming strength.

Captain Nemo gave a shout and rushed out. We were right behind him.

We were met by a terrible sight! The wretched man was being squeezed by the arm of the squid, the suckers clinging to his clothes. He was being tossed about in the air, a mere plaything of that enormous limb. He was gasping for air, choking, shouting 'Help! Help!' *And he was shouting it in French!* The words left me stunned! So I had one fellow countryman on board, perhaps more! I shall hear that desperate call to the end of my days!

The poor man was doomed! Who could save him from that deadly embrace? But Captain Nemo launched himself at the squid and with a single blow of his axe severed another tentacle. His first officer was setting furiously about other monsters that were crawling up the sides of the *Nautilus*. The whole crew were now wielding their axes with a will. The Canadian, Conseil and I were also slashing with our weapons at the flabby bodies. A powerful smell of musk filled the air. It was horrible.

For one moment I thought that the sailor, helpless in the grip

'A long tentacle reached in through the opening'

of the squid, would yet be cut free from the grips of its powerful suckers. Seven of its eight arms had been severed. Just one remained, and it was writhing in the air, waving its victim about as though he were a feather. But just as Captain Nemo and his first officer rushed the animal, it squirted a jet of the blackish liquid which squids secrete from a sac in their abdomen. We were blinded by it. By the time this black cloud had dispersed, the squid had disappeared, and my unfortunate compatriot with it!

Then we renewed out attack on those monsters with redou-bled fury! We were like men possessed. Ten or twelve of them had climbed on to the platform and up the hull of the *Nautilus*. We were virtually wading through segments of severed tenta-cles which twitched and threshed about like serpents on the platform in a welter of blood and black ink. It seemed those slimy arms were about to grow back, like the heads of the Hydra. Each thrust of Ned Land's harpoon went straight into the blue-green eyes of the monsters and blinded them. But sud-denly my fearless companion was knocked over by the tentacles of a squid which he had not been able to duck.

I felt my blood run cold in dismay and horror! The awesome beak of the creature had opened above the dazed harpooner. He was about to be cut in two. I rushed forward, determined to save him. But Captain Nemo got there before me. His axe smashed completely through those enormous mandibles and, saved by a miracle, the Canadian scrambled to his feet and plunged his harpoon into the squid until it vanished into its triple heart.

'Now we're even,' said Captain Nemo to the Canadian.

Ned acknowledged him with a nod but did not answer.

The battle with the squids had lasted a quarter of an hour. The monsters, beaten, butchered, annihilated, finally fled and vanished under the waves.

Captain Nemo, covered in blood, stood motionless by the searchlight, gazing at the sea which had swallowed up one of his companions. Large tears were streaming from his eyes.

19

The Gulf Stream

None of us will ever forget the terrible events of 20 April. I wrote my account of it still in a state of shock. Subsequently, I looked through it again and read it out to Conseil and the Canadian. They found it factually accurate but not dramatic enough. To describe such scenes would require the pen of our most illustrious poet, author of *Les Travailleurs de la mer*.[23]

I was saying that Captain Nemo wept as he stared out at the water. His grief was enormous. It was the second companion he had lost since our arrival on board. And what a terrible death! His friend, crushed, the life choked out of him, broken by the mighty tentacle of the squid, mangled by its iron-like jaws, would never now be laid to rest with his fellow sailors in the peaceful burying ground of the coral cemetery!

Personally, the most heart-rending impression I took away of that battle was the sound of the desperate cries of the doomed victim. That poor Frenchman, forgetting the common language used by the men of the *Nautilus*, had reverted to the tongue of his native land and his mother to make that ultimate cry for help. Among the members of the crew, who were devoted body and soul to Captain Nemo and like him fleeing all contact with humankind, I had had a fellow countryman! Was he the sole representative of France in that mysterious company of men of clearly different nationalities? It was another of the unsolved problems which continued to go round and round inside my head!

Captain Nemo went below to his cabin, and I did not see him again for some time. But how despondent, desperate, irresolute he must have been if I could judge by the atmosphere in the boat of which he was the driving force and which reflected his every mood! The *Nautilus* no longer followed a particular course. She came, she went, she wallowed like a corpse tossed by the waves. Her propeller had been freed and yet it rarely turned. She sailed directionlessly. The captain could not put his most recent battle behind him, he could not forget the sea which had swallowed one of his companions.

Ten days passed by in this fashion. It was only on 1 May that the *Nautilus* resumed her northerly course in earnest, after sighting the Lucayan archipelago at the mouth of the Old Bahama Channel. We were then going with the flow of the greatest current of any sea, which has its own shores, its own fish and its own temperatures. I refer to the Gulf Stream.

It really is a river. It runs freely through the middle of the Atlantic, and its waters do not mix with the waters of the ocean. It is a saltwater river, saltier than the Red Sea. Its average depth is 3,000 feet and mean width 60 miles. In some places, its current reaches a speed of 4 kilometres an hour. The volume of water it moves is constant and greater than that of all the world's rivers combined.

The true source of the Gulf Stream, discovered by Captain Maury, its starting point, if you prefer, is located in the Bay of Biscay. There, its waters, still low in temperature and pale in colour, begin to collect. It moves south, along the coast of equatorial Africa, is warmed by the sun in the Torrid Zone and crosses the Atlantic to San Roque on the coast of Brazil, then divides into two. One branch proceeds to the Caribbean, where it absorbs more heated molecules. At this point the Gulf Stream embarks on a stabilizing role, that is, it sets out to restore a balance of temperatures by mixing water from the tropics with colder, northern water. Raised to very high temperatures in the Gulf of Mexico, it moves up the American coast, reaches Newfoundland, where it is turned by the cold current flowing down through the Davis Strait, resumes its progress through the ocean by following one of the globe's great circles, the loxodromic curve, before splitting into two arms at around the 43rd degree of latitude. One of these, pushed by north-easterly trade winds, returns to the Bay of Biscay and the Azores. The other, after warming the coasts of Ireland and Norway, continues on to Spitzbergen, where its temperature drops to 4° centigrade, and ends in the open water of the Pole.

It was along this ocean current that the *Nautilus* was now cruising. When it emerges from the Old Bahama Channel, the Gulf Stream is 14 leagues wide and 350 metres deep and moves at 8 kilometres an hour. This speed decreases steadily as it moves further northwards, and it is to be hoped that this gradual fall continues for if, as observation seems to suggest, its speed and direction were to change, the climate of Europe would be subjected to a level of disruption whose consequences are incalculable.

Around noon, I was out on the platform with Conseil. I was telling him about various aspects of the Gulf Stream. When I had finished my explanation, I asked him to dip his hand into the current.

He did so and was amazed to find no sensation whatsoever, either of warmth or cold.

'The reason for that,' said I, 'is that the temperature of the water in the Gulf Stream, when it flows out of the Gulf of Mexico, is more or less that of human blood. The Gulf Stream is a huge storage radiator which allows the coasts of Europe to remain permanently green. If Maury is to be believed, the heat contained in the current, if it could be so captured, would supply enough calorific power to sustain a flow of molten iron equal in size to the Amazon or the Missouri.'

At that time the Gulf Stream was flowing at 2.25 metres a second. Its current is so distinct from the seas on both sides of it that its water, compressed between them, is clearly distinguishable, and there is even a difference in level from the cold water around it. Darker and richer in mineral salts, its indigo coloration stands out against the green water that surrounds it. So clear is the line of demarcation that when the *Nautilus* was on a level with the Carolinas, her bow was cutting through the waves of the Gulf Stream while her propeller was still churning the water of the ocean.

All manner of living creatures were carried along by the current. Argonauts, so common in the Mediterranean, sailed along it in large flotillas. Among the cartilaginous fish, the most interesting were rays with very slender tails, accounting for about a third of their bodies, which were shaped like stretched diamonds 25 feet long. There were also small sharks, a metre long, with large heads, small, rounded muzzles, sharp teeth set in rows and bodies which appeared to be covered with scales.

Among the bony fish, I noticed grey wrasse peculiar to these seas; sparids with irises that blazed like fire; scianas a metre long with large mouths bristling with small teeth, which mewed faintly; a black-hued variety of *centronotus*, which I have already mentioned; blue dolphinfish speckled with gold and silver; parrotfish, the rainbows of the sea, whose colours rival those of the most beautiful tropical birds; triangular-headed blennies; bluish brill with no scales; *batrachus* toadfish with a yellow, transversal stripe in the shape of a Greek letter *t*; shoals of brown-speckled small naked gobies; blackfish with silver heads and yellow tails; various species of salmon; slender, shining, softly gleaming *mugilidae*, which Lacépède dedicated to his wife; and lastly, a most handsome fish, the America jack-knife fish, which, done out in the colours of every medal and bedizened with every ribbon, inhabit the shores of that great nation where ribbons and medals are held in such low esteem.

I shall add one further remark. During the night, the phosphorescent waters of the Gulf Stream proved to be almost as bright as the electric radiance of our searchlight, especially during the stormy weather which frequently threatened.

On 8 May, we were still on a level with Cape Hatteras, off the coast of North Carolina. At this point the Gulf Stream is 75 miles wide and 210 metres deep. The *Nautilus* continued to follow an erratic course. All surveillance of us on board seemed to have been lifted. In such circumstances, I could only agree that an escape attempt might well have succeeded, for the shore was inhabited and offered any number of safe refuges. The sea was constantly criss-crossed with numerous steamships which plied regularly between New York or Boston and the Gulf of Mexico, while day and night small schooners formed a regular traffic along various points of the American coast. We could reasonably hope for a warm reception. So here was a good opportunity, despite the 30 miles which separated the *Nautilus* from the shores of the Union.

But then something unfortunate happened which scuppered the Canadian's plans. The weather had turned foul. We were then approaching the zone where storms are frequent, an area of tornadoes and cyclones generated by the Gulf Stream itself. To tackle in a frail rowing boat a sea which often ran high was to risk certain death. Even Ned Land balked at the prospect. He was left champing on the bit in a state of frustrated homesickness which could only be cured by escape.

'Professor,' he said to me on that day, 'this cannot go on. I must know where I stand. Your man Nemo keeps his distance from land and is sailing north. Now, I'm telling you: I've had a bellyful of the South Pole and I have no intention of going to the North.'

'But what can we do, Ned? Escape is out of the question at the moment.'

'I come back to my plan. We must speak to Captain Nemo. You didn't do so when we were near the shores of your country. But now that we're near mine, I intend to have my say. When I think that within days the *Nautilus* will reach the latitude of Nova Scotia, where, once past Newfoundland, we enter the beginning of the huge estuary of the Saint Lawrence, which is my river, the river that flows down from Quebec, where I was born – when I think of all that, I can feel rage glow in my cheeks and my hair stand on end. No, professor, I would rather take my chances in the sea! I will not stay on board! I cannot breathe here!'

The Canadian was clearly at the end of his tether. His forceful nature refused to submit to this prolonged, enforced detention. His expression was growing grimmer by the day. His mood became increasingly intense. I was well aware of what he was going through, for I myself was feeling homesick. Nearly seven months had passed, during which we had received no news of happenings on terra firma. Moreover, Captain Nemo's isolation, the change that had come over him especially since the battle with the squids, his taciturnity, all this made me see everything in a new light. The excitement I had felt at first had evaporated. A man had to be as patient as a Fleming, like my excellent Conseil, to accept our life in a world intended for cetaceans and other denizens of the deep. I truly felt that if he had been born with gills rather than lungs Conseil would have made a pretty good fish!

'Well, professor?' prompted Ned Land when I did not give him an answer.

'Do you want me to ask Captain Nemo what plans he has for us?'

'I do.'

'Despite the fact that he has already told us in no uncertain terms what they are?'

'Yes. I want to know exactly where I stand. Speak to him on my behalf, if you wish. Say it comes from me.'

'But I meet him so infrequently. Actually, he avoids me.'

'All the more reason for going to see him.'

'I'll ask him, Ned.'

'When?' said the Canadian insistently.

'When I see him next.'

'Professor Aronnax, would you like me to go and ask him myself?'

'No. Leave it to me. Tomorrow . . .'

'Today,' said Ned Land.

'Very well. I shall speak to him today,' I told the Canadian, who, if matters had been left to him, would surely have spoiled everything for all three of us.

He left me. Now that the decision had been made, I resolved to get it over with at once. I prefer to get things done rather than leave them hanging.

I returned to my cabin. I could hear the footsteps of Captain Nemo as he paced up and down next door. I could not pass up this opportunity to confront him. I knocked. I got no answer. I knocked again then turned the knob, opened the door and walked in.

Captain Nemo was there. He was bent over his work table and had not heard me. Determined I would not leave without having put the question to him, I went to where he was sitting. Suddenly he looked up, scowled and said peremptorily:

'Why are you here? What do you want?'

'I want to speak to you, captain.'

'I am busy, professor, I am working. Are you not prepared to allow me the same freedom to be alone which I give you?'

It was hardly an encouraging reception. But I was determined to let him vent his mood before I said my piece.

'Captain,' I said coolly, 'I have come to raise a matter which I can put off no longer.'

'And what might that be, professor?' he replied sardonically. 'Have you discovered something I might have missed? Has the sea yielded up some new secret to you?'

We were far from the point. But before I could reply, he motioned to a manuscript which lay open on his work table, then said in the gravest of voices:

'This, Professor Aronnax, is a manuscript written in several languages. It contains a summary of all my studies of the sea and, if it is the will of God, it shall not die with me. This manuscript, signed with my name and completed by an account of my life, will be placed inside an unsinkable container. The last survivor on board the *Nautilus* will cast the container into the sea to drift wherever the waves will carry it.'

His name! An account of his life written by himself! Would the veil of mystery surrounding him be lifted some day? However, at that juncture, all I could see in his words was a way of introducing my subject.

'Captain,' I began, 'I can only applaud the motive which has prompted you to act in this way. The fruit of your labours must not be lost. But the method you propose to use appears to me to be primitive. Who knows where the winds will blow your container or into whose hands it will fall? Can't you find a better way? Could not you or one of your men . . . ?'

'Never, professor!' the captain replied brusquely, interrupting me.

'Captain, I and my companions would be prepared to keep your manuscript safely under lock and key, and if you were to restore our freedom . . .'

'Your freedom!' thundered Captain Nemo, rising to his feet.

'Yes, captain, and that is the subject which I came here to

raise with you. It is now seven months since we came on board your boat, and I now ask on behalf of my companions and myself if it is your intention to keep us here permanently.'

'Professor Aronnax,' said Captain Nemo, 'my answer today is still the answer I gave you seven months ago: whoever boards the *Nautilus* can never leave her.'

'But this is slavery you impose on us!'

'Call it what you will.'

'But no slave anywhere can ever lose the right to attempt to recover his freedom! Whatever means become available to him he is justified in using them!'

'But who,' replied Captain Nemo, 'is denying you that right? Have I ever tried to bind you with an oath?'

The captain folded his arms and looked straight at me.

'Sir!' I replied. 'Covering the same ground twice would not be agreeable to either you or me. But since the matter has been broached, let us get to the end of it once and for all. I say again, this is a question which does not concern only me. I regard my work as something that sustains me; it is a powerful distraction, a means of training the mind, a passion capable of making me forget everything else. Like you, I am a man who is content to remain unknown and obscure, with a faint hope of one day being able to bequeath the results of my labours to the future in a hypothetical container thrown to the mercy of winds and waves. For this reason, I can admire you, I am happy to follow you in those activities that I understand. For there are other areas of your life which give me glimpses of an existence surrounded by complexities and mysteries in which I and my companions play no part. Even when we have felt for you, touched by certain of your sorrows or thrilled by your acts of genius or courage, we have been forced to suppress the smallest gesture of what human beings naturally feel in the presence of something which is fine and good, whether it comes from a friend or an enemy. Well, it is the feeling that we are strangers to everything which affects you that makes our situation here unacceptable, impossible even for me, but absolutely impossible for Ned Land especially. Any man, by the very fact of his being a man, deserves some consideration. Have you never wondered if love of liberty and hatred of slavery are capable of inspiring thoughts of revenge in a character like the Canadian's? Have you asked yourself what such a man might think or actually try, plan and do . . . ?'

At that point, I stopped. Captain Nemo rose to his feet.

'What Ned Land may think, plan and do is of no account to me. I did not invite him here. I do not keep him on board for my own amusement. As for you, Professor Aronnax, you are a man capable of understanding everything, even silence. I have no answer to give you. Let this first occasion when you come to me to speak of this matter also be the last. If it happens again, I shall not even hear you out.'

I withdrew. From that day on, our situation became very strained. I reported my conversation to my two companions.

'At least now we know,' said Ned, 'that we can't expect anything of that man. The *Nautilus* is approaching Long Island. We're going to break out of here, whatever the weather.'

But the skies were looking increasingly threatening. There were signs that a hurricane was brewing. The sky turned white and milky. On the horizon, feathery sprays of cirrus were replaced by banks of nimbocumulus, while other low clouds raced away into the distance. The seas rose higher and rolled in long, undulating swells. Birds began to disappear except for the petrels which are always at home in a storm. The barometer dropped sharply and indicated extreme differences of pressures in the cloud cover. The liquids in the stormglass were separating as a result of the electricity in the atmosphere. A battle of the elements was imminent.

The storm broke during the daylight hours of 18 May, when the *Nautilus* was cruising off Long Island, only a few miles from the entrance to New York harbour. I am able to describe the protracted clash of the elements because, instead of escaping into the depths, Captain Nemo, obeying some inexplicable whim, decided he would face the tempest on the surface.

The wind was blowing from the south-west, first at fresh breeze strength, that is at a speed of 15 metres a second, which had risen to 25 by three in the afternoon, the official definition of storm force.

Captain Nemo, standing foursquare in the teeth of the squalls, had taken up a position outside, on the platform. He had lashed himself fast so that he could withstand the monstrous breaking waves. I had clambered out likewise and was also roped up, dividing my admiration between the storm and the peerless man who defied it.

The raging sea was swept by great shreds of cloud, which dipped down on to the waves. I did not see any of the smaller, intermediate waves which form in the troughs between the large ones. There were only long, murky undulations made of water so tightly compressed that their crests did not break. They rose higher and higher. Each urged the next one on. The *Nautilus*, now blown on to her side and then straightening up like a mast, pitched and rolled horribly.

Around five o'clock began a burst of torrential rain which did not cause either wind or sea to abate. The hurricane broke on us at a speed of 45 metres a second, about 40 leagues an hour. It is in those conditions that it knocks down houses, drives roof tiles into wooden doors, mangles iron gates and blows 24-pounder cannons around. Yet in the middle of the turmoil the *Nautilus* fully justified the remark made by one celebrated highly skilled engineer: 'There is no well-constructed hull which cannot withstand the sea!' She was not an immovable rock which these waves could have demolished, but a steel cylinder without rigging and masts which could move and be manoeuvred, and defied the unchained sea to do its worst.

I looked closely at those furious waves. Some were 15 metres high and 150 to 175 long and the speed at which they travelled was 15 metres a second, half that of the wind. Their volume and power grew in proportion to the depth of the sea. I understood then the role they play in nature's economy: they trap air in their folds and force it down to the bottom of the sea to which they bring life-giving oxygen. The extreme pressures they generate, it has been calculated, may be as much as 3,000 kilograms per square foot of any surface. It was waves like these which once moved a rock weighing 84,000 pounds in the Hebrides. In a storm which struck on 23 December 1864, similar waves flattened part of the city of Tokyo, in Japan, then set off at 700 kilometres an hour and did not stop until they reached the coast of North America on the same day.

The intensity of the storm increased as it grew darker. As happened during the cyclone which struck La Réunion in 1860, the barometer fell to 710 millimetres. As night was falling, I saw a large steamship on the horizon which was making heavy weather of it. It was laid to with its engines turning slowly, giving just enough power to keep her bow to the wind. It was most likely one of the liners which operate the route from New York to Liverpool or Le Havre. Soon it vanished into the murk.

By ten in the evening, the heavens were ablaze. The air was rent by violent flashes of lightning. I could not stand the dazzle, but Captain Nemo gazed directly at them and seemed to be breathing in the very spirit of the storm. The heavens reverberated with a deafening mixture of noise made up of crashing waves, shrieking winds and the roar of thunder. The wind came at us from every point of the horizon, and the cyclone which had started in the east returned to that quarter by way of north, west and south, turning in the opposite direction to that of storms in the southern hemisphere.

Ah, the Gulf Stream! How truly it lived up to its name of Lord of the Tempest! For it is the begetter of the powerful cyclones which are born of the difference in temperature between its flowing current and the layers of air above it.

The rain was followed by a shower of light as water droplets turned into plumes of fire. It was as if Captain Nemo, seeking a death that would be worthy of him, was deliberately offering himself to the thunderbolt. The *Nautilus* pitched horribly, reared, raised her pointed steel prow high in the air, like the rod of a lightning conductor, and from it I saw sparks fly off.

Exhausted, at the very end of my strength, I crawled on my belly towards the hatch. I opened it and went below into the Great Saloon. The storm had now reached a paroxysm of fury. It was impossible to stand up inside the *Nautilus*.

Captain Nemo came back inside around midnight. I heard the water tanks filling slowly, and the *Nautilus* sank gently beneath the surface of the waves.

Through the open viewing panels in the Great Saloon, I saw

'The rain was followed by a shower of light'

large, terrified fish swimming past like ghosts in the fiery water. Some were struck by lightning and died as I watched!

The *Nautilus* went on diving. I thought that we would find calm water at a depth of 15 metres. But no. The upper layers were being too violently disturbed for that. To find stillness, we had to go down to 50 metres, to the belly of the ocean.

But there we found such tranquillity, such silence, such a world of peace! Who would have believed that a deadly hurricane had been unleashed above us, on the surface of the water?

20

Latitude 47° 24', Longitude 17° 28'

By the time the storm had passed, we had been swept eastwards. All hopes of escape to landing places around New York
or the Saint Lawrence were fast receding. Poor Ned, more
frustrated than ever, kept himself to himself, just as Captain
Nemo continued to do. Conseil and I were inseparable.

I noted above that the *Nautilus* had been driven east. I
should have said, more accurately, north-east. For several days
we followed no particular course, sailing sometimes on the
water and sometimes under it, through the fogs which are
so feared by mariners. These are caused mainly by melting
ice-floes which saturate the atmosphere with moisture. How
many vessels have been lost in these waters while attempting to
identify indistinct lights on a coast! How many have foundered
in those opaque mists? How many have run aground on reefs
when the beat of the surf has been muffled by the noise of the
wind? How many ships have collided despite their navigation
lights, the drone of their foghorns and the ringing of alarm
bells?

The floor of those seas were like a battlefield still strewn
with the remains of those overcome by the ocean. Some were
old and blurred by weeds. Others were more recent, and their
metal fittings and copper-bottom hulls reflected the brilliance
of our searchlight. So many vessels comprehensively lost –
cargo, crews and their freight of migrants – on those dangerous
hazards which regularly feature in the statistics: Cape Race,
Saint Paul Island, the Strait of Belle-Isle, the estuary of the
Saint Lawrence! And looking back no further than the last
few years, how many names have been added to the annals

of the dead by the Royal Mail, Inmann and Montreal lines: the *Solway*, the *Isis*, the *Paramatta*, the *Hungarian*, the *Canadian*, the *Anglo-Saxon*, the *Humboldt*, the *United States*, all foundered, the *Arctic* and the *Lyonnais*, sunk by collision, the *President*, the *Pacific* and the *City of Glasgow*, all lost, reasons unknown – grim ruins past which the *Nautilus* sailed as if reviewing a roll-call of the dead!

On 15 May we were at the extreme southern end of the Grand Banks of Newfoundland. They are the product of marine alluvial deposits, a vast accumulation of organic debris brought either up from the Equator by the Gulf Stream or down from the North Pole by a cold counter-current which runs down the American coast. Here too are mounds of stone blocks erratically deposited when the glaciers melted. It is also a vast charnel-house containing the remains of fish, molluscs or zoophytes, which die here by the million.

The sea is not very deep on the Grand Banks, a few hundred fathoms at most. But to the south a deep depression suddenly opens up, a chasm which bottoms at 3,000 metres. At this point, the Gulf Stream widens and mellows. It flows more slowly, cools and turns into a sea.

Among the fish frightened away by the *Nautilus* as she cruised I will mention lumpfish a metre long, black on top, orange underneath, which gives its fellow fish an example of conjugal fidelity which is rarely followed; a huge uarnak, a kind of bright-green moray, delicious to eat; what are called karrak, which have large eyes and a head vaguely resembling that of a dog; blennies, ovoviparous like snakes;[24] gobies of both frillfin and black varieties, 20 centimetres long; long-tailed *macrura*, bright silver and rapid swimmers, which had strayed from their hyperborean home grounds.

The nets also dragged up a bold, audacious, vigorous, strongly muscled fish, with stings on its head and barbs on its fins, a veritable 2–3 metre scorpion, the sworn enemy of blennies, gade and salmon: the bull-head of the northern seas. It has a brown tubercular body and red-edged fins. The fishermen of the *Nautilus* had some difficulty dealing with it, for, because of the way its gill-covers are configured, its respiratory organs survive direct contact with the desiccating effects of the atmosphere, and this enables it to live for some time out of the water.

I will also add, for the record, a small perciform fish which follows ships in northern waters; long-snouted bleak, unique to the North Atlantic; and red scorpion fish. And then there were the gades, mainly varieties of the cod family, which I was able to observe in their favourite habitat, the inexhaustible Grand Banks of Newfoundland.

It could be said that cod are a 'mountain fish', since the Grand Banks are in effect an underwater mountain. Whenever the *Nautilus* pushed its way through their serried ranks, Conseil could not refrain from remarking:

'They can't be cod! I always thought cod were flat, like dab or sole.'

'Don't be naive!' I exclaimed. 'Cod are flat only on a fishmonger's slab, where they have been cleaned and displayed. But in water, they are a fusiform fish, like grey mullet, and perfectly shaped for swimming.'

'If monsieur says so,' replied Conseil. 'But what a swarm! It's a regular ant hill!'

'But there'd be even more if they did not have enemies, scorpion fish and man! Do you know how many eggs have been found in a single female?'

'Let's not stint ourselves,' replied Conseil. 'Five hundred thousand?'

'Eleven million!'

'Eleven million! I could never accept such a figure unless I count them myself.'

'Count them if you wish, Conseil. Or just take my word for it, it would be quicker. It is a fact that French, English, American, Danish and Norwegian fishermen catch them by the thousand! They are eaten in huge quantities, and if it were not for their astounding fertility the seas here would soon be completely cleared of them. In England and America alone 5,000 ships crewed by 75,000 men are employed fishing for cod. Each boat returns with an average catch of 40,000, a total of 20 million. Similar numbers are caught off the coast of Norway.'

'Very well,' replied Conseil, I shall take monsieur's word for it. I won't count them.'

'Count what?'

'The 11 million eggs. But I will make one observation.'

'Which is?'

'It's this. If all the eggs hatched out, four female cod would feed the whole of England, America and Norway.'

While we skimmed over the bed of the Grand Banks, I had a clear view of the long lines, each with 200 hooks, which every boat lays by the dozen. Each line was anchored by a small grappling hook and held up on the surface by a rope tied to a cork buoy. The *Nautilus* had to weave its way carefully through this underwater maze.

However, we did not dally in these busy waters and moved smartly up to the 42nd degree of latitude. That put us on a level with St John's, Newfoundland, and Heart's Content, the terminal point of the transatlantic cable.

Instead of continuing northwards, the *Nautilus* turned east, as though about to sail over the plateau on which the cable was laid. Repeated soundings have mapped the underwater terrain in great detail.

It was on 17 May, when we were about 500 miles from Heart's Content and at a depth of 2,800 metres, that I saw the huge cable snaking across the sea-bed. Indeed, Conseil, to whom I had not spoken of it beforehand, thought at first it was a gigantic sea serpent and was getting ready to classify it in his customary way. But I pointed out his mistake and, to cover his embarrassment, proceeded to tell him the circumstances in which the cable had been laid.

The first cable was rolled out over two years, 1857 and 1858. But after it had transmitted about 400 telegrams it stopped working. In 1863 engineers made a new cable 3,400 kilometres long, weighing 4,500 tons, which was loaded on to the *Great Eastern*. That venture also failed.

Now, on 25 May, the *Nautilus*, at a depth of 3,836 metres, reached the exact spot where the break in the cable had happened and brought the whole project to a full stop. The place was 638 miles from the Irish coast. It became clear at two in the afternoon that contact with Europe had been lost. The electrical engineers on board decided to cut the cable before trying to raise it and by eleven that night had brought up the damaged part. They then rejoined and spliced the ends and lowered the cable again. But a few days later it broke once more, and this time it proved impossible to recover it from the ocean floor.

The Americans did not give up. Cyrus Field, a bold man and the moving spirit of the enterprise on which he was risking his entire fortune, launched a new share issue. It was snapped up immediately. Another cable was made, using an improved design. The core of conducting leads insulated in gutta-percha sleeves was given a protective shield of woven fabric and then inserted into a metal armouring. The *Great Eastern* set sail again on 13 July 1866.

The operation went well. However, there was one incident. Several times as the cable was being run out the electrical engineers had noticed that nails had recently been driven into it with a view to damaging the insulation. Captain Anderson brought his officers and the engineers together and, after discussing the matter, put up notices saying that if any saboteur were to be found on board, he would be tipped into the ocean without any other form of justice. After that, there was no further criminal damage.

On 23 July the *Great Eastern* was just 800 kilometres from Newfoundland when she received a telegram from Ireland announcing the news that an armistice had been signed between Prussia and Austria after the battle of Sadowa.[25] On the 27th, in dense fog, she sighted the port of Heart's Content. The enterprise had reached a successful conclusion and used its first telegraphic wire from young America to send old Europe these sage words which are rarely understood: 'Glory to God in the highest and on earth peace, goodwill to all men.'

I did not expect to find the electric cable in pristine condition, exactly as it was when it left the factory where it was made. The long serpent was covered with shellfish, bristling with foraminiferous protozoa and stuccoed with a stony encrustation which protected it against the depredations of perforating molluscs. It lay peacefully sheltered from the motions of the sea and at a pressure conducive to the transmission of the electric impulse which travels from America to Europe in thirty-two hundredths of a second. The life of the cable is certain to be indefinite given the fact that it has been observed that the gutta-percha insulation becomes more efficient when immersed in sea-water.

Furthermore, on this plateau, which was so judiciously selected for its route, the cable was never placed at depths which might cause it to break. The *Nautilus* tracked it down to its lowest point of 4,431 metres, where it still lay completely free of strain and tension. Then we explored the site where the 1863 cable had been severed.

At that point, the ocean floor was in the form of a valley 120 kilometres wide in which Mont Blanc could have been relocated without its summit showing above the waves. This valley is sealed off at its eastern end by a sheer wall of rock 2,000 metres high. We got there on 28 May when the *Nautilus* was only 150 kilometres from Ireland.

Was Captain Nemo intending to go north and make landfall on the British Isles? No. To my great surprise, he headed back south and returned to European seas. As we sailed round the Emerald Isle, I sighted Cape Clear and the Fastnet Light, which guides the thousands of ships sailing from Glasgow and Liverpool.

An important question then surfaced in my mind. Would the *Nautilus* dare to attempt a passage through the English Channel? Ned Land, who had reappeared when we came close to land again, never stopped plying me with questions. I did not know what to tell him. Captain Nemo remained invisible. Having allowed the Canadian a glimpse of the coast of America, was he now going to give me a sight of France?

Meanwhile, the *Nautilus* still kept her nose pointing south. On 30 May, she passed within sight of Land's End, between the tip of England and the Scillies, which she passed on her starboard side.

If he was going to enter the Channel, he would now have to switch sharply to an easterly course. This he did not do.

Throughout the day of 31 May the *Nautilus* sailed in a series of circles, which greatly puzzled me. She seemed to be looking for a particular spot which she was taking some time to locate. At midday Captain Nemo came out to take our position himself. He did not speak to me. He seemed even grimmer than ever. What could be the reason for his dour mood? Was it his proximity to the coast of Europe? Was it some old memory of the homeland which he had deserted? What was he feeling? Remorse? Regrets? The thought kept going round and round in my head, and I had a presentiment that the captain's secrets were about to be revealed by chance.

The next day, 1 June, the *Nautilus* repeated the same manoeuvres. It was very obvious that she was trying to find a particular location in the ocean. Captain Nemo came out to measure the height of the sun, as he had done the day before. The sea was calm and the sky was blue. Eight miles to the east of us a large steamship appeared on the line of the horizon. She was not flying a flag on her fore-and-aft sail, and I could not tell what nationality she was.

A few minutes before the sun passed the meridian, Captain Nemo reached for his sextant and took his reading with unusual thoroughness. The water was flat calm, which helped. The *Nautilus* was completely motionless, neither pitching nor rolling.

I was still on the platform then. When he had finished, he pronounced these few words:

'This is the place!'

He went below through the hatch. Had he seen the steamer, which had changed course and seemed to be making straight for us? I couldn't be sure.

I returned to the Great Saloon. The hatchway closed behind me, and I heard the hiss of water as it filled the tanks. The *Nautilus* began to sink and continued vertically down, for her screw was not turning and supplied no power.

Minutes later, she stopped and came to rest on the bottom, at a depth of 833 metres.

The ceiling lights in the Great Saloon went out, the viewing panels were opened, and through the glass I saw the sea brilliantly illuminated by the beams of our searchlight over a radius of half a mile.

I looked out to port and saw nothing anywhere in the vastness of the quiet water.

But to starboard loomed a large, bulky mass on the ocean bed which drew my eye. At first glance, it might have been a pile of ruins completely covered with white shells, which looked like a blanket of snow. I studied more closely this apparition and came to the conclusion that what I was seeing was the blurred outline of a ship which had lost its masts and must have sunk bow first. The vessel clearly belonged to a bygone age. The wreck, which was so to speak encrusted with calcareous deposits, had obviously spent many years here on the ocean bed.

What was this ship? Why had the *Nautilus* come visiting its final resting place? Had something other than a straightforward shipwreck been responsible for its presence here under water?

I was still trying to decide when I heard Captain Nemo's voice, in my ear, say slowly:

'This wrecked ship was once the *Marseillais*. She carried seventy-four guns and was launched in 1762. On 13 August 1778, under the command of La Poype-Vertrieux, she courageously engaged the *Preston* in battle. On 4 July 1779 she formed part of the squadron led by Admiral d'Estaing in the capture of Grenada. On 5 September 1781 she was involved in the action led by the Comte de la Grasse in Chesapeake Bay. In 1794 the French Republic changed her name. On 16 April of that same year she made for Brest to join up with the squadron headed by Villaret-Joyeuse, which had been ordered to escort a grain convoy coming from America under the overall command of Admiral von Stabel. On 11 and 12 Prairial of Year 2 of the Revolutionary calendar[26] the Brest squadron ran into a number of English vessels. Today, Professor Aronnax, is 13 Prairial, 1 June 1868. Seventy-four years ago to the day, at this location, latitude 47° 24' and longitude 17° 28', the ship you see there, after putting up a heroic fight, having lost all three masts, with water pouring into her hold, a third of her crew out of action, preferred to go down with its entire company of 356 sailors rather than surrender. Nailing her colours to the poop, she sank beneath the waves to cries of "Vive la République!"

'It's the *Vengeur*!' I cried.[27]

'It is indeed the *Vengeur*, professor! A fine and noble name!' murmured Captain Nemo, folding his arms.

21

Carnage

The tone of that speech, the totally unexpected nature of the incident, the story of that patriotic ship first told dispassionately and then the feeling with which that enigmatic man had spoken these last words, the very name, the *Vengeur*, the significance of which did not escape me, all this combined to imprint an indelible mark on my mind. I could not take my eyes off the captain. He was holding both hands out towards the sea, gazing intently at the illustrious wreck. Perhaps I would never know who he was, where he had come from, where he was going, but I was learning how to distinguish more clearly between the man and the man of science. It was no common, vulgar misanthropy which had driven Captain Nemo and his companions to hide themselves away in the *Nautilus*, but a monstrous – or sublime – hatred which time would never change.

Was such hatred still strong enough to nurture thoughts of revenge? The future was not slow to give me an answer.

Meanwhile the *Nautilus* returned slowly to the surface, and I watched the fuzzy outlines of the *Vengeur* gradually disappear. Soon I was aware of the boat's slight roll, which indicated that we were back in the open air.

At the same moment there came the sound of a muffled explosion. I looked at the captain. He did not move.

'Captain?' I asked.

He did not answer.

I left him and went up on to the platform. Conseil and the Canadian were already there.

'What was that noise?' I asked.

'A shot from a cannon,' answered Ned Land.

I looked in the direction of the steamship I had seen earlier. It was now much closer to the *Nautilus* and was clearly making full speed. There were 6 miles between us.

'What ship is that, Ned?'

'Judging by the rigging and the height of her lower masts,' said the Canadian, 'I'd wager she's a warship. I hope she comes on to us and, if that's what it takes, sinks the blasted *Nautilus*!'

'But Ned,' asked Conseil, 'what harm can it do the *Nautilus*? Will it follow us down beneath the surface and attack us there? Will it shell us at the bottom of the sea?'

'Tell me, Ned,' I said, 'can you make out what nationality that boat is?'

The Canadian frowned, lowering his eyebrows and eyelids, and squinted briefly through screwed-up slits at the boat with all the intentness of his perfect vision.

'No, professor,' he replied. 'I can't tell what nation she belongs to. She isn't flying a flag. But I can confirm that she's a warship because there's a long action pennant hoisted from her top mast.'

For a full quarter of an hour we went on observing the ship, which kept on coming towards us. But I could not confirm that it was able to identify the *Nautilus* at that distance, any more than I could believe it had marked her down as a submarine.

But in short order the Canadian was able to tell me that it was a large warship, with cutwater and two armour-plated decks. Thick smoke poured from her two funnels. Her furled sails were difficult to see against the rigging. There were no flags on her gaff. The distance still made it hard to see the colours of the pennant which streamed out in the wind like a thin ribbon.

It was approaching fast. If Captain Nemo let it come any nearer, the three of us would stand a very good chance of escaping.

'Professor,' said Ned Land, 'if that ship gets within a mile of us, I'm going to jump into the sea and I advise you to do the same.'

I did not respond to the Canadian's proposal and instead went on watching the advancing ship, which was getting bigger by the minute. Whether it was English, French, American or Russian, it would certainly take us on board if we could swim to her.

'Perhaps monsieur would care to remember,' said Conseil, 'that we have some experience of swimming. Monsieur may safely entrust me with the duty of towing him to this ship should he decide to follow the example of Mister Land.'

I was about to reply when white smoke spurted from the bows of the warship. Seconds later, the sea frothed as a heavy body fell into it and splashed water over the stern of the *Nautilus*. After a brief interval, I heard an explosion.

'What on earth . . . ?' I cried. 'They're firing at us!'

'Good for them!' growled the Canadian.

'Well, they certainly don't think we're castaways clinging to floating wreckage!'

'If monsieur won't mind my say . . . Oh!' cried Conseil as he shook off the water which a second shell had showered him with. 'If monsieur won't mind my saying so, they think we're a narwhal. They're shelling a narwhal!'

'But surely they can see,' I cried, 'that they're shooting at men?'

'Maybe that's exactly why they're doing it,' said Ned Land, looking me in the eye.

Suddenly it dawned on me. Everyone now knew very well what to think about the supposed monster. In its clash with the *Abraham Lincoln*, when the Canadian had scored a direct hit on the *Nautilus* with his harpoon, it must have been obvious to Captain Farragut that the supposed narwhal was in fact a submarine boat and infinitely more dangerous than some monster cetacean!

Yes, that had to be the explanation! On the high seas the world over, ships were now hunting down that fearsome engine of destruction!

And fearsome was the right word if, as we had grounds for thinking, Captain Nemo was intending to use the *Nautilus* as the instrument of his revenge! On the night when we had been shut up in our cabins in the middle of the Indian Ocean, had he not already attacked a ship? Had not the man now buried in the coral cemetery been a victim of a collision deliberately engineered by the *Nautilus*? Yes, I repeat: that had to be the way of it! A curtain was being lifted off part of the mysterious life of Captain Nemo. If his exact identity was still not known, at least the coalition of nations now mobilized against him was no longer hunting a chimerical creature but a man who had conceived an implacable hatred for all of them.

The weight of this terrible past now bore down on me. Instead of being reunited with friends on this ship which was now bearing down on us, all we could expect to find were merciless enemies.

Meanwhile, shells kept falling all round us. Some, when they fell, ricocheted off the surface of the water and sped away for considerable distances. None hit on the *Nautilus*.

The armour-plated man o' war was now just 3 miles away. Despite the heavy shelling, Captain Nemo did not come up to the platform. And yet just one of those conical shells, scoring a direct hit on the hull of the *Nautilus*, could have been fatal.

Then the Canadian said:

'Professor, we must do everything we can to get out of the corner we're in. We could signal them! Maybe they'll understand and think that we're on the same side as them!'

Ned Land took out his handkerchief and was about to wave it. But he'd scarcely shaken it out when he was smashed down by a blow from an iron fist and, prodigiously strong though he was, he collapsed on the deck.

'You miserable dog!' cried the captain. 'Would you like me to nail your hide to the cutwater of the *Nautilus* before we ram that ship?'

Captain Nemo, dreadful to hear, was even more terrible to behold. His face had turned deathly pale, such were the convulsions of his heart, which must have stopped beating for a moment. His pupils had contracted alarmingly. His voice had ceased to speak: it thundered. He bent over the Canadian, his strong hands gripping his shoulders, wrenching him this way and that.

Then he let go of him and turned to face the warship, whose shells continued to rain around him.

'You know who I am, ship of an accursed nation!' he cried

'You miserable dog!'

with that powerful voice. 'But I don't need your flags to know who you are! See here! I will show you mine!'

And from the front of the platform, Nemo unfurled a black flag like the one he had planted at the South Pole.

At that instant, a shell struck the hull of the *Nautilus* at an angle, without causing any damage, ricocheted past the captain and fell with a splash into the sea some distance away.

Captain Nemo just shrugged. Then he turned to me:

'Go below,' he said curtly, 'and take your companions with you.'

'Captain!' I cried. 'Are you going to attack that ship?'

'Professor, I am going to sink it!'

'You can't do that!'

'Oh, but I shall,' Captain Nemo replied with cold deliberation. 'Do not think that you can judge me, professor. Fate has shown you what you were not supposed to see. I have been attacked. My answer will be terrible! Now, go below!'

'What is this ship?'

'You don't know? Well now, I'm glad to hear it! At least its nationality will be one secret you do not know. Now go below!'

The Canadian, Conseil and I had no choice but to obey. Fifteen or so sailors surrounded Captain Nemo and stared out with expressions of implacable hatred at the ship which was now bearing down on them. I had a strong sense that they were all filled with the same thirst for revenge.

As I climbed down inside the boat, a new shell raked the hull of the *Nautilus*, and I heard the captain shout:

'Fire away, demented guns! Waste your futile shells! You cannot escape the sting of the *Nautilus*! But you shall not perish here! I will not allow your carcass to mingle with the remains of the *Vengeur*!'

I returned to my cabin, leaving the captain and his first officer out on the platform. Then the screw started turning; the *Nautilus* sped away rapidly and was soon out of range of the warship's guns. The pursuit continued, but Captain Nemo was content to do nothing except keep at a distance.

About four in the afternoon, unable any longer to contain the impatience and apprehension which were consuming me,

I went back to the central stairwell. The hatch was open. I ventured out on to the platform. The captain was still there, pacing restlessly up and down. He kept watching the ship, which now lay 5 or 6 miles off, to leeward. He circled it, like a savage animal, drawing it westward, letting himself be followed. But he did not attack. Perhaps he was still hesitating?

I felt I had to make one last effort to intervene. But I'd barely pronounced his name when he raised his hand for silence.

'I am in the right! I have justice on my side!' he said. 'I am the oppressed, and there is the oppressor! It is on his account that everything I loved, cherished and venerated, my native land, my wife, children, mother, father, was taken from me! All that I hate in the world is there! So hold your tongue!'

I gave one last look at the warship, which was increasing its speed, then went below to rejoin Ned Land and Conseil.

'We must escape!' I cried.

'And so we will. But what ship is that?'

'I don't know. But whatever ship it is, it will be sunk before dark. But I would rather go down with it than be party to an act of retaliation when we have no way of knowing if it is justified or not.'

'My sentiments exactly,' said Ned Land coldly. 'Let's wait until it's dark.'

Night came. All was silence on board. The compass showed that the *Nautilus* had not changed course. I could hear her propeller turning in the water at a steady, rapid rate. She remained on the surface. A slight roll made her sway from side to side.

My companions and I had resolved to make our escape the moment the warship was close enough for them to hear or see us, for the moon, which would be full three days later, was up and shining brightly. Once we were on the ship, if we could not prevent the fate that threatened it, we could at least try to do whatever the circumstances permitted. More than once, I thought the *Nautilus* was preparing to attack. But she was merely allowing the enemy to come closer and would then race away again from her pursuer.

The first part of that night passed without incident. We remained on the alert for an opportunity to act. We spoke little, because of the tension. Ned Land was all for going out and jumping into the sea. I made him hang fire. In my view, the *Nautilus* would attack the armour-plated man o' war on the surface, at which point it would be not just possible but easy to make our escape.

At three in the morning, feeling apprehensive, I went up to the platform. Captain Nemo was still there. He was standing at the forward end under his flag, which was waving gently in a light breeze above his head. He did not take his gaze off the warship. In his eyes was a look of intensity which seemed to be luring it on, mesmerizing it, pulling it along as surely as if the *Nautilus* were towing it!

The moon was then at its zenith. Jupiter was just rising in the east. In the midst of this tranquil seascape, ocean and sky vied to be the more peaceful while the sea provided Selene with the finest mirror that ever caught her reflection.

When I compared the deep calm of nature's elements with all the anger that smouldered inside the hull of the barely visible *Nautilus*, I felt a chill run through my entire being.

The warship was then 2 miles away. It had come nearer, constantly following the phosphorescent glow which indicated the exact position of the *Nautilus*. I saw her navigation lights, green and red, and the white beam of the searchlight positioned on her mizzen mast. A faint tremor in her dimly lit rigging indicated that her boilers were being stoked beyond safety levels. Showers of sparks, which were the smuts and ash from burning coal, flew up from the funnels and added stars to the night.

I remained there until six in the morning, during which time Captain Nemo never appeared to notice my presence. By then, the warship was a mile and a half away, and with the first glimmers of daylight, the bombardment began again. It could not be long now before the *Nautilus* attacked and I and my companions would part company for ever with this man on whom I could not bring myself to pass judgement.

I was about to go below to tell my friends to be prepared to act when the first officer came out on to the platform. Several sailors were with him. Captain Nemo did not see them or perhaps did not want to see them. Various preparations were made, what might be called 'the bustle that precedes the battle'. But not much clearing of decks was needed. The metal posts forming the railing round the platform were laid flat. The housings of the searchlight and the helmsman's cockpit were both lowered so that they no longer showed above the level of the hull. Nothing now projected above the surface of that long metal-plated cigar which might interfere with her handling.

I went back to the Great Saloon. The *Nautilus* was still sailing just above the water line. A few glimmers of the new day penetrated the water. Every now and then undulating waves would fill the viewing panels with red reflections of the rising sun.

And so the terrible day of 2 June dawned.

At five o'clock, I saw from the log that the *Nautilus* was slowing. I took this to mean that she was allowing the enemy to get closer. This was confirmed by the noise of the cannon, which had intensified. The sea around us was peppered by shells which cut through the water with a peculiar whistling hiss.

'It's time, my friends,' I said. 'Let us shake each other by the hand! May God watch over us!'

Ned Land was resolute, Conseil was calm, and I was very nervous and barely in control of myself.

We walked through the library. As I opened the door that led to the central stairwell, I heard the hatch above us slam shut.

The Canadian rushed to the stairs, but I stopped him. I recognized the familiar hissing sound which told me that water was rushing in to fill the tanks. Almost immediately, the *Nautilus* submerged until she was a few metres below the surface.

I knew exactly what was happening, but it was too late for us to prevent it. The *Nautilus* did not intend to ram the warship's impenetrable armour-plating above the water line but below it, where there was no metal sheathing to protect the hull.

We were prisoners once more, forced to witness the abominable drama which was about to unfold. There was barely time to think. We took refuge in my cabin, where we looked at each other without speaking. My wits had been paralysed by my state of total shock. The mechanisms of thought had ground to a halt. I found myself in that painful state of suspension which precedes the certainty of imminent disaster. I waited, I listened, I lived only through my ears!

Meanwhile, the *Nautilus* gradually increased her speed. She was gaining momentum. Her entire hull shook.

Suddenly I cried out. There was a jolt, but it was relatively minor. I could feel the penetrative power of our steel cutwater. I heard the noise of rending and grinding. But the *Nautilus*, propelled by her momentum, smashed clean through the body of a ship as easily as a sailmaker's needle through canvas!

It was too much to take. Frantic, beside myself, I burst out of my cabin and rushed into the Great Saloon.

Captain Nemo was there. Silent, grim, implacable, he was staring out of the portside viewing panel.

Something huge and bulky was sinking beneath the waves. So that he would not miss one second of its death throes, the *Nautilus* was following down into the deep. Ten metres from me I could see the hull which had been split open. Into it water was pouring with a noise like thunder. After the hull the double row of cannon and the bulwarks came into view. The decks were alive with black shadows which writhed and struggled.

As the water rose over them, the poor devils climbed into the shrouds, clung to the masts, struggled in the water. It was a human ant heap which had been overwhelmed by a sudden tide!

Paralysed, rigid with horror, my hair standing on end, eyes almost popping out of my head, breathing with difficulty, gasping, incapable of speaking, I also stood there and watched! I remained glued to the glass as if by some irresistible magnetic power.

The huge ship sank slowly. The *Nautilus* followed it down, tracking its every move. Suddenly there was an explosion. The pressure of the air inside the ship had blown off the decks as if fires were raging in the hold. The shock from the blast was so great that it rocked the *Nautilus*.

After that, the ship sank more quickly. Her shrouds, to which men still clung, came into view. They were followed by

the crosstrees, which bent under the weight of human despera-
tion, and finally the top of the main mast. Then the great dark
mass sank out of sight, taking with it its crew of corpses, which
were dragged down by the force of the undertow.

I turned to Captain Nemo, archangel of hatred, judge, jury
and executioner. He continued to watch. When there was
nothing more to see, he stood up, walked to the door of his
cabin, opened it and went in. My eyes followed him inside.

On the far wall, under the series of portraits of his heroes,
my attention was caught by a picture of a woman, still young,
and two small children. Captain Nemo stared at it for a few
moments, held out his arms to them, then fell to his knees racked
by sobs.

22

Captain Nemo's Last Words

The viewing panels had closed over the hellish vision, but the lights had not been turned back on in the Great Saloon. Inside the *Nautilus* all was darkness and silence. And then, quickly reaching a colossal speed, the boat fled that desolate place at a depth of 100 feet. Where were we going? North? South? Where was Nemo the Justicer going now that he had taken his ghastly revenge?

I had rejoined Ned and Conseil in their cabin, where they sat in silence. I now regarded Captain Nemo with insurmountable horror. Whatever he may have suffered at the hands of men, he had no right to punish his enemies like this. He had made me, if not an accomplice, at least a witness of his act of retribution. I had had more than enough.

At eleven o'clock, the electric lights came on again. I went to the Great Saloon. It was deserted. I inspected various dials. The *Nautilus* was heading north at a speed of 25 miles an hour, sometimes over the surface and sometimes at a depth of 30 feet below it.

Our position having been marked on the planisphere, I saw that we were then passing the entrance to the English Channel and that our course would take us to the northern seas at a phenomenal rate.

I was barely able to take note, as they raced swiftly by, of the long-nosed squali, hammerheads and spotted dogfish which inhabit those waters, nor of the great sea eagles, the huge shoals of seahorses looking for all the world like chessboard knights, eels writhing like squibs in a firework display, whole armies of crabs skeetering sideways with their claws clutched over their shells and, lastly, regiments of porpoises which tried to keep up with the *Nautilus*. But there was absolutely no time to observe, study and classify any of them.

By the evening, we had travelled 200 leagues over and under the Atlantic. Darkness fell and until the moon came up the sea was shrouded in shadows.

I went back to my cabin. I could not sleep. I was assailed by nightmares. I kept seeing the ghastly scene of destruction over and over again.

From that day on who could say where the *Nautilus* took us, to what nooks and corners of the North Atlantic? And always at that same breakneck speed! Always through those hyperborean fogs! Did we graze the tip of Spitzbergen or the cliffs of Novaya Zemlya? Or sail unknown waters, the White Sea, the Kara Sea, the Gulf of Obi, through the Lyarrov Archipelago to the secret havens of Asia's shores? That I could not say. I no longer had track of time. The hands of the clocks on board had been stopped. It seemed that night and day had stopped following their normal pattern, as they do in polar regions. I felt I had been swept up into the strange domain in which the overwrought imagination of Edgar Allan Poe was so at home. At any moment, like the fabulous Gordon Pym, I expected to see 'a shrouded human figure, very far larger in its proportions than any dweller among men. And the hue of the skin of the figure was of the perfect whiteness of the snow'![28]

I estimate – though I may be mistaken – I estimate that the wardering course of the *Nautilus* continued for some two or three weeks. I do not know how long it would have gone on had it not been for the disaster which brought the entire voyage to an end. Of Captain Nemo, there continued to be no sign, nor of his first officer. No member of the crew was ever seen. The *Nautilus* now sailed almost constantly under water. When she surfaced to replenish the air supply, the hatches would open and close automatically. Our position ceased to be marked on the planisphere. I had no idea where we were.

I will also add that the Canadian, at the end of his strength and drained of patience, was never seen. Conseil could not get a single word out of him and was afraid that in a fit of rage or in the grip of a terminal bout of homesickness he might end his life. So he watched over him with constant, unrelenting devotion.

It will be perfectly clear that in these conditions the situation was no longer tenable.

One morning – I could not say what the date was – I was dozing in the early hours in a state of disagreeable and unhealthy half-sleep. When finally I woke, I found Ned Land leaning over me and I heard him whisper:

'We're getting out of here!'

I sat up.

'When?' I asked.

'This very night. It doesn't seem there's any watch being kept on the *Nautilus*. It's as if they're all in a trance. Will you be ready, professor?'

'Yes. What's our position?'

'Within sight of land. I saw it this morning through the fog about 20 miles east of us.'

'What land is it?'

'Couldn't say, but wherever it is, that's where we'll be safe.'

'Indeed we will, Ned! We'll get away tonight, or drown in the attempt!'

'The sea is rough, and the wind is strong, but 20 miles in the dinghy of the *Nautilus* should hold no terrors for me. I've already smuggled some provisions and a few bottles of water on board without any of the crew being any the wiser.'

'I will follow your lead.'

'Anyway,' added the Canadian, 'if I'm caught, I shall defend myself – to the death if needs be!'

'And we'll die together, Ned!'

I was ready for anything. The Canadian left me, and I went up to the platform, where I was barely able to stand against the power of the waves. The sky looked threatening but since there was land hidden somewhere out there in the dense fog, we had no choice but to escape now. We could not afford to waste a day, even an hour.

I returned to the Great Saloon fearing and yet also wanting to meet Captain Nemo, wishing and yet not wishing to see him again. What would I say to him? Could I hide the visceral revulsion he stirred in me? No! Much better not to come face to face with him, and the best thing would be to forget him! And yet . . .

How long that day seemed, the last I would ever spend on board the *Nautilus*! I stayed by myself. Ned Land and Conseil avoided speaking to me in case they were overheard and gave our game away.

I had dinner at six o'clock, though I was not hungry.[29] I made myself eat, though I felt a little sick, because I needed to keep my strength up.

At 6.30, Ned Land came to my cabin.

'We shan't see each other again before we leave,' he said. 'The moon still won't be up at ten. We'll make the most of the darkness before it rises. Come to the dinghy. Conseil and I will be there, waiting for you.'

Then he left, without giving me a chance to say anything.

I wanted to check the *Nautilus*'s course. I went to the Great Saloon and saw that we were travelling north-north-east at a terrifying speed at a depth of 50 metres.

I cast a last look at all the wonders of nature and the priceless works of art which filled the museum, that incomparable collection of marvels which was doomed to perish one day at the bottom of the sea along with the man who had brought them all together. I tried to fix an indelible image of it in my mind. I stayed there for an hour, basking in the electrical illumination flooding down from the ceiling, inspecting all the priceless objects which gleamed in their display cases. Then I returned to my cabin.

There I put on my thickest sea clothes. I gathered my notes together and stowed them safely about my person. My heart was thumping so strongly that I could not control it. I knew that my tense and agitated state would have given me away immediately to Captain Nemo.

What was he doing at that moment? I put my ear to the door to his room. I heard footsteps. Captain Nemo was there. He was not asleep. Every sound made me think that he was about to spring out and ask me why I wanted to escape! Everything made me jump. My imagination magnified my fears, which grew so strong that I began to wonder if it wouldn't be better simply to walk into the captain's cabin, confront him and express my defiance by the way I faced up to him and by the look in my eye!

It was a mad idea, and fortunately I saw sense. Instead, I went back and lay down on my bed to steady my trembling limbs. My nerves calmed down somewhat, but in my overexcited condition the whole of the time I had spent on board the *Nautilus* resurfaced in my memory, everything good or bad that had happened to me since I had fallen from the *Abraham Lincoln*: the underwater hunting forays, the Torres Strait, the tribesmen of Papua, the time we ran aground, the coral cemetery, crossing under Suez, the island of Santorini, the Cretan diver, the Bay of Vigo, Atlantis, the South Pole ice cap, being trapped under the ice, the battle with the squids, the hurricane in the Gulf Stream, the *Vengeur*, the horrific sinking of the warship with the loss of all hands! . . . All these scenes flashed rapidly before my eyes like painted sets which form the backdrop to the drama on the stage. And all the while Captain Nemo loomed larger and larger in this strange decor. Everything about him was amplified and acquired superhuman dimensions. He was no longer a man like me. He was a man of the ocean, the spirit of the sea.

It was then 9.30. I was holding my head in both hands to stop it bursting. I closed my eyes. I tried not to think. Half an hour still to wait! Another half-hour of a nightmare which could drive me mad!

And then I heard the faint strains of an organ, a series of minor chords under an indefinable theme, the anguished lament of a soul seeking to sever all attachment to earthly things. I listened with all my senses simultaneously, barely breathing, as lost as Captain Nemo in the musical ecstasy which was leading him beyond the confines of this world.

Suddenly I was gripped by a terrifying thought. Captain Nemo had come out of his cabin! He was in the Great Saloon, which I would have to pass through if I was going to escape. I would meet him there, for the last time. He would see me, perhaps he would speak. A single gesture from him could destroy me, one word would shackle me to his boat for ever!

But ten o'clock was about to strike. The time had come to leave my cabin and join my companions.

This was not the time to hesitate, even if Captain Nemo were suddenly to rise up out of the ground before me. Even so, I opened the door cautiously, but it seemed to me that as it turned on its hinges it creaked alarmingly. But perhaps I was hearing the noise only in my imagination

I crept along the *Nautilus*'s darkened walkways, pausing with every step to quieten my thumping heart.

I reached the door in the angled wall of the Great Saloon. I opened it and sidled in. The room was in almost complete darkness. The sounds of the organ were even fainter now. Captain Nemo was there. I believe that even if all the lights had been on, he would not have seen me, so completely lost was he in the music.

I edged forward slowly across the carpet, concentrating on not making any sound which might betray my presence. It took me five whole minutes to reach the door leading to the library at the far end.

I was about to open it when Captain Nemo gave a sigh which rooted me to the spot. I knew that he had just stood up. I could even make him out vaguely because a glimmer from the brightly illuminated library filtered into the Great Saloon. He advanced towards me, arms folded over his chest, not speaking, gliding rather than walking and looking for all the world like a ghost. His chest heaved in the effort of choking back his sobs, and I heard him pronounce these words, the last I would ever hear him utter:

'Almighty God! Enough! No more!'

Could it be an expression of remorse escaping from the man's conscience?[30]

Completely disconcerted, I dashed into the library. I climbed the central stairway, hurried along an upper walkway and reached the hatch to the compartment containing the dinghy. I clambered through the opening, which had already been used by my two companions to get inside.

'Let's go!' I cried.

'No time like the present!' retorted the Canadian.

The entry hatch in the plate of the inner skin of the hull was first closed by Ned Land and then bolted shut with a spanner he had managed to get hold of. The outer cover was always kept sealed shut, and the Canadian now began to remove the bolts which held this casing and the dinghy fast to the hull of the *Nautilus*.

At that moment, we heard a hubbub which came from inside the submarine boat. Raised voices were heard calling urgently. What was the matter? Had our absence been noticed? I felt Ned Land slip a dagger into my hand.

'Yes!' I murmured. 'At least we shall die fighting!'

The Canadian had stopped working on the bolts. But there was one word, a word that was repeated a score of times, a sickening word, which explained the cause of the alarm which was spreading all through the *Nautilus*. It was not we who had so roused the crew to action.

'Maelstrom!' came the cry. 'It's the Maelstrom!'[31]

The Maelstrom! In our terrifying predicament, what word more terrifying could we possibly have heard? We were in the dangerous waters of the Norwegian coast! Had the *Nautilus* been caught in a whirlpool at the very moment our dinghy was about to break free of her hull?

As is well enough known, at the height of a tidal race, water squeezed between the Faroes and the Lofoten Islands begins running incredibly fast. It forms a vortex from which no ship has ever emerged. Huge waves roll in from every point on the compass, creating a giant whirlpool rightly called 'the navel of the ocean'. It pulls in everything over a distance of 15 kilometres. Into it are sucked not only ships but whales and polar bears from the distant north.

It was into this giant whirlpool that the *Nautilus* accidentally – or deliberately? – had been driven by her captain. She was turning in an enormous spiral whose radius decreased by the minute. And with her, the dinghy still attached to her hull was also turning at a phenomenal speed. I could feel it. My head began to spin from having been driven round and round for too long. We existed in a state of fear, of the most acute terror, the blood frozen in our veins, our nervous systems numbed; we shivered with a sweat as cold as that of death. And the noise all around our dinghy! The booming, echoing over a distance of several miles! The shattering roar of the water as it crashed on to the exposed rocks below, where even the stoutest objects are mangled and tree-trunks are smashed into 'hair and fur', as the Norwegians say!

Our predicament was impossible! We were thrown about violently. The *Nautilus* reacted like a living thing. Her steel muscles groaned. At times, she stood upright, and we with her!

'We've got to hang on,' shouted Ned, 'and retighten the bolts! If we stay attached to the *Nautilus* we may still stand a chance of—'

Before he could finish what he was saying, there was a loud screech. The bolts had failed, and the dinghy, torn from its compartment, was thrown into the maelstrom like a stone from a sling!

My head collided with a metal stanchion so violently that I lost consciousness.

23
Journey's End

And so ended our voyage under the seas. What happened during that night, how the dinghy escaped the awful swirling underdrag of the Maelstrom, how Ned Land, Conseil and I managed to break free of the vortex, I shall never know. But when I came to, I was lying in a bed in a fisherman's hut on one of the Lofoten Islands. Both my companions, safe and sound, were at my side, holding my hands. We embraced each other with the greatest warmth.

For the time being, any thought that we might return to France soon is out of the question. The means of communication between north and south Norway are intermittent, so I am obliged to wait for the arrival of the steamboat which connects the Islands and Nordkapp twice a month.

So it is here, among the fine people who rescued us, that I have revised the story of our adventures. It is an exact account. Nothing has been omitted, no detail has been exaggerated. It is the faithful narrative of this highly implausible expedition through an environment inaccessible to man, though progress will one day bring it within his reach.[32]

Will I be believed? I do not know. Still, it does not matter. What I can assert now is my right to speak of seas under which, over a period of ten months, I travelled 20,000 leagues in the course of this underwater journey round the world. I was able to see for myself a great many wonders in the Pacific, the Indian Ocean, the Red Sea, the Mediterranean, the Atlantic, and the polar seas of South and North,

But what became of the *Nautilus*? Was she able to free herself from the embrace of the Maelstrom? Is Captain Nemo still alive? Is he still cruising the oceans in pursuit of terrible retributions to inflict? Or has he decided that his most recent act of slaughter would be the last? Will the sea some day wash up on some distant shore the manuscript in which he set out the full story of his life? Will I finally get to know his name? Will the nationality of the boat he rammed reveal the nationality of Captain Nemo?

I hope so. I also hope that his powerful ship won a victory over the sea in its most terrible manifestation and that the *Nautilus* survived where so many ships had foundered! If that is what has happened, if Captain Nemo still dwells beneath the ocean, his adopted land, may the hatred fade from that fierce heart! May the contemplation of so many wonders extinguish the thirst for revenge! May the man of justice wane and the man of science continue his tranquil exploration of the seas! Strange though his destiny may be, it is also sublime. Have I not understood this myself? Did I not live that unnatural life for ten months? In response to the question asked 6,000 years ago in the Book of Ecclesiastes – 'Who has ever descended into the depths of the abyss?'[33] – only two men among all men have the right to give an answer: Captain Nemo and myself.

Notes

PART ONE

1. *Cuvier ... Lacépède ... Duméril ... Quatrefages*: All French naturalists, zoologists or biologists: Georges Jean Léopold Nicolas Frédéric Cuvier (1769–1832); Bernard-Germain-Étienne de La Ville-sur-Illon, comte de Lacépède (1756–1825); André Marie Constant Duméril (1774–1860); Jean Louis Armand de Quatrefages de Bréau (1810–92).

2. *the old Constitutionnel*: *Le Constitutionnel*, a major newspaper reflecting liberal opinion, was published between 1815 and 1914. In the 1840s it acquired a reputation for using sightings of non-existent sea-serpents when news was in short supply. The expression still survives. A 'serpent de mer' is a stock story wheeled out by a newspaper on slow days. It can also mean a topic which recurs regularly in someone's conversation.

3. *Linnaeus' remark ... 'Nature never created a fool'*: 'Natura non facit saltum' appeared as an aphorism in the *Philosophia botanica* (1751) by the Swedish naturalist Carl Linnaeus (1707–88). For *saltum* ('jump', *saut* in French) the witty journalists substitute the homophone *sot* (fool). Linnaeus' view that nature does not proceed by sudden leaps was in vogue at a time when the theory of evolution was being hotly debated. Darwin quoted it six times in *On the Origin of Species* (1859) in defence of continuity, which he saw as the force driving life on earth, against the argument advanced by Georges Cuvier (1769–1832) that nature had consistently created new species after extinction events brought about by natural catastrophes.

4. *like Hippolyte*: In Act V of Racine's *Phèdre*, despite a spirited start, Hippolyte is killed by a monster from the sea.

5. *the Veritas Bureau*: Founded in 1828, a French marine information and insurance service, the French equivalent of Lloyd's Register of London.

6. *an underwater Monitor*: The USS *Monitor*, an iron-hulled steamship built during the American Civil War in Brooklyn in 101 days for the Union Navy, was a warship of revolutionary design. Her crucial role in the battle of Hampton Roads in 1862 made her famous.

7. *thirty-nine stars*: Actually thirty-seven at the time; the current number of fifty was reached with the inclusion of Hawaii in 1960.

8. *the Leviathan*: The Leviathan was a sea monster described in the Book of Job, chapter 41.

9. *Chevalier de Rhodes, a Dieudonné de Gozon*: Dieudonné de Gozon, Grand Master of the Knights of Rhodes 1346–53, slew a troublesome dragon and hung its head on one of the seven gates of the city of Rhodes.

10. *the Argus*: The Latin form of the Greek *Argos*, the name of the ship in which Jason sailed with his company of Argonauts in his quest for the Golden Fleece. Argos was also a many-eyed giant who guarded Io.

11. *the Universal Exhibition of 1867*: The 50,000 exhibits displayed at the Exposition universelle d'art et d'industrie in Paris in 1867 included armaments. In some quarters, it was said that the occasion had been exploited by nations such as Germany and Great Britain to demonstrate their military power

12. *Rabelais*: François Rabelais (between 1483 and 1494–1553), author of *Gargantua and Pantagruel*.

13. *famous reply given by Arago*: The source of the expression, which Verne quotes several times at different dates, is obscure. Jacques Arago (1790–1855), one of four famous brothers, was a novelist, a popular playwright and an indefatigable explorer. He became blind in 1837 but continued to write and travel to the Orient, the Americas and the Antarctic. Verne met him in 1850 and, despite the difference in age, warmed to the man and learned much from his tales of adventure. In 1853 Arago published an engaging *Curieux voyage autour du monde* (*Curious Voyage around the World*), a title which Verne did not forget.

14. *Bowie-knife*: A knife designed for the legendary American frontiersman and revolutionary Jim Bowie (c.1796–1836), who was killed at the battle of the Alamo.

15. *Diderot*: Denis Diderot (1713–84), a prominent figure in the French Enlightenment, best known as chief editor of, and contributor to, the *Encyclopédie*, published between 1751 and 1772.

16. *prosopopoeia, metonymy and hypallage*: Rhetorical devices. Prosopopoeia: speaking or writing as another person or object; metonymy: the use of the name of one object or concept for that of another to which it is related, or of which it is a part; hypallage: an abnormal or unexpected change of two segments of a sentence.

17. *Gratiolet or Engel*: Louis Pierre Gratiolet (1815–65), French anatomist and zoologist. Josef Engel (1816–99), Austrian anatomist.

18. *of Faraday any more than that of Arago*: Michael Faraday (1791–1867), pioneer in the fields of electromagnetism and electricity. François Arago (1786–1853), oldest brother of Jacques, mathematician, physicist and astronomer.

19. *I shall simply be Captain Nemo*: *Nemo* in Latin means 'no one'. The word has many times been used as a *nom de plume* by pamphleteers, satirists, even theatre critics, who have had widely differing reasons for hiding their identity. In the captain's case, it not only conceals his real name and origins but also symbolizes his self-imposed exile from dry land and his citizenship of the submarine world.

20. *passengers on the Nautilus*: The captain's boat is named after a small sea-dwelling mollusc, related to the group of pelagic octopuses of the cephalopod family. It has a thin shell and papery arms which can be used as sails.

21. *Neptune's old shepherd*: Neptune was the Roman god of the sea. Proteus, thought by some to be his son, tended his sea-monsters. A lesser deity, he was reclusive and assumed different shapes to avoid importunate visitors, hence the meaning of 'protean' as changing, capable of change.

22. *as one of your poets put it*: The expression *l'infini vivant* is used as the subtitle of Jules Michelet's *L'Insecte* (1858) and is applied specifically to the sea in his *La Mer* (1861), Book III, chapter 5.

23. *King François I . . . holy water stoops*: François I (1494–1547) was King of France from 1515 until his death. A major patron of the arts, he received many Italian artists, including Leonardo da Vinci, from whom he acquired the *Mona Lisa*.

24. *in the Bunsen batteries*: In 1841, Robert Bunsen (1811–99), a German chemist, developed the Bunsen cell battery, which replaced the expensive platinum electrode with a carbon electrode.

25. *I use Bunsen, not Ruhmkorff, batteries*: In 1851, Heinrich Daniel Ruhmkorff (1803–77), a German instrument maker, patented an improved induction coil. For a further improved design he was presented in 1858 with a prize for 50,000 francs by Napoleon III for services to the application of electricity.

26. *the Dutchman Jansen*: Marin Henri Jansen (1817–93), a rear admiral of the Royal Netherlands Navy. Jansen is quoted by Michelet in *La Mer* (see note 22 above) and was the Dutch translator of *Physical Geography of the Sea* by Mathew Fortaire Maury (see note 27 below).

27. *Maury ... wrecked by political revolution*: When Virginia joined the Confederacy at the start of the American Civil War, Matthew Fontaine Maury (1806–73), an oceanographer and meteorologist much admired by Verne, resigned his commission in the Union Navy and thus ended his career.

28. *Erhemberg's hypothesis*: Christian Gottfried Ehrenberg (*sic*) (1795–1876), German naturalist, zoologist and geologist, who proved that marine phosphorescence was caused by living organisms.

29. *in the time of Lacépède*: Bernard Germain de Lacépède (1756–1825), French naturalist much admired by Verne, who drew heavily on his *Histoire naturelle des poissons* (*Natural History of Fish*) (1793–1803).

30. *north-north-east*: Apparent mistake by Verne – the course given at the start of this chapter and below in chapter 15 is east-north-east.

31. *'Nautron respoc lorni virch'*: At the start of chapter 18, Professor Aronnax says these words, in a language seemingly invented by Verne, probably meaning: 'we have nothing in sight'.

32. *using the Rouquayrol-Denayrouze regulator*: An underwater breathing regulator invented in 1860 by Benoît Rouquayrol as a means of facilitating escape from flooded mines. It was improved in 1864 when Rouquayrol met Auguste Denayrouze, a lieutenant in the French Navy. The following year, it was officially adopted by the French Navy Ministry. An example of the way Verne kept himself abreast of technological developments.

33. *Ruhmkorff apparatus*: An electrical fluorescent lamp based on a tube filled with carbon dioxide (later nitrogen), invented by the German instrument maker Heinrich Daniel Ruhmkorff (see note 25 above).

34. *where the illustrious Cook was killed on 14 February 1779*: Captain James Cook (1728–79), British explorer, the first European to reach the east coast of Australia and the Hawaiian islands. He was killed in a fight with native Hawaiians.

35. *Agora*: The Agora was the assembly point in every Greek city state and the centre of sporting, cultural and political life.

36. *Athenaeus . . . who lived before Galen*: Athenaeus of Naucratis (d. *c.*200 AD) was the author of the *Deipnosophists*, a diffuse commentary on feasting; Galen (*c.*130–*c.*210 AD) was a Greek-speaking Roman physician.

37. *d'Orbigny*: Alcide Charles Victor Marie Dessalines d'Orbigny (1802–57), French naturalist.

38. *Jean Macé entitled The Servants of the Stomach*: Jean Macé (1815–94) was a journalist, politician and educationalist and a friend of Verne. In 1864 he was the co-founder and first editor of *Musée d'éducation et de récréation* (*Museum of Education and Recreation*), a magazine designed to promote the education of the masses. *Les Serviteurs de l'estomac*, a sequel to *Histoire d'une bouchée de pain* (*The Story of a Mouthful of Bread*), was one of the first separate publications of what initially was called the Bibliothèque d'éducation et de récréation (Library of Education and Recreation).

39. *Bougainville's old 'dangerous archipelago'*: Louis-Antoine, Comte de Bougainville (1729–1811), French admiral and explorer.

40. *where Captain de Langle, La Pérouse's friend, was killed*: Paul Antoine Fleuriot de Langle (1744–87), French naval commander and explorer. He was second in command of the La Pérouse expedition, which departed France on 1 August 1785 and was eventually lost in the Pacific. De Langle was killed by natives in what is now American Samoa.

41. *Captain Bureau . . . of the Aimable Joséphine*: The crew of the *Aimable Joséphine*, captained by Bureau, were massacred by Fijian natives in 1834.

42. *d'Entrecasteaux . . . Dumont d'Urville*: Antoine Raymond Joseph de Bruni d'Entrecasteaux (1737–93), French naval officer, explorer and colonial governor, best known for his exploration of the Australian coast in 1792, while searching for the La Pérouse expedition. Jules Sébastien César Dumont d'Urville (1790–1842), French explorer, naval officer and rear admiral, who explored the south and western Pacific, Australia, New Zealand and Antarctica and, as well as his contemporary Peter Dillon (see note below), uncovered evidence of the fate of the La Pérouse expedition.

43. *Captain Dillon*: Peter Dillon (1788–1847) was a sandalwood trader and explorer, who discovered the wreckage of *La Boussole* and *L'Astrolabe*, the two French frigates of the La Pérouse expedition, in Vanikoro in 1827.

44. *Quiros*: Pedro Fernandes de Queirós (1565–1614), a Portuguese navigator in the service of Spain.

45. *the formidable Andamanese people*: The name given to the isolated aboriginal inhabitants of the Andaman Islands in the Bay of Bengal. Although a British report declared them to be close to extinction in 1875, they were widely and erroneously considered to be fierce, even cannibalistic. Grégoire-Louis Domeny de Rienzi (1789–1843), traveller and observer of the ethnology of south-east Asia, was the author (with Casimir Henricy) of *Océanie ou Cinquième partie du monde: revue géographique et ethnographique* (*Oceania or the Fifth Part of the World: A Geographical and Ethnographical Review*) (1836–8).

46. *the strait that Louis Paz de Torrès tackled*: Luís Vaz de Torres (b. 1565, fl. 1607) was part of the expedition noted for the first navigation of the strait between Australia and New Guinea, which now bears his name.

47. *Gueboroar Island*: An island invented by Verne, an avid reader of Defoe and Johann Wyss (*The Swiss Family Robinson*, 1812), as a suitable location for the *Robinsonade* which follows.

48. *Peysonnel*: Jean André Peyssonel (*sic*) (1694–1759), French naturalist. Verne is mistaken on the date here: Peyssonel's experiments to prove the animal nature of coral took place in the 1720s.

49. *'this is perhaps the defining point … its primitive origins'*: Jules Michelet, *La Mer* (1861), 5th edition (1875), Book II, chapter 4, p. 139.

PART TWO

1. *Sirr … Ceylon and the Cingalese*: Here Verne mentions his debt to Henry Charles Sirr (1807–72), a British lawyer and diplomat, and his *Ceylon and the Cingalese*, 2 vols. (London, 1850).

2. *Percival*: Verne does not often acknowledge so clearly the sources on which he depended. Here he draws on the work of Robert Percival, *An Account of the Island of Ceylon* (London, 1803).

3. *a part of that country*: Perhaps an indication that Verne, thwarted by his publisher Hetzel's refusal to accept Nemo's Polish origins, had already decided to make him an Indian, the solution adopted in *L'Ile mystérieuse* (1875). See Introduction.

4. *the Suez railways have already partially restored*: At this point in the narrative (February 1867), the Suez Canal was still under

construction. An international commission had approved the principle of building a canal in 1855. The plan proposed by the project's main mover, Ferdinand de Lesseps (1805–94), was adopted in 1856. Work began in 1859, and the canal was finally opened on 17 November 1869.

5.   *the Libyan coast*: Libya lies west of Egypt and consequently has no Red Sea coast. Another minor slip left uncorrected.

6.   *Henri Milne-Edwards*: (1800–1885), French zoologist.

7.   *the Hebrew word 'Edrom'*: Edom (not Verne's *Edrom*) is the Hebrew word applied in Genesis 25:30 to Esau, elder son of Isaac, who was 'red all over'.

8.   *Monsieur de Lesseps*: See note 4 above.

9.   *Aures habent et non audient*: (Latin) They have ears but hear not.

10. *Est in Carpathio Neptuni gurgite vates / Caeruleus Proteus*: 'In Neptune's Carpathian depths is the abode of a soothsayer, / Sea-green Proteus'. From Virgil, *Georgics*, Book 4, lines 387–8.

11. *says Michelet*: Jules Michelet, *La Mer* (1861), 5th edition (1875), Book I, chapter 3, p. 26.

12. *Atlas . . . never been heard of again*: Perhaps Verne had in mind the loss of the steamship *Atlas*, which left Marseille on 3 December 1863 bound for Algiers and sank without trace with the loss of fifty lives.

13. *Kosciusko . . . Hugo*: Andrzej Tadeusz Bonawentura Kościuszko (1746–1817), Polish-Lithuanian patriot who fought against Russian and Prussian domination as well as in the American War of Independence; General Markos Botsaris (c.1788–1823), hero of the Greek War of Independence (1821–32) against the Ottoman Empire; Daniel O'Connell (1775–1847), Irish political leader who brought about Catholic emancipation; George Washington (1732–99), general in the American War of Independence and first president of the United States; Daniele Manin (1804–57), Italian patriot and statesman and widely considered a hero of Italian unification; Abraham Lincoln (1809–65), sixteenth president of the United States and emancipator of the slaves; John Brown (1800–1859), American abolitionist hanged by the Confederacy, despite the efforts of the French author Victor Hugo (1802–85) to obtain a pardon for him.

14. *King Louis XIV . . . swallow the Pyrenees*: When Louis XIV's grandson became King of Spain on 16 November 1700, it was reported that the Spanish ambassador remarked that 'The Pyrenees have ceased to exist', since the two nations were now

closely related. The remark was later attributed to the King by Voltaire in *Le Siècle de Louis XIV* (*The Century of Louis XIV*) (1751), chapter 28.

15. *now turned to carbon*: Plato's *Timaeus* and *Critias* (*c*.395 BC) indicate that Solon visited Egypt in about 590 BC. But the city referred to in the previous paragraph could not have been 1,000 years older than 800-year-old Sais and at the same time 'nine hundred centuries' old. The confusion, which has misled others better qualified in this area than Verne, has been attributed to an error in the translation of Plato's Greek text into Egyptian which resulted in 'thousands' being given instead of 'hundreds'. Professor Aronnax is thus deluded in his belief that he walks where 'the first men' once walked.

16. *Physical Geography of the Globe*: Maury was greatly admired by Verne, who regularly used his work as a source of up-to-date, reliable scientific information. His *Physical Geography of the Sea*, first published in 1855, was frequently reprinted and translated into many languages.

17. *Now, if bits of cork ... whirl*: M. F. Maury, *The Physical Geography of the Sea* (New York: Harper and Brothers, 1856), p. 30.

18. *worked out all the mines on dry land*: Verne's gloss on Maury's observation is at variance with his progressive scientific attitudes. It revives the naive optimistic interpretation of the universe which emerged at the end of the eighteenth century, which found evidence for the benevolence of both God and nature in the helpful way so many citrus fruits, melons and so on come in user-friendly sizes, handy segments or with helpful markings, all designed by a kindly creation to make their consumption by humans more convenient.

19. *as Frédol puts it*: Alfred Frédol was the pseudonym of the botanist and doctor Alfred Moquin-Tandon (1804–63), author of *Le Monde de la mer* (*The World of the Sea*) (1863).

20. *as in a diorama*: The first diorama, an early form of visual theatre, was opened by Louis Daguerre (1787–1851), the pioneer of photography, in Paris in 1822. A number of painted linen panels, illuminated by redirected sunlight, were rotated, repositioned and generally manipulated in such a way that the painting appeared to change, thus inducing the audience to believe they were seeing a live picture. It was later replaced by the panorama, in which a continuously painted drum was rotated, showing a succession of life-like scenes.

21. *risen by 2 degrees*: Another slip. The difference is 1 degree, not 2, though a water temperature of -12 degrees at the surface seems unlikely.

22. *a certain Olaus Magnus . . . to drill a whole regiment on*: These tales all originate in Scandinavia. Olaus Magnus (1490–1557), scholar and the last Swedish Catholic archbishop, was the author of a *Historia de gentibus septentrionalibus* (*History of the Peoples of the North*) (1555), many times translated. The diocese of Nidaros, Norway, was established in 1068. Erik Pontoppian (1698–1764), scholar and bishop of Bergen, published many works on diverse subjects.

23. *Les Travailleurs de la Mer*: By Victor Hugo, one of Verne's literary heroes, published in 1866. In a famous episode (Part II, Book IV, chapters 1–3), Gilliatt the fisherman fights 'a slimy mass . . . like an umbrella closed and without a handle': an octopus, the 'devil fish'. Hugo's novel is known in English as *Toilers of the Sea*.

24. *ovoviparous like snakes*: Ovoviviparity is a type of reproduction differing from oviparity, in which zygotes are retained in the body of male or female without interaction with the other parent. There are snakes which are viviparous, oviparous and ovoviparous.

25. *the battle of Sadowa*: Decisive battle fought at Sadowa (Bohemia) on 3 July 1866, in which Prussia overcame the might of the Austrian Empire.

26. *On 11 and 12 Prairial of Year 2 of the Revolutionary calendar*: In the wake of the French revolution a new calendar was introduced by the French government, primarily to remove the religious and royalist associations in the old calendar, and also as an attempt to introduce decimalization (for example, ten-day *décades* replacing seven-day weeks). The new month of 'Prairial' ran from around 20 May to 18 June; 'Year 2' was 1794.

27. *the Vengeur!' I cried*: Launched in 1762, the 74-gun ship of the line saw active service in many seas. Renamed the *Vengeur du peuple* during the Revolution, it took part in the most famous naval engagement between the French and British of the Revolutionary Wars. Reports that the ship had gone down with all hands were greatly exaggerated by the press. But her loss was used as fervent propaganda, which turned defeat into victory and stiffened popular resolve. The French view was repeated in overwrought terms by Thomas Carlyle in his *The French Revolution: A History* (1837), which describes the *Vengeur* sinking and 'carrying *Vive la République* along with her, unconquerable, into Eternity' (London: Everyman, 1906, vol. II, p. 324).

28. *'a shrouded human figure ... snow*: *The Narrative of Arthur Gordon Pym of Nantucket* (1838), Poe's only novel. The lines quoted are the last words of the narrator's tale, and in Verne's French text are taken from the translation published in 1858 by Charles Baudelaire, another of Poe's French admirers. Verne published an enthusiastic article on Poe in the *Musée des familles* in April 1864, and his novel *Le Sphinx des glaces* (1897) was a sequel to the story of Arthur Gordon Pym.

29. *I was not hungry*: The professor was presumably served in his cabin by a steward, though earlier he assured the reader that 'No member of the crew was ever seen.'

30. *Could it be ... the man's conscience*: Nemo's words have been interpreted in different ways, as a plea for forgiveness or as a rejection of God.

31. *the Maelstrom*: Originally a Dutch word meaning whirlpool and a useful narrative device used by many writers, including Casanova and Poe, whose story 'A Descent into the Maelstrom' (1841) specified a giant maelstrom, the M9skstraumen, in the western Lofoten Islands, off Norway. Poe's tale is Verne's model here.

32. *bring it within his reach*: For example, Captain Nemo's underwater suit, which allowed divers to move freely on the sea-bed independent of a piped air-supply from the surface, remained a dream for over sixty years. Significant progress in diving-suit design was not made until after the Great War. In 1926 Yves Le Prieu invented an underwater breathing apparatus, and in the 1940s, Jacques Cousteau improved the aqualung, which made underwater exploration viable. Thereafter, the refinement of wetsuits, foot-flippers and goggles paved the way for open-circuit scuba diving.

33. *the depths of the abyss*: The words do not appear in this form anywhere in the Bible, though the thought is many times expressed.